ISBN: 979-86-43510-72-7

Cover design by: Jemima Ridgway
Library of Congress Control Number: 2018675309
Printed in the United States of America

To the ordinary women who inspire me

PART ONE

CLAIRE

David Sutton was my only option. I stared at his address on the card he had given me, though the particulars were now committed to memory and all my deliberations were getting me nowhere. The decision was the only possible choice but I was unable to activate myself, not yet, not until I had worked my last shift at the student bar, not until the landlord came to collect the keys from me. I needed the reality of zero options. In just a few days I would be homeless, unemployed, alone and then I would buy the train ticket and ask a man I hardly knew to honour what had probably only ever been a casual offer of help.

I was 21 years old and I had completed my degree in History, quietly confident that I had secured a First but I had no immediate job prospects, no family to depend upon and I had alienated my best friend Emily Hunt. Her family had given me somewhere to live in the holidays but that option was now removed. The idea of approaching the State for welfare seemed humiliating and likely to fail. Turning up on David Sutton's doorstep would be embarrassing but somehow I trusted him to be, well, honourable.

I watched my clothes tumbling relentlessly in the dryer at the launderette and swallowed hard, trying to keep down the worry and despair, catching glimpses of my face in the glass. I could not entirely fathom how the connection with David Sutton had ever ignited; it was more to do with him than me, something he saw in me. He was twenty years older than me and that made him more knowledgeable and therefore more powerful. If there'd been any other option, I don't suppose I would have placed myself in such a vulnerable situation, empowering him. I fingered the alabaster heart I always wore and my mind floated back to the hotel lounge, at Turnberry, where we first met.

DAVID

The first time I saw you, Claire Sutcliffe, I thought of you as a waif and stray, so sombre for someone so young, like something out of a Charles Dickens novel. Emily Hunt was one of the numerous nieces and nephews I'd had to tolerate, having married into that family. I had recently divorced back out of the family and the women certainly would have preferred me not to have been there. I would have diplomatically skirted around your group that day but I saw you and I was curious.

Emily had grown into an indisputably beautiful young woman and you were like a pretty weed next to her, an intriguing anomaly, the contrast underlined by the different apparel; I was familiar with all the smart labels she was wearing, a perfect ensemble for the summer scene at Turnberry. That large cotton skirt of yours and the tidy blouse; it was too respectable, somehow homely, too old for you. I thought perhaps you were foreign which would have most easily explained such a dire costume.

I introduced myself, much to Emily's annoyance and she was obliged to return the introductions and so my theory was proved wrong; at least, you were not foreign but I was right to find you out of place, wasn't I?

CLAIRE

Joining the Hunt family had introduced me to another world, not just another social class, and that summer, the holiday in Turnberry may as well have been an exotic holiday in the Caribbean. To a working class girl it was dazzling and made me giddy.

Emily Hunt had befriended me within the first few days at University. She told me I was quirky, eccentric and at the age of 18 I sensed rather than categorically knew that her attitude was condescending but I also understand now that it is irrelevant. Frankly, whatever her insecurities and her need to adopt me like some sort of pet, the important thing is that I gained her attention and a foothold in a world starkly different to the one I was trying to climb out of.

Do I want to go over my very murky past, my very humble beginnings? What I told Emily was that I was estranged from my parents and this rendered me tragic and an even more exotic pet. The idea that I had nowhere to call home anymore may even have stirred genuine feelings of compassion in her. Yes, I want to believe that, even now. She settled for the vague summary of my life situation because she did not have the stomach for too many sordid details, being the kind that prefers to make the donation to charity without seeing the depressing video. Her parents were more greedy for facts and I could scarcely live in their home, rent free, without satisfying their need to burrow into my socio economic reality. I suppose they shared their findings with Emily but she never discussed my past. For my part, I invented my background story; the uneducated mother whose chief pleasure in life was a night at the pub or playing bingo; the greasy, foul mouthed step father who gambled most of our money away; the younger sister who showed no promise and was likely to end up on drugs; disinterested other family preoccupied by their battles with money problems. Suffice it to say that this depiction was no better or worse than my actual circumstance but I perversely clung on to my right to privacy. They could feel sorry for me, stare at me, looking for signs of deviance or genetic inferiority but my truth was my truth and they did not have the right to possess it. In this small way, having rejected my parents and my background, I gave my relatives some dignity and respect. No one would know anything about them.

Anyway, Emily took me home with her that first Christmas holiday and I think I probably made the festive season extra holy for them. How their eyes watered at the nativity scene on Christmas Eve and when the vicar spoke of reaching out to the poor and needy, Emily's mother's eyes burned holes in the side of my face. The Easter holiday provided further religious encouragement and by then, her parents had redecorated the spare room I used, not to my taste entirely, the floral wallpaper and white dressing table too overtly feminine but I felt safe and, though they found themselves incapable of ever loving me, perhaps it was enough for God that they were generous, tolerant and mainly kind and now, years later, even though my connection with them was short-lived, I suppose I owe them some small debt of gratitude. It is my natural tendency to be cynical and I am certain that my intellect, my insistence always on correct grammar and not the sloppy ways of most young people and my pretty looks yes, this all made it relatively easy for them to accommodate me. However, the fact is they gave me a home and others would not have obliged.

At the start of that first summer holiday, I was acutely aware that this was a very long holiday and that having me live in their home did not mean they wished to pay for me to fly away with them, that their family holiday abroad might be too sacred an occasion to violate. Emily had promised to try and get me a few hours working at the restaurant where she worked in her holidays, owned by friends. Her parents liked to encourage a work ethic and I certainly had no objection to earning some money. The matter of Italy was mentioned a few times but it was never specified that I would be going. Finally, Emily's Mum settled the uncertainty by explaining that she hoped I would not object to minding the house for them, including the dog and two cats, that she supposed I would wish to carry on with my hours at the restaurant, the money very handy. Of course I was disappointed but this was mingled with relief. I was not part of the family, after all, and some time alone would be welcome. I was so able to be positive in my youth and I straight away focussed on the advantages of having that house to myself.

However, when the excursion up to Turnberry became a topic of dinner conversation (I had no idea where it was and no experience of golf) and Emily insisted I go and her parents so readily agreed, I confess my spirits soared and I had to dig my nails hard into my palms to suppress the urge to squeal; I was going away somewhere, I was headed for a brand new experience. I waited until much later to ask Emily where on earth Turnberry was and to explain that I had no idea how to play golf. She just laughed at me and said.

"Don't be absurd. Daddy and my brother will be playing golf. We'll go to the beach, drink expensive cocktails in the bar, check out any gorgeous guys and I don't know, have a facial.

You know the sort of thing."

I must have looked so blank and she laughed again.

"Relax! You'll love it. I mean, it's not that great. It's just Scotland after all and the weather might be crap but we'll have fun, you'll see."

So, I headed up to Scotland, my modest clothes crammed into an overnight bag and my mind brimming with expectation.

The first two days did not disappoint me. Aided by calm, sunny weather, the quiet beach at Maidens enchanted me with mystical views of Ailsa Craig, its long stretches of sand and the romantic walk at its furthest end, up into castle grounds. We swam, sunbathed, beachcombed, read and ate huge picnics; we might have been part of the Famous Five but for the lack of murder or mystery. There was an incredible simplicity and innocence about it all. By contrast, the hotel was regal and suitably formal for its clientele and though my clothes really were a shambles I enjoyed a feeling of sophistication, perhaps walking a little straighter, determined not to be intimidated but naturally I was because I was entirely out of my depth. I considered myself to be no beauty, especially next to Emily but nevertheless I caught men admiring me, men mostly older and not very attractive themselves but this did not bother me.

Then, the Forster family arrived and within minutes of meeting them it was apparent that the twenty year old son, by the name of Nick, of fine physique and model looks, had some sort of understanding with Emily. Seeing her, he grinned in a telling fashion and she fluttered her eyelashes in a way I found acutely irritating; I thought "You can put the education into a girl but you cannot take the desperate for a man genes out of her." Of course, I admit now that in my case the genes were there but simply not yet activated and Nick Forster, with his public school sporting energy was just not my type. The feeling was mutual and he merely tolerated me.

The Hunt family were kind enough to simply introduce me as Emily's friend from university rather than their charity project and there was no particular reason for me to feel awkward but I wished the Forsters had not come and over the next couple of days Nick and Emily made few efforts to accommodate me into their cosy arrangement, happy for me to carry the bags up the beach whilst they flirted, only occasionally suggesting that I was reading too much and should join in the fun. Only when Nick was off playing at golf did Emily pay me any decent amount of attention and then this was often to bend my ear about the many virtues of Nick.

That day, when David Sutton came over and addressed us, Emily and Nick were brushing up against each other in the usual way, laughing about nothing and I was tense and dreading another day of their infatuation. The older man spoke like one of our lecturers, confidently.

"Hello there Emily. Put young Nicholas down. Do your parents know about this?"

Emily blushed and frowned at him.

"Hello Uncle David, or should I just call you David now?" Her rudeness surprised me. He must have been used to it and remained perfectly serene.

"Mr Sutton if you're going to be impertinent. And who have we here?"

He stared down at me and not sure what to make of the tension I smiled very weakly. I would have introduced myself, should have done but Emily jumped in.

"This is Claire Sutcliffe, a friend from Uni. We're heading off to the beach soon."

David stretched out his hand to me.

"Hello Claire. I'm Emily's ex Uncle, David Sutton. How are you enjoying your time here?"

Confused by how anyone could qualify as an ex-uncle, I shook his hand and just babbled something about the lovely hotel and very pretty beach. It was hard to assess his level of interest but he certainly had time to scan the rest of the room and put a hand up to someone he recognised.

"Great. Well, nice to meet you. Take care of your guest Emily. Nick, you can come with me and caddy and pick up some golf tips. You can join the girls later."

This was a clear instruction, not a suggestion and Nick, in spite of all his previous attentions toward Emily, promptly dropped her like a rock. Emily scarcely waited for them to be out of earshot before venting her outrage at the intrusion.

"What an arrogant shit! I never liked him and I'm glad Auntie Susan married him for his money and took him to the cleaners. Why not?"

She took her time to fill me in on the whole story, totally biased of course. Apparently, her mum's sister married him with no real intention of growing old with her husband, David Sutton being a man of such means that made them seem poor. The marriage lasted less than two years and Aunt Susan declared him impossible to live with and said he had had an affair which Emily said "his type" did all the time. Of course "his type" could afford a top barrister and Aunt Susan had not come out of the divorce at all fairly but she had the house in France and a pretty decent chunk of his cash and nobody had ever liked him much. After much venting, Emily slipped into a quiet sulk. I was not sure quite what to believe.

Later, I took a sly opportunity to quiz Emily's brother about Mr Sutton and his version of the story was different again.

"David Sutton is what you call a smooth operator and loaded. He's not half bad at golf either. My Auntie Susan, that's my mother's younger sister, is determined she is going to be richer than any of us and to be honest, she can be a bit of a cow. Anyway, she came here with us, Dad introduced her to David and she charmed him into marrying her. It was an incredible wedding but not surprisingly it didn't work out. Dad still plays golf with him but obviously my Mum takes her sister's side and Emily too. I think the guy's ok but it's awkward. Rumour has it, some mad French artist lives with him now but that could just be gossip, you know."

I was fascinated. I did not know much about any of this world but it was drawing me in.

DAVID

When I saw you, the following morning, alone, perched awkwardly on that chaise longue, your head tilted to read the newspaper, the sun making your hair shine, I thought you looked like a figure in a painting and I thought of Celeste. Had I considered the matter more carefully I should have concluded that the suggestion was not at all appropriate but I had just played some excellent golf and felt exhilarated and spontaneous. Some of my best decisions are the ones I take quickly.

"Good morning Claire. All alone?"

You started a little and then gave me a very kind smile, although you spoke very carefully, guarded.

"Emily's coming. She needed a lie in. We're going to a different beach today."

"Oh? Who's "we" then?"

"Emily, Nick, and maybe Emily's brother. Nick's going to drive his dad's car."

"Sounds like a plan, although not so great if Emily's brother doesn't tag along. I'm sure you'd rather not play gooseberry all day."

You looked uncertain. You were trying to work out how to respond to that, weighed down by obligation.

"Look, I'm heading back to my place today. It's not so far. My girlfriend Celeste says she's missing me. She's a painter. Perhaps you would like to meet a painter? She's French too and I bet you'd like her. I'm sure Emily and Nick can spare you for one day, if her brother doesn't want in. Think about it. I'll pop by here in say an hour and if you're here you're here. If not, well enjoy your day."

I could see my suggestion had put you in a tail spin so I left you to it and frankly, I did not expect you to be there later on. When you were, looking like a lost child at a railway station, I doubted the wisdom of our excursion but you had committed yourself and I could hardly leave you to be all alone.

As I watched you fumble to put on your seat belt, I mainly

thought of Celeste and how she might react. She was spending too much time by herself. Was I at all attracted to you, at that stage? You were undeniably pretty and slightly mysterious but you were also not very mature for your age and though I had no children, I was conscious that biologically speaking, you could be my daughter. I think, trying to be completely honest with you, that I was aware that you might potentially develop a crush on me and that idea flattered me and made me feel powerful. The way you stared wide eyed at my car and the wonder with which you gazed out of that window I wish Celeste could have painted that but she saw what first drew my attention, the pale waif.

CLAIRE

I should have been afraid. Looking back, it still fills me with a certain horror, to think that I climbed into the car of a stranger and let him drive me away but of course the media teach us that fear and I thought I knew what weird men were like and trusted my instincts. As it was, I only took the precaution of avoiding too much eye contact which was not difficult because he took the approach of a tour guide and kept pointing things out. He told me the drive would take about forty five minutes and I confess I absolutely loved riding in his sporty car and the fact that he drove it so fast. I occasionally had the urge to laugh out loud with the adrenaline and once when I did, he asked me what was so funny and I said "nothing" and there was an awkward silence. I knew I had to avoid repeating that at all costs. So, that was the only thing I recall being afraid of really. I just didn't want to appear stupid. Did I think he was handsome? Yes, I would have had to have been very odd not to have found him so but I was aware that he was taking me to meet his girlfriend and conscious of his age and tenuous connection to Emily's family and above all, his tour guide tone did nothing to make me think he was in any way regarding me in a sexual way.

None of this matters. The important thing is that I took a risk, one that began the connection between us.

We drove up into rounded hills and then down through a valley and then up again, higher this time. David stopped for me to admire the views and talked very knowledgeably of the area and its history. Once we had ceased climbing the narrow, twisty roads, the drive levelled off and now we headed into an area of forestry. David pointed out birds of prey that circled above us and we may only have been less than an hour from the hotel but this was a different kind of place all together, with few obvious signs of human presence. The road started to take us downhill again and we left pine forest behind to descend into deciduous woodland .Then David pulled in next to a large, stone house, strong looking but slightly bleak.

"Oh it's lovely." I said, wishing to be polite.

"Wait there." He jumped out, leaving the engine purring and strode up to the front door, knocking on it firmly.

I saw the door open and an exchange ensued between David and a younger man. The latter laughed at something David said and then disappeared briefly and when he returned he handed David two dead pheasant. They shook hands and David put the pheasant into the boot of his car.

Back beside me, he grinned, evidently very pleased.

"That's the head gamekeeper. Do you like pheasant?"

"I don't know. I've never tried it before."

"Good. You can find out then. Now, about another five minutes and we're there."

Sure enough, after just another few minutes, having traversed a river by means of a very narrow bridge, David pulled up again, now in front of enormous, black metal gates. Just to the other side of these, to the left, was one of the tiniest houses I had ever seen; I thought immediately of fairy tales and elves. To fuel such imaginings, a short, elderly bearded man appeared, touching his cap at David and he proceeded to unlock and open the gates. Once David had pulled past the gates, he stopped and waited for the man to close them again. The man came over and leant in at the window. He had a very strong Scottish accent which made his language sound almost foreign to me. Small, suspicious eyes scrutinised me and my smile was not returned. David did not introduce us. However, as we carried on up the driveway he remarked.

"That's Mr James McDermott, otherwise known as Jimmy but only to his family and friends and now me. It took me a while but we got there in the end. Doesn't much care for English folks. I'm hoping he'll retire in the next couple of years and then I 'll have electronic gates installed."

I was going to ask him why he had bought a house in Scotland but then the house was there before us. I just gasped at its vast, imposing dimensions, making David laugh with satisfaction.

"Not bad eh?"

"Wow! It's incredible Mr Sutton. Really amazing." I am embarrassed to recall such naïve wonder.

"Don't call me Mr Sutton. Call me David. Come on, let's find Celeste."

The house was built of grey stone, with two fairy tale turrets and latticed windows and stone columns either side of the enormous front door. Vines softened the walls and the sunny sky perhaps rendered it more cheerful than it would otherwise have seemed. It was built to withstand more inclement weather. It was embodied dignity and to my inexperienced eyes was quite magnificent. I had so much to learn.

In the hallway, a wood fire was burning gently, though it was a summer's day and I instinctively headed towards it and started to rub my hands because the house was decidedly chilly. David called out for Celeste, speaking French and within moments there she was, descending the wide staircase at a trot, wiping paint from her hands with an old rag, grinning from ear to ear. An old, fat Labrador followed stiffly behind, wagging its tale.

They embraced and spoke French, to me it seemed very quickly but then that is how it seems to the ignorant. Politely, I held back and I enjoyed in those few moments the musicality of their chatter and had chance to study the captivating looks of the woman.

She was dark, Mediterranean, her hair scooped up into a loose, make-do arrangement which was somehow also very becoming. She was about thirty then, though she looked younger, dressed in loose dungarees and a vest top, one strap of the dungarees hanging down seductively. The trousers were rolled up slightly and she wore ankle socks and bendy, leather pumps She had a slight paint smudge on one cheek and she smelled of lavender. Wooden bangles knocked gently on one wrist and there was something about her style that I instantly admired; there and then, without even speaking to her, without knowing anything about her I was besotted. The dog peered up at them longingly.

I think she was oblivious to me until David stepped sideways to make the introductions. The smile on her face fell away but was replaced by undisguised curiosity. I liked her French version of English even better than hearing her native tongue.

"Ello Claire. Enchanted to meet you. "

I stuck out a shy hand for her to shake but she brushed it away and kissed me on both cheeks undaunted by my stiffness. She turned to David.

"But David she is just perfect! I must sketch her tout de suite. She must come and see my work."

She grabbed me by the arms and pulled me towards the stairs. I must have pulled back instinctively, uncertain.

"Don't worry Claire. Celeste can be a bit over enthusiastic but you're in safe hands. Go and see her work. I have some business stuff to do but we'll meet up again for lunch and then I'll show you the rest of the house."

"Yes, yes. Come on Claire. I don't bite. We can 'ave a drink up there and there are cookies and you will see that we can be very good friends you and I. I know it. I can feel it."

There was an intensity about her that I suppose was a bit peculiar and I remembered that Emily's brother had described her as "mad" but she was alluring and her sense of anticipation drew me up the stairs. Again, I am surprised that I was not more fearful, more uncertain, but how glad I am that I followed her up those stairs that day. It was the beginning of another connection, one I can never regret.

The route up to her makeshift studio took us past an array of treasures; paintings of very noble individuals, to my eyes mysterious and romantic, huge oriental pots, musty smelling tapestries depicting the violence of hunting or military campaigns, cabinets full of eclectic ensembles of glass and ceramic ware; I wondered who on earth cleaned all of this, always the practical thinker. I wanted to pause and pose questions but Celeste drew me on with a sense of energetic purpose, apparently well accustomed to the grandeur if not immune to it.

We had climbed to the full height of the stairs and passed down a shadowy corridor and then she stopped and pulled open double doors and we entered into a vast space, mostly devoid of furniture, full lit by a blinding sunlight. One of the floor to ceiling windows had been opened and a fresh breeze wafted over me. The dog had trotted away after David, so we were alone. The window drew me over but the view from this room was limited; just the upper parts of trees and above the rough tops of moorland. She must have read my mind or more likely the look of disappointment on my face.

"'Ere we see not so much. I choose it for that reason. I need no distractions. David can show you the views later, eh? Come and see what I do."

The room was essentially an artist's studio, a selection of different sized canvasses leant up against walls, a couple mounted on easels. There were two large tables pushed together and these were strewn with sketch books, many pages torn and scattered. On another low table, there were paint pots, mixing palettes, brushes, pencils and other tools I was less certain of. I can only imagine how shy and overwhelmed I must have appeared. I held back by the window but she smiled and beckoned me over.

"These I paint to sell. I paint what people want you know?" She indicated the various, abstract creations lining the walls and gave a deep sigh. "But David, 'e brings me 'ere and 'e says I must paint what I really want to paint; I 'ave not done that for a long time. So, 'ere, see, I explore Vanitas. You know this idea, yes?"

I am quite sure I looked dumbstruck. I knew nothing of fine

art. Patiently, she showed me pictures in a large book and talked of the passage of time, man's finite nature and the futility of everything. She explained her project in detail and I maintained a rigid expression of someone listening with interest, nodding, making the odd comment but all the while I was more taken by the wisps of hair at the nape of her neck, a pretty mole on one of her cheeks, the hypnotic melody of her French-English and above all, the grave intensity of her dark lashed eyes. I thought that David Sutton must be madly in love with this woman, that she was the kind to encourage obsession.

She showed me rough sketches that she had repeated, again and again, trying to create a central figure for her project and did not disguise her frustrations. Then she turned to me and brushed my cheek softly with the back of her hand and oddly perhaps, for I was not a tactile person, I was not alarmed or repulsed in any way and gazed back, quite calm.

"You see Claire. You are the face I 'ave been looking for; David, 'e sees this and brings you to me. You are like the white, English rose. In your eyes, you are alone, lost. You can let me sketch you, yes?"

Why would I refuse her? She wanted to stare at me to draw me. I just wanted to stare at her.

"Sure. Why not?" I attempted nonchalance.

She launched into artist mode, explaining that the neck and shoulders were vital; she would add an appropriate costume later. She vanished into a room, off to the side and returned with a cotton top I could slip on, the kind where the sleeves can be pushed down off the shoulders. She ruffled my hair slightly and I could see that I was more of an object to her now, a piece of fruit that needs to be positioned correctly. Then, she muttered something and went off again, returning with a necklace; a dark blue velvet ribbon and hanging from it a stone heart.

I am not sure I had any preconceptions of what it might be like to pose for an artist but I can tell you now that it is mainly uncomfortable and boring and if I shifted now and again, she smiled but scarcely hid her annoyance and re-positioned me.

I tried to talk to her but she asked me not to. So, all I could do was stare back and observe the artist at work and even then, with that first encounter, the level of intensity she was capable of was somehow unsettling, if not yet disturbing. To her and to David I was innocent, and lost perhaps, but it had taken enormous strength and will power to escape to university, and even at that age I had the beginnings of a diamond core and after some time, I arrived abruptly at the end of my tether.

I stood up and roughly pulled off the top.

"There, I've had enough. I'm bored now."

I yanked up the straps of my bra and put my blouse back on. Most students donned the uniform of slogan t-shirts and sweatshirts but I had brought what smart clothes I owned to Turnberry and that dreadful blouse was an example. Celeste might have been annoyed but I saw that she was surprised and then somewhat impressed. As I fussed with the collar of the blouse, I felt the necklace and fumbled to undo it. She put up a hand to stop me.

"Keep it Claire. It suits you. It is an alabaster heart. Not expensive. You are young. You must try always to keep the heart like alabaster no? The heart must be strong but not too strong, the man he must be able to see through it but not so clearly. The heart must never be of glass, you understand?"

I nodded but I did not understand much at all. How could I understand about men and broken hearts? I was vastly immature in that way. I found the way Emily fawned over Nick pathetic and tiresome; my own sexuality had hardly awakened. I understood Celeste was beautiful and had an irresistible quality that made David Sutton want to be with her; it was all a vague, romantic idea, the stuff of films. My own parents had taught me nothing of passion or love. I was not sure such things even existed in the world I had come from.

Celeste invited me into the room from which she had retrieved the top and I discovered it was something of a sitting room from which, by means of another door, one could just glimpse a bedroom. The bed was unmade. Perhaps for this reason, she politely closed the door. Then, she clicked on a kettle and offered me earl grey tea and some buttery French biscuits. I peered out of the window and said how much I was looking forward to exploring the house.

"It's incredible. I have never been in such an amazing house. It's spectacular, don't you think?"

She shrugged her shoulders, seemingly unconvinced.

"These big places, they are buildings of desolation and despair. This is David's dream. It is a rock around his neck. I come 'ere only to paint, with the space and the light. You cannot live in a place like this. I try to tell this to David but he needs to own the past. I tell him, people do not own these places; they blow in them like the wind, in one door and out of the window. You know?"

No, I did not. Celeste knew so much, about ten years older but a hundred years wiser. What I can say now is that we both knew about suffering but mine was directing me to familiar ideas like the pursuit of learning, building a career, amassing wealth. By trying to escape, I connected more strongly to David and aspired to his success. Celeste's suffering was distinct and she was on a different plain of thinking. Yes, it is true that I did not yet understand her illness; that was to come. That day, I only listened with wonder.

She talked to me about her privileged up-bringing in France and her rejection of it and the life she mainly lived, in London, where she had met David. When David himself appeared, all cheery and enthusiastic about the pheasant dinner he had planned for later and poised to give me the grand tour, I confess I was slightly irritated by the intrusion and should have liked to have remained in quiet seclusion with his beautiful girlfriend. They spoke in French again and I guessed that he was urging her to join us but she pouted at him and the word "non" was repeated until finally he gave up and we took our leave of her, David striding ahead of me, like a headmaster. I followed, flustered, trying to adjust. Whereas she was philosophical and hypnotic, he was the great entrepreneur, a little bombastic, proudly recounting the history of his house, his possession, but once I had made the adjustment to his style, I admit it was hard not to be impressed.

He had purchased the house unfurnished and aided by an

interior designer and painstaking research, they had almost completed furnishing it in a wholly authentic style. He was also researching his family history, convinced that sooner or later he must find Scottish blood; how else could he account for his love of this place? His business commitments required him to spend the majority of his time in London or elsewhere but he said that huge technological changes were coming and that eventually he believed he would be able to live there most of the time and still run his affairs; he talked of computers and mobile phones and electronic mail. You must understand that this was at the end of the 1980's and I began to think him a little eccentric, like his girlfriend.

Eventually, we ended up in the kitchen and in this room, at least, the need for authenticity had been abandoned; it was modern and gleaming and he had installed an American sized refrigerator. All the while continuing to recount the colourful history of the area, he pulled out a selection of cheeses, grapes, a green salad and from the immense walk-in pantry he emerged carrying a savoury biscuit selection. He offered me a glass of wine which I accepted only to avoid seeming childish; in those days I rarely drank. He produced olives, something I had never eaten; I will never forget how good those ones tasted; he explained that Celeste had them sent over from family in Provence.

After eating, (he ate well whereas I merely nibbled), he started to properly regard me again and perhaps it occurred to him that I might be finding his chatter boring. He took a large swig from his glass of red wine.

"So, Claire, are you having an adventure? You've lots to tell your parents the next time you see them."

"Well, yes, I'm loving it but as to my parents, I'm not much in contact with them. They were against me going to university. I'm trying to put my past behind me and well, improve my lot in life. That's why I'm staying with Emily and her family."

To my relief, he greeted this not with concern or alarm but was obviously impressed.

"Well, well. Good for you. That takes real guts. From now on, I shall follow the career of Claire Sutcliffe with much interest.

So, after you have your degree, what next? Any thoughts?"

"No, not yet. Possibly, journalism. I don't want to look too far ahead. I want to seize every opportunity as it comes, like today, coming here."

He nodded with approval.

"There's more to you Waif than meets the eye. You're not quite as vulnerable as you look. I'm glad our paths have crossed. Come on, the sun is still shining, we must force Celeste to step out into the grounds with us. We'll work up an appetite for dinner. She takes her art too seriously sometimes, to the detriment of her own health. Isn't that right Obi?"

He rubbed the ears of the grateful Labrador and this prompted the younger dog, a terrier, to step out of its basket and stretch. Both tails started to wag and they began to circle, evidently aware that there was a plan to go outdoors.

David told me to wait there; he would go and fetch Celeste. I was nervous of dogs in those days and hoped he would return quickly. With a peculiar sense of satisfaction I considered the fact that David had coined a nickname for me; it conjured a feeling of belonging, the notion that I had done more than make his acquaintance. Surely our paths would cross again?

When David and Celeste joined me in the kitchen, she looked tired and there was a palpable tension between them. I saw that she had paint on the tips of her fingers. David snapped something at her in French and in an obvious sulk she cut a slither of cheese and tore at the grapes. Then, she insisted on linking arms with me and said in a way clearly intended to provoke him.

"'E thinks he is my papa you know. I must love him, to endure this bullshit." There was more anger than fun in her words and she scowled over at him. I remember how much I blushed. How ironic that David had pretended to be rescuing me from playing gooseberry with Emily and Nick. I felt rather than knew that David was in the right and Celeste was being difficult; I saw a kind of agony in his eyes, though I did not understand it.

The rest of the afternoon might have ended up being unbearable but once we stepped out into the glorious warmth of the gardens, nerves were calmed and soothed by the fragrance of flowers, the hum of insects and the gurgling of the man-made water course. Celeste's spirits rose again and she insisted David row us out onto the small loch. I think both David and I would have been content to have remained stretched out on the main lawn, gazing up at the expanse of cloudless blue but she pulled at his sweater playfully and then kissed him on the mouth, until he laughed and was seduced into fulfilling her wish. Though this was the stuff of lovers, I was less embarrassed by their happiness and in spite of my loathing of boats I decided to insist that yes, a row on the loch was a fabulous idea.

On the water, the mood shifted again, David deep in concentration as he rowed, Celeste pensive as she stroked the chilly water with her hand and I confess, perhaps rudely, I mainly ignored their presence and absorbed every detail of the surroundings, conscious that this was for me an experience I might never repeat.

Later, I would taste pheasant for the first time, flattering my host with over enthusiastic approval, much to the amusement of Celeste who picked at her food, listless again. Finally, she tossed down her fork and embraced me in an abrupt farewell, so that I wondered if I had offended her.

David produced a packet of cigarettes and lit one, without trying to corrupt me to the habit. He took a long drag.

"You mustn't take it personally you know. She likes you. She really likes you. She just loves her bloody work more. God, she can be a pain to live with but I'm not sure I could live without her easily. She's like these rotten fags, addictive. Take it from me Waif, try to avoid love and affairs of the heart for as long as possible. Concentrate on all your other goals. That's my advice."

"Oh I plan never to marry if I can help it, or have children. I want to be a career woman. Don't take this the wrong way, but blokes seem like a waste of time to me."

This made him laugh a lot. I suppose my sincerity must have been, in its own way, enchanting.

"Is that right? Well, another reason for me to keep an eye on you Waif. We must see how far your resolve gets you. Do you read much? Quality literature I mean."

"Well, I've been reading a lot of Orwell and E.M Forster. I can't get on with anything too old fashioned."

"I see. Well, you might find this a bit of a heavy read but let me see if I can find a copy..."

He disappeared for quite a while and returned with a copy of Henry James' Portrait of a Lady.

"Here. Take it with you. Keep it. I don't want it back. If and when you manage to read it, write and tell me (a) what you think of it and (b) why you think I thought to lend it to you. Ok? Here, I suppose I'd better let you have a business card and some contact details and then we'd best make a move and get you back to Turnberry."

I confess, I felt increasingly despondent with every mile that we drove closer to the hotel. It was David's suggestion that he avoid dropping me at the entrance, in full view and that I should, if possible, invent a story about my day, one which did not include him or Celeste. Naturally, I saw the wisdom in this and as far as Emily and the others were concerned, I had spent the most boring day in solitude. I was careful to bury the novel and David's business card in the very bottom of my travel bag. I thought I would probably never touch the paperback and even less probably ever see David Sutton or his French girl-friend again. I thought wrong.

DAVID

When I dropped you off Waif, I watched you walk away and yes, I had a strange gut feeling that we would meet again but this should not be confused with an actual desire to see more of you. Truthfully, there was only one woman on my mind at that point and it was Celeste. She had me on an emotional hook, she was so spell-binding and stirred up within me the kind of longing that generally one only experiences in the first few days of any courtship. Yet, she was even then on my mind for other reasons. A creeping anxiety had started to gnaw at me, like I had some unpaid debt to settle. The day had been, in many ways, magical and I suppose that is why I am still able to recall it so vividly but I could not side step the fact that your visit had been a mixed blessing.

On the one hand, you had charmed some life and energy back into Celeste, much as I had predicted you would. Yet, as I was to discover, there was no obvious on/off tap with Celeste's moods and though I could find ways to elevate her spirits, they then soared out of my control and any subsequent decline could be deeper and darker than before. I was a clumsy amateur; at that stage in denial that this was an illness I was trying to control.

You see, Celeste was like a glittering, dazzling shard of sunlight but there is no sun that does not burn itself out. Two months prior to your visit Waif, I had been to France where she had introduced me to her parents. I was struck by two things; how calm and normal they were compared to their vivacious daughter and a wary look in their eyes. Naturally, I assumed they were being guarded against me, the new suitor and apart from anything there was the fact that I was English, although I expected my command of their language to work some charm on them. Then, the day before we left, her mother drew me to one side and talked about Celeste's unique personality and the need for her life to be a delicate balance. She refrained from using words like "ill" and "medicine" but handed me a cream, embossed business card and explained that they had incurred a great deal of expense supporting Celeste's use of the London Clinic the card described. I noted that it was not Harley Street but an up-market enough location and I admit that I assumed, too readily, that Celeste was consulting with some New Age set-up, that it was some further eccentricity on her part. I pocketed the card and decided not to discuss this with Celeste, not for the time being anyway.

Now, looking back, I realise that Celeste's mother tried to be subtle and a lot was lost in translation and a lot more misunderstood by me because I trusted so blindly in my own strengths. I believed that I was the balance Celeste's edgy temperament needed and that she in return was an antidote to my money oriented, pragmatic approach to life and so, when we returned to London, I strongly encouraged her to pursue her creativity and cast off the structure and restraints of being a commercial artist. I seduced her into embracing the brilliance of her individuality and it was energising to see her float higher and higher but you know what happens when you blow a big bubble. It rises up and up but then suddenly the slightest breeze can send it down and inevitably it must burst.

Perhaps I was not yet at the point where I would have to devote so much of myself to blowing bubbles and then fanning them carefully, in a vain attempt to prolong their fragile existence. No, I did not drive away that day understanding the perils but from that point onward, I found myself regularly checking the delicate soul that was Celeste for any signs of cracks.

After dropping you off, I wanted to stay at Turnberry and play golf but I knew I could not leave Celeste. I knew it but I told myself I was driving back, in such a fury, because I was madly in love with her, which of course, was also the truth.

CLAIRE

The next few months of my life were hectic but fun. I worked the rest of the summer break and then Emily and I moved into our student house, joined by Sarah Maunders and Katherine Richards. I wonder what has become of them. Yes, I am curious but I have avoided University reunions. Anyway, they were more Emily's friends than mine.

The second year course proved demanding and I always felt guilty about enjoying myself too much, convinced that only a First Class degree would be good enough. Amid the busy schedule, I made time to read my way through the Henry James novel, though its wordiness made me want to scream. I thought I should make the effort and get back to David about it, mindful of the one useful thing my mother ever told me; "It's not what you know but who you know."

I finished the novel by the end of the Christmas break and after several aborted attempts, I finally drafted and posted a letter to David, telling him my frank opinion of the work, which was not all that complimentary and I realise now rather arrogant. The more challenging part was trying to second guess his reason for lending it to me. Yes, I understood that Isabel Archer, like me, was young and stepping out into the world, but this was a woman of wealth and a woman from an era when it was entirely the norm to marry and I did not quite see how this was a fit with my impoverished background and determination to have a career. Indeed, I mostly liked Isabel's American friend, the feisty journalist Henrietta Stackpole or was this what David had seen in me?

Years later, now far more mature and wise, I understand that he probably intended me to see a less literal application, that I was to take note of the need for caution, I should be careful in my assessment of others' characters and that I would come to a point in my life, like Isabel, when I might need to accept the consequences of my choices. In any case, I waited and waited for him to respond to that letter but he never did and I felt more disappointed and hurt than I could ever have predicted.

And it was during the Easter holiday that Emily's brother found me at the end of their garden, quietly sulking about it again and, checking over his shoulder to be certain we were alone, he grabbed me rather roughly and snogged me and though shocked and not all that impressed by the crude kiss, I thought "to hell with it" and kissed him back. I decided that to follow through on my policy of avoiding blokes, I should make use of Michael Hunt and endeavour to lose my virginity as soon as possible and be done with it.

So, this great milestone in my life ended up being an awkward, uncomfortable but thankfully brief grinding of pelvises in the woods near their house. I can thank Michael for being sensible enough to use a condom and for not falling in love with me. We agreed after a few repeats which did not ignite any greater passion in me that our fling had been "nice" and that it would be a pity to spoil my friendship with his sister and so I never told Emily. Later that year, Michael went up to Sandhurst.

Relieved to have had sex and not found it to be so compelling as to be likely to interfere with my plans for life, I nevertheless felt a strange new confidence and I decided, much to Emily's amazement, to finally spend some of my earnings from the restaurant job on a swanky, new haircut and some bold, high-street fashion.

I started to wear clothes which accentuated my womanly curves and I began to realise that a sense of my own sexual attractiveness gave me a certain power and not just over the male sex. Everyone noticed me more, listened to me more. I became more interesting to everyone and the fact that David had ignored my letter was now irrelevant.

Then, at the beginning of the summer term, I was informed by a tutor that I should report to the main reception desk and the lady there explained that a gentleman had enquired after me. Naturally, they could not hand out a student's address to him but they had agreed to pass on his message. It was from David. Oddly it made my heart beat fast and I had to re-read it several times.

Dear Waif,

It is generally a good idea to pop an address at the top of a letter. Hope this finds you well and happy. I'm here for one night, staying at the George Hotel. Meet me there for dinner tonight 7.30pm. Hope you can make it. Celeste sends her love. Appalled by your low opinion of great literature but perhaps you would like to see how Celeste painted you?

Regards,

David.

That fluttery sensation and the way I blushed. It struck me that I might just have a crush on the man but I could not fathom it. It made little sense. A big part of me felt I should not go, that there was something dangerous about pursuing the matter, that I had feelings for this man that were not under my control and this was a man much older than me, a man in love with Celeste. Indeed, I screwed the note up in my pocket and walked back to my student house that afternoon, resolved to ignore the invitation. I had lovely memories from that day with them both and I should guard against tampering with them. However, I soon found the company of my housemates irritating and I could not take my eyes off the wall clock.

Obvious questions bombarded my mind. Why not go and see him? Why turn down dinner in a luxury hotel? Didn't I want to see the painting? Wasn't I curious? So, he thought my opinions on Henry James quite unjustified. Shouldn't I defend them?

I chewed half heartily at my heated up leftovers and struggled for half an hour to read more than the first paragraph of a textbook and then furious at my indecision and hesitation, I changed my outfit three times, smeared on some bright, red lipstick and waited for Emily to run her evening bath before slipping out. I could not afford a taxi and there were no direct buses and it would take me about forty minutes to walk there which meant I would be about half an hour late. Actually, I arrived twenty minutes late and when I saw David again, he was sitting on a bar stool, drinking whiskey and looking every bit twenty years older than me. This reassured me. I thought I am just a girl he is taking a kindly interest in and so I walked up to that bar, confident and smiling.

Seeing me, his eyes widened with surprise.

"Good grief! Look at you Waif, you've grown up a bit."

He kissed me on the cheek and I accepted his remark as a compliment.

"Thanks. Yes, I suppose I have. Inevitable really. Like you getting old." It was brazen and rude and made him laugh.

"Heh, love the attitude but spare me a little. I'm about to buy you an expensive dinner, not at all suitable for a student. What would you like to drink then?"

I asked for half a lager but he scowled and ordered me my first gin and tonic which I hated, though it helped me float to our table.

He was entirely the person I remembered, keen to educate me, talking me through the menu, asking me all the right questions about my studies, earnest, well meaning, kind. He was handsome, that was true and perhaps I was more aware of his masculinity and the seductive tone of his voice but we talked a lot about Celeste and I felt comfortable, at least with him if not with our surroundings. The George was an old fashioned, grand hotel, all plaster borders and chandelier, white table linen and too much cutlery. The dining room was huge but there were not many other diners and the waiters fussed over us. This I found awkward, but not David. It was normal for him.

"So, Celeste finished the painting. Between you and me, a reliable source told me it has scarce commercial value but I wasn't about to let her sell it anyway. It's a keeper. Here, I took a photo for you."

She had painted in monochrome. I was the central figure, seated at a desk, surrounded by what I now know and understand to be modern symbols to point the viewer to the vanity of life. I was recognizably me and I looked lost and alone.

"I look so pale and vulnerable. Is that really how I seemed?"

"Of course. Why do you think I call you waif?"

"Ah well, I've grown up since then. You'll have to think of something else."

He stared at me, a faint smile about him and I stared back, suddenly not self-conscious. There was a feeling, a sense that I had always known him.

"Slowly but surely you will find your way in this world and I have no doubt that you will succeed Claire but I think you will always be Waif to me."

"We hardly know each other but you make me feel you know me, understand me."

"Yes, of course. It's because we're alike, two go-getters. Celeste can scorn the pursuit of wealth and prestige because she was born into money and it's funny how an artist always finds someone to pay the bills. I don't resent it though. I love her very much for everything that she is. In fact, we're going to be married."

And so the spell between us was broken. Although, I am being honest when I say that I was genuinely happy for them both.

"Oh that's brilliant news! When? Where?"

"Next month. It's going to be a quiet civil ceremony, in France, with her family. However, we hope to have a party, in London, in September and you're invited, of course."

"London? Sounds expensive. I'm not sure. It might be tricky with Emily and family. If I say I'm going to London, Emily will want to come."

"Well, Celeste insists that you come. We'll make sure you're not out of pocket. You have a while to concoct some sort of story. I think you can probably do deception very well. Here's Celeste's address in London. It's where she paints and sleeps a lot of the time. Drop her a line and she'll keep you posted. You could probably stay there. Don't forget to pop an address on your letters. I have a mobile telephone now but it is expensive for a student to call up, so your best bet is to keep in contact with Celeste. Here, take a look."

He placed a brick like telephone on the table and wanted to dazzle me by making a call on it but he waved it about a bit and complained that there was no signal and I thought he was deluded about his faith in new technology. Time would prove me to be the fool.

And then we talked about Henry James and literature and by contrast about the world of business and how he made all his money and his intellect and knowledge of life towered over me, a magnificent structure that inspired me. I was challenged, encouraged, not overwhelmed and by the time he saw me to a taxi, I had resolved that I did not have a romantic crush on the man; no, he was just someone I aspired to be myself.

His parting words were,

"See you at the party Waif. Meanwhile, go get 'em tiger!" and he made a humorous bow.

My mind raced for most of the night, every part of our conversation recalled and analysed. September would be there in my daily thoughts, hanging. I had never been to London before.

DAVID

Whilst I had found your letter ripping into Henry James amusing, I confess I would not have replied in any hurry, even if you had provided your student address and you have Celeste to thank for my visit.

Your quip about me growing old had hurt more than I was prepared to show. For in truth, I had turned forty and was having the first pangs of a mid-life crisis .Watching you breeze across the room like that, all lipstick and attitude, it struck me that the intensity of youth is a rehearsal for the real drama of life that comes like a tidal wave later on. My instinct was not to warn you of the perils of life, what better response than to take up arms and strike out? I considered your audacity an asset.

I had one disastrous marriage behind me and my crude analysis now, many years later, is that Celeste's fragility was part of the reason I loved her so much, markedly different to my first wife's ruthless and shameless self-promotion. I needed Celeste's need of me and so I had asked her to marry me. When you dissect love, you often find a complicated tangle of desire, need and yes, selfishness. Only an extraordinary man could have stepped back and honestly assessed whether I was the right match for Celeste, if marriage to me was a good idea for her and I mostly forgive myself. I was a man in a state of panic. Yes, business was good but I had turned forty and there was no heir in sight and it seemed to me that Celeste had qualities needed to balance mine out; my logic versus her eccentric, creative instincts, my pragmatism diluted by her spirituality. Easier for me to just say that I was simply in love with her but you and I know that there is nothing simple about what we call love.

Your unrestrained joy at my announcement managed to sweep away all my inner concerns and I am so glad that Celeste nagged me to find you. She went on and on about how you were "an old soul", about our destinies being intertwined and it was always so difficult to separate the wisdom of Celeste from her madness. As you know, she could infect a person with her thinking and when I gazed at that painting of you, perhaps I started to believe in her crazy notions, although I insisted to myself that my reasons for seeing you and inviting you to the party were far more rational; Celeste liked you and your friendship would be good for her and I saw your potential and ought, morally speaking, to do what I could to nurture it. I hope it does not hurt too much if I admit that I regarded you as something of a charity project. There's no point in dishonesty.

What I did not tell you that day was that the painting had cost a lot. The version you saw was completed after several failures and Celeste had ended up exhausted. I agreed with her parents that she should leave London and recuperate in France and that on her return, I would do everything in my power to re-direct her to her commercial painting; it was like painting by numbers for her, boring, routine and I felt guilty asking her to consider it but she was tired and she agreed that she needed the structure and discipline of meeting orders, satisfying customer demand. The money she made was not enough to support her but money was the one thing I had no trouble sourcing and when she had settled again, I decided to propose.

I really believed we had her moods under control. I was David Sutton, entrepreneur and I was poised to marry a beautiful French artist and you were supposed to be the spectator to something incredible and a talisman to our happiness. And then, deep, deep below the surface of my mind was another thought; Claire Sutcliffe was turning into a very lovely woman.

CLAIRE

So, as per David's suggestion, I wrote to Celeste Aubia, congratulating her on the lovely news and saying how much I liked the painting she had done. Actually, I thought I had better say something more than the word "like" though I was no art critic. I opted for saying that it was "a potent blend of haunting and challenging". I am quite sure that amused her. Anyway, my letter prompted a speedy reply and so began the correspondence between us. Nowadays, with e-mail, texting and social media the preferred methods of communication, the letter for me has some sort of special magic and I love to pull out the letters she wrote me. She wrote on hand-made paper, in pastel shades and scented by the soap in the drawer where she kept it and she invariably used turquoise ink which accentuated the prettiness of her French learned calligraphy.

She wrote in English just as she spoke it. At the time, my pathetic knowledge of French did not allow me to fully appreciate the charm of this, as I now can. I re-read them and her voice is clear in my mind and so she continues to live in those letters. They were lively and colourful and in anticipation of my visit to London, a place I confessed to being a little afraid of, she painted the city for me. She adored London and made it her mission to lay the groundwork so that I was guaranteed to feel the same, though I was never capable of feeling anything as powerfully as she did.

Aside from her passionate depictions of her London life, in which David rarely got a mention, she began to make odd references to my being somehow significant and she told me that she had started to paint landscapes which in her own words were "what people without taste desire to marry with their sofas." They were selling well and she said that the only thing that stopped her creative soul from falling into an abyss was the inclusion of a small, mysterious figure in each of them. The clients liked this touch because they imagined that this somehow made the paintings more valuable. Who was the figure? What did she represent? Celeste enjoyed having a secret. Only she knew who the figure was and she laughed that not even David had guessed. She told me that I was the figure and that when she painted me each time, she remembered my visit and rowing out on the loch and that she felt the connection between us.

Now, you will understand, no doubt, that whilst this was flattering, it was also troubling. I went over and over that day, in Scotland, trying to dovetail my own recollections with the strength of her memories. The day had been amazing; taking a risk and driving off in a sports car with a virtual stranger. Seeing that magnificent house. Meeting an artist and sitting for her. Learning all about the history of the place. The beauty of the landscaped gardens. The warm sun on our faces. The tranquillity of the loch and a sense that we managed to slow time for just a while. Meeting someone exotic like Celeste and sense that I would somehow meet them both again. The more I pondered Celeste's words and her insistence upon a connection, the more I believed in that connection. There is no doubt that the power of suggestion should not be underestimated and I was young and impressionable.

However, being far more rational and far less spiritual than Celeste, I placed the connection as the kind of randomly occurring affinity that can spring up between individuals if they meet in a certain context and experience mutual liking. I assumed that had we met in an entirely different place and set of circumstances, then the same level of connection would not have been replicated. In Celeste's eyes this would be a downgrading of our bond. She believed in destiny, not chance. At the time, I calmed any concerns about her rather full on affection by concluding that this was just her Frenchness and her artistic temperament and once I had relaxed about it all, I just made it another reason to like her and invest in the relationship. I endeavoured to make my own letters as engaging as hers and when I discovered one of her pastel envelopes on the doormat I admit I felt a warm glow of childlike happiness, the stuff of Christmas adverts.

In less than a month we exchanged several letters and I can only marvel at the time she was willing to devote to me, given that most brides to be would be rather preoccupied with wedding plans. Then, she wrote and explained that this would have to be the last letter for a while because they were off to be wed and David had planned a surprise honeymoon and she had no idea where she would be. David had been pushed to one side in my mind and upon reading this letter I felt a peculiar unease. They say that marriage is just a piece of paper and these days plenty of people don't even bother but I knew then what I have since experienced ,that a marriage between two people creates ties that no solicitor can easily erase. The "piece of paper" can be put through the legal shredder but something else lingers which we can only try to blot out like an unwanted memory. In my own way, still very young and naïve, I understood that David and Celeste were about to change the dynamic between them and that this had repercussions for everyone that knew them. Before, the idea of their marriage had delighted me but now I suddenly felt a weird kind of dread which I fought hard to dismiss. Too hard.

September came and with it heavy rains. I told Emily and family that it was a great Aunt that had been writing to me (to their credit they had resisted asking) and that she had asked me to visit her in London. Emily made a token offer to go with me but I think the idea of meeting any of my undesirable relatives probably repulsed her and so I made my escape. David was right. I was good at telling lies.

The day I arrived, rain was pounding off the pavements and everything from the window of my taxi was a dreary, grey blur. This was my first, shy encounter with the capital. I wanted to feel Celeste's passion for the city but I actually felt oppressed by the buildings that leant in from every side and the frenzy of the traffic. Sadly, I have never since overcome those first feelings. Yes, I respect the importance of the place and its unique heritage but after every visit, as I leave it behind, I somehow feel cleaner and more alive.

The taxi deposited me at Celeste's residence in Clapham, nothing remarkable at the time but a neighbourhood poised to sky rocket in value. Celeste occupied the middle and top floors and there was no automated way to admit visitors, so I nervously pushed a button and then waited and waited, so that by the time she opened the door, radiant and beaming, I was rain soaked and pathetic. She yanked me inside.

She still smelled of lavender but she had cut her hair into a sleek bob and the red jumper dress revealed a much thinner version of her than I had stored in my memory. She kissed me on both cheeks and laughed at me, as if I had said the funniest thing.

"So then, look, I am Mrs David Sutton." She held out one of her beautiful hands and a slender finger struggled under the weight of a thick, elaborately engraved ring.

"Wow! That's some ring!" I stared at it, absorbing its significance.

"Ah but of course. I am David's most important acquisition, don't you think?"

All the while, our meeting was accompanied by very loud piano music emanating from the ground floor apartment. Naturally, my eyes moved to that door.

"Come .That is my Russian neighbour. She is at least 80 and when she does not play the piano she plays her symphonies on her record player and so you see, I have music while I work. I see her only a few times and I think she wears evening dresses and diamonds all the time. I can say that she never complains if I have parties and so we have our understanding. If you cannot sleep, I can give you earbugs."

"You mean earplugs?"

"Ah yes, exactly."

So, for the second time, Celeste led me up a flight of stairs. She lived on the first floor of her apartment and worked on the uppermost floor, these rooms benefitting from huge skylights. She showed me to my room, a small box room, the bed jammed in and dressed in white bed linen, with a quaint dressing room adjoining, crammed with rails of clothes. There was another, only slightly larger bedroom and a tiny bathroom, most of the floor space sacrificed to an open plan living room and kitchen. I tried to imagine the parties and Celeste's life here.

"So now that you are married, I suppose you won't spend so much time here?"

Celeste was fiddling with a device for making coffee but this remark made her stop and frown.

"But what do you imagine Clare? Do you think that David sleeps in the pyjama and that I prepare his toast? David works a lot. I mean, you cannot imagine. He has a woman called Mrs Jones who is like his mother and me I have my painting. This is not a traditional life. We live our life in sections. Here, David's apartment, the house in Scotland, France. It is like a door which revolves so. It is crazy but I love it."

It sounded exciting to me but I was programmed to think of practicalities.

"Yes, but I suppose when you have children, things will have to change, won't they?"

At this, the colour seemed to drain from her tanned complexion.

"Children? You 'ave been speaking to David of this?"

I had said something wrong, snagged on a trip wire and I froze, my palms sweating.

"Well, no. Of course not. I mean I just assumed..."

And then she did something which I would learn was typical of Celeste, something slightly unconventional and passively aggressive. She pushed the coffee things away and just dismissed the subject.

"My God how stupid of me. You prefer tea, of course. Now, I put the kettle on and you unpack your things and you show me what you are wearing to my party. Ok?"

It was not okay. It was never okay. She shut people down. However close she made you feel, sooner or later you were always back at the perimeter fence, the mansion of her mind impenetrable. The tragedy is that she was stranded there, alone.

So, sent to my room like a naughty child, I unpacked my shameful ensemble of garish disposable fashion, including the polyester dress that had won me over on the day but now seemed hideous and wondered how I was supposed to rescue the mood. I need not have fretted because Celeste was an expert at managing such moments. She took one look at the dress and burst out laughing and embraced me so that I felt forgiven.

"Are you taking drugs Claire? Come on, this dress is terrible."

"Heh, in my defence I'm a poor student and believe it or not I bought this in a very fashionable shop."

"Yes yes. You know that a person can wear anything in a nightclub but David has planned our party in one of London's most beautiful jazz clubs and you must be sophisticated and enchanting ; especially you must not put our friends off the wonderful food. So, go into the dressing room and choose something and prove to me that English girls can dress well."

I question, looking back, why I was not more insulted by this but the open invitation to rummage through all those beautiful clothes was too much for my youthful curiosity and I appreciated that each and every item on those hangers was the essence of Celeste. This, surely, is why it is so painful to sort through the wardrobe of a deceased love one? I did not want to copy Celeste, or try to be her by wearing her clothes but I think I understood that this was a way to be closer to the inner workings of who she was and I believe that when she saw me in her clothes, sometimes, at least, I achieved something she had imagined when she had bought them. As with the painting she had done of me, I completed an idea.

It was a silver grey silk dress by Chanel that most powerfully drew me and she nodded and smiled so knowingly, as if she had foreseen it.

"Ah yes, but of course. I wore it when I was about your age. It was my first kiss in this dress. Well, of course not my absolute first kiss you understand but the first that is really important. He was a man much older than me and gentle and kind."

"What happened? Did he break your heart?"

"No, only the heart of his wife when she found out. Of course, it was only supposed to be a simple romance and we did not want to be together. She was a fool but this is love. But is this dress for you? Come on, put it on. Let's see."

The older me pauses to consider the morality of her carefree attitude regarding adultery but the me of then was too much in awe. So, I just followed her prompt, confident that I liked the dress but not certain it would love me back. In the mirror, I saw the first version of myself that I considered truly eye-catching, good looking enough to mark my presence in a room and it frightened me a little.

Celeste grinned from ear to ear.

"Ah yes, there you are. Not a waif but a powerful, young woman. Are you ready for such a dress?"

"I'm not sure. I don't want too much attention. It makes me nervous."

"Yes, good. This is sensible. But you can find other ways to hide from people Claire. It is more important that you cover your intelligence than your beauty. Your intellect is your true weapon, I think."

Hide my intelligence? I found the suggestion outrageous and sexist and proceeded to give Celeste quite the lecture on the subject which she quietly endured.

"I mean, David respects you for your intelligence doesn't he? You're not telling me you have to dumb yourself down for him?"

"Not exactly. I just don't let him get used to it. I find it effective to surprise him when he is not ready. Of course, David you know is a very intelligent man but there are different kinds of intelligent. This you are yet to learn. Perhaps I should not tell things? Perhaps we can just watch and see?"

She smiled at me and part of me wanted to reject the dress on some sort of vague feminist principle but a stronger part of me loved that dress and the edgy way it made me feel and so it was decided although I resisted the offers of fancy shoes and jewellery. I would wear the patent court shoes, as planned and the alabaster heart.

We spent a further hour perusing her clothes and she insisted I "borrow" some other things and then she started preparations for a dinner party; she had invited a dozen people and I helped her put up trellis tables which we had to carry down from her studio. These were disguised with black table cloths and she later dressed them so that they were most elegant, the cheapness of the tables erased. She further impressed me with her relaxed but effective talents in the small kitchen; my task was to deal with the trail of devastation she caused and though I was asked to sample things, I am quite sure she did not value my opinion in matters of cuisine.

Over the years I have been to many dinner parties and that one is somewhere in my top ten. Celeste's guests were young, creative, fashionable and fun and David never arrived. Half way through the first course he telephoned and Celeste announced with much eye rolling that her husband could not make it, due to work commitments. I do believe that it was only I that felt any degree of disappointment and admittedly, I had trouble seeing how David Sutton, businessman, fitted into this scene. I think even Celeste was unmoved by his absence, in spite of her grumblings about his work addiction and I certainly felt it harsh of her to moan about his working since expensive honeymoons touring South America no doubt depended on his efforts.

Late on in the evening, voices were at an uncomfortable pitch, fuelled by copious amounts of wine and I was happy to accept one guest's suggestion that we go up to the studio and look at Celeste's work. Her name was Angelica and she was American, tall and very blonde. She worked for a fashion magazine and smoked extravagantly, one cigarette after another, taking only occasional light puffs and blowing smoke in all directions. It was all rather dramatic. I paused before opening the door to the studio and remarked that she ought to extinguish her cigarette. She gave me a hard stare but did so.

"Hell, you're far too responsible to be one of Celeste's friends. Where the heck did you guys meet?"

"Well, I met David first and he then introduced us. Up in Scotland."

"Is that right? Interesting. So, what do you make of the groom?" She stared even harder at me now.

"Oh he's very kind and obviously very successful at what he does. I think he and Celeste make a lovely couple."

She looked me up and down, suspicious.

"Now that's what I call a very diplomatic answer. How old are you?"

"Nineteen, nearly twenty."

"For real? That would make you twenty years younger than David Sutton then."

Now she gazed away, pretending to find Celeste's landscapes absorbing.

"I don't get it. What relevance does that have? I mean, age shouldn't be a barrier to friendship, should it?"

She turned and smiled at me. It was an unpleasant sort of smile.

"Oh I don't think it is a barrier to anything. You know none of us here tonight are really David's kind of people. We're all Celeste's friends and very loyal."

She was trying to make a point and I did not like her tone.

"Well, I am friends with them both, in equal measure. Now that they are married, that makes me an ideal friend, don't you think?"

She leant in on one of the paintings, analysing the diminutive figure walking by the lake that was me.

"It's definitely a female figure she always paints. Any guesses as to who it might be?"

She was fixing a stare on me again but I kept my eyes on the painting.

"I'm not sure. Maybe herself?"

"Well now that's an interesting idea! Don't reckon Celeste is the self-obsessed kind though."

"The point is that no one knows. It's a mystery and should stay like that. That's what I think. Are you looking forward to the party tomorrow?" I was keen to change the subject.

"Not going. That's the reason we're all here tonight. We didn't make it onto David's list. We're the rejects, except you it seems. I'm thinking maybe you're the spy in the camp?"

"Why would David want to spy on his own wife and her friends?" It was my turn to fix a mean stare at her.

"Because he's a controlling son of a bitch maybe? You oughta bear that in mind. He's a type, out of a certain mould...."

"And Celeste loves him and I for one look forward to celebrating that with them both." Though her junior, I hoped this was the killer punch in our strange little duel.

She took out a cigarette, lit it and blew smoke defiantly.

"Good for you, honey. Just be careful. You know what they say, two's company etc."

Then, to my relief we were joined by two other guests, both drunk and giggling and I managed to escape back downstairs. It was the only unpleasant part of the evening and it means more now than it did then. After a few more glasses of wine, any tension had vanished and I dismissed the American as jealous and sour.

When the last guest had staggered away, Celeste smiled at me, her eyes sparkling but not drunken.

"Beautiful Clare. Come here. I want to kiss you."

She kissed me on both cheeks and then, her expression more serious, she said.

"I think I love you Claire. Is that okay?"

"Yes, of course." It was no lie. I accepted her proclamation as an extension of her quirkiness and nationality. But I did not say I loved her back because I did not. Not yet.

By the time I woke the next morning, towards eleven, Celeste had left. Naturally she had a lot to do before the party. She had left me a note, next to some croissants and a box of eggs, explaining that I should relax for what remained of the morning and then, at about one o'clock someone would call to take me out on a driving tour of the city sights, as organised by David, including afternoon tea at The Ritz. I would then be dropped at a hair salon, her treat and from there I should take a taxi back to the apartment (the keys were next to the note) and I would be collected again at seven and taken to the venue. I felt just a little hung-over and the apartment was still strewn with remnants of the party but I did not have much chance to question the plan or sulk about any of it because the door to the apartment suddenly opened and a middle aged woman casually walked in, scarcely giving me a glance.

After removing her coat and hanging it up, she peered back at my open mouth.

"Cleaner, dear. Don't mind me. I'll start in here if you'd like to get yourself washed and dressed."

"Oh, ok. Sure. I haven't had breakfast yet. I didn't realise."

"No problem darlin' I'll be done here once you're out and you can have your breakfast nice and quiet, while I do the other rooms."

In the shower, I considered how organised my day was courtesy of others and the one thought most troubling me was the idea of the "someone" scheduled to meet me at one. In all probability, I tried to reassure myself, it would be a knowledgeable taxi driver but then, I further pondered, was I having afternoon tea by myself? On balance, this might be less awkward than having tea with a virtual stranger but my mind raced on to further difficulties. What should I wear for afternoon tea? It was only after I emerged from the shower that I noticed an outfit hanging on the back of my bedroom door and another note from Celeste. "You would be lovely in this. No?"

I very much objected to the overwhelming sense of being controlled but I knew that the jeans and sweatshirt I had arrived in, the day before, were hardly suitable and it would be stupid of me to turn down what was basically a very well-intended gesture. So, with little further hesitation, I put on the skirt, blouse and jacket which required something other than my black, patent shoes but as a small gesture of rebellion I put these on anyway. This gave me a perverse little lift in mood, added to by three croissants, smothered in jam. The Russian lady was also out of bed now and playing her recorded music, loudly. The cleaning lady started to hum the melody.

By a quarter past twelve I was alone again and neither the television nor Celeste's eclectic book selection could dispel the sense of a clock ticking and the "someone" arriving. I just hoped it was a female "someone". By five past one I was feeling a bit sick and blaming the croissants and then almost jumped out of my skin when the bell rang, in short, sharp bursts, the caller either very determined or impatient or perhaps just an idiot.

Flustered, I grabbed my bag and then almost forgot the keys and I was aware of sweaty palms running down the stair rail and so, just before opening the door, I wiped my hands on the skirt and tried to compose my breathing.

When I opened the door, I discovered a tall and very conventionally handsome man, perhaps only four or five years older than me but he fixed such a stern and resolute stare upon me that he might have been much older again and his tone was very business-like.

"Hello Claire. I work for David Sutton and my name's Chris Peterson. I've been asked to show you round the city. That ok with you?"

"Sure. Celeste told me. Nice to meet you." I stuck out my hand and though it seemed a bit formal he did not hesitate to give me a firm handshake and perhaps anything else would have been a challenge for him. He directed me not to his own car but to a chauffeured one, directing me to climb in.

I automatically scrambled across to sit behind the driver but then he opened the door on that side and embarrassed by my mistake, I shuffled back over. When it came to protocol I had absolutely no idea and I already felt that the next few hours would be tense and tough going.

"I'm sorry to be a nuisance. I could have just gone off by myself, on the underground."

"It's no trouble and we're under strict instructions to show you whatever you want. Where would you like to go first?"

"Oh well, perhaps it might be interesting to see where David lives in relation to here and maybe his offices?"

"Really? Well, I'll point that sort of stuff out maybe but how about we head for Westminster first and do all the usual stuff."

It was a polite enough suggestion but he seemed to have concluded that I was a bit hopeless and smoothly took over, giving me a very slick commentary and I just followed where ever he pointed and tried to ask the odd, intelligent question. I wondered what David had imagined when he asked Chris to do this job and whether he had thought we would hit it off. I hoped he was not going to the party. Afternoon tea would be hard enough.

Parts of the tour were enjoyable, namely when I strolled across Hyde Park by myself and when Chris left me to explore Covent Garden. I think he found the tour equally tiresome because when he met me at Covent Garden for the next bit, his breath smelled of beer and I imagined him sitting at a bar, complaining to the barman about the absurd things he was sometimes asked to do. When the car pulled up at The Ritz I considered asking him if I might have tea alone, as I was rather tired and my heart pounded as I struggled to find the courage to make this suggestion but then the door opened and David Sutton leant in, grinning and I am sure I did nothing to disguise the mixture of delight and relief.

"Welcome to London, Waif. Time for tea? Thanks for keeping her out of trouble Chris. Pop back in an hour or so? I think Celeste has an expensive plan to ruin her hair. "

I saw Chris's shoulders fall with obvious relief and he leapt from the car with renewed energy and then stood aside, so that it was David who helped me out and it struck me that it all happened so naturally and that chauffeurs and cars and guests and hotels were all part of the daily scenery for both men.

Afternoon tea at The Ritz might have been a horribly stiff ordeal or a profound let down but David was a man at ease and injected fun and energy into the occasion.

He managed to sprawl himself casually in chairs not designed to such effect and though I remained stiff, correct and upright, I did so because I felt this was how one should enjoy such a first occasion and though I loved his irreverence, I sensed that he enjoyed my attempt at propriety. He studied everything I did, with a faint smile about his lips.

"So, how's married life?"

"Oh life's much the same as before but I confess that knowing that Celeste is Mrs Sutton makes me very happy indeed. Did she strike you as pleased with her new status?"

"Oh yes, definitely. The ring is unbelievable! We had a fun party last night. She has some very interesting friends but one told me that you don't approve of them much."

"Of course I don't. Celeste would hate it if I did. She told you about the club where we're having the party?"

"Yes. It sounds amazing. Did you choose it together?"

"Officially yes but it was Celeste's idea and I'm letting her have her way because that will make it easier for me to have my way about other things."

"You make marriage sound like some sort of power struggle."

"Oh twas ever thus Waif, believe me. Don't get into it for a while. Cherish your independence."

"Well, that's the plan but of course, if I fall in love, perhaps I'll be powerless to avoid it. I mean, these days, a person can avoid actual marriage but living with someone is hardly staying independent, is it?"

"No, no it isn't. The trick is to know when you're not in love which is harder than you think."

"Don't you mean, when you're in love?"

"No. When that happens, everything else will seem obvious but I thought I was in love with my first wife you see and that was a terrible mistake. Anyway, enough of that. How's Uni'?"

And I can marvel now at how patiently he listened to me, asking all the appropriate questions only glancing away occasionally, a very slight nod at anyone he recognized but giving every appearance of being genuinely interested in my studies and then, when I tried to reciprocate by asking about his business, he dismissed the subject with such ease and good humour, as if it were only natural that we should prefer to discuss me. What I see now is how self-absorbed I could be, a self-centred Miss Know-it-all and whilst I know that this rendered me a great source of amusement to him, I can also appreciate the good grace he had to listen.

When Chris Peterson re-appeared, on schedule, I felt like a small child again, being told it was time to put down the toys and David laughed at my obvious disappointment. How this might have seemed to Chris Peterson, I did not question and neither did I make much effort to be civil to him on the journey to the hair salon.

The hairdresser, a Frenchman, peered down at my incongruous shoes, clearly not impressed and proceeded to pick up strands of my hair and drop them with similar disgust and after a deep sigh, clapped his hands and with much French chatter, a girl washed my hair, rubbing at my scalp so hard as to make me wince. If this was Celeste's idea of a treat, then I would have to inform her of just how misguided she was. To this day, I detest visits to the hairdresser's and I regard that day as a defining experience. Yes, the sinister man transformed my everyday hair into a style that was elegant and chic but he made me feel vulnerable, like a dentist and indeed I think I probably prefer a trip to the dentist.

It was only later, when I put on my party dress and applied some make-up that I fully acknowledged the extent to which I had been, not transformed, but beautifully enhanced, not a bunch of daffodils slapped into a pot, but a professional, floral bouquet; I went to the party, no longer the young university student, not David's Waif, but a young beauty, set to dazzle. I went to the party knowing that Celeste would be delighted and this thrilled me.

DAVID

Thinking back to the party at the jazz club, I ought to recollect the superb music, the heady perfume of the flowers, the excellent champagne and wines, the sumptuous food and my ravishing wife in her red velvet gown but all of my sensory based memories are rather blown sideways by what I most sharply recall, my feelings.

To begin with, there was a complete and utter sense of accomplishment. I had married Celeste and it was the best decision of my life. I had secured my future happiness. I made my way round the club, greeting family, friends and significant others, uplifted by the feel of Celeste's hand on my arm. It was a safe, warm feeling mingled with yes, vain, masculine pride. Believing that I was the envy of most men in the room because she loved me and had committed to me, coupled with the warm glow I experienced every time I looked in her eyes, or she spoke one of her charming Frenchisms, or I caught a waft of her scent, why nothing in life could surely surpass those feelings? I was a driven businessman. I lived for the next deal, the next profit and I knew nothing could satiate that particular hunger but Celeste had filled an inner void like no deal ever had or ever would. She was not a distraction from any of my goals for life, she was the force that would power me to go higher, to push on.

Then, there was that particular moment and other feelings. I was talking to one of my cousins about the future of Europe and the possibility of a single currency and the women were rolling their eyes and telling us to stop being so boring when I felt a slight tug on my arm as Celeste pulled away to glance around at her other guests. Then I felt it, a kind of electricity, something tense and alert, running down her arm into her hand and shooting into my arm and it made me look into her eyes and I saw it, a look of breathless wonder, the face of infatuation and naturally I followed the direction of this dreamy gaze and there you were, Claire Sutcliffe, alone, on the top of the stairs, nervous, uncertain, perhaps trying to decide whether to stay or go. Remaining transfixed, no attempt to disguise her emotion, Celeste spoke.

"Look at her David. Look how very beautiful she is. Do you see her?"

Yes, I saw you and a quick scan of the room suggested that many others did too. What we saw was that a very pretty girl had arrived, apparently alone and appearing slightly like an uninvited guest and the longer you hovered there, the greater the impression you made. Yet, I am certain that known of us saw you with Celeste's eyes, so intense, so ardent and when she made to cross the room my instinct was to seize her arm tighter and stop her.

"Wait there. I'll send Chris over to retrieve her. You'll only shine the spotlight on her and make her feel even more shy. She looks like she's about to run away as it is."

So, I pulled Chris Peterson away from his stool at the bar and told him to rescue you and in particular I asked that he only bring you over to talk to us once you had had at least two glasses of champagne and talked to some other guests. I insisted that you were young and would enjoy meeting some of the younger people. I was all matter of fact about it and outwardly calm but my stomach was now churning over and over and I recognised the slight stirrings of jealousy.

As I made my way back over to my wife, politely fending off every guest trying to engage me, I struggled with these feelings, confused by them. Celeste was talking to her guests but all the while peering over to try and glimpse you and yes, I knew all too well the signs of my wife feeling constrained, frustrated, irritated. And you understand, what really perplexed me and disturbed me was my certainty that my wife's feelings for you were not in any measure sexual. Easy for me to say, I suppose, but had you presented any sort of a threat in that way, well it would have been relatively straight forward for me to have challenged her and closed the thing down but I knew two facts; first, this strange infatuation was non-sexual and complex and secondly, you, the object, were most probably oblivious to it, unaware of your growing power.

You can hopefully understand my coolness toward you that evening, why I stubbornly refused to please Celeste by dancing with you, why I refused to pay any attention to Celeste when she expressed concerns about Chris Peterson; truthfully, the way I felt, if he had not tried to seduce you I might have paid him to and when I saw you leave with him, I confess I was both relieved and satisfied.

In this bizarre way, I was blinded to any attraction I myself felt for you. Those feelings were driven down and suppressed. If I had gone to the top of those steps and rescued you Waif, how different our story might be.

CLAIRE

Chris Peterson had been a boring tour guide but when he appeared at the top of those stairs, I was ecstatic with relief and when he prescribed champagne for my nerves I revered him like an esteemed doctor. He introduced me to several guests, all young and aspiring members of David's enterprise and though they all stared at me too much, I began to feel a little more at ease.

After the first glass of champagne, I felt confident enough to say to him

"I think I must be slightly paranoid but I feel like everyone is staring at me a little."

He smiled and I noted that he was handsome in his dinner suit.

"Well, people are bound to stare a bit. I mean, you are an exceptionally pretty girl and to be honest, if you don't believe that yourself well, that makes you rather cute with it. A modest, beautiful woman. That's a rare thing."

He sounded different and this unexpected charm made me blush. He held my gaze and the attraction between us was quickly sealed. Flattery was getting him everywhere. He suggested we dance and when I explained that I had no idea how to dance to that kind of music he just took my hand and confidently moved me about the dancefloor, so that all I could do was laugh and I lost myself in him and the music. He was no longer distant and boring and we were just two young people connecting.

Then Celeste and David appeared next to us and we stopped our dancing and moved over to the edge of the dancefloor. Celeste was beaming at me. David seemed distracted and was looking about at the other guests a lot, as if trying to locate someone in particular.

"Are you aving fun Claire?" Celeste gazed from me to Chris and back again, her eyes teasing.

"Yes, thank you. This place is amazing and you look stunning Celeste. Congratulations to you both."

I stared over at David but he was still peering around and I thought perhaps he was ignoring me, though this seemed a bit irrational. I reminded myself that he was the groom and probably felt the need to keep circulating. Celeste frowned at him and pulled on his sleeve so that he had to look at us.

"David, I think now you must dance with Claire. You must show her your skills, no?"

David's eyes were directed at me but he seemed to look right through me and he spoke rather curtly.

"Oh I think I can't compete with Chris here and we should leave the youngsters alone. Claire won't mind, will you?"

"No, of course not. Please, I'm sure you have lots of guests to speak to."

Celeste's face crumpled in a pretend sulk and then she raised a hand and stroked my cheek fondly.

"Yes, yes. Always the duty to perform but listen Claire, we two will cause a storm and dance together later, the carnation and the lily. I don't care about my grumpy husband who suddenly wants to speak French to my cousins. He is such a show-off. Come on then my love, allons-y."

She was smiling at us but as she slipped her hand onto David's arm she gave him a very dark look, as if he had said something terribly wrong. He nodded at us, no warmth, no friendliness and they walked away, muttering at each other. It had all been peculiar and I might have worried and worried about it but Chris insisted we dance again and I was easily distracted.

By my fourth drink, I felt pleasantly drunk and though Celeste was wearing a very distinctive, red dress, I never seemed to be able to spot her .Chris left me briefly with some other people, enough time for me to lament his absence, though I fought hard to disguise such feelings from him. By the time I had finished my sixth drink, I had decided that Chris Peterson was the most attractive and interesting guy ever but I was sober enough to realise that if I stayed at the party any longer I would regret it and in the interests of not shaming my hosts, I should take my leave.

I wanted to thank them and say goodbye properly but still I could not locate them, though there had been a fleeting moment when perhaps I had noticed Celeste's eyes staring at me anxiously, but this picture was soon swallowed up by a multitude of other faces, in a room that was beginning to spin.

Chris walked me out to a taxi, the cold air exhilarating and my heart pounding. He held open the door, ever the gentleman. I snatched hold of one of his lapels.

"Why don't you leave with me? I think you're ok, really. You were very boring earlier, dull and very public school but I like you now."

"Is that right? Well, I suppose I'd better make sure you get up all those stairs in one piece. Go on then."

The taxi had scarcely pulled away and I started to kiss him, though the right word is snog because there was nothing delicate or graceful about it and he pulled back laughing at me and then taking my face in his hands, he kissed me slowly, skilfully, passionately and when the taxi stopped at Celeste's flat I said something half robotically about him coming up for a coffee but of course, neither of us nor the taxi driver believed there would be any need of a kettle.

Odd how what I mostly remember of that night is insisting that I remove the borrowed dress myself, as it was vintage Chanel(I may have repeated that to him a few times) and I remember glancing at my hair in the mirror and feeling a bit sad that it would all be ruined by the morning. I was sober enough to have such concerns and sober enough to appreciate that Chris Peterson was much better at sex than Emily Hunt's brother Michael, though of course I admit the venue was much improved .He may not have transported me to giddy heights of ecstasy but he definitely achieved something on a par with a very professional back rub, conjuring strange groans of pleasure from me which seemed to encourage his ardour and thanks to the convenient location of a mirror I recall much admiring the beauty of his physique as he laboured and a very particular sense of satisfaction when he secured his own peak of pleasure .I felt a strange sense of honour that he had chosen me as a vessel for his bodily fluids and though he had seemed far more sober, I lay awake long after he had fallen asleep, admiring his nakedness, studying it in the moonlight.

I awoke when he clicked the door of the apartment shut. It was daylight. There was a note on the bedside table.

"Call me when you are next in London." And he had scribbled his telephone number down. It was Sunday morning and to my surprise, already nine o'clock.

I was wrapped in a bedsheet, leaning on the kitchen counter, trying to decide whether to shower or have breakfast first when the apartment door opened and David appeared.

I am sure I turned bright red but he was oh so matter of fact and almost business like.

"Come on lazy bones. Get washed and dressed. I'm taking you out for breakfast."

DAVID

When I arrived outside Celeste's place, I saw the door open and Chris Peterson emerged, a little dishevelled but yes, I think the satisfaction was there in the eyes. He had managed a smooth exit. I could have let him sneak away but it was not in my nature to do so.

"Morning Chris. Enjoy the party?"

It was mean of me to make him squirm.

"Er, hi! Yep, great thanks."

He looked down at the ground and away to the end of the street. It was like I had caught him stealing my wallet.

"Go on then. Off you go. Make the most of the rest of the day. I'll see you at the office tomorrow."

"Sure. Thanks. Tell Claire I'm sorry I had to dash. I've left her a note."

"Of course you have. Now go on, sod off."

When I entered the flat, you were all tied up in that bed sheet, like a mermaid in a net and your embarrassment touched me; I saw how young you were and perhaps if I had been just a little older I may have felt quite paternal towards you but as I watched you scurry away to the shower, I distinctly felt the first clear erotic thought about you but then there were a lot of other thoughts and feelings on my mind. My wife adored you and I loved my wife very much.

By the time you came back, dressed like a student again, I had prepared what to say.

"Chris is a nice guy and I'm glad you two had a nice time together but you need to forget about him now. Stay focussed on getting that degree nailed."

"That sounds like fatherly advice. I'm not big on parents."

"Take it as the advice of someone older and wiser and all advice is easier to swallow on a full stomach, so let's go. Come on."

The English think they are the kings of breakfast but I took you to an American place and blew your sleepy head with all the choices. As you scanned the menu over and over, wide-eyed, I realised that this child-like excitement, this pleasure in relatively simple things, it was something I could never quite manage with Celeste. My wife had come from money and privilege and had a complex relationship with materialism, the kind that in itself is a luxury. It was refreshing to be with you but without you realising it, you were also a threat to me.

"So, my wonderful wife has become extremely fond of you. You do know that?"

"Yes. Actually, she went and told me she loved me. I'm guessing that's just a very French thing going on. We write letters to each other and hers are amazing."

"Yes, I'm sure they are. And you're the figure in her paintings of course."

"Oh she told you did she? It's just Celeste having a little joke. I don't mind."

"The thing is though Claire, I'm worried that she might distract you from your studies this year. This final year is going to be very demanding for you and Celeste won't appreciate that. You won't have much time for a pen pal and I have lots of plans too so Celeste is also going to be very busy, plans she doesn't know about as yet. So, I just wanted to say that you mustn't be too disappointed if Celeste doesn't keep in touch as much but of course, if you ever need anything, you must not hesitate to contact me and I'll do whatever I can."

You had been enjoying a blueberry pancake and your lips were stained with the juice. Now you put down your fork and frowned at me. You were young yes, but very bright and I was not hiding my tension very well.

"Honestly David, I don't think you need to manage our friendship. Celeste and I can figure it out. I know you call me Waif and see me as all vulnerable and naïve and perhaps I am compared to you but you don't have to go out of your way to protect me. I know both you and Celeste have your life together and I get what it is to be a third wheel. Has Celeste said or done something?"

To be successful in business, you need nerves of steel and I was determined this situation would not get away from me.

"No but I know Celeste far better than anyone. She can be intense and demand a lot of people and I want you to trust me on this. You are too young to be so involved with her and she won't mean to be selfish about you but she's come from money and knows nothing of your struggles, your ambitions and the sacrifice required. When I introduced you to my world, I meant to help you, encourage you... I'm just suggesting a bit of distance that's all. Trust me on this."

There was no sign of trust in your eyes, only suspicion and un-certainty and I remember thinking that if you were a witness to my crime then I had no assurance that I had silenced you and that in the movie I would have to kill you .I felt dirty, a moral reprobate.

"Like you say David, I'm going to be very busy this coming year. If Celeste writes then of course I'll write back but I'm sure she's going to be too busy herself to keep a pen pal thing going so I think you are worrying about nothing. Is Celeste ok? She's not ill or anything?"

You stared at me, so wide-eyed, so unblemished by life. Ce-leste's mental health was a dark secret that I had to guard and you certainly did not deserve to have your youth, vigour and optimism tarnished by it.

"No, just badly hung-over. She is not a huge fan of breakfast. Come on, eat up. We need to collect your things and get you to the station."

And so I side stepped your question and rushed you along, like some unwanted relative and I could see how awkward this was for you but you had the good sense to know when to give up .When I finally waved you off on the train, I decided that overall things had not gone too badly, though badly enough perhaps that we might never see you again. It was a pity. Or did it feel a greater loss? When I returned to my apartment it felt stuffy and I had to open several windows.

CLAIRE

I had done something wrong. I had hours on the train to go over every detail of that week-end and the most obvious conclusion was that David had chosen some very evasive, cir-cuitous explanation for why I was being effectively banished back to university, pointing to Celeste as somehow to blame, nudging me out of their picture when in fact it was all be-cause I had slept with his employee Chris Peterson. Once I had grasped hold of this "truth", I analysed the only two possible explanations for why my sexual exploits had compromised our friendship. Either he and Celeste or perhaps just David thought I was a slut and not after all a lovely sweet girl OR David in particular disapproved of my nocturnal activities because I was supposed to be his charming waif and perhaps all along he had desired me and had only been waiting to seduce me; Celeste was to be the perfect trophy wife and bearer of children and I would be the young mistress. Glancing around at my fellow passengers, at the normality of everything, my theories seemed absurd but I kept coming back to the same start point, that I done something wrong and that David had managed me out of their lives.

After breakfast, we had driven back to Celeste's apartment and when I attempted to strip my bed David snapped at me to leave it for the cleaner and urged me to pack speedily, insisting that traffic to the station might be bad. I stuffed what few things I had in my bag and placed my wedding gift for them on the bedside table. I had forgotten to take it to the party. It was a pretty dreadful but heartfelt gift. I had crocheted two cushion covers in white. It was my only such skill and I thought that crochet was probably a French thing, that white was inoffensive and that a handmade gift was appropriate for two wealthy people from an impoverished student. Moreover, my story to Emily and family about my correspondence with a great Aunt was conveniently reinforced by my making such a gift. Emily's Mum found it very endearing. Perhaps she secretly hoped that said Aunt was going to step in and offer me a place to stay?

Naturally, once I returned, there would be a barrage of questions about my week-end and so I had to desist from thinking about David's eagerness to put me on the train and start thinking about my cover story. By the time the train started to pull slowly into my station stop, my poor head was spinning and I felt exhausted. It was certainly hard to believe, as I hauled myself and my bag up the platform staircase, that the best parts of the experience of my week-end away made up for all the subsequent feelings of guilt and stress.

Then, two days before Emily and I were due to return to University, I was summoned into her Dad's study by her mum and confronted by a page of society photographs, taken at the London wedding reception for Mr and Mrs David Sutton and there I was with Chris Peterson and the caption read "Budding entrepreneur and employee of David Sutton, Christopher Peterson and Miss Claire Sutcliffe, a friend of both bride and groom. Miss Sutcliffe wowed onlookers in this vintage cocktail gown by Chanel." Emily's Mum turned out to be the very controlled, sinister type when enraged.

"We invited you into our home, we have shown you every kindness and you have chosen to not only lie to us but to betray every ounce of trust we had in you. I have no idea how you managed to ingratiate yourself with the likes of David Sutton or what you hope to achieve from it. I am not going to make a huge scene for Emily's sake. You will make an excuse and leave for uni today, by yourself. I will explain to Emily everything in due course and you can be sure she will expect you to find another student house, as soon as possible and our connection with you ceases. If David Sutton is so wonderful then I suggest you ask him to put you up in the holidays but let me do you one last kindness and warn you, the man is a complete shit and you have made a terrible mistake by getting involved. Now, just go and pack your things. The sooner you are gone the better."

I felt humiliated and dreadfully ashamed yes and naturally anxious and overcome by a sense of being quite alone but what I mostly felt was a sense of awe at the smooth and breath controlled delivery of this judgment and it compelled me to be likewise very dignified. So, I did not attempt to argue or defend myself and did just as she had instructed me to, even managing to calmly inform Emily that I had decided to leave early as I needed to sort out something at the university campus branch of my bank, one last lie, beautifully executed. And I was very composed also, when I returned to the study and quietly retrieved the society pages from the waste paper bin where Emily's mum had tossed them. I looked incredible in that photo and Chris Peterson had been quite a catch.

So, the rest of that last academic year was destined to be a hard slog. There was all the studying to do, of course, and I took up as many shifts as I could at the student bar to help fund the squalid room I was obliged to take in a house with other misfits, a house where I was now forced to spend the holidays, including Christmas. I resisted any temptation to go home to my parents .They were waiting for me to fail. I wrote to Celeste informing her of my change of address and telling her not to post anything to Emily's. She wrote only several weeks later, on white office paper, in type, saying thank you for the "remarkable cushion covers" lamenting the distance between us, not just geographical but "the disparity of our situations." She told me David was making lots of changes, that she was opening a new gallery in Chelsea, that she was exhausted and she urged me to come to London. I wrote back explaining that I could not miss lectures or afford to give up work shifts and she did not write again until the early spring.

David was right. Celeste was an unhealthy distraction from my reality and when I thought of her, I imagined her sipping champagne at gallery evenings, dark and enchanting and though she bemoaned her exhausting life, it was a life of comparative luxury and with every week that passed Mr and Mrs Sutton became a bizarre chapter in my life, a set of experiences I had been immensely privileged to enjoy but it was over now. Gone. Finished.

Except that I still believed that David had been sincere when he had reiterated the offer to help me, if the need arose and it was comforting to have his business card tucked into my sock drawer and now and again I pulled it out and fingered it and pressed it against my mouth like a good catholic girl might do with her rosary. The option of going to him made me feel safe, comforted me in some very bleak hours.

Then, at Easter time, when I found myself up to my neck in revision and ground down by too many late night bar shifts, I received a very strange letter from Celeste, written on the lavender paper, in the turquoise ink.

My beautiful Claire,

I lament you much. I never forget you. I think of you with your head into all those big books and your pretty hair falling against your cheeks and I wonder why you do not come to London. I plan a adventure for us in France but David tells me you must study but you know, life is not in books and I want to teach you so much. So, I wait for you. You see how patient I can be. I hope that you wear better clothes. Everywhere I see things and I think "Yes, she would be adorable in this" and "That is made for Claire."

I send you all my love,

Celeste

I could not comprehend it but the letter filled me with a sense of desperation, a terrible anguish for her. I actually thought about abandoning my revision timetable and spending money I could not spare on a ticket to London but wisely I tucked the letter away and promised myself that I should let some time pass and with that time came reason. It would be a total disaster to go running off to London, to risk everything and in due course, I sent her a pretty card, thanking her for her kind thoughts of me, explaining that I might be able to come to London after my finals, that students had no need of lovely clothes and that I hoped she continued to paint. I sent her best wishes, not love.

She never replied and I confess it was a relief. Deep down, I believed I had let her down, that she expressed a kind of need of me but I refused her and so, when my own hour of need came, it was to her husband I turned. David was my only option.

PART TWO

DAVID

In the months after our wedding party, I worked hard to keep Celeste busy but balanced which was no mean feat given the demands of my business dealings but your name was like a dripping tap. Every time I thought I had finally cured the problem, she mentioned you, lamenting your absence, trying to procure a visit. As if to spite me, for she must have sensed my resistance, she started on some sketches of you and these were left about the place. Drip. Drip. Drip.

I took her away at Christmas and being away from London seemed to offer some respite from her longing and sulking but almost as soon as we returned she announced a compelling desire to paint you again and insisted that she would need you to sit for her. All the while, I struggled to erase from my own mind an image of you, your hair tangled, caught up in a bedsheet, young, spirited and not so very innocent. I was mature enough to know the difference between my love for my wife and what was probably no more than a niggling fantasy but how was I supposed to get past it when my wife seemed even more mesmerised by the same woman?

I was tempted to invite you to London myself, to confront and somehow overcome whatever was at the heart of my wife's obsession but instead I called up a man I had used on many prior occasions, to have him carry out a background check on you. It was my standard approach to any person considered a potential threat in the business domain and honestly, it seemed a good idea to know more about who Claire Sutcliffe really was from an objective standpoint. I hope this does not make you feel too violated. It seemed quite logical at the time.

He came to see me on a bitterly cold February day. He was explain clothes police and had poker winning eyes. He was expensive but did whatever necessary. I had seen him carry in great dossiers on people but I straight away saw that yours was a very thin file.

"I hope you don't mind me saying this David but this job has troubled me a bit. Before we go any further, can you explain a bit about your precise interest in this young girl?"

I looked him straight in the eye. I didn't dare not.

"It will strike you as peculiar perhaps but my wife seems to have developed a sort of adolescent crush on her. If I can speak frankly, this concerns me from just about everybody's point of view. Perhaps it is rather ridiculous but I confess I feel a bit jealous. I am also genuinely concerned for my wife who has, shall we say a delicate and fanciful nature and I am also anxious for Miss Sutcliffe, insofar as she may not appreciate the impact she has made on my wife nor feel anything remotely similar. I don't think my wife feels sexual feelings toward her but her affections are definitely strong. I need to know if Miss Sutcliffe has any dark secrets. I suppose I need you to confirm that my instincts have been perfectly correct and that the young lady is totally harmless."

He nodded and tossed the file on to my desk.

"There it is then. No dark secrets. Humble background, verging on poverty, smart enough to get herself a scholarship at the local independent school. Of course, get yourself enough education, start pronouncing your words properly and it drives a wedge, doesn't it? The only question worth asking is one I am not qualified to answer but believe me, I've asked myself that question before. How do uneducated, ordinary folk produce such smart kids? I did confirm that she was never adopted, just in case .Seems like it's just another genetic anomaly. Course, rumour is they didn't want her going off to university, waste of time etc. but Miss Sutcliffe has ambitions and coming from a town like that, dull as dishwater, well we can't hold that against her. As for ambition, well you don't need me to point out the dangers. It's a puzzle that she doesn't go back perhaps but then I think I can understand it. She drew a line. Takes a lot of guts. When she's older, made her way a bit, then she can return the conquering hero I suppose. According to the neighbours, the parents are too proud to go chasing after her. They were furious about her going. She's a looker but that won't be any great revelation to you nor that brains and beauty are a potent combination. Is she any kind of threat? Well, she has a spotless school record, no bullying, so I can see no reason to suspect she might blackmail anyone. Are you being totally straight with me on this David? I mean, I like to think we're sort of friends by now."

I had been staring at a photograph of you all the while.

"What do you mean?"

"I mean there's a bit of an age gap but it wouldn't be anything illegal. Yet, you only recently married. Affairs are always a risk. After all, I found out about your ex-wife's didn't I?"

I closed the file on you.

"I am not intending to have an affair with Claire. I told you, it's my wife that can't shut up about her."

"Well then I can offer you some advice if you want. Take it or leave it. No extra charge."

"Which is?"

"Whatever this connection is, don't try to block your wife. It will probably die a natural death. It's the 1990's. Women are so touchy, banging on about their rights. Just cos your last wife was a bitch don't be too controlling. As for Claire, no doubt she can take care of herself."

As if to prove a point, I handed the file back to him.

"Thanks. You can destroy it. Don't need to know any more. One more question. Since you have sort of raised the issue, do you think there is any chance she might have a thing for me?"

"Ah well, let's see. You're a rich, handsome bastard. Why wouldn't she think about it? You're the one with the ring on their finger. I meant what I said. Be careful of yourself David. You've got a lovely wife. It would be a shame to screw it up, not to mention expensive."

After he left, I cancelled all my appointments and spent the rest of the afternoon pretending to work but thinking about you. Finally, I rang the florist and ordered roses for Celeste.

At the beginning of March Celeste hosted a successful evening at her new gallery, selling many paintings and crucially some of the larger canvasses. I remember how radiant she looked and how proud I felt, yet later, back at our apartment, when she kicked off her shoes and fell onto the sofa, there was a pout about her lips and I did not want her to say anything because I knew she would take away the moment, pull the plug on the joy. I tried to head it off by speaking myself, telling her how superb she had been, how much I respected her but I was fighting a losing battle. She propped herself up on one elbow and arched her eyebrows at me.

"You know David, you are a brilliant man but please darling, do not pretend to be a critic of art. People buy my paintings because they like me and most of them are stupid fools with too much money. They buy my paintings like they buy their cocaine. Puff! Up it goes, the moment of consumer pleasure. One day you will find my paintings in a quiet showroom and who will buy them then?"

I was determined to remain upbeat and light hearted.

"Spoken like a true artist. You are all so self-critical, so self-doubting."

To my surprise she just smiled and seemed willing to let me be right but actually she had something else on her mind. She sat up with a sudden burst of energy but I don't believe there was anything spontaneous about the idea.

"I'm tired David. I want to go to Scotland."

I poured myself a whiskey and took a large swallow.

"Any particular bit of it?"

"Well to the house of course. It is calming. I need a break from here." She said this in French. It was her way of being more assertive.

"You said you hated that house, that it was too big, that it made me pretentious."

"Claire made me see it differently. So impressed, so full of wonder and I want to love it because it is special to you. The light is good there. I can paint well."

"I can't possibly get away right now. There's too much going on."

"I'm not a child. I can be alone. You can order the staff to spy on me if you like. Anyway, you can fly up at the week-ends. What is the point of your money if you can never be free?"

She never understood the freedom I felt in being an entrepreneur, soaring on all that adrenaline. She always scorned my work, though not so much the life style it afforded us. In that sense she was very spoiled.

"So I'm reduced to week-end sex? I'm not madly in love with that."

She smiled seductively. She knew how to work me.

"We will have sex in every room. I promise you darling. Anyway, I am thinking just two or maybe three weeks and if you say yes, I will pleasure you now until you beg for mercy."

She ran the tip of her tongue playfully over her upper lip and we laughed.

"Damn it! How do I turn down that kind of a deal? Ok, Scotland it is. I hope you realise how bloody freezing it will be."

She said nothing but stood up and slipped out of her dress. A deal was a deal.

She left two days later and yes, I did brief the staff to keep an eye on her. She was to eat regularly, she should be encouraged to walk every day and I should be told immediately if she started drinking heavily or lying in a lot or if her behaviour appeared at all erratic. I knew all the signs of descent.

Imagine then my surprise and delight to learn that she walked the grounds twice daily, ate well and was especially enjoying the house library, consumed by an unexpected enthusiasm for local history and that no, she rarely painted. The first week-end, I could not make it up there but I was content that she was healthy and enjoying the place and I planned to take three days the following week-end to spend some quality time with my lovely wife.

My flight up was delayed and when I arrived I was greeted by the housekeeper Maggie Stewart. She looked tense, nervous.

"Mrs Sutton has been in a very excitable mood today Sir. She has been anxious to see you. She's in the library and I should tell you she has had no dinner but she has made a start on the wine. I hope that's ok. I did not feel I could say otherwise."

Now I too was tense and nervous.

"That's fine. Thanks for warning me. I'll go straight there and see what all the fuss is about."

When I entered the library, she practically flew across the room and jumped into my arms. I felt the nervous energy in every fibre of her and smelled the wine on her breath. She spoke in French and so quickly that I had trouble adjusting and with irritation I told her to calm down. I wasn't angry with her. I was angry at her mania, how it possessed her.

"Oh David I am going mad with my discovery. Please, don't be so English and boring. I won't speak in French then. I can see you are tired."

She caught me by the arm and led me across the dark, musty room to a large reading table, covered in books.

"You see David, I wanted to please you. I wanted to prove that you have Scottish family, a connection perhaps even to this place."

"Ok but how about we go and have something to eat first? I'm famished and you want me to pay attention right?"

I watched her mind twist and turn, tormented and her hands bunch into fists. She hovered over her own manic energy because I made her see it. Her shoulders sagged in momentary defeat.

"Yes but of course my darling. I am selfish. Very well, we must eat. You are right."

It took enormous strength and will power for her to walk out of that library with me and over dinner she slowly slipped into fatigue, aided by the alcohol. If I had suggested an early night, she might just have acquiesced but then there was the reality of depression and I was determined that she should still have her moment in the library, whatever it concerned. By the library door she hesitated, questioning the wisdom but the embers of excitement still glowed. It was not too late.

She made me sit at the table and she picked up a ruler and swung it about, quite the professor as she made her presentation to me.

"I am so sorry but you are not in any way Scottish my love. I go back a long way and not a tiny bit of Scottish blood. But then I ask myself if something else can draw you to this place? So, I see all these books are here about the history of this house and you know it is not so old. Before, there was a castle but that was destroyed and then the land was given to another family and they built this house in the 18th century. To begin with, it was a hunting lodge and then it is expanded. Here is a painting of the man who did that. His name is William Munroe."

She showed me a painting of a bearded man, moderately handsome, posing with a pair of fine hunting dogs. I made every effort to appear intrigued.

"And this man, he had a younger brother called James and a sister called Margaret and Margaret she liked to keep a diary and the diaries are impossible for me to read but the local history experts, they have produced transcripts and here we have a copy. And you see, her brother William needed a wife but he could not decide. It was a very political time and he had to be careful because the families here were always in argument and he had to choose with care. Then, his brother James who is a soldier, he comes here and he brings his beautiful French girlfriend, you see?"

She showed me a portrait in one of the larger books of a pretty dark girl, like Celeste yes, insofar as they were both French.

"William is immediately in love with this French beauty and of course he has the money, the house etc. so we cannot blame her that she transfers her affections to him and so Margaret describes to us, James is very understanding and he accepts that William and Marguerite, for that is her name, that they will marry and so they do. I think this is too easy when I read it but I accept that these people were very different to us perhaps. Marriage is a matter of business no? And then, poor Marguerite, she does not enjoy the Scottish weather and she is often ill and there are no babies and the love between William and her it begins to fade. Then, James he returns again and I think you know what happens next yes?"

"Er, they have an affair?"

"Exactly and Marguerite she falls in love with James and then she is pregnant and of course, William is very angry and he uses his power and influence so that his brother is called away and then it is very sad because Marguerite gives birth to James' son but poor James he is killed in a battle and so he never returns."

"And?"

"Well, it seems that William and Marguerite remain together and in fact she has three more children with William but he takes a lover and Marguerite she lives a sad and lonely life and then one day she goes out on the lake and she is drowned and no one knows if this is suicide or an accident. Her eldest son dies of fever two years later. It is all so tragic but now I must show you the most incredible thing. Close your eyes."

Very reluctantly I did as I was told. Upon her command I opened them and she was holding up a portrait printed in an immense volume, of a very dashing man in uniform who I correctly assumed was the unfortunate James. Celeste's eyes flitted from the page to my face and back again repeatedly and her eyebrows arched in enquiry.

"Don't you see David? It is dark in here perhaps. Look closer."

And she used a piece of paper to cover the bottom of his face so that my attention would be more fixed on the eyes and it took every bit of my nerve not to show that I did see. I saw completely. It filled me with a sickening fear, a deep dread of where this was all going.

"Sorry, I don't know what you mean. See what exactly?"

Was she remotely convinced by my feigned ignorance? I don't think so.

"It is Claire of course. They are the same eyes you see in the painting I did of her."

"Are they? I suppose eyes can come in types and you're the artist. You would see that sort of thing."

"Don't be stupid David. You know what this means, why the three of us came together in this house."

"Er, I don't but no doubt your wonderful imagination has concocted a theory!"

I tried to sound jovial, light hearted but my heart was pounding.

"We are the same souls David. You were drawn to Claire because she was once your brother and you brought her here to me because I loved her and your soul needs to find peace. Don't you see?"

"What? And what happens next I suppose is that you tell me you're a lesbian and that you and Claire are going to ride off into the sunset? Are you actually crazy?"

It was like I had struck her across the cheek and I immediately hated myself. It isn't pleasant for the strong to crush the weak. Or was it fear that made me react that way? I put out a conciliatory hand but she was furious and smacked it away and then I seized her arm and she struck me with a surprising force and for a second, just a second, I may have wanted to kill her but never her in fact, just the madness. Horrified by her own violence, her eyes filled with tears and it seemed the most natural thing in the world to enfold her in my arms and kiss her hair and tell her I was sorry for being such an idiot and as can sometimes happen this strange cocktail of emotion spilled into immense passion. I locked the door of the library and pushed all of the books off the table onto the floor and if it is not too inappropriate to say, I do believe that is how my child was conceived

CLAIRE

The decision to head to the house in Scotland rather than to London was instinctive and I confess partly rooted in cowardice. London was huge and alien and even if it did offer countless job prospects, it was also where David and Celeste shared their apartment together and a hectic life; I believed I would be less of an intruder in Scotland. I could hide away in one of the many rooms until I secured the funding for a law conversion course, for I had more or less decided that this was what I wanted to do next. Organising the course was relatively straightforward but I knew living costs would be an issue and I hoped that I could persuade David to make me an affordable loan. Contacting my parents was not an option. They would just feel that my being unemployed was proof that a university education had been a complete waste of time.

I really had no idea to what extent David would be a man of his word and help me out but I knew that Celeste was fond of me and that he was inclined to keep her happy. Though I headed there with a reasonable level of conviction, when the taxi pulled up at the wrought iron gates, I stepped out into the wind and horizontal rain, unpleasant even in summer and my hand began shaking as I reached for the newly installed, electronic intercom. I had paid up the driver and he had headed off, so I was entirely at the mercy of whoever responded. I saw the curtains twitch at the window of the gate house but no one came out.

I buzzed again and then a woman's voice came on. It was sharp and crisp against the background hiss.

"Yes? Can I help you?"

I leant in and shouted, probably needlessly.

"Hello. My name is Claire Sutcliffe. I'm a friend of Mr and Mrs Sutton. I have his business card. He said I should feel free to look them up, if I ever needed anything."

"Mr and Mrs Sutton are not here. "

"Oh, but I've sent the taxi away and you see I really have nowhere to go for tonight at least. I have come a long way. Perhaps you remember me? I'm the girl in the painting?" It all sounded dubious, even to me. There was a long pause.

"Come up to the house and out of the rain. I'll have to call Mr Sutton about this."

"Yes but…"

She had activated the gate and for now our conversation was over. I had two huge bags and neither had wheels and I was already soaking wet. I glanced in at the gatehouse. A light was on but no one attempted to come to my aid and so I began the tortuous walk up the drive, bags bumping against my legs, rain running down the back of my neck, great drops falling from the tree tops above, my hands sore beneath the pressure of the handles. I was obliged to stop every fifty yards or so to catch my breath but the rain came on relentlessly and by the time the house came into view I was thoroughly drenched and very weary. I rang at the front door but she appeared from a side entrance and summoned me over. I started to feel angry and quite determined that I was getting a bed for one night if nothing else. However, some of this abated when I saw that the eyes which looked me up and down were not unsympathetic.

"Ah but you're soaked through. Come in to here and wait a bit. I've not managed to get hold of him but he has a mobile telephone and his secretary said she would get him to call. You'll be wanting a cup of tea and a towel for your hair."

She had a firm, matron like manner which reassured me. She led me into a cosy kitchen, heated by an aga, not a kitchen I had previously seen and I guessed that these must be separate quarters for staff. She poured me an enormous mug of tea and offered me a tin containing homemade shortbread and then produced a warm towel which had been hanging over the aga. She told me to wrap it around my head and then offered to take my dripping coat. She had indicated a kitchen chair and I flopped down, exhausted. Then her telephone started to ring and I felt my gut twist anxiously.

"Ah yes hello Mr Sutton Sir. I have a young lady here calling herself Claire Sutcliffe and she says she's nowhere to go and that you offered to help her. She's like a drowned rat the poor wee thing." There was what seemed a very long silence whilst she listened to David's lengthy response. How was I to interpret her furrowed brow, the many "Ahas" and the way she twisted that phone cord? I kept waiting to be put onto the telephone to speak to him and ran over my prepared speech but then she was saying goodbye and replacing the handset.

"Right then young lady. That's ok then. You've to stay with me until Mr Sutton can come up. He's not due for another few weeks when we've the shoot and there's so much to get ready.

We've a lot of Americans coming and he says you're to earn your keep. You can help with the other girls. They'll show you what to do. Meanwhile, I'll find you jobs don't you worry. Now, drink up and you can help me make up the bed in the spare room. My name is Maggie Stewart. You've to call me Mrs Stewart because everyone else does."

Though she was firm, she smiled at me warmly and I felt every muscle in me loosen with the relief. This was not quite what I had imagined, joining the staff, but for now I had a roof over my head and the smells emanating from the oven suggested I would be well nourished.

Mrs Stewart had me make up my bed under her scrutiny and instructed me on the correct way to tuck sheets. My room was small and dingy but later I gratefully fell into that bed, my stomach pleasantly full and listening to the rain which continued to pour outside, I drifted into a wonderful sleep.

David's housekeeper had me out of bed by seven every morning, filled me with a huge breakfast but true to her word, found plenty of work for me to do. For the first few days, we worked as a duo and I was very much under her instruction but then girls from the nearest village joined us, girls mainly younger than me but they knew what they were about and had a knack for making me look rather dim. They spoke very quickly in their curled Scottish accents, with interesting bits of slang thrown in and took delight at my ignorance. Mrs Stewart saw plainly enough how they made me suffer this but never came to my defence. Then two weeks into my stay, after supper, she congratulated me on my hard work and progress and added.

"I looked at that painting and I see that it's you. You're very bonny and it's only natural that the local girls make it hard for you but they're going nowhere whereas I've no doubt you'll be going places. Mr Sutton likes a hard worker."

"Yes, I think he does. Has he called at all?"

"Ah yes, all the time."

"Does he never ask to speak to me? Or Mrs Sutton perhaps?"

"Mrs Sutton is away to France with her family. She'll come for the shoot perhaps. I've not had instructions as yet. Mr Sutton asks after your progress and I assume I tell him everything he wishes to hear. He arrives next Tuesday, if nothing changes."

She had a way of closing a matter on me, so I did not enquire further.

Then, two days before David's scheduled arrival, we were dusting one of the smaller rooms in the main house when Mrs Stewart made a surprise announcement.

"So, you're to move your things in here and you're to make yourself known to the head gamekeeper today. You'll be helping out on the shoot. There are suitable clothes in the wardrobe. Everything should fit ok."

"Oh ok. Thing is, I don't know anything about shooting."

"You know how to follow instructions well enough. Mrs Sutton won't be coming. She's staying in France a wee bit longer. You'll be known to the guests as a close friend of Mrs Sutton. Mr Sutton says it will be a chance for you to make some very useful contacts."

"I see. But I want to study the law. I don't want contacts."

She smiled at me, at my innocence.

"Young lady, it's not what you know it's who you know. Surely you know that well enough."

Over the next two days, the head gamekeeper put me through my paces very severely, though to be fair, guns and bullets are not to be messed with. I felt I looked ridiculous in the tweed clothes but I was reassured by his son that I would fit right in. The wardrobe also contained some pretty evening dresses. I wondered if they were Celeste's old things.

The gamekeeper's son was by no means unattractive and flirted in a style which somehow always kept me on the back foot and slightly embarrassed. He regarded me as a bit of English fun I assumed but then that all changed the day David arrived.

I was part way down the main staircase when I heard his voice distinctly. I paused on the landing and I felt a strange mixture of apprehension and almost regret. I had been enjoying my unusual work placement and now everything would change.

He underscored the reality of my situation and now I remembered anew how he had bundled me back off to university from London and it struck me that I really was a huge source of inconvenience. I slowly continued down the stairs and there he was, in the hallway, fussing over the dogs. He glanced up and it was impossible for me to determine quite what his expression meant.

"Hello David. Here I am again. Back to haunt you."

Though he smiled, I'm not sure he found this very witty.

"Hello Waif. There you are indeed. Celeste sends her love. Come on, let's go get a drink."

It was a strange greeting. No embrace no handshake. He did not even wait for me to reach the bottom of the stairs but headed off for the sitting room and I could not decide if this was him being rather distant or whether this meant I was just an accepted part of the place. If he offered me whiskey I intended to accept.

DAVID

You meant it as a joke but that day you said you had returned to haunt me and you looked pale and ghost like on the stairs. Naturally, Celeste's bizarre notion that we were all somehow connected by a previous life sprang to mind but I pushed this away with every rational fibre of my being. Without even asking you what you would like, I decided to pour us both a whiskey and drinking it made you shudder, reminding me that you were really not much older than a child. Indeed, it was preferable to see you this way, it was safer. That said, you ought to have been safe enough regardless because I had just come from France and seeing Celeste and I could not have loved her more. She had survived horrendous morning sickness and was in the full bloom of pregnancy, aided by the love of her parents and the warm sunshine of her native country. Her parents continued to express great anxiety about the pregnancy but Celeste's buoyant but stable mood seemed to defy their concerns. I wondered how long it would take you to ask about Celeste; we managed all of two minutes perhaps.

"How come Celeste didn't come? Does she object to shooting?"

"No way! She's actually not a bad shot but it didn't seem suitable, given the pregnancy."

It was an unceremonious way to tell you. Your face glowed with joyful surprise.

"Wow, that's amazing news! I didn't think Celeste was so keen on the idea of children. Oh that's great news David. Many congratulations."

"Thank you. We're both pretty excited. Anyway, like I said, Celeste sends her love. You can catch up another time."

Celeste had no idea you were in Scotland. She had not mentioned you recently and I preferred it that way. I changed the subject.

"So, you've been earning your keep here. During the shoot, I'll introduce you to James Brookes. He owns several businesses including a London based estate agency. Very classy, top end stuff. Impress him and you've got yourself a job selling property. The basic won't be all that exciting but no doubt you can earn yourself some pretty good bonuses. I'll see what I can do about accommodation just to help you out a bit extra."

"Oh but I was actually hoping to carry on studying. I want to go into the law. I've found a good course and it's not too late to apply. I was hoping for a small loan towards to my living costs. I 'll pay back every penny."

"I see. Well, I don't do loans. Not the kind that earns me rubbish interest. Work for James for a year and you can fund yourself AND you'll have notched up some excellent experience."

You put down your glass. You were crestfallen.

"But I don't like London and I haven't got a clue how to sell houses and this James Brookes doesn't know me from adam."

"Relax. I have every confidence in you. You'll get used to London and besides, James is coming here to meet the Americans. It's my favour to him so he owes me one. It's the way the world goes round Waif."

"And how exactly am I supposed to impress him? If he's some sort of dirty old man...."

"Calm down! What do you take me for? Anyway, just be yourself. Trust me .He'll see that you're smart, ambitious, charming enough and yes, easy on the eye never hurts. You'll be shown the ropes and I'm sure you're a fast learner. It's my best offer, take it or leave it."

"But why can't you give me a job, if it comes to that? I'd sooner work for you like I am now."

"I don't employ little waifs with history degrees. Not outside of Scotland. It's a rule of mine."

You did a funny little pout. The whiskey had put some colour in your cheeks and perhaps because I was now the expectant father, I felt almost paternal towards you.

"I'll think about it but I'm not doing it if I don't like him, if I don't respect him."

"Fair enough. Now run along and see if you're needed. I need to speak to the gamekeeper and then make some calls .Oh and Waif?"

"Yes?"

"After this, you'll owe me. Remember that."

That news came sideways at you but you maintained your composure and I thought that there really were few limits to your potential. Barring a serious derailment, you were destined to succeed in life.

CLAIRE

After our first conversation over a whisky, during which I fought hard to maintain my composure, I found myself running on fear induced adrenaline. My fears were not unreasonable. I was about to spend most of the next two weeks in the company of multiple entrepreneurs, some of them Americans (I had had few trans cultural experiences) and one of them my potential boss for the next year, entering a profession I knew nothing about. All of this would occur in the bizarre context of my tenuous connection with David and everyone would be working on the information that I was a friend of Celeste, David's absent wife. I am not sure quite how David sold this to them, how embellished the story was, but I will say that all of the awkward questions I feared, how had I met Celeste, how was she coping with the pregnancy etc., none of these questions were ever put to me.

James Brookes, notwithstanding some of his objectionable political views and his preference for smoking toxic cigars, was a mostly amiable man in his early sixties and for the most part he was intent on establishing a connection with the Americans. He came with his quiet, Thai wife and most of the other wives and girlfriends, like her, showed no interest in the shooting, fishing and golf or the business talk but were content to enjoy the splendour of their setting which was rendered exceptionally beautiful by two uncharacteristic weeks of uninterrupted sunshine. I began to wonder in fact if Mr Brookes had any idea that he was supposed to be offering me a job, such was his scant interest in interviewing me but then towards the end of his stay, when we were gathered round the dining table, he threw an orange over to me and instructed me to sell it to him. I was to imagine that it was no ordinary orange but one with a ridiculous price tag. This, I should explain, attracted the interest of all the other guests and with David sitting opposite me. Apparently, I was that evening's entertainment.

After turning bright red, I swallowed hard and rose to my feet, lifting the orange high, for all to see. Inside, my guts were in knots, but from somewhere, by some miracle, a little speech managed to flow.

"One orange can appear much the same as another and indeed they all ultimately serve the same purpose but if you are the sort of person looking for a unique and unforgettable assault on your taste buds, not to mention a heavenly aroma which will transport your soul to unimaginable heights, then this Sir is the orange for you. At this price, you may be asking if you can really afford to tear into its flesh. Is it a trophy purchase, the sort of orange you acquire to impress others? Well, yes, certainly everyone will be impressed but what you will be buying is an experience they will only ever be able to vaguely conceive of. Believe me, you will never regret owning this orange. In a market place crowded with fruit, most of it mass produced and tasteless, you will possess something utterly exquisite and life transforming."

This caused most of the guests a great deal of amusement and I was duly applauded. David gave me a nod of respect. James Brookes who had listened to me as though I were delivering a critical speech looked less convinced but then said.

"Young lady, you are going to be on a steep learning curve but I'm willing to give you a chance. Make no mistake, selling any-thing is a highly skilled task, derided by intellectuals but it's selling that makes this world go round, whether it's a house, a deal, an idea, doesn't matter what. You have yourself a six week trial, starting the first of September. Don't blow it."

There was another helpful round of applause and I practically collapsed back into my chair. It must have taken at least half an hour for the warmth to fade from my face.

I remember every word of that speech to this day and the con-stant sense of being on stage throughout those two weeks. The rest is more of a blur. The shooting days were very hard phys-ical work. The evenings revolved around some of the finest meals I think I have ever eaten, aided by copious amounts of alcohol. David was an exemplary host. I admired his constant energy, his skills of diplomacy and I discovered that he could be quite the entertainer .He could make a room of people laugh.

The little I heard of the business talk left me in no doubt as to the real purpose of the whole show and I realised that the huge house, fancy car and general life style were the result of a certain type of hard graft. Of course, I came from the working classes and I was conscious too of all the running around and strenuous efforts of David Sutton's staff and I observed that the other guests were somehow less aware of this; they were so used to being served, food arriving over a shoulder, drinks seamlessly replenished, coats passing on and off like a magic trick but the staff were never invisible to me. I wondered how long it would take me to develop their immunity. It was not as if they never thanked the staff but it was done on automatic pilot and never allowed to distract them. Did I want to ever possess that immunity? Was it inevitable?

When the last guest had driven off down the driveway, I saw David's shoulders fall with relief and weariness crossed his face.

"Are any of those people your friends David?"

He smiled.

"Of a kind, yes. I admit that money can have a habit of forming the glue and without removing it, one can never be too sure what holds it all together. I prefer to measure relationships in terms of levels of connection. With some people the signal is stronger and never goes out of tune. You'll learn to tell the difference. Don't worry."

"I don't think I want to be as wealthy as you, to live in your world."

He lit a cigarette, the first I had seen him smoke that whole time. We were still standing on the edge of the driveway. Some shrubs had been hacked back and the stump of one remained. He raised a foot and placed it on this and watching him smoke, pensive, deciding on how to respond to me, I realised, beyond any previous doubt, that I was attracted to this man. This older, happily married man was activating me, stirring up all sorts of hormonal responses. In my mind, I tried to fix on a picture of Celeste. I could not possibly allow these feelings. It would be a disaster. I avoided eye contact, as far as it was normal to do so.

"Well Waif, you'll have to be a little less brilliant then and curb that natural ambition of yours. Or, you'll adapt. We'll have to see won't we?"

"Can I have a cigarette please?"

"No. It's a very bad habit. I'm trying to shake it myself, with a baby on the way. Come on, let's go in. You look done in."

He was right. I was exhausted. Yet, as I brushed out my hair later, I was struck by a certain radiance about me, perhaps the result of all that sun and fresh air. The gamekeeper's son called on me.

There was to be a gathering at the village pub. Was I interested? I wanted to be with David. That was the honest truth of the matter but that desire was dangerous and so I said yes and glancing over at my rugged, Scottish partner for the evening, I thought "He'll do."

DAVID

The evening before that most memorable sales pitch you did on an orange, I had stayed up late with James Brookes and we got drunk together.

James had made the connection between you and the painting and it was only natural that he be more curious about your connection to my wife, given that I was asking him to give you a job.

"So, tell me David, how precisely did your Miss Sutcliffe come to know Celeste?"

"Oh we met at Turnberry and Celeste invited her to sit for that painting." This was more or less the truth, was it not?

"I see. And they just hit it off? I mean, there's a bit of an age gap and she was just a student wasn't she?"

"Yes, well I suppose Celeste didn't know many people up here and Claire was a lovely distraction. Celeste regards her as a bit of a protégé, or younger sister. She invited her to our wedding party in London and made a point of showing her the sights. I like her too. She's bright. She has potential. I suppose she has become a bit of a joint project of ours. She's not from money. Getting that First class degree was a struggle. She had to do bar work to make ends meet. We both love a trier. I promise you James, she'll sell your houses. No worries."

"Mmm. We'll see. She gets a chance but I make no promises. Business is business."

"Sure. Can't ask for more."

"And Celeste doesn't mind her husband spending time round such a pretty young thing? And don't give me the old line about age differences. Remember I've married someone thirty years younger."

I twisted my glass round and round and although I was already quite drunk, I considered my next words very carefully.

"Celeste has nothing to worry about but of course I have noticed Claire that way. What man wouldn't? Putting the matter of adultery to one side, do I think Claire is too young for me? No, of course not. I mean, no man wants to think that way. But if I put it the other way. Am I too old for Claire? Then, yes, I think I am and don't bullshit me that it doesn't trouble you, having a much younger wife. Hey, it's none of my business. Anyway, bottom line is that I love Celeste, the woman carrying my child. I feel protective towards Claire, almost like her father."

"So, you mean that under no circumstances would you try and get your leg over?"

We were both drunk, you understand. This was a private conversation between two drunken blokes. I didn't need to lie.

"I'd say no, not under any circumstances but then she is beautiful. Keep that to yourself though."

We started to laugh in the stupid way drunks do and I like to think that that conversation was forgotten by James. But the next morning I remembered every word of it and it made me uneasy.

CLAIRE

The following day, I woke up late, nursing a huge hangover; the night at the pub had been pretty wild. When Mrs Stewart told me David wanted to see me in his study, I remembered having the gamekeeper's son's tongue down my throat, followed by an unromantic grope in the woods and went half expecting some sort of lecture. Though feeling quite ill I conjured some defiance. David was not my father and what I did on a night off was my concern.

However, when I entered the study, he looked up all relaxed and smiling and it struck me that this was not at all his agenda.

He began by pushing an envelope towards me.

"There you go. Your wages. A good job done. Well done. Now, I'm off back to your favourite city. Enjoy the next week here.

Rest up. Here's the address of the office you are to report to and the name of the manager you'll be working under."

"Oh, not James Brookes then?"

"Don't be daft. It's one of several businesses he owns. He doesn't run it, not in that way. You'll really have to impress the manager. He didn't pick you himself so you've everything to prove. But you can do it, I'm sure. Here's my secretary's number. She's arranging a small flat for you. It will be pretty basic but you'll cope with that."

I picked up the other pieces of paper he had slid across the table and did not know what to say. I mainly wanted to throw up.

Then, he sat up a little straighter.

"Okay, so that brings me to discuss something a little awkward with you."

"Oh?" I wondered if I looked as ill as I felt. Was this going to be the lecture?

"I haven't told Celeste you were here. She was happy in France and I worried she might make a fuss and think she had to come over. She wouldn't approve of me making you work either. So, if she finds out she finds out but I'd prefer you never to mention it. You'll come and have dinner with us naturally. That okay?"

"Er yes, I think so. I don't like telling lies but I suppose it's a white one right?"

"Exactly. So, what that means Claire is that if you ever come here to Scotland again, you won't be staff. That was just a bit of work experience for you, a way to keep you out of mischief."

"Fine, I get it. Our secret."

"Good. And so the thing is Claire, staff are staff and friends are friends." This last point left me a bit perplexed and I did not disguise my confusion. He looked determined to clarify his point.

"I gather a great time was had by all at the pub last night but for the rest of your stay here you should avoid Craig. He's staff."

Craig was the gamekeeper's son and it was all I could do not to throw up now. I should have been angry, outraged but I felt, in that first instant, too ill and too humiliated.

"I see. At least I think I do. Well, thank you for everything David. Please give my love to Celeste when you see her."

I stood up and he offered me his hand and so we shook hands which felt completely wrong. I walked to the door to leave but it was as if the fog lifted and my true self rose up, indignant. I went back to the table and leant over it aggressively.

"Actually, I don't see David. I mean, you have been very kind and helpful to me and I know I should be totally grateful but my private life is my private life and you're not my keeper. Craig works for you but you don't own him. If we want to have a bit of fun, I can't see the harm or how it's any of your business really."

David stood up and I immediately regretted my outburst. He was stern and it occurred to me that I had never made him angry before and that he was probably quite imposing if crossed. He must have seen the fear this produced, the way I stepped back and I think he wrestled with how to respond.

"Fine. Have it your own way. First, Chris Peterson and now Craig. I employ a lot of people Claire, so if you're gonna screw every vaguely attractive one then you've got your work cut out but be my guest. I'm not sure it's none of my business and frankly it shows me a great deal of disrespect but if you can't take good advice you'll sure as hell learn the hard way."

What on earth was I doing? I was taking a chunk out of the hand that was very generously feeding me. I owed this person a huge debt and I had spoken to him like a petulant teenager.

"I'm sorry. You're right, even if it pains me to admit it. I mean, I shouldn't get so drunk. I don't know what to say…"

David let out a huge sigh which only seemed to underline the fact that I was an enormous pain in the arse.

"Go back to bed Claire. Sleep it off. We'll see you in London. Just don't mess it up."

So, my head throbbing, my stomach churning, I crawled back

up to my room where I immediately threw up. I was so angry with myself but too ill to vent it for now. I fell back into bed and woke several hours later. David had left.

DAVID

I could have flown down to London or taken the train but I decided to drive. It would take me longer but I needed the time to think and straighten out my thoughts. Driving helped me that way. On the one hand, I genuinely had your best interests at heart and I had not enjoyed over-hearing Craig talk about his nocturnal exploits with the English lassie. Yet, when you had leant over my desk, all defiant, it was only then that I felt just how much it bothered me, your night with Chris Peterson and the trouble was, it was not just all about me being protective. Yes, yes, I did have a certain duty to advise you, to look out for you but I was old enough, experienced enough to know when I was feeling jealous and possessive.

I had a beautiful wife and she was expecting our first child. Why the hell would I entertain such feelings? I kept going back to the drunken conversation with James Brookes and blamed him for planting a poisonous seed but then my private detective friend had also warned me about straying with you. Was I tainted by the corrupt thoughts of others or were they facing a reality that I had foolishly denied?

I went over every encounter between us but, whilst I primarily did so to fathom how and at what point an attraction had formed (there did not seem to be a defining moment other than seeing you wrapped in that bed sheet but then I thought I had moved beyond that), I admit I also searched for any slight sign, any faint indication that you might have been attracted to me. There was again, no obvious moment but I had to admit that there was, in every encounter, a gentle buzz, the tell-tale sign of connection, the same sort of vibration I had felt run down Celeste's arm, when you arrived at our party.

Then, suddenly, recalling Celeste's revelations in the library and her bizarre fantasy that we were three connected souls, it dawned on me that my wife had known from the very first meeting with you that I was drawn to you. All that stuff in

London, dressing you up, commenting over and over about how beautiful you were, had it all been a perverse kind of testing, trying to measure just what sort of threat you posed? And was Celeste's mad story a peculiar way to place you off limits? Why, I was being defied to fall for someone who I had wronged in a previous life and that person had been my brother so naturally, sleeping with you would be a version of incest. This all sounded completely insane but I placed nothing beyond the complexity of my wife's mind.

I arrived in London feeling totally confused and emotionally drained. I had done my best for you. You had somewhere to live and a solid job opportunity. I had to remain focussed on my marriage and my child. Whatever the truth of the matter, whichever way I looked at it, you were a toxic force and I resolved to put any dinner invitations on the back burner.

The next day, I instructed my secretary that if Miss Sutcliffe called, unless it were absolutely an emergency, my secretary should handle matters and I did not wish to be involved. I made up my mind that if Celeste did not push the matter, I need not tell her that you were even in London. London was a big enough place and I hoped, beyond reason, that it would swallow you up. Without knowing it, you were dangerous.

CLAIRE

When my train pulled into London, I resisted getting up and exiting with my fellow passengers. The train wasn't going anywhere for a bit and I wanted to take a moment. I was about to commence a new chapter and I did not want these feelings of trepidation. I had had the courage to leave my home town and family to go to university. I had been brave enough to take a chance and live with the Hunts. I had climbed in the car with David Sutton that day and subsequently taken a risk in trusting in his offer of help by turning up unannounced on his doorstep. I had proven in Scotland that I could learn fast and rise to new challenges. Now, faced with fresh challenges in a vast, alien city, I did not want to begin that journey filled with fear. I had every reason to believe in myself, to trust that I could and would deliver, and I wanted to exit that train feeling bold and resilient. The only baggage I wished to carry off that train was the physical kind, so I slowed down my breathing and conjured in my mind a sense of excitement. I was poised to begin a new adventure. I needed adrenaline yes, but it should be the right kind.

I can look back at the young woman that stepped off that train and be amused by her confident strides, the head held high, the chin jutting out in defiance. I can see it for what it was, the false optimism and over confidence of zealous youth. Could I have been any more naïve? Yet, knowing now just how little wisdom I possessed, how untested I was, I can only admire that young woman too. London, like other major cities, is capable of devouring people, crushing them, ruining them. I strutted headlong into its jaws that day and if that young woman had been my daughter I should have been justifiably terrified for her.

The flat David paid for was small, functional and uninspiring but not badly located and I was in no position to complain. My new boss, Graham Arkwright, was ex-military, efficient, organised, only charismatic strategically, demanding and certainly not inclined to suffer fools, even young, pretty ones. I never grew to like the man but he was an excellent instructor and understood a great deal about the battlefield that is the London property market.

It sounds a cliché but I walked the common path of apprenticeship, from tea girl, to errand girl, given only the most basic office duties initially, obliged to shadow other sales members and observe them perform, which itself was confusing because each had a unique, personal style. It was only after what seemed like the longest, most intense month of my life that I was allowed to properly speak to customers and then longer again before I was accompanied on a showing and permitted to take some of the lead. The first sale which could be at all attributed to me was one of the greatest thrills of my life and, though my resolve to re-train and enter the law never disappeared and I walked away from that lucrative, job I fully acknowledge the value of that experience. David was never too far wrong about those sorts of decisions.

Though professionally speaking, I adapted to my new life with relative ease, the first weeks were a profoundly lonely time for me. I called David's office several times and his secretary informed me each time that he was unavailable; in a meeting, away from the office, out of the country etc. Then, when I next called she explained, in a firm, efficient manner, that if I had any issues she was responsible for assisting me and it dawned on me that David did not wish to speak to me and of course I could not stop going over and over that last conversation of ours. So, it appeared David thought me a bit of a slut and he had washed his hands of me, albeit he was honourable enough to keep paying my rent.

I sulked for a week. I considered finding my own flat but the numbers didn't add up. I would have to re-locate further out of London and then have to meet with the inconvenience and costs of commuting. I could not afford to be quite so petulant. More than anything, it annoyed me that he had spoken about inviting me to dinner but then left me hanging.

Then, one day, I decided, on a whim, to satisfy my curiosity and visit Celeste's new gallery. I did not expect her to be there, for she had to be very near to having the baby, but part of me knew that David, for whatever reason, would not want me to see her and I was driven by a perverse desire to go against him. I had every right to make contact with her and she had expressed huge affection for me after all. David had told me to keep quiet about Scotland and I realised that this gave me a peculiar sort of power. If he had caused me injury by blocking my contact, then just visiting the gallery, whether she were there or not, presented itself as a subtle form of defiance. There was a small risk, if he found out, that I might annoy him enough to make him pull the rent but that day I just blocked this out.

I located the gallery quite easily and from across the street I saw that Celeste was there. The size of her left me stunned but I noted that she was nevertheless still very beautiful and she managed to make maternity clothes seem stylish. My heart began to pound and I had decided not to go any nearer when she suddenly glanced over and her eyes widened in surprise and she grinned in such a way as to dispel any doubts as to whether I was a welcome sight. I stayed frozen to the spot and she signalled for me to come over and stepped out of the shop when she observed my failure to respond. I would look like some sort of psychotic stalker if I walked away now so I smiled and crossed over.

"My God Claire look at you! You look wonderful but what are you doing in London and wearing a suit like that? Come in, please."

We went inside and she turned the sign to closed.

"You look radiant Celeste. When's the baby due?"

"Not for two more weeks and I am so fat and so bored! Come to the back and we will take an infusion."

She led me into a small office and at the back there was a tiny kitchenette. She put a kettle on and then embraced me, as far as the immense bump would allow.

"So, come, tell me about this suit. What does it mean?"

"Well, I have a job selling property. I've been in London almost two months now. It's just for a few months and then I'm going back to university to study law."

"Really? Well, I won't say that sounds interesting because I'm not so sure but the main thing is that you are in London and this is exciting. David will be very surprised."

Right there and then, her dark eyes fixed on mine, I knew I was not going to lie to her.

"Well, not so much. He helped me get the job and he's paying for my flat. I guess he hasn't wanted to worry you, given the baby and all."

For a second, the light went out of those eyes as she processed this information but she had the ability to flit from emotion to emotion the way of butterfly from flower to flower.

"Okay. That's interesting. I'm not sure why he has not told me that but I tell you what, I like secrets too so let's not tell David we have seen each other. What do you think?"

I thought it sounded complicated and hazardous and that I was getting myself into deep waters but Celeste smiled at me, shining with mischief. She had this ability to enchant, to place me under a kind of spell, there was something irresistible about her eccentricity so I waded into those waters though it felt counter-intuitive.

"Alright. Sounds fun. Though you'll have to tell him eventually, I suppose."

"Yes, yes but we decide. Now, let's 'ave this drink and then I want to take you to visit a friend. He's wonderful fun and I am going to introduce you to lots of interesting people, not boring office workers."

"Heh, maybe I'm a boring office worker you know!"

"Yes there is a risk of this but I can give you immunity. Trust me."

We travelled by taxi to an old warehouse in the East End and we must have looked utterly incongruous, she so heavily pregnant and yet seeming to float in her dress, me all prim and proper with my suit and briefcase. Inside, she introduced me to Gary, tall, thin, a fussy moustache and exaggerated hand gestures. He stared me up and down and then raised his eyebrows at Celeste but she just laughed and this was apparently enough for him to accept me. He had converted the warehouse into an artist's studio cum residence and though it was all very urban and edgy, I knew that there was a not insignificant amount of money behind it all.

He was drinking red wine and offered us both a glass. Celeste sighed and patted her bump and refused but to fend off Gary's sulk about this insisted that I have a very large glass which went straight to my head quite nicely.

Gary started an amusing anecdote about his day but then the door buzzer went and the first of several other guests began to assemble. This was not a planned party I concluded but just an ordinary day in the life of that building. Visitors came with bottles of wine and helped themselves and in the cavernous building, the combined sound of human chatter and electronic music created a throbbing energy not conducive to relaxation at the end of the working day, and I marvelled at Celeste's stamina, only sitting down after an hour or so, though it is true that she drank only water whilst the rest of us had to contend with varying degrees of intoxication. The only food was bowls of olives and crisps and chunks of baguette crudely tossed into baskets which people occasionally served up with a potent smelling selection of cheese. I was too excited to eat to begin with and then, as I grew tipsier, I discovered a sudden appetite and everything, though so simple, tasted wonderful. I was introduced to everyone and remembered not one single name. One or two faces were familiar and they remembered meeting me at Celeste's flat and then I saw Angelica, the prying American and I knew it was only a matter of time before she spoke to me.

She came over, said she wanted to smoke and suggested we move upstairs where it was quieter. I had no desire to speak to her but no wish to upset her either, so I followed. When she offered me a cigarette I recalled David's censure and decided to take one. I was careful not to inhale too deeply, not wishing to choke like an amateur.

We stared down at the others, Celeste very much the queen, surrounded by her courtiers.

"Not long now and David Sutton gets an heir." As before, she expressed no affection for David.

"You always make him sound like a complete tyrant. They love each other you know."

"You think two people being in love is always a good thing?"

"Yes, I think so. I know marriages don't always work out, I'm not stupid but David and Celeste have as good a chance as any. No money problems to start with."

"Kid, money is always a potential problem, especially too much of it."

I hated the way she condescended to me but I begrudgingly accepted that she was older, had lived more, seen more. It was tricky to know how much was wisdom and how much was bitterness. She glanced at my suit and neatly arranged hair.

"So, what are you doing to earn a buck?"

"Estate agency. It's sort of work experience before I study law."

"Sounds a lot of laughs and the sort of thing her husband would approve of. This (she used a sweep of her hand to indicate our colourful surroundings), this is not his thing at all and I'm not sure Celeste has thought through the whole mother thing. Gonna be shit going down, mark my words. Do you see any of us doing walks in the park with the baby stroller?"

I peered down at the others and it was true that none of them seemed the parenting kind. It was typical of me to feel the need to work out an answer to any problem.

"Well, they can afford a nanny, so I'm sure Celeste can still enjoy some of this side to her life. She's an artist, David must get that."

"Being an artist isn't the problem, it's being Celeste. Do you really know her?"

It was a straight forward question and deserved an honest answer.

"No, not really. She's magical, a bit eccentric you could say but I think she will be a wonderful mother, not boring and limiting like mine."

I had dared to share some personal information and she nodded at me respectfully and moved closer.

"She goes up, she comes crashing down. This is her being up and yes, she's incredible. Look at them, like bees round the honey pot. You been there for her when she's down?"

"No, no I haven't really seen that. All pregnant women have mood swings though, don't they?"

"This is a swing like an axe. Watch your head kid. I don't like David. I think he's a controlling son of a bitch but I get why he feels he needs to control her. He just keeps getting it wrong. This baby is a big mistake. If I didn't love Celeste, I'd tell you to run and keep running but you make her eyes light up. Maybe you're the sort of friend she needs. Be careful, that's all I can say."

In case I thought she was actually becoming my friend, she blew smoke in my face and then looked away, conversation over. Feeling dismissed I went back down the stairs and Celeste grinned at me and summoned me over. She struggled to her feet from the soft sofa and took hold of my hand.

"Come on Claire. These people are too drunk and I'm too sober. Let's go."

We took another taxi and she insisted we drive around a bit so that she could give me the Celeste tour and by the time we pulled up outside my place, she looked exhausted. A phone started to ring in her handbag. She glanced in at it.

"It's David. My time is up. Do you have a phone in that dump?"

"Hey, it's not that bad and, yes, there is such a thing as a phone. Here, I'll write down the number."

"Good and the number where you work too. I don't suppose you have an answer machine or a mobile?"

"No and not yet. Work might be giving me a mobile soon but anyway, I'm in most evenings. My life after work is very boring."

"No boyfriend?"

"No, I don't seem to be very good at boyfriends, just the odd drunken mistake."

She smiled and tucked an escaped tendril of hair behind my ear tenderly.

"Be patient. The man that wins you, he must be formidable, handsome, intelligent, not in any way average. When he finds you, you have only not to be afraid but remember, always the heart of alabaster."

I had not worn the necklace in a while and felt somehow embarrassed, like I had forgotten some homework. She smiled at my blush and gestured at my chest.

"There, not around your neck. Now go on, David is worrying about me."

Still a little drunk, it took me hours to be able to wind down for sleep, conversations spinning in my head, the smell of Celeste somehow lingering and as I finally drifted away I still had a strong sense of satisfaction derived from having taken the initiative and re-established contact with Celeste and yes, a perverse pleasure from keeping it all a secret from David.

The next couple of weeks were sheer madness. Full and demanding work days, with barely enough time to eat lunch, followed by Celeste's crazy entertainment schedule; trips to the theatre, to the ballet, to friends' galleries, to a fashion designer's studio, to Gary's place and shopping, shopping and shopping. Every night I fell into my bed exhausted and still I can marvel at how Celeste kept going, though I suspect she spent a lot of the daytime resting. As the due date arrived, I expected her to make her apologies and for our happy time to end but she insisted that we keep going, that she needed to stay busy. Of course, I wondered what David thought of his wife's activities but she told me he was mostly working and that evening, when her waters broke all over Gary's suede sofa, I was shocked to discover that David had actually flown over to New York and was not due in until the following morning and when Celeste gripped hold of my hand and pressed me to go with her to the hospital, I could hardly refuse.

Yet, what did I know about babies and giving birth? What I learned is that it is all extremely painful, though the medical staff seemed unperturbed, that it takes longer than I had imagined, that nothing I said was any help to poor Celeste and this was a time when I had no mobile, no instant means of contacting David or any of her family. In fact, Celeste was adamant she did not want David there, that he had attended no ante-natal classes and would be quite useless. Every now and then, she spoke in French and seemed almost delirious. Then, shortly after midnight, the sleepy looking registrar announced that Celeste would need an emergency caesarean and she was wheeled away on a trolley and I spent the next while staring into a vending machine, palms all sweaty yet feeling chilly.

Finally, in the early hours, a midwife informed me that Mr and Mrs Sutton's daughter had been safely delivered and mother and baby were well. Celeste was asleep and should not be disturbed but I could take a peep at the baby if I wished. Then, it was advisable for me to go home but without David yet in Britain, let alone at the hospital, I felt I could not and should not leave. If Celeste awoke, I felt I needed to be there. So, I spent the next few hours attempting and failing to sleep in the waiting area. Celeste asked to see me around seven. I walked in to find a small, thin, dark haired lady, most of her concealed beneath sheets and it took me a moment to recognize Celeste. She looked so suddenly old, as if her life not just a child had been extracted from her. She turned her head to signal that I should look in on the cot to the left of her bed and there she was, smaller than I had imagined, cocooned in a blanket, dark and olive skinned like her mother but it was somehow a female, infant version of David. She opened her eyes and regarded me. It felt like a long, wise look and made me uneasy but instead I pronounced her to be very beautiful.

"She is called Amélie. Please Claire, pick her up, hold her. I feel too weak but I do not want her to be alone. Don't be scared. She won't break."

I did as she asked but held the child away from me, awkward, not wishing to breathe on her flawlessness. When I finally dared look over to Celeste, I saw that she had drifted asleep again.

When David arrived at midday, Amélie had discovered the full power of her lungs and was all milky around the mouth with the latest listless feed. I had managed to phone work to explain my absence but I was desperate to be able to go home to shower and change, as well as ravenous. My arms were stiff from nursing the baby so rigidly. Celeste had fed on demand but was somehow detached which I attributed to tiredness and/or the anaesthetic.

Into this weary, pathetic scene he strolled, all aftershave, relaxed and handsome in a short sleeved polo shirt. He stopped short to register that it was me, not paying much attention to his daughter and went first to place a soft kiss on the fore head of his tired wife. She smiled faintly but rolled over to fall asleep.

"Hello Waif. What a surprise. You look dreadful."

"Thank you David. It was a long night. I need to go. I need to get to work."

I am not sure if he listened to this because now he was transfixed by the stirring bundle in my arms.

"Here. Take her. Celeste says she is called Amélie. She looks like you, I think."

I expected it to be an awkward transfer but David seemed to know what he was doing and cradled her confidently in the crook of one arm, peeling back some of the blanket to study her and though by no means overpowered by emotion, I saw clear, proud satisfaction.

"Congratulations David. You're a father."

"Thank you, yes, yes I am. Thank you for being there Claire. You can go now. We'll be in touch."

It was a rather curt dismissal which cut me to the core but I was too tired to raise any objection.

Then, as I went to leave the room he added.

"Guess this makes us even. You don't owe me. I hear good things about your work. Still going to follow the law or might London have seduced you?"

I was tired but from somewhere I found the strength to say: "The money is good but only Celeste has made London enjoyable for me. I'll probably see out the year but then it's off to study the law. I think I'll make a great lawyer."

This made him hesitate though I did not give him the satisfaction of a response but left, striding out down the corridor, only letting my shoulders collapse once I was descending in the lift. It struck me that I had not said a goodbye to Celeste but she was safe, with her husband and baby. They were a family. I was alone again.

DAVID

I can make no serious defence of the way I spoke to you that day, in the hospital. You were there for Celeste when she really needed you. I should have been kind to you and expressed far more gratitude but, seeing you there, holding my child, it was like some sort of bad dream. Can you begin to comprehend how Celeste's warped theory about us being souls reunited played in the background, a grotesque, unmelodious composition which I had to keep trying to block out with every part of my rational mind? There was also the plain fact that I had been deceived by both of you; all the while you had been seeing each other and I had no idea if you had told her about Scotland, though I mainly trusted you not to have done so.

Celeste had been adamant she would go at least a week over her due date and I had been a complete idiot to heed her. Now I even wondered if she had witch-like conspired for me to be unavailable, choosing you to share my child's birth. Honestly, my mind raced with every possible, paranoid theory and only one thing saved me from falling into an abyss of jealous obsession. The dynamic businessman, the man who scarcely knows how to be still, he held his beautiful daughter, so tiny, so pure and he clung onto her innocence for his salvation.

Celeste asked about where you had gone, naturally. She was so worn out by her most magnificent creation that she seemed to resign herself to my logical reasoning, accepting that you had your work and your life and that this time needed to be our time, though I comprehend now that post-natal depression played its part in her easy surrender. It was soon apparent that Celeste was not well and I arranged for her transfer to a private clinic and from there out to her dependable family in France. When the medication started to help and she began to smile again, I left my family and returned to London. I told myself I was being practical. I could not put my business responsibilities on hold for long and this was how I would provide for Amélie's security and happiness but I admit I needed my world of work. It defined me.

All the while, an image of you striding off down that hospital corridor troubled me, a small thorn wedged in, superficially insignificant but so irritating and I knew I would have to see you again and try to resolve matters.

I had already formed another idea. I knew Celeste would have to return to London before too long. Part of her belonged there and I certainly did not belong to France but I decided we should aim for a different London, now that we were a family, suburban London. The idea morphed at speed. Yes, I should like our daughter to grow up in an affluent, middle class area, something vaguely normal. I did not want her to be too spoiled. The house in Scotland was too much. Perhaps she would grow up thinking of it as somewhere we went on holiday but by no means the norm? And so my mind raced and was it a moment of genius when I joined the two schemes and decided that Claire Sutcliffe, young estate agent, could be procured to show me round a suitable property? Except that being a man who likes, no needs, to be in control, I did all the research beforehand, selected a suitable house and then arranged for you to show it to me because of course, I was never seeing you to make a decision about a house. The agenda was quite different and quite specific.

And so, you clipped along the pavement in your high heels, rummaging in your bag for the house keys, nervous but ready to perform and no wonder that when I stepped out of my car to greet you, you moved back with surprise and promptly dropped the keys. It was just the beginning I had hoped for, giving me all the advantage. I scooped up the keys.

"Good morning Waif. Ready to sell me a house?"

Guilt is a futile emotion, but noble, and I ought to say how guilty I feel for having you try so hard to be professional, escorting me round a house I had already decided to buy and recalling it now, yes, there is the odd twinge of guilt, but frankly I loved every minute of it and still do smile about your vulnerability and your determination to put on a good show, mingled with confusion. That day, it was the last of your youth and innocence squeezed out for my consumption and recalling it all, it tastes just as sweet. Sooner or later, you were going to acquire wisdom, maturity. Youth and its charming naivety must fade and it seems to me a privilege that I saw you make the transition.

So I let you perform and I was a fantastic listener was I not? Then, having agreed on the merits of a spacious, mature garden I made you sit down in the garden room for the little talk I had planned. You were outwardly anxious, twiddling with the edge of that pile of papers, glancing about a lot and I must have seemed very calm but, even as I recall that exchange, my heart is beating faster and I can tell you that it took every part of my self-control not to reveal the tumult of emotions that that encounter provoked.

"Well, Waif, I think you may have just sold me a house but before we conclude the business end of things, you must realise that I also want to speak to you as a friend and say how sorry I am for the last conversation we had. I was too abrupt and not at all as thankful as I might have been."

Your fingers continued with their twiddling.

"Oh that's ok. It must be an emotional time, becoming a parent. So, you said Celeste and Amélie are fine."

You sounded calm and accepting but your body language spoke differently.

"Yes, they are both doing well. You see, when I saw you at the hospital, it was a bit of a shock but I don't blame you for seeing Celeste and I know how fond you are of each other."

Your eyes sparked with suppressed emotions.

"I never told her about Scotland, if that's what you're worried about, not that Scotland was any big deal. Surely Celeste would be happy that you helped me out? Is there something I am missing?"

Considering how nervous you were, you managed to express yourself quite to the point and I realised it was going to be tough for me to follow my script. I had been around the block of life enough times to know that I was attracted to you and that I was about to attempt something rather difficult and perilous. You see, I had not just arranged for you to be there for an apology. I wanted to discover if *you* were attracted to *me*. I had no clear idea of starting an affair; I loved Celeste, the mother of my child, but like many arrogant men I wanted to know what my options were. To put it in brutal terms, I was curious to know if I could have you and I was more intrigued by the potential, by the notion of options. I had been married to an adulterous woman, yes, I knew all about the pain involved but still my ego propelled me to explore the parameters of our connection. I wanted to know just how much power I had over you. You adored my wife but what precisely did you feel about me?

With the passage of time, perhaps I over simplify my emotions and motives that day or is it that I distort them? I think at the time that I told myself it was wise to determine whether you nurtured any feelings for me, that there was the risk of an awkward, bizarre love triangle, that I had a responsibility even to be certain not to hurt you but now, looking back, I think my feelings were more primitive and yes, egotistical. Let's face it, what man my age would not have desired you to want me?

"Well Claire, you know that there is a world of difference between how things are and how they can appear to be. For instance, we both know that that back bedroom upstairs is small and dark but the sellers have put up a large mirror. It's an old trick. So, we both know, for example, that I made the right decision to persuade Celeste not to go to the shoot, in her condition and that fussing over you and your predicament would not have been ideal. Now, I could have given Celeste the choice but you know how strong willed and emotional she can get, so I didn't tell her about you. Those are the facts. However, someone at the shoot pointed out to me, rather unhelpfully, that people might have looked at that circumstance and judged differently. That is, they might have thought I had motive for you being there without Celeste knowing, a sexual motive. Of course, I rejected that stupid notion straight away but then it struck me that Celeste, if she were to find out about my lack of honesty, well, she might just put two and two together and come up with five. Pregnant women are particularly sensitive."

We stared at each other for just a few seconds and the energy between us intensified.

"Well I told her you helped me get this job and that you're funding my flat, so I don't see what the difference is. Anyway..."

This is when you stood up and went over to the window, so that your back was turned to me. You sounded so calm, so reassured but then, I could not see into the windows of your soul, could I?

"I am sure Celeste is mature and perceptive enough to know what *you* already know, that nothing would ever happen between us because I am not attracted to you. I mean, no offence, but you are technically old enough to be my dad so the idea of you and me...well, sorry but no way. And, even if that were not an obstacle then there's the fact that you and Celeste are a match because you both come from money and I'm not saying you don't work hard and I really am grateful for all your help but you don't know anything about me really, I mean where I come from. I'm assuming that that's what has motivated you and Celeste to be so kind. I'm a sort of project for you."

"Ouch, that makes us sound pretty bad. I don't want you to think...."

"No, it's fine, really. It's not like I don't have a dad but yes, that's sort of the way I see you, like a father figure and if you don't mind me saying, you should just be a lot more honest with Celeste and a lot less controlling."

Then, you turned around and the expression on your face was so stony, so resolute and yet, somehow I wanted to take you in my arms there and then and kiss you and perhaps you recall that cough of mine? I wasn't clearing my throat, I was trying to compose myself.

"Okay, well that clears things up then, doesn't it? We all know where we stand. Look, I've got some other appointments and I suppose you had better get back to work. "

"Sure. So, you know how the process goes for buying a house. I can miss out that speech. We'll be in touch."

"Fine. That's great. Look Claire, I don't know how you were planning to get back but I insist on giving you a lift."

"Oh thanks. Actually, the office will be closing soon so you may as well drop me back at my flat."

"OK. Let's get going then."

Could the atmosphere have been more awkward? I called you Claire not Waif and we hardly spoke in the car. When we pulled up outside your building, it felt like you were floating off down a river and that I really ought to do something to stop it happening but I was floundering myself.

"Hey, once we move in, Celeste will want to host a huge party. You must definitely come."

"That sounds nice. Give her my love and a kiss for the baby."

I heard your voice crack slightly at the end but I didn't move. I didn't even get out of the car to open the door for you. I just watched you walk away.

Then, instead of driving off, I took a moment to try to convince myself that perhaps it had all gone as it should have, though it didn't feel that way. I glanced over at the passenger seat and saw that you had dropped your scarf. It was a sign. Me, Mr Rational, I was suddenly willing to grab at signs!

I scooped up your scarf and headed into your building. I knew where you lived. I was paying the rent.

When I arrived at your flat, I was about to ring but then I heard you through the flimsy door. Why, you must have been just on the other side, on the floor perhaps. You were sobbing, intensely, bleeding out and I knew exactly what it meant; everything you had said at the house had been a lie and Waif, you must believe me when I say that I wanted so much to do what any man in the movies would, ring the bell, make you open the door, throw my arms around you, let the passion engulf us but I hesitated and I know that hesitation is primarily a good thing. It has saved me from many a bad business decision. My instincts are important yes, but you know that I am a rational thinker and so I paused and I took in the bigger picture. What I want you to know now, quite clearly, is that I walked back to my car that day, not because I loved Celeste more. I took that scarf of yours, I kept it because I needed to hold on to some part of you. I knew that we would never be a fling, a dirty affair, that if I went to you then, it was the start of something huge. No, I went back to my car and drove away because of another woman, my daughter. I remembered and thank God I remembered that I was a father, that Celeste had made me a father and that I had to fight for that. I could have made that choice for many other valid reasons but I say again, that day I chose Amélie.

CLAIRE

After Amélie arrived, I put my whole self into my work, determined to accumulate bonuses and developed a sophisticated persona for the purpose. It worked well. Then, one day, I was told to head out to the leafy suburbs to show a house to an important client and though always nervous I travelled there unafraid.

It was naturally a shock to discover that I was going to be showing that house to David and I was still angry about his dismissive attitude at the hospital but these emotions had to compete with the real reason for my blush and pounding heart, the fact that I was attracted to him. Whatever line I had wandered over in Scotland, there was no finding my way back. I quickly retreated behind my professional persona and after exchanging some very awkward, initial pleasantries I can honestly say I did a brilliant job of show-casing that house.

In every room I tried to picture Celeste and her baby, I must have repeated the phrase "ideal family home" dozens and dozens of times. Who was I attempting to convince? Nothing could dim my senses, smelling him, the tone of his voice running like a feather down my spine, noticing the hairs on his arms when he pushed up his sleeves and then flashes, moments of previous times together, in his car when he drove me away from Turnberry, out on the lake as he strained at the oars of the boat, watching me intently as I balanced an orange in my hand, leaning his foot on a tree stump, smoking. Every moment together, every conversation was infused with fresh significance, meant something different. In collision with these feelings, like a powerful cross current, ran my thoughts about Celeste, enchanting, vibrant and then an image of her in that hospital bed, so diminished, so vulnerable. She had kissed me, told me she loved me. Had she always known me as a Judas?

In the garden room, he started to apologise to me about his rudeness at the hospital and so it began, the descent over white rapids, with my limited experience of life and love and relationships to keep me afloat and only my wits and intellect and bravado as oars. The rocks were everywhere. This man was paying my rent. I could not afford London without him, not if I wanted the money to study law. His wife trusted me and had shown nothing but kindness and generosity but now I wanted more, I wanted her husband. How could a person be so damned greedy? Why would he ever love me when I hated myself? I came with a track record. I had walked out on my family, betrayed the trust of Emily and her parents and then my behaviour with men to date did nothing to redeem me. Feelings, lust, love, they were perilous and better to cut off an arm than sacrifice the whole body.

He started up some sort of speech about how our relationship might be misconstrued and it was like he handed me the blade to begin the surgical task. He provoked just enough loathing in me then to make the incision and so I stared out over what would be the perfect garden setting for his beautiful little family dream and I made the first cut, a small tentative slice, a lie: "I am not attracted to you." And I must have been in shock because it didn't seem to hurt so much and so I cut again deeper. Not only was I not attracted to him, why he was obviously far too old and naturally I regarded him like a father. Then, thinking of my own father, I took up a bigger blade and pointed out that money, class, background, that these formed the impenetrable barrier between us and I told him that he didn't even know me, that I was nothing but a project for him and Celeste. Those lies, they were the darkest because truthfully David absolutely got me, we were both rooted in ambition and Celeste, whatever her feelings were towards me, never once had she pitied me.

It was a dreadful speech but if there was any chance the limb could still be saved, well he made no great effort to do so. He wavered a little yes but then business-like thanked me for clarifying the situation, and I must have been a terrible stain on his dream, family home because he could scarcely wait to see me off the premises. I had hurt his pride, given him a categorical rejection speech, ended brutally any connection between us. There, it was done. Whatever we ever were was over.

When I closed the door to my flat, I thought "The important thing is that he will carry on paying the rent for his place." But my head went down and I suddenly felt it. Oh my God, my arm was missing. I had just made it impossible for David to ever love me and he was never going to invite me to their party because I had said it loud and clear; I was nothing but a project and projects are completed and all he now required was a nicely typed letter, in a few years hence, informing him of my success in the legal profession, thanking him and Celeste for their patronage and he would smile and think "Oh yes, do you remember Celeste? That thin, waif of a girl, practically an orphan. We helped her out, got her started. Good to know it has all worked out." But Celeste will not care about my job. She will want to know if I met anyone and fell in love and she will be so disappointed to learn that I am a dry, cold spinster, my beauty all wasted and thank goodness she captured it all in a painting about futility...

My legs went from under me, I slid to the floor and I started to sob and the pain, the pain was like nothing I had ever felt. I had been caught up in some wonderful adventure but it had all unravelled and this was what it felt to be utterly alone.

I'm not sure how long it took me to cry it all out but eventually I got up. It was cold in the flat and I could not stop shivering. Gradually, rational thoughts began to creep back and so I pulled out my latest bank statement and a calculator and started on the maths. Another month in London perhaps and I would have just enough to leave and head north. I could maybe find a bar job and it would not be too long and my law studies would begin. The same girl who effectively ran away from home would run again. I was good at running.

PART THREE

CLAIRE

I tried very hard indeed to forget about Mr and Mrs Sutton. When I pictured them, strangely it was never in their London suburban home, playing in the garden with Amélie, hosting family barbeques on the terrace. He was always outside the house in Scotland, foot resting on a tree stump, smoking. She was always upstairs in that house, art materials everywhere, brow furrowed as she sketched away and then I recalled the three of us, rowing on the lake and, tormented by these repeating images, I made myself remember the cold flat and the sound of my own sobbing and this was always my way back to reality. Of course, studying to enter the law, combined with late work shifts serving in pubs, and the minimum amount of social life had played their part in distracting me and then, shortly after commencing my work placement at a Leeds firm of solicitors, I decided to allow the senior partner, a married man, to seduce me. It was an arrangement that suited us both. He was having a second life crisis and I made it clear from the start that I would never fall in love with him. I was a boost for his struggling ego and he took the edge off my solitude. The relationship was rooted in another kind of attraction; my boss was mature, seasoned by experience and radiated the power that provides. There were moments in those protective arms when it occurred to me that this was what David could have offered and so, I could never entirely forget him. As for Celeste, it was pure guilt that did not enable me to put her aside; guilt that she had shown nothing but love for me but I had formed a crush on her husband; guilt at walking out of her life at an evidently challenging time; guilt at having discarded such an exquisite, enchanting individual, as if such connections could be found anywhere, at any given time.

After one year at the solicitors, my boss and lover dangled the offer of a job, once I had finished my Articles, but I surprised myself with my own ruthlessness and used his matrimonial indiscretion as leverage to exploit his powers of influence otherwise, and he reluctantly helped me secure a pupillage in Chambers. Whilst he agreed to do this, it was clear he felt poorly used and the relationship ended.

I was working out the last part of my employment in his offices and growing excited about my forthcoming pupillage, when Caroline Summers, a solicitor from London, presented herself. From her hands to her ankles, she had sharp, city edges and her ice blue eyes and clipped southern accent rendered her so imposing that she had raised all kinds of speculation in the offices from the moment of her arrival. She was shown to the boardroom by my boss, where she awaited my arrival in stubborn silence and when I appeared, she dispatched him as if he were a junior clerk which I confess made me have to stifle a nervous laugh.

She pulled out a pair of spectacles and several papers from a beautiful, leather case.

"Miss Sutcliffe, I represent Mr David Sutton." The way she spoke his name, he might have been the Prime Minister.

Suddenly filled with panic, my intelligence and its reserve departed out the window.

"Oh God, I still owe him for the flat in London. I meant to pay him back as soon as possible."

She peered down her elegant nose at me and I thought she might request proof of my identity, such was the unlikelihood of my having any connection with her client.

"I am not here to discuss any such thing. First, I must inform you of some extremely grave news and Mr Sutton asked that I do so delicately."

It was hard to imagine Ms Summers doing anything delicately. I clasped my hands tightly together and forced myself to take a deep breath.

"I regret to inform you that eight months ago, Mrs Celeste Sutton died, as the result of a tragic, boating accident in Scotland. I understand from Mr Sutton that you were very fond of her. So, allow me first to express my condolences and if you like you may take a moment to digest this very sad news."

It was odd, the way she gave me permission to react and maybe it impacted the way I did. I rose to my feet and was overcome with a surprising anger, strung together by so many questions.

"What the hell? She's dead? I don't believe it. Hang on, I don't get this. You say 8 months ago? Why am I finding out now and how come David isn't telling me this himself? Oh God, her poor daughter. I need to speak to David about this. I'm sorry but you being here is a complete waste of time. I need to go to London. I'm sorry you'll have to leave now. I have a lot to sort out. Oh God...."

I lost momentum and fell back into my seat. I saw Celeste coming down the stairs in Scotland, I heard her sweet, lyrical language and smelled lavender and my hands reached instinctively to where an alabaster heart had once adorned me and my real heart felt a great pressure, a huge weight upon it. She was gone and not just now but eight months ago which meant that every thought of her reality since then had been a lie, which meant I had not been to her funeral, had never said goodbye. Leaving her to her life the way I had, that was one thing, but now she had left me, she had vanished from reality, she was beyond contact. I realised that I had had a sort of plan all the time, that I had been waiting to arrive at some tangible point of success in my life, perhaps expecting that with that would come love and then the grand reveal to her shining eyes; "Look, see, I've made it." I wanted, I needed her approval.

I would have lost control entirely but for Ms Summers' steel, blue eyes and determination to represent her client to the utmost professional degree. Like a judge pronouncing the death penalty, she did not falter at my weakness.

"Mr Sutton saw fit to have me inform you of the news. You must appreciate that he is still struggling to come to terms with his loss. The circumstances surrounding his wife's death meant there had to be a post mortem and an inquest and it has been a dreadful ordeal for her entire family. In the circumstances, a quiet family funeral in France was arranged. Now, if you will bear with me, I have not simply come to inform you of Mrs Sutton's death. There are other matters arising."

I did not realise I had started to cry until I glanced over then and she was a blur. I wiped the tears away, ashamed at my own emotion.

"Please, say whatever it is you have to say. I am listening."

My voice was small, childlike.

"So, it was the express wish of Mrs Sutton that you be god-mother to her daughter Amélie and she had urged Mr Sutton to contact you. It took him some time to find you but when he did, for reasons he perhaps may wish to discuss with you, he felt the connection was imprudent and informed his wife that you could not be found. He wishes you to know that he also gave great consideration to your own best interests. Meanwhile, Mrs Sutton purchased a small property in Brittany and instructed me, separately, that this house was intended for you and for the purpose of you having holidays there with her and her daughter, once you had been traced. I believe that at my last meeting with Mrs Sutton, she was on the point of making her own enquiries to find you but she became unwell and she and her daughter moved over to the south of France where her other family resides. I did not inform Mr Sutton of the existence of the house in Brittany, as per Mrs Sutton's instructions to me. This became disclosed as a result of her tragic death, at the reading of her will. In short, she left you the house and recorded her wish that you be god-mother to her daughter Amélie. There is a letter for you which I will leave you to read. Mr Sutton is very sorry that this will all come as a terrible shock. He desires that his wife's wishes be fulfilled as far as is possible but stresses that he will understand entirely if you feel you are not in a position so to do, as regards forming a connection with his daughter. The house is yours without prejudice. There is the inevitable paper work of course. Mr Sutton has suggested that you take the time to reflect on everything and then, if it is convenient, you might come down to London to go over your decision. Naturally any travel expenses will be met by my client."

She had pushed a small, lavender envelope over towards me, my name inscribed in turquoise ink. It looked so small and lost on the vast, oak table and I thought of an empty boat, bobbing up and down on cold, dark water.

"Did she die on the loch at their house in Scotland?"

"Yes, I am afraid that is correct."

It was *the* loch, our loch, the one we must have all recalled.

"He should have come and told me himself."

She shuffled in her seat and something of her professional veneer seemed to slip slightly.

"David has been through hell. He believes his wife killed herself and gave testimony to that at the inquest. It was concluded that there was insufficient evidence to reach that verdict. Young and inexperienced as you are, you must try to imagine what this horrible business has been like for him. I suggest you think carefully before throwing accusations at him."

I knew then that David was not just her client but a friend yet she quickly composed herself before there was any risk of us connecting over that. I did not like to be reminded of my relative youth and inexperience. I stood up again.

"Please inform your client that I am very sad indeed to learn of his wife's death. I will take some time to reflect on it all and I will inform him of my decision when I am ready. I don't much like London so I may or may not take the trouble of speaking to him in person. I'll think about it. Please just leave his contact details. If you don't mind, I would like some time alone now."

She gave me her most severe stare yet and gathered her things.

"Very well Claire. I can see you need to do some thinking."

She moved over to the door but stopped and turned.

"I understand you wish to be a barrister. What area of law interests you?"

"Not sure. Matrimonial stuff maybe? Do you think I'll be any good?"

She studied me, deliberated.

"I should think you will be quite capable. Time will tell. Good luck. At any rate, you own a very nice property in France now."

She peered over at the other papers she had left and I felt it was a test and so feigned scant interest. Once she had closed the door, it was to these papers I turned. I wasn't ready for turquoise ink.

Later, after a glass of wine, I turned to her letter.

My dear sweet Claire,

I look for you. I think of you so often. I am in France with my family. It is not easy being a mother. Amélie is so beautiful. I know she can enchant you. I feel a long way from you here and in London I look and look but I never see you and I remember that you do not love London the way I do. Perhaps, if I go to Scotland, I will find you? Do you remember our wonderful day there?

You must be Amélie's god-mother. You were there when she was born. I know that you are not religious. You are like David, always rational, always thinking of logic and I do not insist that you be a catholic. Her French family take care of all that. I simply want you to know her, to love her, to help her.

I carry on my search for you. I write this only as a precaution, you understand. I have found a pretty house in Brittany. I think that Brittany suits you, that you will like the sea there. I don't see you in the south of France. Brittany is French and English mixed, like you and me and like Amélie.

I know this is difficult for you to hear but I love you. I see you blushing, even now. You cannot avoid love. You must accept it, even if you do not understand it. I told you to wear an alabaster heart, not one of steel. Be careful.

I love you always,

Celeste

DAVID

Who would be a coroner? It was no easy matter to give a title to the manner of my wife's death and he frowned and sighed and gave every indication of due diligence in considering the facts before him. Though numb, I confess I was never deaf to the whisperings in my ear. They told a story about a woman obsessed with another story, set in a time long ago, a tragic love triangle linked to the house in Scotland. Yet, enough of my rational mind still functioned and, though I was happy to talk about my wife's mood swings and medication, I held back from speaking of her obsessions. I looked into the large brown innocent eyes of my daughter and had the good sense to stay silent. Though I believed in my heart that suicide was most probably the correct verdict, how could I deny my child a verdict of misadventure? Better for Amélie to believe that her mother, in a moment of ill-advised spontaneity, had been a victim of inclement weather on a Scottish loch rather than have the shame and stigma of suicide cast a bleak cloud over her origins and heritage. Either way, poor Amélie would have to learn a tragic story.

So, although I muttered against the coroner's verdict (she went out on a squally loch without a life jacket for heaven's sake), I did not wrestle too hard and had the sense to let it be so. And then, I was generous enough to return Celeste's body to her family and country of origin. I surrendered her to a catholic burial which she probably would have despised because frankly her wishes were no longer my primary concern. Far better to satisfy the needs of the living and they had a definite preference whereas I was, as I have said, quite numb and indifferent to the options. Celeste was pulled from a cold, cold loch and eventually transported to the dazzling sunshine of a Mediterranean grave yard. Perhaps even the less rational part of me favoured this plan, lest she rise from the grave a second time to haunt me. To haunt us.

Then, I found out about the house she had purchased and her grand plan for you. I confess that I took some considerable amount of legal advice on the matter before determining how to proceed. The conclusion was that you had a legal right to that house which would be difficult but not impossible for me to block. As for you having any connection to my daughter, that was more a matter of moral conscience. Only having wrestled with these aspects did I then permit myself the luxury of recollection, lingering over every memory of you, from the innocent girl sitting in the hotel reception at Turnberry, to the confident and defiant young woman who had walked away from me in the hospital and then the trembling, deceitful woman who had sworn she had no feelings of attraction toward me.

In the brief but intense time of our acquaintance I had certainly grown attracted to you and so, when you announced your willingness to travel down to London, done all very correctly through the solicitor, I admit I was more than satisfied and the greyness of grief parted to let some of the brightness of possibility shine through. How could I not look forward to seeing the latest version of Claire Sutcliffe, poised to train as a barrister? Would there be any of Waif left? I doubted it. You were a grown woman now and nothing of our difference in age would constitute an obstacle but there were other difficulties, not least the painful recollections of a dead woman. Celeste had created a wonderful drama for us. Would we agree to participate?

CLAIRE

I arrived at the Sutton family home, resolved to try to forget the last time I was there and when Mrs Jones, David's housekeeper, greeted me and led me through to the garden room this was made easier by the transformation of the place. I saw that it was a most beautiful home now, although not in any way reminiscent of Celeste and her character. I studied the carefully crafted décor and furnishings of the garden room and concluded that this was the creation of an interior designer. There was nothing eclectic or interesting about it and the only reference to Celeste was a photograph of her. It was in black and white but all her colours radiated from it and I bit down on the inside of my mouth to maintain my composure. My grief surely must give way to David's? And Amélie? Did small children grieve?

I never heard him approach and when he entered the room he seemed taller than I remembered and in spite of grey hairs not by any means less handsome. I stared back at the photo of Celeste, as if it might provide refuge.

"Hello David. I'm so very sorry. I can't believe she's gone."

"Hello Claire. Yes, it's not easy to accept. It is kind of you to come down."

He appraised me, from head to toe and I knew that in that instant he regarded me as a woman although he knew how to disguise any conclusions. He too glanced over at the photo.

"She was never herself entirely after Amélie was born. That photo was taken before we were married. She would want you to remember her like that."

"I can only remember her like that. Actually, I only have one photo of her, a newspaper cutting from your wedding party. She wore that red, velvet dress. You looked like the perfect couple."

There was a long difficult silence and thankfully Mrs Jones appeared with a tea tray. While she served us, David stared at me until I had to look away. An annoying blush crept up my face and our mutual attraction plonked its elephant behind between us.

Mrs Jones sniffed at the air and muttered about the damp weather we were experiencing but I wondered if it wasn't our stinking elephant that she smelled. She left.

"So, you have a very nice property in Brittany to enjoy."

"Well, yes, eventually. I'm going to be rather busy in Leeds. Perhaps I should rent it out for an income?"

"I can certainly help you arrange that, if you like. I don't suppose you've learned any French in the last few years?"

"No, not a bit. Your help would be very much appreciated. I should learn French though, I suppose. I mean, for Amélie."

"You should speak English to her. She has a French nanny and naturally she can assist you. You do want to be part of my daughter's life then?"

"Yes, yes of course. I mean, I'm not sure what Celeste quite pictured but I'll do my best. "

Another silence fell but this time it rested between us more easily and I realised that aside from mutual attraction there had always been another level of connection between us and we could depend upon it now. We exchanged smiles.

"No one ever really got inside Celeste's head, let's face it. I think you should just be yourself and Amélie will love you. When she's older she'll have a ton of questions about her mother and all any of us can do is offer her a glimpse, our own perspective. As an artist, Celeste understood entirely about subjective interpretation."

"It's just I have never had a relationship with a small child. I don't know how to behave, what to say…"

"Oh that's easy. We'll take her to the zoo this afternoon and you'll laugh at the monkeys and penguins with her and you'll buy her a balloon and like magic she will love you. With children, there are no barriers."

There was no time to reflect on this observation because the door opened again and in she rushed, followed by the French nanny who was clearly remonstrating with her, to no avail. David raised a hand to convey that the interruption was quite ok and exchanged French with the excited child who had barely given me the time of day. She clambered onto her father's lap, stuck a thumb in her mouth and now stared at me, not hostile but I felt she saw through to my soul.

"So, this is Claire. She doesn't speak French so you must speak in English, ok? Say hello."

She looked up at him and then at me and her brow furrowed. This new situation perplexed her. Whilst she had her mother's colouring, she was the image of her father. Her version of him was very cute and I suspected she got away with just about anything. I decided attack was the best form of defence.

"Hello Amélie. It's lovely to meet you." I smiled, instinctively no teeth.

She responded by saying something in French and then leapt off his lap and ran out of the room.

"Oh dear. That didn't go too well."

"No, she's gone to get something, something she wants to show you I think. Don't worry. This is normal."

And quickly she returned, waving a rag doll with straw, yellow hair. She spoke to her father again, clearly not willing to address the strange woman who did not speak French. David was stern, insisting in English that it was rude to speak French in front of me but nevertheless he fell into the role of interpreter.

"So, apparently, this doll is called Claire. Celeste's idea no doubt."

Then, Amélie crossed the room and placed the doll in my lap, trying to assess my reaction. I picked up the doll, stroked its unruly hair and thanked her and this produced a guarded smile. She snatched the doll back and ran back to the safety of her father but overall it felt a connection had been established...engineered by the child. She talked and talked a mesmerising version of French that had me quite hooked and David patiently decoded and summarised.

"She tells me you are the lady in the painting and that mummy loved you and said you were special. Zoo or no zoo, you've nothing to worry about. Celeste prepared the way it seems. She adores you."

A quick nod of his head at the nanny and Amélie was efficiently escorted away, unprotesting. David glanced at his watch.

"Lunch time already. Fancy something stronger than tea?"

Without waiting for a reply he led us away into a fantastic, remodelled kitchen, dismissed Mrs Jones and set about cooking for us, having uncorked a delicious white wine which I sipped very slowly, deliberately restrained and I kept thinking "whatever you do, don't fall for the gorgeous widower. Stay detached."

Easier said than done.

DAVID

When I walked into the garden room that day, it was immediately apparent that the young woman in the stylish cut jeans and polo neck sweater was no waif. You had matured into a striking and confident woman, though I was glad to note that you still allowed your wayward hair to mainly do its own thing.

In the exchanges that ensued and judging by your blushes, it was obvious that there was an attraction between us which a few years apart had done nothing to diminish. The obstacles to us developing our level of connection were not by any means negligible. Something of Celeste hovered over us (I deliberately avoid the word ghost) but it was not primarily a dead woman that rendered a relationship tricky. No, it was more so my very much alive daughter, on the one hand the primary link keeping us connected but in a bigger sense a permanent reminder that I had loved her mother, had been married to her mother. Was it me being over sensitive, or had Celeste been rather devious in assigning you the specific role of God-mother? Moreover, Amélie had been carefully prepared for your role in her life, her mother's beloved friend, someone so special to her mother, why even a doll had been named after you. In life, Celeste had had the ability to often frustrate me and in death her powers were not wholly diminished.

The trip to the zoo went well, beyond my greatest expectations. Amélie was happy, you seemed to enjoy the experience and for just those few hours I managed to cast off the troubled thoughts that I had been wrestling with since Celeste's death. We were all three of us, if only for that afternoon, carefree and content.

You agreed to stay for a couple of nights. Amélie ate her early supper without protest and I read her one of her favourite bedtime stories whilst Mrs Jones cooked dinner and you retired to your room to unpack. Over dinner, we re-lived the highlights of the zoo but by the conclusion of dessert, when we withdrew into the sitting room, it was evident that Amélie was no longer a distraction. I poured us a whiskey and just for a while we were able to rest in an easy silence, alone with our thoughts. Me, I thought about the fact that I was twenty years older than you and decided I really ought to be the one to take the lead, to be more forthright.

"You know Claire, I have plenty of contacts and could easily arrange for you to attend Chambers here in London. It would be far more prestigious and fast track your career as a barrister. It would make it easier for you to see Amélie."

You gave me a hard stare and sat up straighter.

"I like the North and I love Leeds. The cost of living is far cheaper and anyway, I'm not sure a child is required to see that much of their God-mother."

I took a necessary slug of whiskey.

"And what if *I* prefer to see you more often?"

You put down your glass and crossed your arms.

"Why? Because I remind you of Celeste and happier times?"

I put down my glass and leaned forward, unflinching.

"No, because I think we like each other and I see no reason not to explore that."

The arms stayed folded and colour daintily infused your cheeks. You shuffled in your seat.

"Oh, I see. I didn't see that coming. I mean, you don't mess about."

I shrugged.

"I can't really afford to Claire. I'm 20 years older than you and it doesn't need to be complicated. Just to be clear, I'm not looking for another mother for Amélie. The nanny does just fine. I'm not suggesting anything too full on. We just explore the options."

"Well, that sounds like a preamble to a business deal David and not very romantic but in any case you presume a lot. I'm not sure I'm interested in an older man."

This, I confess, irritated me, rubbed up against my ego. I also recalled a previous conversation when you had claimed I was like a father-figure and it had been pure bluff.

"Oh? Novelty worn off? There are rumours you were involved with your much older boss."

Not surprisingly, that was enough to flick your switch.

"What? How the hell do you know that? Have you been spying on me?" And there it was, a complete confession.

"No, actually Caroline told me. That is, it was merely her suspicion but I see that she was spot on then."

Now you rose to your feet.

"Well it is absolutely none of your damn business but as it happens maybe I now prefer the idea of a younger man, someone with a bit more stamina. Either way, I'm not sure what makes you so confident that I fancy you."

I stood up too and we were just feet apart so I could hear your rapid breathing.

"Oh come on now, I know when there is an attraction. Think very carefully before you say another word. Do you really want to deny it?"

We stared at each other for what seemed an age and I could see you struggle with yourself.

"It's getting late. It has been a long day for me. I think I should go to bed before we ruin a perfectly good friendship."

"Ah, so that's a no then, just to be clear." I heard myself and I did sound a lot like the ruthless person I could be.

"No, it's a polite request for you to back the hell off right now. I have a life in Leeds and a plan for my career. You can't just expect me to drop it all."

"Drop it? Of course not but Claire..."

You had started to walk past me but I stopped you, lightly taking the top of your arm.

"Yes?" Your huge angry eyes made me want to kiss you so much but I have always been good under pressure.

"Just bear in mind that I am not the sort of man prepared to come second place to a career, a career that at best will be worth a fraction of what I make in a year. I get it. You're a very intelligent and determined woman and you have to weigh up all your options. I'm just not sure I can wait in the wings while you try to catch up on life. I'm not *that* patient."

You shook off my hand.

"Oh I think I understand perfectly David. You have set your terms very clearly. Now if you don't mind, I'm going to bed. "

"Alright. Goodnight then Claire."

"Goodnight. I'll see you in the morning." You flicked back your hair and started to open the door.

"Er no actually you won't. I thought you, the nanny and Amélie might spend the day together. I have a number of meetings scheduled. I have tickets for the opera tomorrow night, if you're interested."

You wavered, only for a moment and then pursed those lovely lips.

"I'll see how I feel. Child minding can be exhausting."

"Very well. Goodnight waif."

You stretched yourself up taller and jutted out a defiant chin.

"No David, I'm not "waif" anymore."

A strand of your unruly hair had fallen across one cheek and I scooped it gently upward, tucking it behind your ear and right on cue your pupils dilated.

"No, no you're not. I can see that."

I had managed the last word and it made you furious so I did what seemed like the gentlemanly thing and turned away, to let you go. I waited to hear if you would slam your bedroom door but you clicked it quietly shut and perhaps that was the last word, after all.

CLAIRE

That night, I went to my bed absolutely fuming but what was I really angry about? First and foremost, I was mad at myself. Not only had I plainly gone against my own counsel and fallen for the attractive widower (how had I deluded myself that it was any other way?) but far, from keeping an alabaster heart, my feelings must have been practically inscribed on my forehead because David had called it crystal clear. Yes, I fancied him and it was that obvious. Neither was I able to pretend that I disliked him being attracted to me.

All this was hugely aggravating for my pride but my wrath was galvanised by something else. As I lay in bed, staring up at the ceiling, I just went over and over the intense fury I suddenly felt towards David and its root cause? My goodness, his arrogance, his basic assumption of professional supremacy and the notion that whatever my career pretensions were, ultimately he was the great, male provider and nothing could get in the way of his empire. If I had intentions of being someone important in his life, then I would have to fit into an available slot in his schedule. He seriously expected me to move to London? Oh and I really shouldn't take too long to think about it all because he was not a patient man!

I should perhaps have packed my bags and left that very night but then there was Celeste. Rightly or wrongly, I felt indebted to her and she had made it clear what she wanted. I was to be part of her daughter's life and if David really could be that selfish and over-bearing well then surely that child needed me?

I can set out all these thoughts and feelings with clarity now but that night they were all tangled up into a confusing melange and it took hours for me to finally drift asleep. When I woke up, David had left as he had predicted, and I resolved to make my day with Amélie as positive as possible. This was not difficult because she was a delight. Though she looked like

David, she had her mother's soulful radiance and irresistible vivacity. All her practical needs were handled by the nanny and we spent a very enjoyable day, walking in Hyde Park, riding on a big, red bus and visiting Hamley's toy shop.

Come six o'clock, Amélie having started the long bedtime routine, my mind turned to the prospect of an evening with David at the opera and once again, confronted by emotional complexity, I preferred to find a way out of the situation. I was not ready to leave London and say goodbye to Amélie but I decided to make my own plan for the evening. I would go and visit Celeste's friend Gary. Before tackling David again, I would seek wise counsel. Mrs Jones was informed of my plans and I left a little gleeful at the idea of David returning to find me gone.

I arrived at Gary's place and it was as if time had stopped there because the music was still throbbing and the ground floor was already jammed with colourful people, the wine in full flow. Except Gary looked older, older than he should have done after just 4 years. I saw that he was wearing a black band on one arm. He spotted me straight away and gestured towards the stairs. It was quieter above. We embraced, a light token gesture and I asked him about the black band.

"That's for Celeste and two other friends recently passed. I've lost four friends to AIDS and I know dozens who are HIV Positive."

"Oh, oh I'm sorry. That's horrible."

He scrutinised me suspiciously. I felt he didn't much like me.

"Where did you go? Celeste was looking for you. It was like you had died."

"I went back up north. Celeste was a mum. I didn't think she needed me around."

"Well, you were wrong about that but then again David did a good job of keeping us all out of her way."

"You don't like him, do you?

"Oh it's nothing personal. I mean, he was a catch by anyone's standards but Celeste should have had her fun and thrown him back in. He wasn't right for her."

I decided I had nothing to lose with Gary and to get straight to the point.

"I'm here because Celeste asked me to be Amélie's God-mother. Now David wants us to be more than friends. What do you think?"

He glanced me up and down again but in an almost pitying way, as if I had just told him I too was HIV Positive.

"Well, with Celeste gone, there can't be any harm I suppose but be sure to throw him back into the water when you've finished with him. Learn from her mistakes."

"So, you think it's me catching him and not the other way around?"

"Oh I'd say you're a fair match for each other but he's the one supposed to be grieving, remember?"

"Do you think he really loved Celeste?"

"Yes, I can't say otherwise. I think he loved her but love is not always a good thing. It doesn't always end with happily ever after. He was wrong for her. She needed some control yes but he was too full on with it. He didn't get her creative spirit. He's not the type. In fact, you're more his type."

He cast another critical eye over me.

"If I got involved with David, do you think he would just end up controlling me?"

"Well, I'd like to see him try! Maybe you wouldn't make him feel so threatened. You're more like him. What is it you do again? Property?"

"No, actually I'm training to be a barrister right now."

At that, he almost choked on the sip of wine he had just taken.

"Really? Good for you! Well then, you've got no worries. Any trouble from David and you can sue his pants off. Just tie him up in loads of red tape and if it all goes pear shaped, take him for every penny."

We both laughed at the idea but deep down I felt no reassurance and no clearer.

Gary spotted some other guests arriving and promptly dumped me. I stayed for a while, having one conversation with a would-be fashion designer who gave a very negative appraisal of London life and another with a freelance journalist who, once she discovered my connection to David Sutton, wanted lots of information about his business dealings and quickly lost interest when I failed to oblige.

Celeste would have been at home with this crowd, whilst never just blending in but they made me feel boring, dry and somehow rigid, like I was made of cardboard and they were all colours of plastacene. Perhaps Celeste liked me because I was actually like David but a younger, less threatening version? She had always liked to make fun of my ambition and my business suit but perhaps it was also endearing? I liked to think I brought out something good in her, something less self-centred.

I left Gary's place feeling light headed and more confused. By the time I arrived back at the Sutton Residence, I had decided that if David pressed me that evening, then perhaps I should take a risk and go with it. Perhaps as Gary suggested, I had more power in the situation? I had had enough to drink to take the risk (this was how I dealt with men and sex) but when Mrs Jones came to the door, she explained that Mr Sutton was not home yet. He had gone to the opera as planned.

In the morning, I discovered that David had not returned home and drew my own conclusions. He had however, telephoned to say that a cab would collect me and Amélie and we would be taken to join him for breakfast. The cab duly arrived and took us to the American place where David had treated me to breakfast the morning after the wedding party. David was there, not dressed for an opera, looking as fresh as a daisy. He grinned at me, clearly relaxed and in a good mood.

"Good morning! Remember this place? I thought I would treat you to some of those pancakes you loved. Amélie likes them too."

Amélie was buzzing for the pancakes, oblivious to any adult tensions.

"Nice time at the opera?"

"Wonderful thank you. And I trust you had an enjoyable evening too?"

"It was very interesting. Celeste's friend Gary is very insightful. It was fun to catch up."

If this annoyed David, he gave nothing away but studied the menu.

After the pancakes, as ever delicious, Amélie was happy to scribble on paper with crayons whilst the adults were decidedly serious.

"So, you head back to Leeds this afternoon?"

"Yes, my train is at three. I'll keep in touch with Amélie. Maybe in the summer, I could take her to the house in Brittany?"

"Yes, I'm sure that can be arranged. I've asked Caroline Summers to look into an agent to manage the property for you. Any dates you want to keep it for your own use, you'll have to let them know. Any problems and I can lend a hand with the French."

"Ok. Thank you very much. I hope you can understand David that right now I need to concentrate on my career. It's what I have worked so hard for."

"Of course I understand. I just don't accept that you have to train in Leeds and in fact I think you are being bloody stupid, independent for the sake of it."

"You think you are such an irresistible catch don't you? Anyway, judging by last night, there are plenty of other fish in the sea for you."

He smiled at this and looked into my eyes in a way that made parts of me swoon though I was determined not to show this and tried to stay deadpan.

"All kinds of fish Claire but you're no fish and I wouldn't dream of trying to get you on a hook. I've had chance to reflect and if it's a career you want more than anything, then far be it for me to distract you. I'm sure you will do very well, even in Leeds. In fact, Leeds just won't be able to contain you. When you get bored and realise you need to be in London, I'll be here."

"But not exactly waiting if last night is anything to go by."

"I'll be getting on with my life Claire whilst you get on with yours. "

He summoned the waiter for the bill, satisfied with this arrangement but it did not satisfy me. I now realised that I had negotiated myself into a place I didn't want to be. Yet, I could not find it within me to ask for new terms. It was not my career that was more important than David, otherwise London would have been the obvious compromise. It was something else. We both knew it and maybe he understood better than I did what it was but he was going to leave me to figure it out.

Later, he drove me to the station. The mood was suitably sombre but not awkward. He walked me to the ticket barrier and kissed me lightly on the cheek.

"See you Claire. My e-mail address is on the card I gave you. Everyone will be using e-mail soon, even barristers. Keep in touch."

"And what if I say that suddenly I don't want to go, that I'm afraid I've made a mistake?"

"I'd say some mistakes should be made and lessons learned.

Now off you go. Leeds awaits."

And he just turned and walked away from me, never looked back and I got on that train feeling utterly crushed which perhaps was exactly what he wanted.

DAVID

Did it annoy me that you decided not to go to the opera with me? Well, I won't deny that it was a little like a slap in the face initially but then I could not stop smiling about it. I showered and prepared myself for an evening at the opera and felt a certain admiration for you. Let's face it, a man like me always enjoys a challenge. Your feisty attitude was a positive and as I adjusted my tie in the mirror I thought about Celeste and the fact that my extraordinary wife had loved to collect niche pieces of art and that some of those had accumulated a not insubstantial amount of value. In you, she had recognized potential and unique qualities. She had wanted so much to see what became of you. I did too.

Naturally, I would go to the opera regardless and so I called Caroline Summers and she was more than willing. The two of us already had an understanding. She had decided early on in our relationship that we would make better associates than lovers, that our mutual business interests were best secured by a platonic connection and perhaps you do not know to this day that it was she who introduced me to Celeste? She had encouraged the romance and carried a certain burden of guilt for it.

She has a refined appreciation of the arts and a ticket to the opera would never be wasted on her. I allowed her to savour its wonders and only brought you up in conversation as we headed back to my city apartment for drinks.

"So, tell me again Caroline. What do you make of Claire Sutcliffe, so favoured by Celeste?"

"Ah yes, the beautiful Claire. Has she come down to see you yet, to meet her God-daughter?"

"Well, as a matter of fact she's staying at mine right now only she wanted to go and catch up with some other friends tonight. Amélie loves her already and if I'm honest I'm finding myself pretty enchanted. She's grown-up."

Caroline gave me the look, the one she gives her clients if they dare question her legal opinion, the one that makes me feel a bit ignorant.

"Oh dear David, now be careful. She's VERY ambitious and there was definitely something going on with her boss which shows she'll stop at nothing."

"So, do you think *she* was using *him* or the other way round? There's no chance she was at all besotted with him?"

Caroline gave me a weary side-glance and perhaps it occurred to her that the trip to the opera had had an agenda. She smoothed her dress and composed her thoughts but could not disguise the irritation.

"How the hell should I know? Don't you have a man to snoop for you?"

"Yes, but I value your insight. I've annoyed you. Sorry. We can change the subject if you like."

"Look, I met her briefly and the circumstances were pretty dramatic but I don't know, I think she can probably take care of herself. Just remember, you've had two marriages. Do yourself a favour and try being single for a while."

"Er, did I mention the word marriage?"

Again, she managed to regard me in a way that made me feel rather silly.

"Well now David, if you wanted to just bed her I don't think you would be asking these questions. You must intend at least something half serious?"

"Damned if I know exactly what I want but I know it's complicated. She wants a relationship with my daughter apart from anything. Call me paranoid, but I can't help thinking Celeste has engineered things. She was obsessed with Claire and didn't want me and Claire to ever be anything and then she makes her Amélie's God-mother, like she was Celeste's special friend and confidante."

Caroline looked at me intently.

"Tell me, when Celeste was alive, did you ever give her any cause to think you might stray with Claire?"

"Absolutely not. I loved Celeste and Claire was just a girl trying to make her way in life. I almost felt sorry for her. If you must know, if anyone had a right to be jealous in that marriage then it was me. You know, I even began to wonder if Celeste had some hidden lesbian thing going on."

Caroline turned away. Clearly, none of this was easy for her.

"David, you know Celeste was my friend too and I won't go into any detail but I really don't think it was anything sexual. She clearly felt something for Claire but now she's dead and frankly what happens between you and Claire is entirely your affair. I'm assuming you think she might be interested in you?"

"Yes, I believe she is but she's ambitious and insists on pursuing her career in bloody Leeds. I'm not sure if I can be bothered to play second fiddle to all that."

Caroline arched an eyebrow at me, akin to a sharp smack on the hand.

"No, I can believe that. Look David, do you really want my advice?"

I made a point of sitting more upright.

"I'm all ears."

"Good. Well then, back right off. Let her go and pursue her career in Leeds. In the end, if she's a real contender as far as the law goes well then she'll come crawling down here soon enough. She'll outgrow Leeds. Put your feelings on hold. Give yourself time to get over Celeste. What's the great rush?"

"Er the fact that I'm twenty years older than her?"

"So? You'll still be rich and handsome in a couple of years' time. You bastard men only get better with age. Right now, let her go and focus on your daughter. I'm no expert but children allegedly grow up fast."

"Mm. Maybe you're right."

"Of course I am. Now for pity's sake, can we talk about something else?"

So, we returned to my apartment and had drinks. Caroline always knew when to call a taxi but I decided to stay at the flat anyway, thought it wouldn't hurt for you to think that I had stayed over with someone.

They were silly games that we played, scoring points against each other's egos. I want you to know how very hard it was for me to take you to the station the next day and let you leave on that train. I made every effort to seem calm and in control but I walked away with a bad feeling inside.

When I got home, Amélie told me she missed you already. So did I.

I had to make a decision about the house in Scotland. It was a costly second home but it employed a lot of people. On the way there, I concentrated on all the practicalities of the matter and not all the emotional baggage, nor the uppermost reason for my visit, to mark the anniversary of my wife's tragic death. I decided not to tell you, not to include you and neither did I take Amélie.

It's hard for me to think about all of this, so painful to admit that as I passed through the gates and headed up the driveway, I still felt so angry with Celeste. Whether her decision to go out on a loch had been a moment of rash stupidity or whether she had pushed out in that boat because she felt too wretched to go on living, that distinction did not matter so much anymore. Either way, she had placed herself at enormous risk and left her little girl motherless and I had been left to pick up the pieces.

Then there were other feelings, a memory of you seated next to me, all wide eyed and ready to be impressed in a way that Celeste had never been. She had mainly disliked the house and had mocked me for being pretentious.

Yet, according to her, we had a former life tied up in that house. Again and again, I rejected her story as absurd but I could never entirely erase its narrative from my mind.

In the entrance hall, I stared up at the painting of you and I felt I would probably not sell the house because it was as much about you as anyone. Celeste had painted you into a theme of futility, life crumbling away at our fingertips but you looked youthful and so full of possibility and it gave me hope. One day, maybe you would return to this place and create another chapter in its history, a fresh tale?

The next day, the staff assembled in front of the house and we walked in a slow procession, down to the loch and I placed a wreath of red roses onto the water and gently pushed it out. Celeste was not there anymore. She was decaying in a French cemetery but I think we all hoped that, as those roses bobbed up and down, a final bolt had been slid across, leaving Celeste the other side of an impenetrable door. No part of her belonged to that house and the living. We all just wanted her gone.

As we strolled back to the house, I felt the tension and anger of months slip from my shoulders and though I had elements of grief still to negotiate, I felt optimistic. Surely everything would be easier.

CLAIRE

I worked in a frenzy over the next months, always driving myself that much harder because of my humble origins and the insecurities it entailed. Training to be a barrister is never easy and even the majority of my social life was about networking. Arranging to use the house in Brittany as a holiday let was more complicated than I had imagined and highly subject to seasonal demand and so I did not enjoy the steady supplementary income from my acquisition that I had hoped for. To the extent that David and I shared any communication it was mainly to establish this arrangement, interspersed with news of Amélie. E-mail was efficient to this end and no one reading those exchanges would have found evidence of anything romantic.

I had devised a plan. I would take the minimal amount of holiday and so leave myself two and half weeks in July to enjoy the house in Brittany, a few days by myself to appreciate my inheritance, a week with Amélie and her nanny and then David could join us. He intended to take Amélie on to her family in the south of France for August and so our plans neatly dovetailed. This was all very sound in theory but the schedule pushed me to the brink of exhaustion. Looking back, I cannot believe how I managed it and all the while, though surrounded by people, I was so alone and any attempts to seduce me into any intimacy were ruthlessly defeated even if it meant I cried myself to sleep.

At Christmas, David invited me to join him and his family in Scotland but I declined. I could not afford the time off and the idea of returning to a place so full of memories scared me. On Christmas Eve, I regretted this decision and was so depressed that I contemplated showing up at my parents but I was rescued from this drama by flowers, a hamper and a cheque from "Amélie" who apparently wished her favourite God-mother to spoil herself a little. If David had appeared on my doorstep then I should have just melted into his arms pathetic and desperate. Yes, it was tempting to pick up the shovel and go for gold and I stared at that cheque for quite a while but then neatly folded it away. I would only use it if my life depended on it.

So, naturally it was hard for me to stay focussed on my work in the days leading up to my summer holiday. The anticipation of a trip abroad, the idea of sunny beaches, the possibility of being able to eat and sleep whenever I wished, these almost outweighed any desire to see Amélie or David but I won't deny that I was eager not to feel so alone. Deep down, I yearned for their human affection. In the case of David I knew I was likely to let this go to my head but by the time I had reservations about this, it was too late to change the plans.

PART FOUR

CLAIRE

David offered me a first class flight to Paris from where I could take a train to Quimper. The house was near Benodet, to the south. I had refused to cash the Christmas cheque but I had the sense to allow him this gesture because I was exhausted and keen to simplify the journey. He telephoned me to discuss the details. It was a strange business like call and when he said he was looking forward to seeing me it was said in an off-hand way, no subtle undertones and I contemplated the fact that whilst I had been living a celibate life, he had perhaps been enjoying every opportunity an attractive, wealthy person in London might. This in turn triggered a whole range of emotions, including regret, frustration, indignation and denial and I knew that this holiday would not be entirely relaxing.

However, once I set off, the anxious traveller in me mingled with awe struck childish wonder and I lost myself in every detail of the experience. From the moment I took my seat on the train for Brittany it was Celeste who dominated my thoughts. This journey and everything waiting for me was her vision finally being lived out, except that she was in my head and not seated next to me. Over and over, I asked myself "And how would she want me to feel about that view?" Or, "Would she want me to try eating that?" and "Would she find my reaction to that amusing?" She was gone but always there.

I was at the point of collapse when I finally unlocked the door of the house in Beg Meil; white walls, a grey roof and blue grey shutters, modest looking but mine and certainly more than I could afford to buy. Sheer adrenaline powered me from room to room, every corner, each embellishment a carefully crafted expression of Celeste. In the master bedroom I found myself frozen to the spot. There, painted by Celeste on the opposing wall, was a picture of a dark haired woman, the wind blowing her hair across her face, a white cotton top exposing pretty tanned shoulders, a full-flowing skirt, the hem slightly damp and bare feet dappled with the beach she was walking on. In one hand she carried a bucket full of oysters and the other hand clasped that of a small child, the face obscured by a large sunhat. It was a joyous, uplifting depiction of pleasure and the bond of mother and child made my heart ache. The next bedroom afforded me no comfort because there I was, painted on the wall, my face not hidden, my identity explicit. She had painted me as a mermaid and the painting reminded me of something I had overlooked for some time; I was a beautiful woman. My hair was longer and partly covered my breasts which she had proportioned generously (this made me laugh and blush) and surprisingly it wasn't odd to see myself with a tail but beyond the playful fantasy she had captured me, more vividly than in the painting in Scotland. The eyes conveyed neither youth nor innocence and exposed a part of me that was rather terrifying; passion, sensuality, the bits of me I worked hard to control and disguise. If I had ever doubted it, it revealed how much she had loved me, how deeply she had looked into my soul. And then I found myself saying out loud "the tempting siren, luring men onto rocks." There was no sign of an alabaster heart! She had cautioned restraint but not too much, not control. Well, this sea creature before me was holding nothing back. It was not a contradiction of her advice to me. She showed me what I might be capable of, she revealed my power. I thought I heard her whisper in my ear. "Be careful."

I went into the next room and discovered a room with twin beds, decorated for a child and leading off it a smaller room perhaps intended for the nanny. Down the hall I found a luxurious bathroom and next a staircase which led up to an attic room, a large round window framing a view of the sea, a room designed perhaps for reading and painting or a space in which simply to ponder and it was only when I was back downstairs, exploring kitchen cupboards that it suddenly occurred to me; nothing about David, not even a photo. Would she ever have invited him here? Well, I had and he was going to see it all. I felt tired and slightly sick and went to bed, avoiding the room with the mermaid.

I woke early the next day, the curtains only able to defend me from some of the brilliant sunshine and gulls screaming at the sky. Though my first encounter with the house still made me uneasy, I felt elated to have days of holiday stretching out in front of me and excited about exploring the area. I had had the foresight to pack tea bags and made myself a mug of black tea, then dressed and headed out in the direction of the local baker's I had spotted the previous day. There was also a small grocer's so I could buy milk and orange juice. The plan was to live from moment to moment, free of routine.

Oh, I recall it all so vividly that first week, falling in love with the beach, all the tension bleeding out of me, making me feel weak to begin with but then gradually more alive than I had felt in a long time. I was alone but never lonely. I was content to observe the goings-on of people around me, happy to have permission to be an outsider because I was one of the tourists who didn't speak French and yes, sometimes there were pangs of guilt. I was supposed to be here with Celeste and Amélie and I would never be able to thank Celeste for gifting me such a fantastic haven and then even more guilt when, as the day of Amélie's arrival drew closer, I did not feel ready for her interruption.

Yet, when the day arrived, I discovered how foolish I had been to nurture such reservations because she rushed in on my space like a blast of cold sea air and, watching her explore the house and smelling her lavender hair against my cheek, I felt uplifted. Her exuberance brushed away any lingering cobwebs left from Leeds. She scarcely knew me, had not seen me for months but she could overcome anything and everything with her child magic. She spoke alarmingly fast in French but the nanny, Natalie, patiently persisted with the encouragement for her to speak English to me and when she began to utter those first words, it was adorable and with a much limited vocabulary we surprisingly connected. Like her mother, she was generous with her hugs and kisses and my controlled reciprocations never defeated her. She persisted and we learned our particular code. She would hug my legs, rooting me to the spot and I would tug gently on her pigtails as if to say "Yes, I love you too and now you can release me" and it worked.

Amélie's skin tanned easily, whereas I was pink and blotchy, but the sun lightened my hair and Natalie remarked that I was looking well. In her role as nanny, she remained behind a screen of etiquette and professionalism and, though I was not Amélie's mother, she knew expertly when and how to give us space, facilitated our contact but knew when to intervene. In the evenings, when Amélie was asleep, she engaged with me, answered all my questions politely but there was never a sense that we would become friends and when, on a couple of occasions, I attempted to ask her about Celeste she steered the conversation away and so I understood that this was not something she wished to discuss.

However, the evening before David's arrival, she managed to completely wrong-foot me.

"Mr Sutton has suggested I can take some days of holiday when he is here but I can stay if you prefer."

To my horror this made me blush which then made me blush further.

"Oh, um, well, have you made plans? I don't want to spoil anything for you."

"No plans really. My family is in Paris and of course they will be happy to see me but I can see them in August anyway. Mr Sutton will be in the south with Amélie's French family and then I go to Normandy where my family stays in August. If I go to Paris I can perhaps see some friends but it is not important."

"Well, I'm not sure. I mean, I suppose Da... I mean Mr Sutton is your boss so if he has said that then..."

She looked at me then in such a way as to make me feel naïve and silly.

"This is your house and your holiday and I think maybe you can choose what you want, no?"

"Well, this is the first I have heard of you having a holiday so it's a bit awkward." My mind was racing and my stomach struggling to catch up. Without the nanny, I would be spending evenings alone with David. He had moved a pretty important chess piece. I should have stopped the clock and considered my move but Natalie's unfaltering gaze made me panic.

"Look, let's just do that then. You go and enjoy some time in Paris. I suppose Mr Sutton would like some time alone with his daughter."

She frowned at me as if I had just said something illogical and just for a moment the real her, not the nanny, decided to speak up.

"Ok but of course he wants to spend time with you. You understand that?"

I had been relaxing on holiday, all my normal defences were dismantled but I managed to rummage inside me and cobbled together a response.

"As a friend yes. We have only ever been friends. Our friendship is important and I do not want any complications."

Her gaze remained constant.

"Men are not complicated but we women are. Be careful."

With that she stood up to leave but this comment irritated me.

"Hang on a minute. Be careful of what?"

Just to further annoy me she appeared to find my question amusing.

"Be careful of love of course. You have fallen in love with Amélie so easily. To fall in love with her father is not so difficult."

"Oh, I don't agree, they're two different kinds of love you're talking about. I think I know the difference." I sounded so indignant now and with that her face glazed over and she decided she should be the nanny again.

"Ok. Well, I will go to bed now. Goodnight."

Well, maybe she slept soundly that night but I did not. Again and again, I considered speaking to her in the morning to change the plan but then how would David respond to me doing that? Months ago, in London, I had stalled David and since then he had been distant, kind but detached. I knew he was not a patient person and perhaps now he thought it was time for us to move our relationship on? I had invited him here without thinking it through but I could not deny my feelings over the last couple of days. I was looking forward to his arrival, eager to see him. What was there to prevent us from becoming lovers? Why did the nanny warn me against it? I was not about to compromise my career for HIM. In that sense nothing had changed except that he had proved he could respect my wishes and that was a good sign wasn't it?

In bed, I stared at the painting of a mother and child walking on the beach together. Celeste and Amélie. She had loved David and she had loved me. Surely that made us the perfect match and that was by no means a betrayal of her? Yet, David had been a controlling husband and Celeste had counselled me to be careful in affairs of the heart. How should I act? What should I do?

"Have sex with him. Just do it and get it over with and maybe you'll both just realise that that's all there is to it. Just frustrated sexual curiosity. It might all settle down and then you can be properly friends."

I knew that any advice to myself at two in the morning was never rational or sound but with this conclusion I finally managed to drift asleep. In the morning, I considered my thinking unbalanced. I had a headache but Amélie was bursting with energy. We had no idea when exactly Daddy would arrive so we headed to the beach, with the usual plethora of bags. I had a plan for the next couple of hours but beyond that nothing.

My mother had a favourite necklace. Nothing valuable because we were poor. A string of beads, in assorted autumnal colours, in a pattern, graduating from small to large and then back to small and so on and the largest of the beads, burnt orange and ribbed, it stood out as intended. It was the highlight, the moment of splendour, the glimpse of extraordinary, the most costly of the beads. I often liken my experience of life to that necklace, the vivid, powerful moments a few visually striking beads and when David arrived at the beach that day, it was one of that kind.

I was helping Amélie fly her kite which was not easy because the wind kept gusting and because she was reluctant to let me do anything more than loosely guide her tiny hands and my hair kept blowing across my face. We had persevered, a credit to her remarkable attention span for one so young and we had reached a sweet spot and the kite was soaring like a free spirit. I released one hand to try to tether my annoying hair and then I saw him, making his way towards us. The bottoms of his trousers were rolled up and he was barefoot. He was wearing a short sleeved polo shirt, navy with a minute designer label, unbuttoned at the neck. He was surprisingly tanned for someone who spent most of his time in London. He was smiling but

I could not see his eyes, obscured by sunglasses. He was wearing a watch, an expensive one but what I noticed was that it drew me to his forearm and I remember thinking that a man's forearm can be very beautiful, displaying his strength.

I hesitated, something holding me back from returning the smile but the closer he came, the more I felt compelled to mirror his warmth and then I smiled and there it was, a moment of dazzling splendour, the two of us connected like the kite to its string, hovering, in lovely suspense. Then Amélie saw her Dad and with her there was never any hesitation. She let go of the kite and ran to him, leaping into his arms and he gathered her, laughing, whilst I struggled to rescue the kite. The strings just seemed to become more and more tangled, the wind unhelpfully gusting again and then, there it was, his hand on mine.

"Oh dear. Come on, take a well-deserved break. I'll get this."

In spite of that previous moment, nothing of the power struggle between us had shifted and I felt the usual resistance surge up in me.

"Er, I think I can handle it. You take care of Amélie. Go buy her an ice-cream or something."

He pushed his sunglasses up onto his head, knowing instinctively that he could project authority from those eyes and pulled my hand from the handle of the kite.

"Let go of this Claire. Come on, be nice. Let me do the dad thing and fix the kite."

So, I gave in but then stretched out on my beach towel and laughed almost vindictively at each of his failed attempts to tame the kite. Amélie joined in, unaware of the real game but David never flinched. The kite could only resist him for so long and he persevered until there it was, all gathered in and detangled and folded up on the sand. He might have said something or looked at me smugly but instead he projected his attentions onto his daughter, taking her by the hands and spinning her, until she squealed for respite. They spoke in

French, rapidly and though I smiled, pretending to enjoy their happiness, I felt excluded and it was like the sting of the sea salt on the small cut I had acquired from the kite string. It grew harder and harder to smile. Twenty years more experience of life made him better at such games and he knew when to stop.

"Ok, enough French. Remember Claire doesn't speak it much. It's getting too hot to be on the beach. We'll burn. Time for lunch. Come on, Daddy will give you a piggy back up to the house."

I followed them up and struggled not with the bags of beach stuff but with the sudden, uncontrollable rushes of emotion, finding him attractive, wanting to be with him, afraid of his confidence, determined not to be Waif, resenting the twenty year advantage. Once the house came into sight, there was Celeste watching, interested, but I had no idea what she was ever thinking.

David said he would like to look around the house and my irrational instinct was to say no because this was my house and the house I was intended to enjoy with Celeste and now that he had entered it, his masculinity seemed to throw it all off balance but again, Amélie did not share any of my sensitivities and she grabbed his hand and led him off on a tour, leaving me to sort out beach towels. As I rummaged and sorted, sand speckling the floor, I could only speculate at his reaction to the paintings, especially me as a mermaid and then there was the fact that there was nothing of him and no obvious room for him. I had asked Natalie to strip her bed and make it up for him. He could sleep in his daughter's room. It was the safe choice. I had prompted Amélie to draw a picture of her Dad and stuck it on the wall by the bed, a diplomatic gesture.

When they joined me downstairs, he just remarked that the place was very nice and I thought we would avoid any awkwardness but when Amélie had finished downing her glass of water, wiping her mouth with the back of her hand, she pro-claimed,

"Papa likes the picture of you."

The child wandered over to her toy box, oblivious to her bombshell. The adults met each other's stare, each unwilling to give much away and then he said.

"Let me make us some lunch then."

"Actually, now that you're here, I think I'll go out and explore by myself a bit and leave you two together, if that's ok."

His mind contemplated the chess board and my move. I saw this, in the slight tightening of his jaw.

"Sure. Go for it."

I practically raced up the stairs and my heart pounded as I gathered my things, checking over and over that I had every-thing for my impromptu excursion. I had underestimated the unresolved tensions between us and for now, he would let me retreat but then, as I headed for the door to leave them, he made another move, shifted another piece.

"Just a minute."

I stopped my hand on the door handle. He came over and gently brushed the top of my shoulder, bare because I was wearing a sleeveless sundress.

"You've burned a little there. You should cover up."

And I blushed. Damn him, of course I did.

"I've got a cardigan. I'll pop it on. Have to go. There's a bus I want to catch. See you later."

I went to open the door and right on cue it managed to stick. He took a pace back, no doubt delighted to see me squirm.

I was furious all the way to the bus stop but oddly, as the bus started to pull away I found myself smiling, a kind of excite-ment spilling out. I was losing the game but maybe I didn't care.

That evening, I am embarrassed to say that I was shockingly predictable. I put on my prettiest dress, pinned up my hair to enhance my neck and shoulders and applied lipstick. David cooked a delectable meal and Amélie was more than willing after three stories and several yawns to be tucked up in bed. I rearranged myself on the sofa several times, attractive, available but not too keen. This was it and I felt ok about it.

When David came in, he smiled at me and I think if he had thrown himself upon me there and then, I would not have objected in the slightest. Instead he stretched himself, yawned and reached for his jacket.

"Where are you going?" Could I have sounded any more desperate?

"Oh I thought I'd like to go and explore a bit too. There's a few nice looking bars and it would be fun to chat to the locals. Don't wait up. I'll see you tomorrow."

Again and again, he managed a more clever move and I think in that moment I even hated him.

"Wait up for you? I'd never do that David."

He must have stared at me but his face was obscured by shade. I waited for a clever response but he just said goodnight and left. I waited and then picked up a cushion and screamed into it. He was too good at this and the game was driving me mad.

Over the next two days, I sulked and maintained a stand-off, unashamed to use Amélie to such ends, all my energy focussed on her. In the evenings, worn out by it all, I kept hoping David would break the deadlock but to my increasing dismay it seemed he *could* resist me and the night before our final day together I lay in bed and actually felt rising panic. I had played the game all wrong, he had tired of my resistance, thought better of things. I had given him enough time and space to apply wisdom and rational thought to the subject of a possible us. I was just a girl, no way mature enough for him, too caught up in my career, too much effort for him after all.

That last day, we each played a starring role in a production entitled happy families. Why, no wonder people stared at us. We looked such a beautiful family, any tensions between the adults meticulously managed and disguised. Come the evening, I regarded myself in my bedroom mirror and even to my critical eye I was lovely and I decided that David must be holding back out of respect for my modernity, sensitive to the age gap and my anxieties about control. He was leaving me to break the deadlock and giving me the choice.

During dinner, I sipped again and again at my wine, sensing the clock hand's every movement and as I cleared the table, David having gone up to put Amélie to bed, I felt myself floating on all the powerful emotions, waves of it crashing over my head and when David finally came into the kitchen, I just rushed over to him, threw my arms around his neck and all those words came spilling out, my voice sounding odd to me and surely to him too.

"Oh David, I give in. I mean, I'm ready to admit it. I don't want us just to be friends. I think I've always fancied you maybe. I'm not sure. But what's the point in all these games?"

I tilted my head back and expected him to kiss me but he brushed my hair to one side in an almost fatherly manner and I suddenly understood that he was sober and I was quite drunk.

I moved away and straightened up.

"What's the matter David? You said in London you wanted us to explore things. Now you're looking at me as if I have something yucky on my face."

He shrugged, distant.

"I don't know Claire. Biology might be telling me one thing but then something is stopping me."

"Well what is it? Is it grief? Is it thinking about Celeste?"

"No, no it's not any of that. I think it's a kind of pride, a sort of principled position."

"What the hell? I don't get it." The energy seemed to go out of me and I felt my balance fail and grabbed at the back of a chair to hold myself steady.

"I think Claire that it's because you're drunk, that you got drunk to do this and I don't think I want to be another fumble in the bedsheets because frankly it diminishes you, and if you and I are going to go there then I think you should be sober. I think I deserve that. I'm sorry but maybe we're still better as friends for tonight."

"Friends? We can't really be that! It's too late. Oh come on, I'm not so drunk. You're just making an excuse, for reasons that are not very obvious."

"Well, you may be right but then I shouldn't need an excuse. If I am holding back, there must be a reason. It might be the age gap, our history, or maybe it is Celeste but right now, I think making love to you would be a terrible mistake."

And then, because I was drunk and young and still quite immature, I lost control.

"Well screw you, David Sutton because I am sick of this and your reason and your logic. I'll tell you what it is. You know you would never be able to control me. I'm too strong. You're afraid I might take you to bed and then toss you aside and maybe you're right. Maybe you would just be an experiment for me. You're old and I'm young and I'd just outgrow you. Well, I see everything clearly now. I may be a bit drunk but I'm not that drunk."

I went to leave and there were these stupid tears running out of my eyes, unwanted. He grabbed hold of me.

"I've hurt you. I'm sorry. You must know how much I care for you."

I threw his hand away.

"Get off me! Whatever it was, it's over. I've had enough. You are

141

so boring! Yes, that's it. You are bloody boring. Celeste got it and now I do."

It was a brutal blow and in that moment I saw how ugly a wounded human can be and the way he just bore it, that made it even more painful.

I climbed the stairs to my room and half expected to find blood on my hands. I had said horrible things, something perhaps neither I nor he could undo. I pulled the bedcovers over my face and thought "That's it. It's over."

DAVID

So now, Waif, I need to talk about what happened in Brittany and the passage of time does not make it any easier or clearer for me. First, I want to say that there are few recollections of mine more beautiful than an image of you and Amélie flying that kite together. You must know that I planned for us to become lovers that summer, hence sending Natalie away. I had been very patient, something I am not known for. The palpable tension between us, the little games we played, I was certain that we were acting out a particular form of courtship with the outcome inevitable. I saw the mermaid on the wall and I saw no reason not to swim to her. Yet, that evening, when you seized the initiative, waiting for me to kiss you, something made me draw back. How can I explain that? Disliking the fact that you had sought courage in a wine bottle, I did not lie about that but it was something else too, something I can only describe as a nagging instinct.

You know, over the years, I have been repeatedly asked "What is the secret of your success as an entrepreneur?" and I have actually been approached several times to write a book on the subject. It has always amused me because the secret of my success can never stretch to a book. It's quite simple. I have good instincts and I listen to them. Now, I will be the first to admit that good at business does not equate to good at love and relationships but I think I am guided by my instincts in all respects and we cannot regret that because it was instinct that made me offer you an excursion at Turnberry. It was instinct that guided me in every point of contact with you thereafter. As to that evening in Brittany, of course I often consider what might have happened subsequently had I listened to lust and not something else. What was it, exactly? A strange kind of perfectionism that demanded that the physical consummation of us be conducted in total sobriety? Few women would believe me capable of such scruples but then you are not women but a woman, a very particular woman and I can only repeat that my instinct was to hold back. I think I wanted you to want me with the same confidence and resolute determination that you applied to the rest of your life, all doubts cast aside, no need to embolden yourself with wine. There was just a hint of desperation in the way you offered yourself up to me and so, instinctively, I backed away from the deal.

I believe I made a terrible mistake and have suffered the consequences. I am quite sure you see it differently and of course it makes no logical sense to nurture regrets. However, for what it is worth, I regret my behaviour that night. Always have, always will. Then again, I saw my rejection that evening as a mere postponement whereas you subsequently chose a course of action which made our union impossible, as you well know.

CLAIRE

When I reflect upon events that summer, I admit their significance but I refuse to taint Brittany in any way, and uphold that magical place to stubbornly guard it in my heart as a place of happiness, honouring Celeste's intention. Whereas London, London is my scapegoat. From the word go I never fell for its charms, mistrusted it, felt it close in on me, resisted its egotistical power and London was to be the scene of the real turning point in my relationship with David.

The parting in Brittany was a dreadful stiff, English performance, awkward enough to contaminate Amélie. She kept looking at us in such a puzzled way and David had to bundle a crying, inconsolable child into his car. It was horrendous. He muttered that we should keep in touch and I turned to walk into the house before he had driven away.

True to his word, he did make every effort to keep in touch. He sent me regular, informative e-mails about my god-daughter and made polite, kind enquiries about me. I wrote all my replies to Amélie, in a childish style, requesting that she say hello to Daddy for me. We had no plan agreed for contact and no amount of my being busy with my work as a newly qualified barrister could erase a sense of Christmas looming large on the horizon. A month before, he emailed me to suggest that I was welcome to join them for Christmas; they would spend it in London and go to Scotland for New Year. I replied that I had already made plans (a lie) but knew a case would take me to London at the beginning of December and decided that I would drop round to the Sutton residence. I could deliver Amélie's present and by calling in unannounced I thought I could more easily control any awkwardness.

Such a visit required three changes of clothes before I was satisfied, my hair went up, down and then back up, make-up went on, off and then on again more lightly. It was ridiculous. I recall walking up to David's front door more anxious than I have ever felt before any judge.

I knocked and waited for Mrs Jones to do the honours. The door opened but no Mrs Jones. A man, not as tall as David and a thicker build. He was unshaven but attractive. On one side of his face there was a thin scar which connected to the outer edge of his eye. Oddly, it rendered him more striking, more appealing to me and his aftershave had a crisp, linen quality that I very much approved of. He was holding a beer bottle, half the contents gone.

"Oh hello. I'm Amélie's god-mother. I've just popped by to leave a Christmas present for her."

I held up the package for his inspection but it was me he scrutinized.

"Ah well everyone is out but do come in. Amélie thinks Father Christmas will be bringing all the presents so we'd better find a secure location. Mrs Jones is still shopping, nanny is fetching Amélie from somewhere and his Lordship is still in New York. Gets back tomorrow. "

He had turned and walked away, into the house, leaving me to follow. I closed the door behind me and watched his denim arse as he ambled away, relaxed, very much at home. I followed him into the kitchen, where he offered me, tea, coffee, wine or a beer. I opted for the beer which he unceremoniously uncapped and pressed into my hand and I thought who the hell is this man? His thoughts were along similar lines.

"And Amélie's god-mother is otherwise known as?"

"Claire, Claire Sutcliffe. I was a friend of Celeste's." It was instinctive to say that.

"Ah, ok. Well, I'm Rob, David's younger brother, half-brother to be precise."

"Brother? David has never mentioned you. Funny how our paths have never crossed."

"Er well not really. I've been in the army and away most of the time and I should probably explain straight away that we share the same dad but my mum was the cow that broke up his parents' marriage. Actually, that's not exactly true. His parents had already split but my mum getting pregnant sort of sealed the deal, or should I say divorce! Anyway, they're all dead now. May as well say that David and I are not incredibly close. He's ten years older to start with. So you were one of Celeste's pals. An artist by any chance?"

145

He took a hearty swig from the bottle and unashamedly stared at my breasts which somehow I did not mind.

"Er no. I'm a barrister actually. I modelled for her a little, when I was younger."

"Really? I thought she only did abstracts and some landscapes. I must find out where David is hiding those. So you and David..." He arched one of his fabulous eyebrows at me and yes, I blushed.

"We're friends. Just friends. "He was noticeably pleased with this answer. I took a swig of my beer and thought that it was an acceptable version of the truth, though it felt like a deception.

"Well Claire, very pleased to meet you. Amélie has a doll called Claire come to think of it. Blonde but nowhere near as pretty."

He saluted me with his beer bottle and enjoyed seeing me blush. It rattled me and so I took the offensive.

"That's quite some scar. How did you get it?"

I had never met a former soldier before and had never tested their defences.

"That was David, believe it or not. Wasn't thrilled about having a baby brother." He was matter of fact, nothing in his face or voice to denote a lie but as a barrister I was trained to think of the facts, to weigh everything very carefully and logically.

"That seems improbable. Try the real story on me." This impressed him. I saw it in his eyes but he was not the sort of witness to crumble under pressure.

"A work related incident. That's all you need to know."

Things could have become uncomfortable but the front door had opened and within seconds Amélie burst into the kitchen. Seeing me she squealed with delight and threw herself into my arms. I was just able to safely discard the beer bottle and saw Rob deftly scoop up the Christmas present and place it in one of the high cupboards. There was an initial gush of French but then she switched into an equally charming version of English, no polite enquiries as to my health, my reason for being in London or my plans but detail after detail concerning her day's events, her life the centre of the universe. She was wearing a school uniform that made her older than her years and she smelled the smell of schools which triggered a strange nostalgia in me. I listened diligently. She had to come up for breath eventually. Natalie had appeared and seemed matter of fact about my being there. She made toast for Amélie and poured out a glass of milk. With skill, she unobtrusively removed the child's hat and coat and waited until the child had come to the end of one of her complicated sentences before ordering her to go and wash her hands. This was Amélie's routine and she did as she was told. It was then that I registered that Rob had slipped away.

I stayed for an afternoon snack and answered the peculiar and random questions that Amélie eventually posed. Mrs Jones then arrived, more surprised to discover me there and when she asked if I would be staying for dinner, it seemed only polite to decline the offer and I explained that I had an early train back to Leeds the following morning, had had a busy day in court and that a quiet evening at my hotel was very much in order. She was clearly relieved.

I stayed another hour and then Amélie was summoned for her next meal. I reassured her that I would come again soon, conscious that we had different ideas about time and the meaning of "soon" and I confess that, as she walked away I felt a small lump in my throat. Was I being the god-mother Celeste had intended? I was trying my best but I felt inadequate, a failure. When Rob appeared, there wasn't time to disguise the gloominess.

"I should get back to my hotel. Can I use the phone to call a taxi please?"

"Nope. Not my phone and no way are you paying for a taxi from here to the city. I'll run you in, I insist."

I was in no mood to decline this kind offer but imagine my face when he led me into the garage and presented me with a motorcycle helmet.

"Er, I thought you meant in a car. I've never been on a motor-bike before."

"Great. Then it will be a real adventure for you."

"But my clothes..."

"You're wearing trousers. It'll be fine. Here, let's get this on you."

He had the helmet on in seconds and then proceeded to issue lots of instructions and to all intents and purposes he may as well have been preparing me for a skydive. I am not the kind of woman to be pressured into much so I concede that alongside fear there was adrenaline and a compelling desire to have the adventure. Once on the bike, the engine purring, I was acutely aware of our physical proximity, as I am sure he was and the electric buzz of attraction was palpable.

He drove carefully to begin with, just a few blocks before pull-ing over. He asked me if I felt comfortable and was getting the hang of it and when we next pulled away, he increased the speed. Then, he pulled over again before the slip road onto the dual carriageway and reminded me to hold on tight. As we sped up that slip road and raced onto the inside lane, I felt fear overtake excitement again and gripped onto him, slightly desperately. He might have slowed down but instead he ac-celerated and I heard myself screaming as we moved into the outside lane. The scream lasted only a few seconds and then subsided into hysterical laughter, making it hard to breathe. This was madness and I loved it.

So it was Rob Sutton who introduced me to motorbikes, one of my unhealthier obsessions. By the time we were in the centre of London, I had decided I would be buying one, that it was the only way to travel. He pulled over, not outside my hotel and when our helmets were off, he was wearing a smile of complete satisfaction and surely my whole face was radiant with every positive brain chemical known to humans?

"Fun?"

I laughed.

"Yes, I loved it. But this isn't my hotel."

"No, well I thought we could have a bite to eat first. I know the chef here. It's nothing too fancy. Just good, Italian food. Sound good?"

I stared in at the warm, softly lit interior and suddenly felt hungry.

"Sure. Why not? But I'll pay and claim on expenses. I insist."

It was a test, to see if I could regain some control. He showed no sign of hesitation.

"Sounds great. Let's go."

That evening and that meal, I was so happy, not in the way of Scotland and my time with David and Celeste. It was far less intense, much simpler. For the next few hours I didn't think about David. Rob didn't look like him, wasn't like him. The only tension between us was sexual attraction and our conversation, it was a light, fun sort of dancing, moving around each other playfully, some clumsy moments yes but nothing that we couldn't laugh about. When we arrived outside my hotel, I had few doubts about inviting him in.

He smiled, brushed a strand of hair away from my face, leant in and kissed me, a long, lingering kiss but then he wrong footed me.

"I'm tired and you have an early train tomorrow. I'm in Catterick next week-end, to catch up with army mates, not a million miles from Leeds. How about I come by and see you on the Sunday?"

"Oh ok. Sure. That should be ok. I may have casework but I'm sure I can keep the afternoon free. Are you sure you don't want to come in for coffee?" It sounded like a plea and I hated myself.

He looked up at the hotel. I think he had already made up his mind but perhaps this was a kind gesture.

"Thanks but I'm gonna head back. I'll take your phone number shall I?"

"Sure. Hang on." I rummaged and produced a business card which made me feel somehow stupid.

"It's a work one but you can reach me on that. Thanks again for a lovely evening." I despised the sound of my own voice.

It was only after I had watched him ride away and as I replayed every part of the evening, not least the long kiss, that David came back into my mind. I had never kissed David but now I had kissed his brother. On one level it was thrilling but there was no denying that other feeling. Guilt.

DAVID

My business trip to New York had been very successful and it had eased a great many pressures. I arrived in London looking forward to Christmas and in particular spending it with you but when I entered the house Mrs Jones immediately informed me of your unexpected visit and the fact that you had left a gift for Amélie which meant of course that you did not intend to accept my invitation. This annoyed me and I bombarded her with many questions about your visit until she managed to explain that actually she had arrived towards the end of your visit and my brother had taken you off back to your hotel on his motorbike. She added that he had not returned until very late.

My brother. He was a thorn in my side yes but I did have a lot of affection for him. Before his death, my father reminded me that my mother had received a generous divorce settlement and that I stood to inherit decent sums of money from both parents. My father never married Rob's mother and when he died she received only a modest amount, most of the estate passing to me. What my father expected from me was generosity to Rob yes, but also kindness and a willingness to help him. I was assisted toward this by one simple thing. Though it is true we did not look like brothers, *he* most resembled our father and this encouraged my regard for him. He joined the army and I had the utmost respect for this profession and admired his courage, though it meant we saw little of each other. After his injury in Kuwait, he started to communicate to me a desire to leave the army and I did what I could to help him make sensible plans toward this. He loved motorbikes and proposed setting up business as a motorcycle mechanic and I thought this was a reasonable scheme. He had managed to fritter away most of the money from my father but I agreed to assist in any way I could. Amélie adored her fun uncle and so I never objected to his visits. Thus, he became a more prominent part of my life.

I had always intended for you to meet him that Christmas but now you had met him without me being there and the picture of the two of you speeding off on a motorbike and him not returning until quite late well it went over and over in my mind and I knew of course that I was jealous. However, I held back from raising this with him. I wanted to know what he would choose to say about it.

He said nothing until after dinner. He offered to make up a fire in the sitting room. He was good at it. I poured us each a whiskey.

"So, Celeste's friend Claire Sutcliffe was here to see Amélie. What is she to you David, if you don't mind me asking?"

"Did you ask *her* that?"

"Well, she led me to believe things were pretty neutral between you. Is that right?"

The notion of neutrality pierced me. Surely we were anything but that?

"I see. Well, I'd like to think we were closer than neutral but she is certainly a free agent. Do you like her?"

"Oh I like women David. You know me. I said I might go to Leeds to see her but if it is in any way awkward, I won't. Simple as."

"Mrs Jones says you got back late after taking her to her hotel."

"Fairly. We had a meal together and then I dropped her in front of the hotel. That's all. Question is, do I see her in Leeds or would you prefer me not to?"

I knocked back my whiskey and maybe it inclined me towards risk.

"To be honest, I thought Claire had feelings for me but maybe I've read her wrong. I invited her for Christmas but she's not coming. That has to mean something, right? I have no right to tell you not to go and no doubt she would despise me for trying to exert any control. Do whatever you think best."

I sounded quite unperturbed but Rob stared at me and reached his own assessment.

"Whatever you guys are, it's not neutral. I won't see her but maybe you should go up there and then you can figure out what you both want."

He sounded irritated, frustrated and jabbed at the fire with the poker. I let out a huge weary sigh.

"Celeste was a very complex woman and I think maybe Claire is even more so. What I want is a simple life. I'm getting too old for this shit."

He nodded and raised his glass to me.

"Here's to a simple life."

We carried on drinking whiskey and forgot about you for a few hours. I dreamt uneasily of mermaids.

CLAIRE

Rob never came to Leeds. He sent a short text explaining a change of plan and I could not think of a single text that did not make me sound desperate, disappointed or falsely indifferent so I did not respond. I hated the whole format of texting and agonised over whether or not to call but behind every thought lingered a picture of David's face, stern, disapproving, enough to prevent me from acting. Christmas came and went, a lonely business. Not for the first time, I considered going to see my parents but I had managed to find out that they were doing pretty well without me, the same house, the same town, the same friends. That Christmas, I sent them a large cheque. I wanted them to know that I was earning good money, making my way, that the decision to go to university had been so right. They returned it. They said thank you but they had everything they needed which I took to mean that not only did they not need the money, they did not need me either. Throughout, work was my most loyal friend. I enjoyed being a barrister, I was very good at it. I met a lot of people. There were plenty of men who showed an interest in me. Most were declined. I was strategic in my few dalliances, never anyone too connected to work, detached loners like myself, passing ships. I can look back on that period and acknowledge that I was not just robed in black for the courtroom appearances; everything was black, formal, rationalised, bound up in almost contractual constraint, emotions pushed to the periphery.

David sent me a very charming photo of Amélie for Christmas. Though she was the image of her father, the smile reminded me of Celeste. The photo went back under the tissue paper, the lid of the box was resealed. Any kind of love was unhelpful to me, threatened to undo me. Next came an adorable thank you note, painstakingly trying to follow the lines on the paper, the letters all sizes and then a postcard from David, from a French ski resort, detailing her love of snow and her confidence. He had retreated behind his daughter. After the rejection in Brittany it appeared this was to be the revised version of our connection.

In February I lost a case. I had lost cases before but this defeat must have visibly crushed me because a colleague suggested I probably needed a break. I felt I was not sufficiently well established to turn down cases and that stepping away after losing a case would be foolish, so I took on three challenging cases, won all three and of course this only led to more cases. Nevertheless, I carved out a week's break. It was not long enough to justify a journey to Brittany but it was London I had in mind.

These days, a few clicks with a mouse would have found me Rob's new work premises but I had to show a little more diligence. When I arrived he was concentrating hard on a large section of motorbike engine, hands and forearms smeared with oil. A radio was blasting out pop music and a phone on the wall was ringing which Rob was ignoring. He didn't seem shocked or surprised to see me.

"Do me a favour and get that will you? Just take a message. The apprentice is off sick. I need to finish this."

It was a peculiar introduction but I took it as a good sign. He was not exactly thrilled to see me but he trusted me to answer his telephone. I took the call, then two others followed. By the time I had scribbled down the last message, he seemed satisfied with his progress and was scrubbing up at a sink. He clicked off the radio and finally there we were together.

"I was disappointed you never came to Leeds."

"Yeah, sorry about that. Had loads to get on with here. You look cold. Come up to the flat. Time for lunch anyway."

We went into a back room and up over some narrow stairs into what was a minimalist, bachelor pad, clean and warm. He put the kettle on.

"So, been to see David and Amélie then?"

"No, not yet. Wanted to see you first. This is great. You've achieved a lot already."

"Yep, it's going ok. How 'bout you? Winning lots of cases?"

"Winning more than losing overall, building my reputation. It takes time."

I was growing used to being direct with people and Rob made me want to get to the point.

"Anyway, I wanted to see you again. Question is, have you even thought about me?" I smiled flirtatiously.

He regarded me thoughtfully and then turned away to make the tea.

"Well, I spoke to David about you and concluded that maybe I shouldn't think about you. Seems to me, you guys have unfinished business."

I didn't like this answer. It annoyed me.

"I told you. As far as I'm concerned, we're friends."

"Well he invited his "friend" to spend Christmas with him but she declined which tells me things are a bit awkward and I have no plans to get in the middle of that. You know, he is seeing someone at the moment? She's about my age, attractive, confident, very very nice."

I knew this required a clever, dispassionate response, though the words cut at my insides. He stared at me mercilessly.

"Well good for him. So you see, nothing between us for you to worry about. We're both free agents."

He placed a huge mug of tea down in front of me. Suddenly, all the light seemed to disappear out of him. There was a threatening darkness about his eyes and mouth and I remembered he had been a soldier, capable of looking at a person and killing them.

"Don't bullshit me Claire. Tell me the truth or just fuck off."

Was this what it felt like to be one of the witnesses I calmly interrogated? I was not used to being on the receiving end.

"Ok. So, at one point, I admit I had a big crush on him. I loved Celeste, they were a family, so I did the right thing and went away. After she died, David contacted me to say she had bought me a house in Brittany and had planned for me to be Amélie's god-mother. He came out to Brittany last summer and our feelings were pretty confused. I thought he wanted me but I made a pass and he decided against it. We just aren't meant to be like that, I suppose. Anyway, there's a big age gap. Honestly, we're done. You said yourself, he's seeing someone."

I thought I had spoken frankly and it all sounded plausible, even if it didn't quite feel the truth.

He drank some of his tea, weighing my words.

"Fine. You've convinced me. Come on then, take off your clothes. Let's do it."

The flat was too small and airless. On the back of his motorbike I had felt incredibly safe. Now, I felt in danger. I stood up.

"No, no way. Look, just forget it. This was clearly a mistake. I read you all wrong. I'll go." I grabbed my jacket and bag and headed for the door.

"Wait Claire." There was something different in his voice that made me turn to look back at him. "Do you know that there's a fine line between fear and aggression?"

"I suppose there is. So what?"

"So you and me, we're very alike. We act all front, when really we're nervous. The way I just spoke to you then, I tried to frighten you away but if you go, we'll both regret it. I don't want you to go. Please."

"I don't know. I think maybe I should." He came over and brushed my cheek with his forefinger, conjuring something electric between us.

"I think maybe you shouldn't. Trust me."

And he leant in and started to kiss me and nothing that followed was about knowledge and trust. It was all a kind of beautiful desperation. Later, in our tangle of bedsheets, it was agreed that we would carry on seeing each other but that we would not be telling David. Not yet.

Of course, I can analyse it all now, pull it apart, coldly dissect the strange melange of need and desire which drew me into Rob's embrace and had him take me into his bed and his damaged heart. We were both cut adrift, orphans, trying to make it alone. I had left my working class roots and he had left the army. That scar on his face, it was just the outward confirmation of other damage and, being so messed up myself, his vulnerability gave me permission to let go, where David's strength had only made me hold back, fearful of surrender. David had once warned me that a person can make the mistake of not understanding that they are *not* in love and Celeste had counselled me to keep an alabaster heart but wisdom and caution were dead to me then, drowned out by passion. Yet, I will speak frankly and admit that David's rejection of me in Brittany, his pulling back, his hesitation, like a courtroom defeat that would always define my career, the lingering hurt was there, under the bedsheets, between our skins, a curling mist. Deep down, Rob knew, in spite of anything I said to contradict it, that there was a definite something between David and me, and so it was easy for us to agree that David should not know about us. We both felt the instinct to protect and defend our connection and a kind of shame.

DAVID

I was angry with you. I kept picturing you on the back of my brother's motorbike and then there was an invitation for him to go to Leeds versus a decision not to spend Christmas with me. It never occurred to me that you could ever fall in love with Rob. It struck me all as a childish attempt at hurting me, getting back at me over Brittany and though I told myself I was too old, too experienced to be drawn into such games, yet I tried to make some clever moves myself, exploiting the connection to Amélie and then picking up with someone else, pretending to move on but hoping to make you jealous. My ultimate arrogance was to disregard my baby brother's advice to me, not to go and see you and resolve things. Somehow, I was stuck in Brittany, frozen by a moment's hesitation but that was not all. Celeste's story played over and over, a constant torment. In a previous life I had denied my brother happiness and now, in this life, my brother threatened to steal away mine and the terrible coincidence, both men soldiers, it was just enough to deny me a rational dismissal. Poor Celeste, she was dead and buried and she and our love should have been safe, beyond reproach and yet, that story, those words, they were corrosive and they stirred up a pointless hatred. Why hate the dead? Then, every time I looked at my daughter, that hatred, that bitterness, it twisted into guilt and when Amélie spoke of you, your name was like a knife to my gut. Small wonder that every time my mind drifted to thinking about you, I pulled back and you were less of the enchanting mermaid and more of a perilous lure onto rocks.

What I failed to feel was any sense of urgency to push past this and it was this overall inclination to hesitation and not a moment's reluctance in Brittany that allowed events to unfurl. I had Easter on the horizon and decided I would make sure I saw you then and it is true that my hectic working life fooled me into thinking that that was not so far away, that things could wait. It was a fatal error.

At the beginning of March I arranged to catch up with Caroline

Summers. We conducted business with the usual degree of efficiency which led us neatly up to lunchtime and the opportunity to share our love of fine cuisine. Our relationship was an entirely frank one.

"So, I hear all sorts of enthusiasm about enticing Claire Sutcliffe to Chambers here but strangely not from you and then last week, I had to go up to the frozen North myself and imagine my surprise when I learn that said, promising barrister is seeing a man called Sutton, only not you but your brother."

I have dealt with enough shock revelations in boardrooms to maintain my composure but Caroline had known me a while. She put a hand across the table and covered mine.

"Oh God, you didn't know. I am so sorry."

I pulled back my hand.

"Yes and no. Rob met her before Christmas and I thought we had an understanding."

"But you've been seeing someone else yourself David. Pretty confusing all round. Anyway, I'm sorry if I am at all to blame. I know you weren't sure what to do. Maybe I got in the way of something..."

My tie felt too tight and I yanked it off, throwing it onto the table. I was in a very uncomfortable place, somewhere between despair and fury.

"I'm not sure how I feel right now. Cheated on? Out manoeuvred? Deceived?"

Caroline smiled sympathetically but she respected me too much to be gentle.

"You've been a bloody fool David. This thing with your brother, a line has been crossed but it's not as if they're married. It's not too late; I mean if you love her..."

"And if Robbie loves her? And if she loves him?"

"Well I'd say it's still a case of speak now or forever hold your peace."

I was so livid, almost trembling but not at Robbie. I didn't believe you could be in love him for one minute. It was a tactic, and so beneath the belt, and was that Celeste laughing at me, enjoying me out of control?

"So much for giving her space, respecting her age and her need to grow a career. You know she practically offered herself up to me in Brittany and some weird perfectionism in me made me hold back? I've probably loved her from the first moment I saw her but I was married and already in love with Celeste and Claire was just a kid really. I did everything to be honourable and Celeste, she always knew and she played a very clever game, got in my head, contaminated my thinking. I loved Celeste but there were parts of her...well, you knew her. Fucking hell, if Claire had used any other man to get at me..."

"So you think she still cares for you, that this is just her trying to hurt you? You're not being too arrogant David?"

I stared into Caroline's questioning eyes and she reached her own assessment.

"Look David, if it isn't already too late, I suggest you get yourself up to Leeds and talk to her. No tactics now and stuff your pride. Tell her you love her and if she loves you then, if only for your brother's sake, this needs sorting out."

"And Robbie? What do I say to him?"

"Well, frankly, whether you and he like it or not, Claire gets to decide here. She gets to choose."

I glanced down at my watch and remembered my schedule. I was due to fly out to Chicago the next day. I telephoned my secretary and left her to sort out the mess. As I left the restaurant, Caroline wished me luck but what I needed was a miracle.

CLAIRE

That morning in court, I remember thinking that I was beginning to find my stride. Though I lacked the gravitas and experience of my senior colleagues, I was beginning to play the game with more ease, finding the shots, not over hitting as much and finding the angles. I had been approached by a couple of London barristers already and there was a sense that it would be perversely stupid of me to resist the lure of London for long. If Rob had pushed for me to move there, I would have had no hesitation but he seemed to enjoy every trip North, often calling to Catterick to see army buddies and so I stayed uncommitted, in truth as uncommitted as the relationship was. We never mentioned David's name but there was a sense of him always lurking in the background and whereas not telling David had been logical at the start, with each encounter the arrangement and the secrecy grew ever more incongruous, yet we could not break the deadlock. Sometimes, I felt Rob looked at me, weighing up the potential cost, questioning whether or not to sacrifice loyalty on the altar of a woman. As long as we stayed in the North, away from David, we could postpone any announcement and all of its consequences.

That day, as I say, I flew in court, performed with confidence and expertise and it was only as I tidied away my papers, the session adjourned, that I glanced up at the gallery and saw David, relaxed in a leather jacket, a smile on his face. He nodded a gesture of approval and it was enough to make me blush. I wondered if I would ever quite feel his equal, if he would always be a mentor to me and I started to feel irritated; he was no lawyer and in no position to offer me approval. This was *my* world and he had no grounds to assess me. Or was my irritation self-directed because I valued his approval so much?

He stood up and made towards the door, on his way down to me and I tried to compose my suddenly ruffled mind. I greeted him with a radiant smile, carefully composed.

"Wow David! What a huge surprise. To what do I owe the pleasure?"

"Well, we haven't seen you in ages and I thought I could stop off on my way up to Scotland. No idea what your schedule is but I was thinking lunch?"

"Er well, lunch sounds fine. As it happens, I'm not meeting clients until half four. I've got the usual mountain of paperwork but nothing that can't wait. You're lucky. I might have been booked for court all day."

He smiled at me, warmly appreciative, pleased to see the latest version of me but there was another nagging sense that he had come with an agenda. Men like David usually ran to an agenda, nothing was that spontaneous. I was already so cynical.

I explained that I could pop back to Chambers and get changed there and recommended we rendez-vous at one of the more glamorous city centre bistros but he said he had something different in mind. I only needed to pop on something casual and he had his car outside so he could drop me at my place. My heart sank. It would be a posh sports car, naturally, and the terraced house I was renting was not in a particularly chic neighbourhood. He walked out ahead of me, no opportunity for negotiations and there it was, a dark, panther like car and he soon had the door held open for me. He had parked in a drop-off space and managed not to get a ticket. As I lowered myself in, trying to gather up my robes, I realised there was something utterly incongruous about me in that car. Two local solicitors were on their way to court and nodded at me but it was David they were really interested in.

I didn't bother to invite David into my house. It made more sense for him to guard his car. Some of the local youngsters checked it out from across the street and I could only try to imagine what they were thinking. A law lady and a probable drug lord and the stench of corruption. There was no way David could be a professional footballer and they only knew two types of people who drove cars like that.

It was the just about the fastest change of clothes ever. When I explained matters to David, he just found it all very amusing and to impress the kids he revved the engine and pulled away fast. Part of me was infuriated, though I could see the hilarity. I remained stubbornly deadpan.

"Thanks David. You've done a lot to win their respect for the law."

"They'll all want you to represent them."

"Actually, I've been offered a job, in London. It's not what I originally had in mind. I was thinking of staying loyal to the north but you were right, London is pulling me in."

This was met with a short but somehow significant silence and it occurred to me that maybe he knew about Rob and another motive for moving there.

"Well Claire, money alone is never a good motivation. Of course, I do what I do to make money and I enjoy what money can do but it's not really what drives me and I've seen plenty of people destroy themselves with greed. You should get yourself a mortgage sooner rather than later. Property in London is only headed in one, general direction. I assume you plan to get your driver's license. You can live without a car in London but if you want to be able to escape from it…"

This was all good advice but his mentoring tone was exasperating.

I noticed we were heading out of Leeds, towards the Dales and I looked forward to seeing more greenery. Bricks and stone had a way of weighing a person down.

"Well, actually I was thinking of getting a motorbike."

I thought he would laugh but instead he gave me a dark glance and I knew then that he knew about Rob. As the first fields appeared and the landscape and sky opened up, he accelerated and I shifted nervously in my seat. He knew but I did not know how. If Rob had spoken to him, he would have let me know, surely?

"I love a trip in the Dales David but I have a feeling this isn't quite a spontaneous adventure. Is there something you wanted to discuss with me?"

As he moved up and down the gears to move us round a steep set of curves in the road, I saw that the veins were raised in his hand where he gripped the gear stick and his jaw was set into a stern grimace. All the while, tension and anger had been just beneath the surface and now I had no means to avoid it. He had me captive, the way I liked to have a witness under cross examination, except that his eyes were on the road not burning into mine, a small mercy.

"Your legal world is actually quite a small pond Claire. Caroline Summers thought I would be interested to know that you are seeing my brother."

There it was, the reason he was here and the sense of a power play was tangible. I wasn't Waif and neither the age difference nor the favours he had previously bestowed upon me should be allowed to undermine me. What hampered me was persistent, lingering attraction and a tangled knot of confused feelings. I was still hurt by his rejection in Brittany and my relationship with Rob did nothing to temper this. Not seeing David had allowed me to deny a great deal and though my feelings for Rob were sincere, I realised, in part, I had been using him. Well, here was the reaction in David but exactly where were we headed now? I stared blankly ahead at the winding road.

"I see. I'm sorry we haven't got round to telling you. We've been just waiting to see how things progressed, I suppose. I'd say it's more than a fling but Rob hasn't told me loves me as yet."

"Oh so it's mainly just a physical thing. Well that's ok then."

I had seen David annoyed before but this was building up to something bigger. I felt the momentum gathering. Anger begets anger and though I feared provoking his, my own outrage was being stirred up.

"Er look David, I know you've been seeing someone and in Brittany you made it pretty clear you weren't interested so this jealous, possessive stuff is bullshit. The way I see it, we both loved Celeste and there's no way past that. We owe it to her memory and to Amélie to keep it simple, just friends."

"You think sharing a bed with Amélie's uncle keeps it simple for her? And I never ever said I just wanted friendship. I don't think preferring to make love to you sober was so unreasonable. You over-reacted because you're immature and I think given the age gap it was reasonable for me to start seeing someone closer to my age. I wanted to test out my feelings for you and I was trying to give you space. Throwing yourself into bed with another guy is really not the issue here. My brother? Honestly, you didn't feel that was crossing a line?"

"Well you know, Rob crossed that line. Why don't you take out your temper tantrum on him?"

"I know you Claire and I saw you in that courtroom today. You convinced him that there was absolutely no "us" but he knows the truth in his gut. He's been avoiding me. The couple of times I've dropped into the garage he does a good job of being totally absorbed in an engine. He hasn't been able to look me in the eyes."

"There is no "us" David. There can't be. And what if I'm in love with Rob?"

He laughed at this, a feigned humour slamming into me.

"Oh please. You don't know him and you said it yourself, he hasn't told you he loves you. Well, don't hold your breath. He's already married."

This winded me as effectively as any actual blow might and I could feel the colour drop out of my face. We had entered a village and David pulled over in front of a vine covered pub. A different set of circumstances and we might have been climbing out of the car, smiling, caught up in romance but we stayed in the car, very still, weighed down by tension.

"What's her name? What's she like?"

"She's called The Army, Claire, and he'll never leave her."

I didn't even attempt to disguise the relief.

"But he already has. He has the business now. Motorbikes are his passion."

He stared at with pity and, behind it, I knew it, was love. Something stubborn in me resented it.

"You've crossed a line with me Claire but I am begging you, don't do this. Go any further and there's no way back for us. Think carefully. You were angry with me. You wanted to hurt me, to make me jealous but that's enough now. Finish it with Rob and we'll try to work things out."

I thought about Rob. Everything seemed easier with him.

David undid his seat belt.

"Come on, let's get a bite to eat and a drink and talk this through Claire."

Talking things through with David would mean somehow giving into him, yielding to age, experience and wisdom. There was a clear sense that "us" would never be played out on level ground. Whilst a part of me desperately wanted to let him have the advantage, to stop struggling, it felt like it would be loving him at the expense of respecting myself. Looking back, perhaps I was still too young. He wasn't too old. I can picture him now. He was so handsome and his maturity, experience, they had a hold on me. If I had had any sense, I would have taken the medicine he had to offer me. I could have fallen into the healing and security he offered to the waif inside me but pride prevented it. Pride, not love for Rob.

"I'm not really hungry and to be honest it's too late David. I love Rob. I'm sorry but I'd like you to take me back."

With that simple declaration, said without passion but stated as a cold fact, I saw just how much David loved me because it brought him right down, a decisive blow. Then, in that moment, he looked old and weary.

"I see." Then, he gathered himself, renewed his strength and without placing a hand anywhere near my throat, calmly strangled me.

"Very well. It's already over then. I'll drive you back. I won't stop you seeing Amélie but don't expect happy families. I'm fond of Rob and I know him better than you. For your sake, I can only hope that you can succeed where so many women have failed and actually change a man."

"I don't need to change him. I love him the way he is."

I will never forget the look on his face then. Disappointment. I had gone down in his estimation, I was diminished. It filled me with shame and I turned away and stared out of the window. He started the engine and in a gesture of mercy to us both put on some loud music and we drove back to Leeds, firmly apart, in our heads. There was nothing more to say, only an awkward goodbye.

When I next saw Rob, I told him I loved him and wanted to marry him. He thought this was the funniest thing, apparently, and though he said he loved me too it was said with little conviction. I told him David had been to see me and we had sorted things out and that I really wanted to elope with Rob. Well, it was clearly a stupid idea but Rob and I both knew how to gain inspiration from a bottle and we drank until eloping seemed like the best idea. In truth, we got married the way some couples decide on Italian versus Chinese. It was crazy and I postponed thinking about David's warning to me; I really didn't know Rob Sutton.

PART FIVE

DAVID

What happened in Leeds was a childish, stupid attempt to win a power game which cost us both. When I heard about the impromptu marriage(a postcard from Rob) I was torn up with fury and for a few days contemplated every extreme response from assaulting Rob to exercising my power to financially ruin him and I even considered going against my assurances to you by preventing you from seeing Amélie. My first wife had committed adultery and had never provoked such rage. Celeste had frustrated me but it was nothing on this scale. It was only by avoiding the two of you and throwing myself into my work, taking every opportunity to be out of London that a complete meltdown was avoided. It was six weeks after the marriage before I finally went to see Rob. Perhaps strangely, as soon as I saw him I decided he was the victim and my anger fell away. In my eyes, he was *always* the victim, first the unfortunate love child and now a naïve participant in your aggressive strategy to wound me. In essence, as you know, Rob was not like us. Every mistake he made in his life, every bad choice was textbook, never the result of complex deliberations. In a warzone, the decision to kill someone must be made quickly. There is not much room for subtlety. In civilian life, he was impulsive, inclined to take foolish risks and you were just another example. We went out for a pint together and passed an oddly pleasant couple of hours speaking little of you and the marriage, except that towards the end, when I politely said for him to pass on my best wishes, he chose to remark that he had probably bitten off a bit more than he could chew. I said nothing.

Later, after my anger towards you had dissipated, I remained furious about my own behaviour in Leeds. You see, there is no getting away from the plain fact that I was twenty years older and that day my judgement and my behaviour were undeniably poor. It had nothing to do with Celeste and a lingering story. I watched you perform in that courtroom and there was no question that I loved you and had always loved you. It was a love like no other, a meandering river, sometimes quiet and murmuring, other times fast and noisy and it really ought to have been entirely simple; all we had to do was go with it. Celeste, Rob, the age difference, they were rocks yes but nothing that the waters couldn't push past. That day, I told you that Rob was a stranger to you but stopped short of spelling out any of the facts and instead of making a simple, passionate declaration of my love for you, I alluded to boundaries and was more like a father dishing out measured advice, provoking your inner child. Damn it, I made a mess of things, didn't I?

You went and married him. Could I forgive you? Could I forgive myself?

CLAIRE

In some moral universe it may be considered sinful of me to regard my elopement, honeymoon and initial period of marriage to Rob through a golden lens but I feel compelled to do so. Rob, poor Rob, he maybe deserves this. In spite of everything, I feel I owe him. In fact, the first weeks were rather lovely and if only for a moment, I want to disregard the terrible unravelling that occurred later. The wedding took place at Leeds Town Hall. I wore a cream generic dress and only the flowers dispersed in my hair suggested matrimony. I had no bouquet but the groom indulged me with an elaborate ring, sterling silver. It would hardly endure but it would not have to. He refused a ring, considering it less than manly and it is true that nothing would have seemed right on his rough, weathered hands. We had lunch at a fast food place and then back to my place for a quick change of gear and off we went on the motorbike, bound for Newcastle and a ferry to Holland. I should have liked a honeymoon in Brittany but that required more planning workwise; colleagues were most disgruntled at my sudden need of leave. I did not explain I was popping off to get married. They would have thought me deranged and it is the required characteristic of a barrister that they be rational.

Rob was a lot of fun and applied himself to being a wonderful lover. He had a sizeable male ego but enough intelligence to comprehend that what worked for me would ultimately work in his favour. We were not naturally good lovers together, as depicted in films but we made sex our labour of love and it was with Rob that I began to comprehend what all the fuss was about. Of course love and sex are not one and the same thing and in a true romance love should come first. I told myself I was in love. I told Rob I loved him but I cannot vouch for that being the case for us. Yet, I do know that with each successive moment of ecstasy during that time together, under a spell called honeymoon, I fell a little deeper for him. I loved his smell, each of his scars, the way he stretched to yawn, the creases on his face when he laughed, some particular quality of his voice when he felt he needed to be firm with me. Every time I woke to find him next to me, I meditated on these growing feelings and felt vindicated in the choice to marry him. I believed that with every passing month and year the love could only deepen. Such was the optimism of my youth. Only very occasionally was I troubled by a fleeting image in my mind of his brother. Any such moments made me kiss Rob a little harder, cuddle him more, laugh a little louder at his jokes. It was all quite manageable.

It was on the way home that I explained to Rob that there were opportunities for me in London and that I was ready to make the move. London would be our home. Rob seemed a bit surprised, as if he imagined we would just revert to our previous arrangement, as if it were the most natural thing for married people to live apart. I just laughed this off.

It was only when I moved my boxes into the tiny flat above his garage that I realised quite how compact the place was. I did not dislike his having his work on hand though. He would stay below, pottering away, whilst I spread my work papers everywhere and when he had had enough, he would shower and cook and whistle. He was a good chef and I opted to do the tidying up afterwards. Doing the dishes would often assist me in thinking through the final strands of a case and I would glance over at Rob, stretched out dog like on the sofa, sipping his beer and honestly, it seemed to me a perfect scene of domestic bliss. We had a structure and rhythm that seemed to flow and it was only after the first few weeks that the initial signs of disturbance occurred.

I had finished in the kitchen and was pouring myself a glass of wine. I had had a stressful day at work, with a difficult client and suddenly the flat walls seemed to lean in on me.

"You know we really should start looking at properties and find something more spacious. The market is only headed one way so it makes sense to invest. My earnings should be able to raise a pretty respectable mortgage but I'll need your figures too. It should be a joint thing."

Rob propped himself up on an elbow on the sofa and stared at me as if I had just blurted out some very surprising news.

"Er well, I don't think my "figures" will do much to impress you."

"What do you mean? This flat and the business have value Rob. It just needs to be something official for them to look at."

He sat up right now and was clearly uneasy.

"Er the thing is Claire, the flat and the business mainly belong to David. He bank rolled the whole project for me. Business is doing ok but it will be a while before I have paid him back and that is kind of a priority."

I put down the glass of wine and most of the colour in my face departed from me too.

"You are joking! It all belongs to your brother? You never thought to point that out?"

"Er no because I didn't think you were marrying me for my money! Look, it's no big deal. You earn plenty enough and luckily I'm not the proud, chauvinist type. Though, if it's a problem, just put the new place in your name only. I can live with that."

He was calm, reasonable but I was devastated by the notion that I was living in a place that belonged to David.

"No Rob. No way. Ok, well we will have to postpone getting a bigger place for now. I'll look into raising the finance to buy this off David first." I glanced around the tiny flat and felt suddenly very trapped.

Rob frowned at me. He came over, picked up my glass of wine and swigged most of it down. That close to me, I could not avoid a penetrating stare.

"Bollocks to that. I'm no businessman but that makes no sense. He is charging me no interest and there's no fixed repayments as such. He's my brother and rolling in it. He doesn't care when I pay him back, how long it takes. That means I have been able to keep investing in equipment and parts. Besides, I like having David overseeing things. I trust him."

"Oh yes, I forgot, he's an expert on motorbike repair businesses. I hardly think he'd care if I paid him off."

"Why though? Why even bother?"

"Well it's obvious. He's your brother. Surely you'd prefer to be independent of him, now that you are married? I mean, it's one thing for *you* to be dependent on his generosity but you can hardly expect me to feel comfortable with it."

There was a certain something in my voice, an audible tremor, a controlled rage for which there was only one likely explanation. It suggested I did not like David which we both knew to be untrue which meant that it could only mean that I liked him a lot, still had feelings for him, feelings I had always strenuously denied. Rob looked weary then, like he had managed to forget to collect something for a third time. He knew women. I was a woman. Of course I had lied. Women often lied to get what they wanted. He had fallen for it.

"You are not buying this off David. It's between me and him. You want a bigger place, then go ahead. I have a small amount of savings which I can chip in for furnishings. You're the lawyer Claire. You should have talked through all the detail before rushing into a marriage, if any of it's a problem for you. Me, I'm cool with things."

He gave me a chance, an opportunity to pretend that it was all ok, to move past what had just been revealed. He still loved me. I hesitated and took a necessary deep breath.

"Alright. We'll leave it then. We don't need anything that big anyway. It's not as if my parents will be coming to stay."

We laughed, a pathetic, polite effort. He went onto bed before me but once I had settled in under the covers, he moved up against me and we began to make love. It was necessary. It was a kind of healing.

It was during our third month of marriage that the next blow was struck. I had started looking at properties but it was a struggle to gain Rob's interest. By way of a compromise I had given the flat a clean lick of paint, added some feminine touches. Any Scandinavian would have been proud of my organisational skills, maximising every inch of space. Rob always complimented me on my efforts but took no active part and for the most part I was happy to enjoy complete control. However, I always arrived at the same conclusion; we needed a bigger place.

Then, one evening, I became particularly enthusiastic about one possible property and frustrated by Rob's nonchalance.

"This place might just be too good to pass up. I worked selling property in London for a short time and a mate from there has passed me the details. It has a huge double bedroom and another room which would be perfect for guests and well, a baby eventually. It would be a squeeze to swing the mortgage but…"

"Hang on, hang on. Did you say "baby"?" I had his full attention now.

"Ok, don't panic. Not for ages yet but time moves on and yes, we'll want a family eventually."

"Er well, I don't know about that. I thought you were a solid career type and loved motorbikes."

"Yes, yes that's right but everyone wants children eventually. At least one."

"I don't. Or more's the point, I can't. Doctors told me. I got exposed to some stuff in the army and a bunch of us have next to no useful ammo left. I mean, I never thought for one minute that you would want to do the mum thing."

The flat was hot and stuffy and I felt a crack run up through another wall in our marriage, a more important wall. I was not yearning for motherhood, a baby was more of an abstract notion but to suddenly discover that Rob could not give me a child, it made me feel quite desperate.

"My God Rob. I can't believe you never mentioned that. I mean, that is quite a serious fact that you really should have shared."

"Er maybe you should have asked me but if it's a big deal for you, to have kids I mean, well we could adopt. I'd consider it."

"You're ten years older than me and that whole process can take ages. I'm not ready to be a mum just yet. And besides, we'd both want to want it and you said you don't even want kids."

"Honestly, no I'm not all that keen but I love Amélie and I'm sure I could love another child if push came to shove. But you know all my flaws. Do you think I'd make a good dad?"

I stared at him and thought of the interminable scrutiny of an adoption process and my heart sank. I also caught a quick glimpse of my own dad in my mind, fully aware of the consequences of inferior parenting. The fact that I had no contact with my own parents would hardly count in our favour. Besides, what about biology and the clock within? Its tick was inaudible yet it existed, as sure as my eggs.

"I don't know Rob. Look, this has come as a bit of a revelation. The whole matter can go on hold. It's just something I had assumed and I need time to take it in. That's all. What do you think about this house though? Shall I arrange a viewing?"

I pointed to the particulars, but all my enthusiasm withered. I must have looked abject and pathetic.

"Sure. Why not? Whatever makes you happy."

He meant it. He cared about my happiness but what was abundantly clear was that our happiness was not inextricably linked. Like the nightmares which woke him, born of experiences I could not even begin to imagine, this man, his wants, needs, his motivation, everything was out of my sphere. He cared for me but he remained detached and there was no prospect of a biological child uniting us. It was a connection but so half-hearted and though we were married I knew that the bond with David had been stronger. Looking over at Rob then, I saw that despite my fondness for him and what had been the ease of our compatibility, it was not love and never had been. I had been a complete idiot.

Yet, I was a stubborn woman, not a quitter and I resolved to make my marriage work, against the glaring odds. Trouble is, Rob needed to share my determination but he did not. Without consulting me, he decided mending motorbikes was not all that enthralling, neither was having a wife and enquired about a position as a civilian advisor to the UN peace keeping forces deployed in former Yugoslavia. It was as David had told me. He was married to the army. He could not stay away. He told me about the job after the fact and announced his imminent departure in the same tone he might have announced what was for dinner. There was a bitter row, a pointless thing, my every objection kicked into the grass. I tried so hard to block it, insisting on my fears for his safety but he brushed this aside, a flick of his hand enough to squish the pathetic, irritating fly that his wife had become to him. I had bought the new place and I am ashamed to recall trying to persuade him to stay because it needed decorating. The day after he left decorators turned up at the house. He had spoken to David and his brother had sent a reliable, efficient crew, all to be paid for by him. I snapped. I called a taxi and headed for the offices of David Sutton.

DAVID

Try as I might, I cannot recall what you were wearing when you burst into my office but your hair was loose and your eyes fierce and the effect was quite stunning. Perhaps you were hoping to interrupt a meeting and humiliate me, or cut me off in the midst of a crucial, international call but actually I had just been staring out of the window, hands in my pockets and I was quite able to absorb your indignation. I had twenty more years of life experience and I had seen just about everything.

"Did you know of your brother's plan to go off to a bloody war zone? If so, did you make any slight attempt to dissuade him?"

I paused and waited until your breathing slowed just a little.

"Yes. That is, he told me after he had signed on the dotted line. Had he asked my opinion, I seriously doubt I could have made any difference. Sooner or later, he was bound to go back, in one way or another. I did think you might keep him grounded a little longer but you have managed to see him off quite quickly."

It was harsh of me to say that. Perhaps I should have tried more kindness but you were so angry, angry enough to take kindness and burn it to a crisp.

"You think I even entered into the calculation? And what about the fact that he can't have children? Did you know about that?"

Here I took more time to consider my words. It felt like one of those moments when one would prefer to have a lawyer present, any comment ready to ensnare me. You were the only lawyer there and definitely not on my side.

"He came to me after you had that particular discussion. He felt terrible for letting you down. Of course, you should have both had a proper talk before you got married but then you insisted on doing everything in such a blinding rush. As it is, I'm sorry for your disappointment. I don't think I can say much more than that."

You stared at me for an uncomfortable amount of time, struggling to contain a great deal of rage, so frustrated, ensnared yourself.

"You know David, I think I was practically in love with you once but right now I utterly despise you."

Any animal caught in a trap will try to break free but mostly it is futile. I was sorry to see you in so much pain but yes there was a perverse sense of satisfaction at the notion that the balance of power was with me now. You had made a terrible mistake by marrying my brother and though you wanted to blame me there was scarcely sufficient grounds. As a lawyer you knew you were drowning and as a human being you tried to grab hold of me and pull me under.

"No you don't. You're mad at yourself and that must really hurt and somehow lashing out at me seems like it might ease the misery but it doesn't does it?"

"Er I think I know my own heart and I definitely hate you right now."

"Yes, well the lines between love and hate are easy to blur. For my part, though I find you and your decisions a gigantic pain in the arse, I cannot deny that I still care about you and probably always will. The dilemma remains what it is. You are my sister-in-law and I love my brother."

"And I love Rob." You blurted it out. Was it heartfelt or just said out of obligation? It sounded hollow.

"Well then, there we are. Not much else to say is there?"

Your shoulders dropped and wearily you fell into the nearest chair, tears pricking at your eyes. You covered your face with your hands and groaned.

"Oh God, David. Just explain this to me. When you came to Leeds you were angry about me seeing him but you never actually said that you loved me, wanted me. I mean, you spoke to me as if I were a child or worse some kind of ward, needing to be steered in a sensible direction."

"Would it have made any difference? You told me you had fallen in love with my brother. I suppose I hoped it might be a passing thing but then you went and got married."

"And in Brittany? Remind me why you held back then? I practically threw myself at you."

Part of me yearned to walk round the desk between us and kiss you but you had a wedding ring on your finger and yes, that crazy story of Celeste's still haunted me. *She* did.

"It didn't feel the right time, not the way it should be. Do you think Celeste would have wanted us together?"

You frowned. Was it only me who considered Celeste?

"Do you think you would have bothered to find me if she hadn't made me Amélie's God mother and left me the house?"

"I'm not sure. My first wife committed adultery. My second wife went out in a boat and didn't come back. I think I would have tried to avoid love for a while. It isn't kind to me."

I surprised myself with that honesty. I rarely show my belly.

The mood was now so different. Subdued and reflective and perhaps the first time we had ever tried to communicate as equals.

You rose from the chair.

"Do you love me David?"

Trust a barrister to land a direct question on me like that.

"For what it is worth, yes I do. In one way or another, I probably always have."

You stared down at your hand and twisted the ring round on your finger.

"And we both love Rob so I guess that's how we leave it. I suppose I'd better get back to the house."

You sounded broken and that is how I felt and yet I was unwilling to feel more vulnerability. I summoned strength from my sensible, rational core.

"Yes, probably for the best. But look, if you need anything, anything at all, just let me know. I promised Rob I'd look out for you."

"Alright, I will. Sorry for the outburst. At least we know where we stand now."

"Yes, yes we do."

You smiled at me, defeated and resigned and left, closing the door quietly behind you.

Did you feel the depth of pain that I did? As if your insides were dissolving in acid? If you did, you had managed to disguise this, wandering away like some unearthly apparition, only the faint scent of you hanging there. Now it was my turn to sit down. I should have cried but instead I picked up a mug of coffee and slammed it against the wall. Anger was easier although nothing really helped.

CLAIRE

David had told me he loved me but life and all its demands did not permit me the luxury of pulling apart the tangle of emotions this left me with. A primitive feeling in my gut convinced me that I had to calmly carry on. Now, years later, I can comment on the contrasting feelings I experienced and managed, whilst appearing to be so together. There were pangs of mental anguish, knowing that by choosing Rob I had sacrificed David and to the extent that love is a choice, I had made the wrong one. Then there was the anger directed at David because he had not blocked me in Leeds. He should have tried so much harder for our love. His age and experience and therefore judgment had been squandered. Then, there were occasional moments of euphoria, when I dispensed with the reality of our circumstances and just thought about the fact that David loved me and had said so. Finally, there was another emotion, quieter but growing. Indignation. Marrying Rob had enticed me to London, a place for which I had no easy affection and there was the career itself, not as exciting as I had imagined. I was a brilliant barrister ascending the ladder but beginning to doubt the substance of my ambition. After an effective and ruthless kill, my colleagues would pat me on the shoulder but I felt detached from this version of myself. The young woman who had walked away from her home and family to pursue an education had aspired to far less. The teenage me had walked past the semi-detached houses with stained glass porches thinking that the day I owned one I would have made it but David drove me through those gates in Scotland into another world and when Celeste sketched me I fell under some spell. He had seen a small flame of ambition and blown on it and she saw beauty and told me to harness its power. Both had beguiled me to reach higher. No one had forced me to pursue success but I held them largely accountable. Perversely, my unhappiness made me work even harder and I was wandering further and further into a spiritual desert. I had a few friends but doubted they would comprehend this and David was not poised to ride in and rescue me.

There was still the remote chance that my marriage could redeem me but when Rob returned from Bosnia he was a changed man.

DAVID

Bosnia changed my brother. He sustained no serious physical injuries but he had seen the kinds of things which alter the human mind and spirit, like ivy strangles a tree. I think we both hoped it was just exhaustion. As far as possible I attempted to avoid being in your lives, based on the accepted wisdom that all relationships require space. My connection to Caroline meant that I was always well informed as to your general state. She never made me specifically enquire but dropped bits of information into our conversation and pretended not to notice my keen interest. She told me how hard you were working, of your success, the fact that you had lost weight, the common piece of knowledge that Claire Sutcliffe always kept expensive whiskey in her office but of course drinking was a part of the culture, so no special cause for concern. Amélie often wanted to see you but this was rationed and it was Uncle Rob consistently tasked with collecting her and dropping her back. On these occasions, Rob and I talked but he always seemed distracted, more vague than ever about plans. He never showed me the other side, the depth to his darkness.

Then, one day, Caroline telephoned and requested that we meet promptly to discuss something "personal." I knew instantly that the matter concerned you and knowing Caroline not to be easily flustered about anything, I was prepared for it

181

to be grim news. I had her come to the house and when she arrived her facial expression did nothing to allay my concern.

"Thanks for coming here. As you said it was a personal matter I thought it best."

"Yes, that's fine. You haven't heard anything yourself I take it?"

"If it concerns my sister-in-law then I've heard nothing of any interest but you have then?"

"Yes David, I have, and it isn't good. She dropped out of a case this week and has gone on extended leave. It's dreadful."

"Exhaustion? Burned out? Too much heavy drinking?"

"No. A reliable source tells me she has been the victim of a serious, physical assault. Apparently quite a mess."

"Oh my God. Well, have the police been involved? I should call Rob straight away."

Then Caroline flinched, shifting her gaze awkwardly and I wish it had taken me far longer to join the dots but they connected in a flash and I felt sick to my stomach.

"Sorry, please don't tell me *he* did it. My brother is a fucking wife beater? Please tell me this is twisted gossip. Damn it, I am going to kill him."

She put out an arm and blocked me from making a furious exit.

"That would be a disaster and you know it. First, you should go and see Claire and get the full story or I can if you prefer."

"You? No way. I'm not a coward. I'll go but I am telling you I don't care what shit he went through in Bosnia. He has crossed a line that is non-negotiable."

"Agreed but how are you going to play this David? The knight in very shiny armour?"

Then the door opened and Amélie appeared, just home from school and all excited with news from the playground and we put aside the darkness of adult lives and let her carry us into a world of childhood wonder. I should have told her we were busy and sent her away but frankly I was more than eager to take refuge from thinking about you, bruised and battered and my brother, damaged perhaps beyond help, the two of you in a marriage that never should have happened. It was a dreadful mess and Amélie arrived at just the right moment, preventing me from acting in haste. She could certainly talk but eventually she stopped just long enough to register that she was hungry and disappeared in search of Mrs Jones and toasted crumpets, leaving an abrupt and awkward void for the adults.

"My goodness David, she's adorable. You're very fortunate."

"Do you think so? It doesn't feel that way right now. This is a mess."

Caroline rose to her feet and placed a comforting hand on my shoulder.

"You create order out of chaos all the time. Just keep your head and you'll see the solution."

"You think I should use my head on this then? Not my heart?"

She gave me the sort of stern stare that always accompanied any difficult legal advice she was compelled to offer.

"Someone in this situation needs to keep their head, don't you think?"

I sighed and felt masses of tension bleed out of me and already the beginnings of a plan started to form in my mind.

"Of course. Far be it for me to lose my cool."

She smiled, reassured and, after she had left, I started on the action plan. I was a calm, rational trouble shooter, no romantic knight and you, after all, were no princess. I was certain you would not make any attempt at rescue easy.

CLAIRE

I never would have opened the door to David. I was in hiding, so ashamed, stuck with the ridiculous notion that somehow Rob's attack was my fault though none of the facts supported this. I was even attempting to hold myself solely responsible for his decision to go to Bosnia which was quite absurd. I was nursing the shame with a bottle of gin, scarcely sober from the previous day. Drinking gin at ten in the morning is never a good sign, nor very helpful. I was curled up on the sofa in sweaty pyjamas, my hair dragged back into an unflattering pony tail, lending maximum exposure to my battered face. If there were prizes for being a complete wreck then I was a definite for the short-list.

I heard the front door open and grabbed at a cushion, terrified that it was my husband but it was my brother-in-law who stuck his head round the door. In a panic, I lifted the cushion to cover my face and then with the other hand tried to scramble the gin bottle out of sight. It fell with a clatter and gin started to pour out across the glass coffee table.

"Oh fuck. David, how the hell did you get in?"

He placed the gin bottle upright and snatched the cushion away, tossing it into another chair and stared at me mercilessly and for what seemed a very long time, though I know it can only have been a few seconds. He clearly did not like what he saw and my emotions were so muddled that I assumed the angry eyes were accusing me and I recoiled in the sofa, tears pricking at my damaged eyes.

"It's ok. Don't be afraid. Caroline told me and Rob gave me a spare key when he went away to Bosnia, in case of emergency. I had no idea it would ever come to this. How much have you had to drink? Have you eaten anything?"

"I've had a few and no, I'm not hungry. Really, this has nothing to do with you. You don't need to stay. In fact, I'd prefer to be on my own."

He gazed at me, more paternal than he had ever been before, or so it felt.

"Drinking won't help, so stop it. Where is he then?"

"Not sure but I'm guessing up to Catterick to see his army mates. He's in trouble David. Bosnia screwed him up."

"You sound like a wife already contemplating forgiveness. Have you taken a long look in the mirror?"

"Well, we can't just abandon him...can we?"

"Can *you*? Absolutely. Will I? No. I'll take care of him. Leave it to me. Meanwhile, go and get showered and dressed and pack some things. I'm taking you up to Scotland. Mrs Stewart will look after you until you are better."

I stood up to protest but infused with gin immediately fell back into the sofa.

"I don't want to go to Scotland. I don't want you to help me or be nice to me. You told me not to get involved with him and I did exactly the opposite and in a weird way I think I deserve this. I should suffer. I've been a complete idiot. He did to me what I have wanted to do to myself for ages, only he should have hit me harder, put me in hospital. I fucking hate myself." The words were true but the intensity gin-fuelled. I started to blubber.

"Yeah well you can talk to me more about that self-loathing on the way up to Scotland but meanwhile up you get. Come on, you'll feel better after a wash. A sleep in the car will help too."

I was so tired. Self-hatred is exhausting and being forced to stop working had totally derailed me. I was too tired to argue and so I did as I was told. Even packed my own bag with what turned out to be completely inappropriate clothes and an inadequate supply of socks. He was right. I did feel better after a wash and we had scarcely driven for half an hour before I fell asleep. By the time I woke up we were half way to Scotland where our story had begun.

DAVID

Whilst you slept in the car, it was easy for me to allow the full range of emotions to run free in my mind, trying to decide who had let you down the most, Rob or I, guilt, frustration, rage endlessly circling. My Father had asked me to take care of Rob but frankly all I had ever really done was furnish him with money. I had never really understood him and his love of the army and authority. What we both enjoyed was risk but in my business dealings, apart from having as much respect for law, contracts and the taxman as any entrepreneur could reasonably get away with, I believed I played with a pretty free hand. What risks I took were largely my decision and I had never let a board order me around the way Rob submitted to the chain of command. When Rob had told me about his posting to Bosnia, not officially army but as part of a UN peacekeeping force, it sounded plausible and I had not given the plan any proper scrutiny. Now, I felt flimsy for that. Perhaps I should have used my weight as a much older brother to press him into staying with the motorbike venture and lectured him on the responsibilities of marriage, but then, he had not married just any girl had he? Damn you. Yet, looking at you now, how could I find you deserving of any blame? Absolutely no one should be treated like that. Driving up to Scotland made me vividly recall our first drive to that house, how young you were, how innocent, fresh and wide-eyed, eager to grab at every life opportunity, having had the courage to walk away from a life and a family that would have kept you safe but stuck. Powering up the motorway, I tried to re-examine all the twists and turns of our connection and figure out just how we had ended up here but it was a changing maze. Marrying Rob had been a fatal wrong turn on your part and to have not prevented it the greatest error of judgment I had ever shown but then, alive and dead, Celeste had worked her power. When I buried her in France, I should have left her stupid story there too but even as we drove further and further towards the house in Scotland, the story repeated its whisperings...a powerful love triangle, trapping us on every side, in the past and now again in this present. I looked at how serenely you slept and wondered when I might reasonably wake you. I needed some fresh air and a coffee.

I drove on for about another 2 hours and then decided that I had to stop and, as the motion in the car altered, so you stirred.

"Where is this?"

"Services on M1, just south of Sheffield."

You tried to sit more comfortably and licked at dry lips.

"Shit I feel like hell. My head is pounding."

"Yeah well, we probably should have flown up but this was an easier escape. You're dehydrated. You can stretch your legs here and we'll get you some water."

"You don't mind being seen with me like this? People will blame you, you know."

"Stuff'em."

"Is there even a VIP bit at services for posh, rich gits like you?" You managed to say this with a very faint twinkle about your spoiled eyes.

"Nope but with a peasant like you beside me I'm sure I can blend in."

"If you put on a bit of a limp and look like you really care about me, they'll probably think you're my dad rescuing me from my swine of a husband."

"Er I think I'm only technically old enough to be your dad but in no way look like it."

You smiled, glints of mischief which looked strange in the setting of a damaged face. I waited for you to say something kind about my age but there was a long pause.

"Oh don't expect me to comment on that. I expect a lot of women of various ages would find you attractive but I won't say further than that."

"Spoken as ever by a true lawyer. Come on. Let's get on with it."

People really did stare and if some gave me dirty looks I could stand it. Some fresh air, water, coffee and a Danish pastry and you started to look much better.

You managed to sleep a little more and we spoke few words until after the next stop in the Scottish Borders. Then, you remarked how good it was to have left London, how you really had not gained any affection for the capital and I asked you about your home town. For the first time you gave me an earnest, detailed account of your childhood. The background check I had carried out on you years before had provided the facts but here was the authentic narrative, the shape and character of the building blocks that the Claire I knew was constructed upon. The first time I saw you at Turnberry, I sensed you were damaged, lost but determined to survive. I fell in love with your courage, not just your vulnerability. By opening up to me about your childhood you demonstrated both traits to me and I drank up every precious word. Then, I offered you something no other woman had ever been given, a frank narrative of my own childhood. Girlfriends had never got a crumb, my first wife had never really cared enough and Celeste had repeatedly failed to make it past the outer wall but then she had been layer upon layer of mystery to me. It had been a mutual standoff. Your childhood was rooted in deprivation, mine in affluence yet somehow we had a connection. Celeste had wanted to convince me that the connection was in the distant past, in some prior existence, that ridiculous idea that had contaminated me, that I could never completely dismiss. As we talked, I looked for any clue as to how our totally different life experiences had bizarrely created common factors but the only obvious shared feature was ambition. I could accept that it was important that we both had ambition but it was hardly the basis for love. There was the obvious physical attraction, but if that was it then I probably would have taken advantage of you in London and had an affair and I definitely would not have rejected you in Brittany. In business, I held out on a deal for various reasons; because I saw too many flaws, because I thought I could negotiate for something better. Had I really been stupid enough to treat you like a business deal?

As we drove through the gates and up the driveway to the house, the talk subsided, there was a spiritual hush as if we had entered a church. I never returned there without fully appreciating the beauty of the place and this time my admiration was wrapped about with huge nostalgia because I had brought you here, all those years ago, scarcely an adult, thrilled to see you dazzled by it all. With equal delight I saw you swallow hard and a solitary tear slip down one cheek, clearly moved by everything you saw and then, as we pulled up in front of the house you turned and exclaimed in what was almost childlike wonder.

"Wow! I feel like I've come home."

I should have been wholly pleased with that remark but as I was pulling the bags from the car I thought for just a moment that I heard Celeste laughing. I had buried her in France but would she ever be gone from here?

CLAIRE

The house in Scotland made me feel instantly safe. David had done absolutely the right thing by making me go there. I walked on jelly legs towards a smiling Mrs Stewart. Ever the professional, she showed no reaction to my interesting face but threw warm arms about me and her Celtic chatter was a mesmerising distraction as we moved indoors. She set about preparing tea and arranged fingers of homemade shortbread on one of her flowery, eccentric plates. It was David's house but this was her way of saying that she was taking care of me now and David duly made an excuse about catching up with other staff and left us to it.

After tea, she took me upstairs and to my surprise showed me into what had been David's marital chamber.

"Oh but this was David and Celeste's room."

"Aye and so he has no use for it now and it's a beautiful room. The light is special here. It has been totally redecorated of course. There's still a few of her things in the cupboard in the dressing room but don't say a word to him. She had beautiful taste and I just thought wee Amélie might be interested when she's older. I keep meaning to fold them away but there's always plenty to do."

"David still comes here then, in spite of what happened?"

"Oh yes, as often as he can with Amélie but more often than not to wine and dine the business folk. Well, you remember all that. It's funny. He always says how it's important for Amélie to have the fresh air and tells me he makes the best business deals after coming here but never admits that he just loves the place to the depths of his soul. I never see him in London. He has Mrs Jones down there but I think this is where he comes to life. Have you noticed at all?"

"Er well, I'm not sure. I haven't seen so much of him in a while. After I married Robbie… well er…"

I had turned very red. Just saying my husband's name had made my breathing shallow.

Mrs Stewart blushed herself.

"Oh dear. I didn't mean to make you uncomfortable. Don't try to say another word for now. I'll leave you to sort yourself out. Perhaps a nice soak in the bath?"

"Yeah, sounds like a good plan. Thanks Mrs Stewart."

I thought she might insist that I call her Maggie but the housekeeper veneer fell over her like a veil and she left the room full of brisk purpose.

As I ran the bath and unpacked my things, I kept thinking of the cupboard and Celeste's clothes but resisted what was a very strong temptation to look at them. In the bath, all I could think about was the fact that she had lived, breathed and died here. I refused to think about Robbie or David. As I very carefully applied moisturiser to my bruised face I was relieved that she never lived to see this happen to me. I thought about the alabaster heart and her efforts to steer me safely through the dangerous channels of love and I pictured my heart, cracked and chipped and as I stared into a mirror which must have so often contained her, I thought, and said out loud.

"And on top of everything, I'm in love with your husband. No idea what you would say about that. Something clever and witty?"

Then, finally and instinctively, I went to the cupboard, opened it and raised the sleeve of a silk dress to my face. It still smelled of lavender.

DAVID

Dinner was a subdued affair and you looked exhausted. You soon went on to bed. I walked the gardens, smoked two cigarettes and considered going to the village pub but Mrs Stewart appeared yielding a bottle of my favourite malt. After Celeste died she had decided to be more maternal towards me and a visit never passed without us having a whiskey in her parlour, just a brief social encounter so she could assess me, remind me not to keep smoking, nag me about my eating habits in London, etc. She had no idea how supervised I was by Mrs Jones and I was gracious enough to allow both women to feel they were taking care of me and keeping me right.

We drank the first whiskey with all the respect and concentration it deserved. I waited for her to start up about the smoking but she had someone else on her mind this time.

"I just can't believe he did that to her. I've always warmed to

Robbie. He's got bags of charm. I know the army does things to a person but can you believe it of him?"

"It's hard to stomach. Part of me wants to throttle him but I don't know, I need to try and understand it too. Of course, he is going to need help. I've started making enquiries. There's a place in America."

"You mean like a clinic?"

"Yes, exactly. A complete change of scene, away from his army mates. I blame myself partly. I didn't push him hard enough with the motorbike business, make him take responsibility. I should have talked him out of Bosnia. I didn't think he would listen but I should have tried."

"A man his age knows his own mind."

"For sure."

"It was his wife he might have listened to. Did she not try to stop him?"

"She wanted to. She came to see me but he was already pretty committed by then and well, it was complicated."

"Ah yes, I know."

I had been staring into my whiskey glass but something in her tone made me look across at her. I saw her immediately gather herself. She was wise, perceptive and aware of many delicate boundaries.

"Really? What do you know?"

She drained her glass and placed it carefully on the table, straightening the coaster underneath.

"Well, I knew the very first time that you brought wee Claire here to the house that as much as Celeste adored her, it was delicate. When Claire came here after, all drowned like a rat, asking for help, I almost called your wife but then you were the boss. You've always been very correct about things but after your poor wife died the photos were put away but that portrait stayed, didn't it? She's very lovely and when I heard she had up and married your brother, I couldn't believe it. More than that, I shan't say because I know it's none of my business."

"I see." Mrs Stewart knew and understood a lot then and though it partly irritated me, I was not inclined to waste an opportunity.

"Claire shouldn't have married Rob. Some mistakes can't be undone."

"Oh I think divorce is easy enough these days and she's reasonable grounds has she not? She made a mistake but no one would want to punish her for it."

"Punish her?"

"Oh yes, you know. Hold it against her. Make her feel it can't be undone."

"Well, I certainly won't get in the way of a divorce if that's her decision."

"No, well she wouldn't let you. She's strong. She'll work it out but…no, I shan't interfere. It's not my place."

"No please, say whatever it is. Maybe I need to hear it." I leant forward in my chair, eager.

"Well then, you're a man who knows how to make decisions. Be decisive. Listen to your instincts and don't let pride or anything else get in the way of it."

I stood up. I smiled down at her, wanting to reassure her that it was all ok and that her opinion was reasonable and not out of place.

"Thank you for your honesty and the drink. I'll think about what you've said but I 'm tired now. It's been a long day."

More than that I was not able or willing to say. I went into the large hallway and stared up at your portrait and considered my happiness and yours. As I climbed the stairs, I felt older than my years.

CLAIRE

When I woke up the following day, I felt better than I had felt in a very long time and, as if the bed itself was the secret, I was reluctant to leave it but then I started to feel hungry and as I dressed I started to think about David, the conversation we had had in the car driving up, the strange blend of emotions that had come over me as we approached the house. Then my mind drifted further back, hearing him say he loved me in his London office, various pictures of him which I kept stored in my mind; walking out of a courtroom and him opening a door whilst I climbed into his sports car, feeling proud, of him or myself or both? A picture of him walking across the beach in Brittany, not such the business man for a change, an early definitive image of him, smoking, a foot on a log, and another faint picture of his arms, rowing us out on the loch.

Whatever I had ever felt for Rob had been destroyed. It was finished, just the lifeless body of a marriage to dispose of now. There would need to be a respectable period of mourning and a chance to process everything. I wanted to go down to breakfast with a fresh sense of resolve, but in truth, there was no golden sun in a clear sky. The more I thought about it and the closer I got to the bottom of the stairs, the more clouds I saw, drifting relentlessly across, threatening to obscure the sun entirely. David had rejected me in Brittany, failed to talk me out of being with his brother and made it known that he regarded my decision to marry Rob as definitive, a solid, insurmountable obstacle, a storm that could never pass. When Mrs Stewart appeared and explained I would be having breakfast on my own, that David had been making business calls and had now gone out for a run, I felt relieved. I wasn't ready for breakfast for two. I was a mess and only partly because of Rob. At some point working life had started to consume me, I had been drinking heavily, I had no clear idea what I wanted anymore. If I loved David and if he loved me, then now was probably not the time for us. Half way through breakfast, I already had a headache. I went into the cloakroom off the hallway, found some old wellies and one of David's many old coats and decided to go out for a walk.

I walked for a long time, almost unaware of my surroundings but instinctively not in the direction of the loch. I was not up to that today. It started to rain, only a light, warm drizzle. By the time I found myself outside of the cottage, it was raining harder. I peered in through the windows. All was neat and tidy, no signs of human occupancy. It was perhaps a holiday cottage. On a whim, I lifted a flower pot by the door and yes, there was a key. The cottage was within the confines of the estate so perhaps no greater security was considered necessary. Every fairy-tale warns of the perils of entering a house uninvited and I would have hesitated longer had not the rain begun to really lash down. Inside, I shivered over and over and rubbed my arms. I was cold now. I set about making a bad effort to light a fire and the stress and strain helped warm me and then finally a spark and some small flames. There were blankets in a basket next to the sofa and I wrapped two around me. The wind drove the rain up against the small window panes, compounding a sense of comfort and security. After a while, going over and over in my mind just how crap my life was, seeing no easy solutions, I felt exhausted all over again, the benefit of a good night's sleep cancelled out. Depressed, I closed my eyes and eventually drifted asleep.

The crunch and grinding hiss of feed-back on a walkie talkie woke me abruptly and the outline of a man peering in at the window made me gasp. He immediately put up a hand to reassure me and I heard him say sorry. Then he spoke into the handset and told someone that he had found me and went on to listen to some instructions I couldn't quite make out. He didn't attempt to enter the cottage but spoke to me through the window.

"Mr Sutton is on his way here. Please wait for him and he'll take you back to the house."

Sure enough it did not take David long to arrive, still in running clothes, wet looking. He was obviously pleased to see me and smiled warmly enough but after the other man had left us alone and once he had closed the door of the cottage behind him something shifted in his countenance and I recognised irritation.

"We have all been frantic. You left without a word, your breakfast half eaten and no idea where you were headed. Are you ok?"

Whatever fairy-tale world I had drifted away to, now the reality came crashing back in. I was a victim and my life had derailed. David had brought me here, springing to the rescue and it was possible that the twenty year age gap was wider than ever now and that these were almost paternal feelings he had for me or at best plain pity. For some reason, this just made me angry.

"Of course I am. I just went for a walk and when it started to tip down this place seemed like a good idea. I figured it was just part of the estate and the key was under the pot. I'm not a child, David."

"Well, under the circumstances it was natural for us to be concerned."

I hated more than anything that he said "us", Mrs Stewart my presumed mother in the situation. I grew even angrier.

"Honestly, so you ordered a bloody search party? What was I gonna do, throw myself in the loch?"

My hand went up to my mouth but it was too late. I had said something stupid and cruel. He just stared at me, probably stunned.

"Oh God David. Please, I don't know what made me say that.

196

Please, you're right, I'm not really behaving very sensibly right now. I should have just told Mrs Stewart I was stepping out for a walk. I can totally understand your concern. Can we just go back to the house now and forget the mix-up?"

He looked at me then without any hint of affection never mind love.

"Do what you like Claire. You always do." He turned to leave.

"No David, please. Come on, I've apologised. Don't sulk." Wow! All the great words were coming out and there was yet another cause for regret.

He turned back and yes he was furious but not for one instant was I afraid of him because he was not like his brother and I knew he would never hurt me. This anger came from a different place.

"Damn it Claire, let's do it, let's have the conversation, whilst we're on a roll. Just tell me, whilst I try to get over my little "tantrum", why did you do it? Why did you have to marry him?"

The question did not wrong foot me. It felt like we had been waiting to discuss this for ages.

"Because I thought I was in love with him. You once told me how important it was to know when you were not actually in love with someone and I thought it was a strange piece of advice but now I get it. I found out the hard way that what I felt for him was mainly because I was in love with you. It was all very reactionary. I resented you for rejecting me in Brittany and when you came to Leeds I wanted you to put it all right again, to win me over. I mean it sounds stupid, like life is ever like the movies but instead you treated me like, oh I don't know, a silly, confused child and it pushed me further and further into his arms."

It was odd how easily I was able to explain all of this, almost eloquently. Had I rehearsed this at some level?

"Did you ever love him then?"

It was a question which felt like, however I answered, I was doomed. So, I decided simple honesty was the best option.

"In a romantic, sort of adolescent way yes. I can't pretend that it was *all* to make you jealous, that I had no feelings for him at all. If only you had fought for me and you know, finding out that you were right, that I really didn't even know him. God, he has a talent for being economical with the truth."

"If he hadn't gone to Bosnia, if he hadn't hit you like that, where were you headed? Do you really know?"

"Oh, probably along a twisting road to separation and divorce. We had as far as pride would take me but when he came back he just put a sledgehammer through it all."

"So, you regard the relationship as entirely over?"

"Well yes, of course. The same way you felt free to marry Celeste after your divorce, I imagine."

Until now, he had regarded me with such intensity but now something seemed to drain out of him and he came over and took me by the hands. It felt …it unnerved me. He stared into my eyes, unflinching. He intended to be understood.

"Oh Claire, one thing I've learned is that a divorce is not just paperwork. I left my wife legally and emotionally yes, I mean I certainly didn't love her anymore but when I married Celeste I had baggage. I never really trusted her. I don't mean that I thought she would have an affair exactly. I just never entirely believed that she could love me and I'm sure you know that I was quite controlling, AM quite controlling. The fact that she was mentally unstable, that just added another layer of complexity. I look at you now and as much as I love you and I DO love you, I see my baggage and yours and think maybe enough is enough."

He let go of my hands but I grabbed hold of one of his arms with both hands, suddenly desperate.

"No David please, don't do this again. You take risks all the time and I need you to take one now. There isn't ever going to be anyone else for me, I know it."

And in a panic I pulled him towards me and put my mouth on his and started to kiss him, badly, like a crazy person and it was horrible because he was static, unyielding and just when I was about to concede total defeat and humiliation, he pulled away and then covered my mouth with his and as I had always assumed, he was the most artful kisser, passionate but controlled. I had experienced many different kinds of fear but as he led me upstairs to the bedroom I felt a kind of electric terror. This was it, we were committing to an "us", after so many evasions and postponements.

Weird as it sounds, though the chemistry was there between us, I felt something distracting me from him and it was then that she chose to haunt me. I thought the book on Celeste was closed and already gathering dust but I had smelled her clothes hadn't I? When David entered me, I thought I heard her laughing, not a happy laugh, but the kind we fall into when we feel desperate and afterwards, whilst he dozed, I was alone with my thoughts, difficult, troubling thoughts. Rob had never been the true obstacle. It was Celeste Aubia Sutton, my feelings for her, and his. She was not just a memory. I did not believe in ghosts but I believed in enduring significance and there it was, a fragrance that distracted from everything else. For the first time in a while, I remembered Amélie and wondered what she was doing. Lying next to her father, I should have felt content but in truth my feelings were completely confused. How could a dead woman make me feel so guilty?

DAVID

So, we had sex. Let's not pretend it was making love. It was all too desperate and the outcome was relief more than anything, the conclusion to a huge, absurd struggle. Now that I am speaking frankly on the subject, I will go further to say that it wasn't great sex either. You were oddly passive and perhaps even distracted. None of this really concerned me. Now we had finally, clumsily crossed the line and the courtship of your mind, body and soul could begin. You were so young, so beautiful and if you held back a little it was, I concluded, because you were still inconveniently my brother's wife and yes, as I had warned there was baggage to deal with but, just like the bruises on your face, it would all fade with time. Ah, time. As you know I am not a patient man and so when I stirred from my brief nap and saw your porcelain back (you had turned away onto your side) and caught the scent of your sweet body and thought of the greatness, the complexity of Claire Sutcliffe, I resolved there and then that a talk with my brother was number one item on the agenda. I loved my brother and fully intended to help him but nothing now could be allowed to mess with our connection. As baggage goes I felt he was the easy one to fumble out the door but there was still the matter of a female ghost. She was a large, cumbersome trunk with sharp steel corners. It would take two of us to put her out onto the pavement but I was determined.

I kissed you on the shoulder, got up and dressed. You moved onto your back and watched me, silently, as if we were old lovers going through a ritual encounter.

"Now what?" You asked.

"Now we get dressed and go back to the house. I have a few more calls to make but I had planned to head down to see my brother today anyway and there's a place, in the States, a clinic that can help him. The sooner the better."

"Will you tell him about us?"

"I won't lie to him about anything. Let's just see what he says. Come on, up you get."

So, we left the cottage and returned to the main house. In the large hall, I glanced up at Celeste's painting of you and decided to postpone my departure until the next day. I had that nagging feeling about something, a vague sense of a task undone but it is only now, writing this, that I can speak of it with clarity. I went to your room that night, wishing to explore you further but you said you were tired and it is true that you were pale and so we exchanged a polite kiss and the next morning I got up and left. I can concede now that I made a mistake leaving you there, at the mercy of memories and ghosts. I went off, the real man of action, all grit and determination, expecting you to play the part of the princess, ready to patiently await my return. What an idiot.

CLAIRE

The day after we had sex at the cottage, I woke up with the same headache that had accompanied me to bed. David had left me a scribbled note on the bedside table which meant he had crept in and watched me sleeping and which indicated that he had now left. He suggested I relax, enjoy the surroundings and further advised me to eat a hearty breakfast. His advice was duly screwed up and binned, though I *was* hungry and Mrs Stewart cooked amazing scrambled eggs. I dressed quickly and set off to find her. I discovered her in the laundry room ironing bed sheets. I recognised the floral print of the cottage bedding and turned adolescent pink, as if my mother had found a packet of condoms. However, I was by no means a child anymore and decided to tackle matters directly.

"David should have asked me to sort all that out. I suppose living with staff means no such thing as a private life. Do you think us very immoral? Or maybe just predictable?"

"Oh I just do my job. I am not paid to have opinions. Ready for some breakfast?"

She guided me through to the kitchen and without asking immediately started on the scrambled eggs. Predictable as far as breakfast went anyway.

"I can bring it through to the dining room if you like."

"No, I want to eat here with you. Besides, I need to talk to you."

She turned from the stove and looked nervous.

"I need to talk about Celeste and what happened to her. You know I cared very much for her, don't you?"

"Ah well, I know she was very, very fond of you. I mean, you can see that in the painting she did and I believe you were the figure that appeared in all her later landscapes. She was trying to find you actually and Mr Sutton could have helped but was minded not to. I suppose he was already in love with you and was trying to save his marriage."

I took a huge swallow of the coffee she had poured me. I had not anticipated that she would speak quite so freely and my heart had started to pound but I was more excited than anxious.

"Really? Do you think he loved me then? After Amélie was born?"

"I have no idea but Mr Sutton is no adulterer and though their relationship was difficult, he loved her too, very much."

All the while, she had been readying the toast and now dished out the steaming eggs but I was not hungry now, just obsessed with the conversation.

"What happened to her on the loch? In your opinion was it suicide?"

She pushed the plate closer to me and obliged me to eat something first whilst she efficiently tidied up. Then, she removed her apron, folded it thoughtfully and took the chair opposite, carefully composing her response.

"The verdict was as it should be. No one can be certain about what happened. She was certainly up and down after the baby and sometimes behaved a bit oddly and I daresay she was often a bit depressed but it's hard to say because she preferred London to here and I only ever saw her here. She liked to paint in this house but she always complained about the size of the place you know and Mr Sutton trying to be the lord of the manor. Actually, she was fond of that little cottage you found. She joked that she was like Marie Antoinette with her pretend farm down there. It always makes me think of the house on the beach in the novel Rebecca, not that she entertained anyone there. All her friends were down in London you see. Here, it was just them, as a family, unless he had business visitors and she wasn't keen on all that either. She said they were the dullest crowd and certainly they weren't the artistic kind."

I tried to digest the fact that David and I had consummated our relationship in Celeste's special place. Did David know that? I felt a bit sick though the eggs had been delicious.

"I feel so guilty about loving him and it is far more to do with Celeste than with the fact that I married his brother. I mean Rob was just a stupid, confused decision, on both our parts and look where it's got me." I gestured at the bruises and she smiled sympathetically. "Celeste requested that I be Amélie's god-mother but what would she think about me and David getting together?"

"Well, she loved you both. She might be very happy for you. The dead are the dead, Claire. She's at peace in France now, so all you've to worry about is whether Mr Sutton is the right one for you."

"And please tell me, what do you think about that?"

She moved back from the table and for the first time looked very uncomfortable and pursed her lips tightly, unsure what to say.

"I'm his housekeeper so I don't think I should say anymore."

"Yes, but we're friends and you can talk to me as your friend can't you?"

"Friends? I feel more like your mother! Look, he's a lot older and you've not even divorced yet. If you love him you love him but don't rush into things. It seems pretty obvious how *he* feels but you must decide on *your* heart. Now, I've things to be getting on with. It's a fair day. Why don't you go for a walk and have a think about it all?"

I acquiesced. I had no right to push her any harder. I found wellies and another of David's coats and headed outdoors. I instinctively made my way across the lawn and towards the loch. It was time to deal with her last journey.

DAVID

I found Rob much how I expected to, nursing a permanent hangover, unshaven and tense, eager to hit someone or at least something. He was sleeping on an army mate's sofa and the friend gave me a very anxious stare before leaving us alone. Clearly, Rob needed help. As ever, I saw the resemblance to my father and every dutiful chord in me chimed.

He lit a cigarette and inhaled sharply. He stood against the wall by an open window and blew the smoke outside. I was keenly aware of his physical strength and his eyes betrayed the anger he felt for me. That he had used that strength against Claire made me angry too but I had to be the one to show control. He didn't offer me a cigarette.

"How is she then?" He did not sound all that concerned for your wellbeing.

"Healing. She's in Scotland. Mrs Stewart is taking care of her."

He took another long draw and I saw how he flexed the other hand and was reminded of a tiger's paw.

"What happened was fucking messed up and I'm sorry she got in the way. It should have been *you*. I knew when I married her it was gonna be a train crash and you were the one who should have stopped it. You do get that?"

"Yes but you know she only wanted to marry you because I advised her to stop seeing you. I'm not sure what else I could have done."

"Er not pissed about and just told her you loved her? Or how about being honest with me? Anyway, I don't give a shit about you or her. Tell her she can have a divorce on her terms. I've got other stuff to deal with. I can't fucking sleep. I can't concentrate. I'm going mad."

For the first time I saw fear and not anger. A terrible anguish.

"Let me help you Rob. There's a clinic in the States. They have a lot of experience treating veterans. You can fly out this week-end. A friend will meet you. All you have to do is get on a plane."

He stubbed out the cigarette but had already pulled out another.

"Easy then. Problem brother solved. "There was a long, agonising pause. "Screwed her yet?"

I took this verbal punch in the gut but held my ground.

"Do you care, really?"

He nodded his head slowly and lit the cigarette, smiling at something he found funny. It provoked the anger in me again but I absolutely needed to keep my head.

"Do I care about the two of you? No, just curious. It's going be quite something, the two of you competing for control and my money is on Claire. You've got twenty years on her and all that money but it will take a lot to break her. Even when I left her curled up on the floor I could smell the defiance. She is very strong."

"I have no desire to dominate her. I love her and respect her."

He laughed out loud.

"Oh you can't help it David. You have to be in control. You're just like Dad. Seriously though, I wish you luck. Two marriages crashed and burned so maybe third time lucky? I hope you guys work it out, for Amélie's sake, if nothing else. She's a great kid."

I decided it was time to end the conversation. I loved my brother but if he said any more…

"Here are the flight details and tickets. I'll come and see you once you've settled in. In spite of everything, I want you to know that I care about you. Don't waste this opportunity, please."

I threw every last drop of sincerity and brotherly care into this please and it stopped his attitude in its tracks. Unsure what to do or say next he turned away and stared out of the window and I left, closing the door quietly behind me.

When I drove away, Rob should have been my nagging preoccupation, there being no certainty about quite what would happen next but all I could think about was you. They were not exactly romantic, tender thoughts. I wanted to see you naked again and make you groan with pleasure. Rob's accusations niggled at me but I was certain I didn't want to control you, or break you. I just wanted to be with you.

CLAIRE

The loch was very calm and though I tried to imagine Celeste, in some heightened emotional state, struggling out onto its vast expanse in one of the rowing boats, the picture which dominated my mind was that of the three of us, on a bright, enchanting day, heading onto the water to share some sort of magical flash of human connection. How many times had that afternoon been played back, so many replays, so that its intensity and significance was something probably far beyond the original experience? It was a painting that had been retouched many times, each new stroke adding further embellishment. The cascade of her laughter, her delicate fingers caressing the surface of the water, the bend and twist of David's arms as he rowed, the handsome profile of his face which I was too shy to linger on and the air, so clean and pure that my lungs struggled to cope, or was that just my nerves? If Celeste remained with me, it was not as a sad woman about to die but as a vibrant, charismatic, soulful being and though I wanted to always remember her that way, like a vase of lilies, this was too powerful, too pungent and if David and I stood a chance I needed to put her out and open the windows. I turned and looked back at the house and from this angle it seemed bigger than ever. David had an attachment to it that the tragedy of Celeste's death had not unravelled. I wondered if Amélie understood that her mummy had died here. For aristocratic families it was normal to remain connected to a place where life, death and every intervening human drama had occurred but David did not have the burden of inheritance. It was a very special place but he had money enough to find another. Should wife number three insist on a break with all this past?

I had said it. Wife number three. Poor Amélie would have to try and understand that I was her God-mother, Auntie and now step mother. It all seemed absurd and the enormity of actions and consequences pressed in on me as I hurried back toward the house. David was right. A divorce was never just a piece of paper and as I climbed the staircase to my room, I remembered the lighter step of a young girl who climbed them for the first time and felt by comparison the effort it all seemed to require now. I had cast off shyness, lack of confidence, naivety and uncertainty about my place in life and how to pay the bills, but my load did not feel lighter. For the first time in days, my mind turned to my career and my life in London and I recalled the huge sacrifices that had been made to secure this. I had abandoned my family and my roots, I had studied and worked to my limits and though I could picture dozens of admiring colleagues and associates, where the hell were the friends now? Did I really love David so very much or was it all just a desperate, lonely grasp at his offer of protection? At the top of the stairs, I turned and looked again at the painting. I was not intended to be seen as a woman but as a symbol. It was a depiction of the vanity of human existence except that Celeste had failed because there was too much hope in the eyes.

I was not willing to surrender hope. I found the nearest telephone and called Chambers and as I familiarised myself with all the latest developments, adrenaline flowed through me. I hated London, the job was like a drug, my house was an uninspiring project but as I made arrangements I felt the same drive and power that made David get out of bed every day. I could wait for him to return, fall into the safety of his loving arms, I could opt for the state of being that is love or I could choose to act, focus on doing. I was not choosing never to be with him but it was impossible to see myself with him right now as anything other than a creature of passivity. Oh it would feel so warm and safe and the prospect of returning to London filled me with dread but it felt necessary, the right thing to do.

I went to his office, sat in his chair, smelled him and almost changed my mind but then took a sheet of paper and wrote one of the most important letters of my life.

DAVID

I don't know if you can believe me when I say that finding you gone and Mrs Stewart handing me the letter, it made me so proud of you and oddly elated. Oh I was bloody furious too and frustrated, annoyed at you, myself, and quite frankly the lack of sexual gratification played its part. In my muddle of emotions I threw the letter on the fire and I have always regretted that because it was a wonderful, clever letter which pretty well showcased your brilliant mind. If I possessed your remarkable capacity for remembering things which perhaps I once did then I could reproduce it. As it is, I can only summarise.

You began by thanking me for bringing you away to Scotland and spoke of happy memories and culminated this by saying that you loved me. It was kind, gracious and sincere and measured.

You said you were sorry that you had married Rob and had reflected a great deal on the fact that a divorce is a beginning and not an ending. You believed that I would be a vital part of that beginning but the divorce needed to happen first and meanwhile you had a career to manage. It was quite something, how you managed to request the cliché space and time from me without mentioning either word, or making me feel shunned, or at best put on hold. You showed that you understood the rocks of male pride and my addiction to control and sailed gracefully past and I could not but smile in admiration.

You told me, audaciously, *why* I loved you and though in fact you did not grasp the complexity of that emotion, you outlined its basic roots perfectly; your strong independent spirit, your beauty, naturally, your vulnerabilities (and you understood that the age gap would always preserve this). You explained that it all had to be maintained in delicate balance and that you were afraid rash choices and actions endangered us.

The final card you laid was of course the winning one. We had to think of Amélie and how any relationship would be explained to her and of course, when you spoke of Amélie, Celeste was there, hovering.

The letter defeated me. It took every next move from me. I was held in an arm lock and had no choice but to yield.

I returned to London myself two days later. I was poised to be a new man, to be patient, willing to wait. Then, I met Audrey

Hopper.

PART SIX

CLAIRE

Going back to the house in London propelled me into a whirl-
pool of regret but after a strong coffee I forced myself to focus
only on the facts. The house was mortgaged but I did not
suppose Rob would insist on its sale and his half share of the
relatively meagre equity. I was inclined not to sell what was
a fantastic investment, as prices were set to climb. In fact, I
reminded myself, Rob had put money into the place that was
actually David's money, as David had financed the motorbike
business. Anyway, I decided with much deserved bitterness
that Rob did not have much claim to anything after beating
me. The furnishings and décor had all been chosen by me with
Rob pretending to care; nothing I could not alter again, in due
course. I had tried to cater for Rob's modern tastes, as exem-
plified in his bachelor pad whereas my real sympathies rested
with eclectic and old. Over time I could make the place more
expressive of my identity. I would keep the house, one way or
another. It was better located than David's place, though he
had the beautiful garden. He could sell his apartment, or rent
it out. Struck by the semi absurdity of this rambling thought
process, I started to put Rob's clothes into a suitcase and
turned to thinking about work instead. It was hard to explain
even to myself how I could be so attached to a career that
eroded a person's soul. I had not quite sold my soul to the devil
but it was in a long term lease arrangement with costly get out
clauses. I made a living out of making clever arguments which
were only ever a devious version of the truth, navigating a system which claimed to represent justice but justice is such a
relative term. If I helped people, it certainly came at a price to

them. Jokes about lawyers were not that funny because they were too close to the truth.

Finally, I thought about the importance of having actual friends and not just a network of contacts. It was challenging for me to trust and like others but if I intended to attach myself to a man twenty years older, then it made sense to have a circle of friends more my own age. I would have to think of some hobbies, as lame as that sounded. Join a gym, get a dog or take up a new class? The career was very exacting and inclined to deny me all leisure time if I let it.

When I thought of my life as a pie, I wondered if there would even be a thin slice left for David and Amélie. By the time I had packed away the last possessions of the man I was going to divorce, I was ready to fall onto the bed, exhausted from so much thinking. I fell asleep in my clothes.

DAVID

When I returned to London, Amélie leapt at me like an affectionate Labrador and I was bombarded with the triviality of her life until she ran out of steam. Mrs Jones was skilled at bribing her away with something toasted. She had looked after me long enough to read the levels of my fatigue and was wise to pick an appropriate moment for any required briefings about domestic matters. On this occasion, she saw that she must delay until the following morning. So it was that I was enjoying coffee and toast, with the chaos of the nanny and Amélie's preparations to leave kept muted by my heading into the haven of the garden room, when Mrs Jones stepped in with my post and the pad on which she scribbled messages. The world was growing used to e-mail but I still had boundaries and the computer never went on until after breakfast.

I picked up the first newspaper and scanned my way through whilst she informed me of the gardener's intention to cut back a tree subject to my approval, the odd job guy's apologies for the delay in quoting me for a repair to the garage door, a reminder that I should attend parents evening to review my daughter's early educational progress (a formality if the latest written report were reliable), the usual messages from the office threatening the collapse of my entire business if I did not make certain decisions imminently (apparently, I was the only person capable of staying calm at the roulette table), messages which would be duplicated on my phone and computer and then there was a shift in Mrs Jones's tone and she straightened her apron which was always a sign that something irritated her. So I put down the newspaper and paid full attention.

"So, she has now left about three messages, all in a terrible, untidy scrawl and pushed into the letter box at the back presumably because she comes up through the garden which I think is a bit of a cheek but then I suppose she is very patient with Amélie and of course Amélie just goes on and on about her. Anyway, I told you that reducing the nanny's hours was a mistake and that Amélie would be bored with me after school but there you are. I'm a housekeeper, not a nanny. Anyhow, she seems to think you need to "pop in" for a "chat" and I don't think you can politely put her off any longer, so if there is any chance you can go and see what she wants."

I had missed the name of the person in question as I had been distracted by some share prices.

"Sorry, who are we talking about again?"

"Your neighbour, Audrey Hopper. She lives in the big house with the garden which backs on at the end there, beyond the orchard. There's a connecting gate which I advised you to padlock. Not sure why it's there. Anyway, Amélie, the little madam, must have gone through and well, the lady seems to have taken a shine to her, well who wouldn't? She is very good with her. Presumably she wants to meet you to discuss Amélie's little visits."

"So my daughter has been spending time with a stranger?"

"Well, yes. I suppose that is true but not a bad person as such."

"How old is she? What does she do?"

"Oh about your age and whatever she does she makes time for Amélie. It's a big house that one, so she's not short of a penny. Other than that, you will have to go and see her and ask."

"I see. Well, notwithstanding her apparent kindness, I am not used to being summoned by a neighbour and there is no way I have time to "pop by" today. Amélie is not to go down to her again, until I have met her myself. I will try tomorrow evening but meanwhile Amélie must not leave our garden."

"Ah well, she has ballet tonight anyway and she is usually tired after that."

"Good, that's fine then."

"Should I tell Mrs Hopper that you will see her tomorrow evening?"

"No no. I will "pop in for a chat." Leave it at that. Anything else?"

"No, that's all for now. More coffee?"

"No thank you. I must get to the office and save the sinking empire. Thank you Mrs Jones."

The following evening I was very tired and inclined to go to the club for an energising swim but remembered my persistent neighbour. I considered quizzing my daughter about the mystery woman first but Amélie was happily distracted with a scented mound of play dough, so I quietly crept away and took a rare stroll up my garden. It was a lovely evening. I had to stoop low to pass under branches and reach the gate, what to Amélie must have seemed a magic entrance to a secret kingdom.

My neighbour's garden was very beautiful, obviously not merely maintained but cherished and nurtured. I passed through a slightly wild area which buzzed with insects, then past a netted pond adorned with lily pads where I paused to observe some rather large fish. As I moved up closer towards the back of the house, the garden became increasingly formal and on the back of the red brick edifice, a large conservatory housed a more exotic collection of plants. To the left of this, the rear of a huge kitchen which oozed money and fine taste. I paused at the window and saw that my neighbour, her back to me, was busy tending to a steaming pan of something which smelled delicious, kitchen implement in one hand, a glass of wine in the other. She was tall and lean, in jeans and cotton, hooded top. Her long, slightly wispy hair which was silver in colour had been quickly scooped into a very untidy bun which reminded me of the wild part of her pretty garden. I tapped on the window.

She turned, unstartled, perhaps expecting Amélie, a faint smile about her lips which did not fade away upon seeing me. Her eyes were a very clear grey–blue, the skin to the corners marked with laughter lines. She was about my age and the beauty of her youth discoloured like an old print but you could imagine what had once been vivid and striking and what was left had some charm. She had a long, prominent nose, full lips and the overall structure of a face which denoted a strong, intelligent presence. I thought a lecturer perhaps, or a doctor. These were my first impressions.

She crossed over to the rear door and opened it. Her fragrance was sweet, floral and old-fashioned and not overpowered by the smell of her meal. I was not prepared for the North American accent.

"Hey there. Thanks for coming. Come on in. I'm Audrey. Amélie has told me you are called David, right?"

"Ah so you know who I am then?"

"Well sure. For one thing no other guy is likely to wander up my back garden and it just so happens your daughter looks a lot like you. Glass of wine?"

"Er well, I didn't intend to stay. I gather my daughter is being a bit of a nuisance to you."

She had turned and walked back into the kitchen, obliging me to follow. She poured me some wine anyway and then did a quick scoop and tidy up of her hair, before rummaging around and producing olives and some crisps.

"Your daughter is such a cutie and once we had the talk about the pond I was more than happy for her to come by but I do have some concerns."

I decided to have a swig of the wine before she filled me in. She opened a drawer and placed a selection of Amélie's drawings on the table in front of me.

"So, her mom is deceased, right?" She pointed at a picture which featured a mother, standing by a lake, the dark hair and red lipstick the main clues that this was indeed Celeste. I guessed that it was the loch in Scotland and my daughter liked to think of her mother forever next to it, not lying at the bottom.

"Yes, I'm afraid so. She died in an accident at our home in Scotland. Amélie probably can't remember that much about her."

"Oh I am so sorry. Amélie told me she had gone and I just sensed she didn't mean that her mom had just left. So then there's you of course". She pointed with a long, elegant index finger at two or three pictures where I was unmistakably portrayed, large and in a suit with ties and was that a briefcase? I noted that I never smiled. "And then there is her mystery friend which to begin with I thought was maybe a favourite doll but then she mainly draws her as a mermaid and she insists that she is real. I feel like your daughter is a bit lonely and has invented this character."

I was looking at pictures of you, clearly Amélie's favourite topic.

"No, that's Claire, her God-mother. She's real. Are you some

216

kind of child psychologist or something?"

At this, she clearly noted my irritation though I had tried to keep it low and this was met with a hard, merciless stare. This was a woman not to be messed with.

"Er no. Actually, I just raised three kids by myself. All went to college. All doing well and along the way I set up and ran a very successful business so what I can say is that being a lone parent is never an excuse for weak parenting. You must have had a tough time adjusting to the loss of her mom but I think you could step up a bit more now. You need to spend TIME with your daughter. A nanny and a housekeeper and maybe even this amazing God-mother she clearly idolises, none of them are more important than you."

I had been pushed onto my back foot but was more than capable of pushing back at any given opponent.

"Er well, according to what you just said, your kids did just fine without a dad so maybe my daughter doesn't need me all that much after all?"

"It's not a man versus woman thing. You are the parent, simple as. But tell me, why is her God-mother a mermaid?"

"There's a house in Brittany, left by my wife to Claire. They were close. My wife was an artist and she painted Claire as a mermaid on one of the walls there. Just a bit of fun. Really, Amélie is just fine. The school are very happy with her progress. I have no concerns. I will talk to her and explain that you are a busy person and that she really shouldn't bother you."

I got up to leave.

"Oh really? Well, that's being a bit melodramatic David. Obviously, I have upset you and I'm sorry but I think it would be a shame if you stopped your daughter from being my friend."

She made me bristle. She was very direct and I was more at ease in a boardroom but I was determined not to let her make me feel somehow pathetic.

"Look we really don't know each other and I don't have the time to change that. I thank you for being so kind to my daughter and for raising your concerns and I admit that I should devote more time to her myself, so you have achieved what you wanted. I won't so much stop Amélie from coming here, as make sure she spends more time with me. That sound amicable enough?"

She smiled at me. It was quite clear she pitied me and I had never been the object of another's pity. It annoyed me so much. I had to erase the pity.

"Would you like to go out to dinner with me Mrs Hopper? " I astonished myself with the question.

She raised one eyebrow sharply and reminded me of a demanding maths teacher who had always kept pushing me and never accepted silly errors.

"Please just call me Audrey. As for dinner, I don't think the signs are too promising but I believe in giving people a chance. I would be pleased to come and eat dinner, at your place, cooked by you. How does that sound?"

I am not sure if this was designed to skilfully deter me but as you know, I am at ease cooking and was ready to accept her challenge.

"Ok. Why not? I can do tomorrow evening. Otherwise, it will have to wait another week or so. I have some important visitors from Hong Kong." As I said this I realised it was an admission that Amélie really did not get to spend much time with me.

"Tomorrow it is then. I'll come about nine. That way you will have some time with your daughter first."

"Ok, tomorrow at nine."

I put out my hand and she hesitated before acquiescing to a very Brtish handshake.

I do not mind admitting that I returned to my house that

evening feeling flustered, a bit out of control and yet already thinking about what I would cook for her and yes, oddly excited. All the while, I did not forget you. I had every intention of contacting you and was aware that when someone asks to be given some space there is a danger in giving too much and failing a commitment test. When I thought about you and "us", I had no clear strategy. Audrey Hopper had presented herself as a distraction.

CLAIRE

I don't mean to brag but hardly a week could go by without a man asking me out. I had a stock way of turning them down which deterred all from persisting.

"That's very flattering but I am busy taking my ex-husband to the cleaners. When I've finished nailing his balls to the wall I'll maybe call you." Some actually turned pale. Most looked sorry for asking.

Then there were the well intentioned female colleagues who felt obliged to confirm their solidarity by suggesting fix-ups with guys who were "great fun" and "not looking for anything serious." My stock answer? "Ah but I am not looking for anything at all."

It struck me that for all the progress of feminism, people still defined themselves through relationships, men and women alike. To one or two people that I knew better, I divulged that I was in a relationship with someone but it was complicated. I never clarified just how complicated by explaining that he was my brother-in-law.

In my letter to David, I had effectively asked him to give me space and he was doing just that. All I could do was imaginatively speculate as to how and what he was thinking. It occurred to me that I might approach Caroline Summers for intelligence; she had been an effective spy for him. She saw him quite regularly. How did he seem? Had he asked after me? Then there was Amélie. I could make her an excuse to go to his house but nothing ever developed from this thinking. Matters were in a state of paralysis except that my divorce was progressing and work was keeping me mainly occupied. I made up my mind to take the next opportunity to go to Brittany and have a complete break and seize that time to fully assess my relationship with David and our possible future together. The one scenario which never presented itself was the notion of David meeting someone else and moving on. However, the plan to take a breather in Brittany collapsed when a very juicy case landed on my desk, the sort of case that could shoulder me several rungs up the professional ladder and when one considered how many broad shouldered men stared down at me on that ladder, it was an opportunity I knew I had to take. I was weary but the adrenaline would carry me through. Thoughts about David were pushed away.

He had told me he loved me. I trusted him. I trusted that love could wait.

DAVID

Audrey arrived bang on time but then she had not far to go. She had done something more sophisticated with her hair and wore a simple, silk dress and with small heels was tall, sleek and her eyes sparkled. I was attracted to her and this rendered me uneasy, only partly because of my feelings towards you and everything yet to be resolved. It was also because she was unlike any woman I had been drawn to before. There was no fragility, nothing delicate. She was like a shimmering steel blade. I had met women in boardrooms like her but their strength always seemed to be a performance, not quite authentic, something modelled on what they perceived as strength. This energy was born of genuine confidence rooted in the success of her life. She had made it in business and raised her children without a man and nothing could take that away from her. She had managed without marriage and perhaps a man was only ever an appendage. After two marriages and with our relationship drifting in swamp land, can you blame me for fluttering around this strange new light?

I was confident in my kitchen, even under her steady gaze. The conversation was easy. We exchanged notes on our business dealings. Her numbers were small compared to mine but then I was making a lousy job of raising one child so there were no grounds for me to feel too superior. She thought nothing of tasting my sauce and suggesting improvements. I asked her to make a salad and she produced something artful whilst not agreeing with several points I made and keeping me on the back foot in our discussion. This was a fresh experience for me and I was willing to go with it.

After dinner, she was enthusiastic about trying my finest malt. We retired to the garden room and she spread herself on the chaise longue, a fine, athletic lurcher. I felt more relaxed than I had felt in ages yet pleasantly poised for something to happen and sat forward in my armchair. I wanted to smoke but sensed she would disapprove and this woman made me want her approval.

She took a good swig from her glass and smiled at me.

"Good food, nice company and great scotch. Wonderful David. I'd like to see you again and I don't mean to discuss parenting issues. What do you say?"

The scotch caught in my throat and I coughed slightly.

"Er yeah sure, why not? Though just to be clear, I am sort of involved with someone right now."

White flames flared in her stunning blue eyes.

"Oh really? Tell me about her." Just to prove her interest she sat up and forward.

"Well, it's a cliché thing to say but it's complicated. It's Claire, the mermaid, Amélie's God-mother."

She pursed her lips and the eyes scanned me from head to toe.

"Your late wife's friend?"

"Well yes, she was friends with both of us. Actually it was me who introduced her to my wife. Look, there was never any adultery. I loved my wife very much. Claire loved her too." Why did she compel me to defend myself?

She was clearly processing every word, every part of my tone, hand gestures, body language.

"She's quite a bit younger than you I'm guessing. Is that why you're hesitating?"

For a moment I questioned whether this was any of her business but the whiskey inclined me to confession.

"The age gap is real, yes, but there have been other issues. She did something stupid, something to force my hand and it kind of back fired."

"She had a fling?"

Describing us to her made it all seem ridiculous and hopeless.

"Er a bit more than that. She married my younger brother. It's over now. They're divorcing."

Her eyebrows arched and I felt like an idiot.

"My my, she really goes for it. I can only imagine that she is as beautiful and magical as Amélie draws her. Mermaid sounds about right. You know they lure guys onto rocks don't you?"

I smacked my glass down onto the table. Always the instinct to protect and now to defend you.

"Like I said it's complicated. I've had a nice evening Audrey but I think we should call it a day. I have a packed schedule tomorrow and I am sure you do too."

I stood up; ready to politely escort her to the door. She sighed, insisted on emptying her glass and seemed to rise oh so slowly. She took me by the arm which disarmed me.

"I feel for you David. Believe me, if you love her then I hope you guys can work it out."

She moved in and kissed me softly on the cheek and yes, every part of my manly passion was provoked. If you were a mermaid, maybe she was the cruel, ice queen, casting her spell.

"If not, well, call me. Trust me, I'm straight forward. No games."

"Maybe I enjoy games." The urge to flirt was intense.

"Only if you get to win, I'm sure." No flirtation. A cold statement of the truth.

I looked as far into her eyes as she would let me and thought that this was a woman who never played a losing game. If I loved you, then why even bother with Audrey Hopper?

Still, I watched her walk away up the garden and thought about what it would be like to take her on. Would it be any more complicated and demanding as we had become? You had made no contact, time was opening up between us and time for someone my age was a commodity soaring in value.

Yet, I would respect every word of that letter you wrote. No calls, no surprise visits. It was your move.

CLAIRE

I won the case. It was a victory against the odds which earned me the esteem of my professional friends and rivals alike. I had scarcely had a chance to shake hands with my client before being swept off to one of our preferred drinking holes to celebrate. They flocked to toast my success and successive glasses of wine were pressed into my hand, albeit I was only able to grab quick sips between responding to the barrage of praise. However, clearly I had had more than the legal limit by the time I made the decision to go and get changed, and pop round to surprise David. My ego was pumped, the adrenaline made a heady cocktail with the wine and it was time to see him again. I wanted to share my success with the only person who really mattered. The decision to head off on my motorbike was clearly reckless but was indicative of my euphoria. How I got to his house in one piece is beyond me but it was only when I climbed off it and made my way to the front door that I registered quite how dizzy I felt. I pushed my finger nails into the palms of my hand to try to sober up.

Mrs Jones opened the door and did not immediately invite me in. She was rather stern.

"He's not back yet. He has been in Los Angeles. His flight is only due in much later. He'll be very tired. It would be better to call on Sunday perhaps, after he has had a chance to recover."

I was not in the mood to be sensible and not entirely confident about getting back on my bike.

"Well, it would be lovely to spend some time with my beautiful god-daughter in the meantime. Where is she?"

I pushed past Mrs Jones. I knew this house. I went to the kitchen. A coffee would be a good idea. I took up the kettle but Mrs Jones seized it from me and insisted she could do the honours.

"Amélie is with the neighbour, doing some baking. They're not due back for another half hour or so. Then it will be time for her supper and her normal bedtime routine so please don't get her all excited. The nanny is off for the evening and I am not up for any fuss."

"Oh but I love a bit of fuss Mrs Jones. Leave it to me. What's for supper? It smells amazing."

I normally had a reasonable rapport with David's housekeeper but I probably showed all the signs of having had a few drinks, the flushed cheeks, daft eyes, speaking louder than necessary and she did not appear pleased. The strange effect of this critical stance was that I changed my mind about the coffee and helped myself to some of David's fine Rioja. I was happy. It had been a great day and I did not want her to kill my mood. I told her about the case but she did not seem impressed. She kept glancing at the clock, distracted. Eventually, I took my wine and my happiness and headed off to the garden room. I searched through David's music collection and put on something suitably cheerful. I sipped, I danced, went over parts of my glorious performance in the courtroom. I could not wait to see David. I checked myself in the mirror several times. I thought I looked better than I had done in a while. I paused before the photo of Celeste, part of me missing her but of course, if she were here then David and I could not be together at last. As I finished my large glass of wine it was clearer than it had ever been that that was what I wanted. I wanted him. I thought about Celeste's idea of wearing an alabaster heart and it seemed stupid.

I was half way through a refill and a bowl of peanuts which I had managed to scrounge from Mrs Jones when the lady came up the garden towards the house, Amélie skipping along in front. She was older but striking. She walked with confidence and I observed the wonderful rapport she had with Amélie. When Mrs Jones had said Amélie was baking with the neighbour I had imagined someone short and round, in a pinafore, someone akin to a grandmother. As they neared the house I was also struck by her American accent which rendered her exotic. I waved excitedly at my god-daughter and she squealed with reciprocal joy. She ran to the house, discarding her companion.

Amélie was only half way through sharing with me every detail of her charming life, when Mrs Jones ushered her away to wash her hands and then the older lady joined me. She came directly over and shook me by the hand. Hers was cool and dry, mine was warm and clammy. She said her name but I was too taken in by her metallic eyes, the grey but chic hair and the way her silk blouse lay perfectly over the contours of her form. She had the advantage of knowing who I was, thanks to

Amélie who adored me.

"You know, David isn't due back until really late. I guess he is gonna be pretty jet lagged too."

She stared at my glass of wine. I felt judged but that was not the main problem. There was something about the way she said David's name that resonated familiarity and I objected to that. It was some kind of signal and I would not be handled.

"Oh David will get over it when he sees me, believe me. Anyway, I plan to have supper with my amazing god daughter and if necessary, I can crash here for the night and see David tomorrow. It won't be a problem. Thank you for spending time with Amélie. We can take it from here. It's Friday night. I'm sure you have plans."

She smiled at me. Nothing in her expression showed defeat.

"Ok well I will leave you to it. It has been very interesting to finally meet you Claire. Take care now."

She touched me lightly on the arm, almost maternal, which really seemed patronising and left, leaving her delectable perfume behind her. When I went through to join Amélie for supper, I had a list of questions ready, all worded for a child but designed to extract key information. Was the lady (I learned that her name was Audrey and this time it stuck) a friend of daddy's too? Did they see a lot of her? What did Amélie love about her? What had Amélie told her about me?

I continued to drink through supper but my mood was deteriorating. I swayed a little when I got up from the table and admitted to Mrs Jones that it might be better if she supervised bath time and after a gruelling day perhaps I was not up to doing a bedtime story. After strong protests from Amélie we agreed we would watch a video together instead. By the time the child was tucked up asleep, the desire to see David had become a desperate need. When Mrs Jones informed me that the flight was delayed, I fell into despondency and started on his whiskey. I put the television news on but all I cared about was my own state of affairs. The clocks hands tormented me. At some point, horribly drunk, I fell asleep.

DAVID

Jet lag was not growing any easier with age and when I finally stepped through my front door, a little after midnight, I was thoroughly done in. Mrs Jones surprised me by still being up, even though I had sent her a text and told her not to do so. She was wringing her hands anxiously and I immediately panicked. Was Amélie unwell? It was therefore primarily a relief to discover that the problem was a drunken you, asleep in the armchair. She had tried to move you, having prepared a bed, but you had protested and she was too old to handle you. She made a point of saying you had used dreadful bad language which briefly amused me.

I went into the sitting room and there you were. Your hair was cascading softly over the side of the chair. There was dribble around the slightly open mouth. You stank of alcohol. Yet still I looked at you and loved you. You only grumbled slightly, in words inaudible, as I scooped you up and took you up to the waiting bed. As I took each stair, it occurred to me that another few years and I would be past managing this. There was no possible way of getting those tight jeans off without a lot of struggle, so I dispensed with the duvet and placed a light blanket over you instead. You would sleep in your clothes and no doubt waken with a crashing hangover.

I knew I was beyond much sleep myself, so I made a mint tea and settled into the armchair near your bed and watched you. I drifted under for a couple of hours but by five I was awake again. You looked peaceful. I had the time and opportunity to study you and to think about it all. I decided to wake you up.

CLAIRE

"Come on Claire. Wake up." He must have said it a dozen times before my mind scrambled free from my subconscious and registered that his voice was coming at me from reality. My instinct was to shoot upright out of the bed but then I hit a wall of pain and fell back, groaning. My mouth was incredibly dry and there was that familiar nausea. With horror I mentally ticked off all my vital signs and concluded that this was one hell of a hangover. Then, I remembered what had dragged me awake. Oh no, it was really his voice and he was there, sitting near me, seeing me. I was in his house.

I did not want to but of course I had to open my eyes. Yes, there he was, staring at me. Yep, I looked appalling and he thought it was amusing.

"Oh damn. What time is it?"

"A little after five."

I had to close my eyes to concentrate and process this information.

"What the hell? Why have you woken me? Let me go back to sleep, please. I feel like shit."

I opened my eyes to implore him to pity but he was no longer smiling. Actually, he looked very grey and tired. Had he had any sleep?

"No Claire come on. We need to talk before Amélie wakes up. She never lies in. Only teenagers understand week-ends. Here, have some water."

So, I forced myself up, swallowed the tablets he held out and finished off the water. I said I needed the toilet but mainly I wanted to check just how bad I looked. I splashed water on my face and summoned some colour. I combed my hair with my fingers. I remembered Audrey and her natural poise. I crashed back onto the bed, moaning.

"What the hell do we need to talk about that is so urgent?" Then, managing to smile at him. "Why don't we just skip to sex? Missed me?"

I did my best to be alluring but every part of me was stiff and aching. It would be an effort but I was willing. He sighed. It suggested a lot of things, mainly disappointment I thought.

"Really? You just turn up out of the blue, get drunk and now expect me to desire you? You ought to have worked out by now that I am attracted to sober Claire. Anyway, the last time we had sex you decided to up and leave me. You really want to go again?"

In a dramatic gesture he stood up and started to unbutton his shirt. I put up my hand in surrender. No, he was right, it was hardly the moment.

"Ok, ok. You're right. Bad idea. But I want you to know that I came here last night because yesterday was a huge day for me. I won a massive case and I came here because you're the only person I wanted to celebrate with. I love you and I don't want to mess about any more. I want us to be together. "

"I see." He sat back in the chair again and balanced his chin on clasped hands, contemplating my little speech. I felt instantly uneasy. Something had changed.

"You know, I have been staring at you a lot and quite frankly, even drunk, you ARE beautiful and intelligent and funny and feisty and I DO love you, very much. Here's the thing though. Love isn't the consideration it used to be for me. I'm twenty years older than you Claire, two marriages down and a child to care for and you know, nothing has been straightforward between us, least of all you marrying my brother. I think it is time for us to accept that we are just not meant to be, not as lovers. I will always care about you deeply and always be your friend but maybe the rest is just not what I need, nor you really."

I watched each word framed by his mouth as if in slow motion but it was processed internally at high speed, a network of neurones fired up and blazing, examining all the information, making connections and crucially arriving at conclusions.

I sat upright, throwing off the blanket.

"Fucking hell. You are going to trade me in for an older model! I met her you know, your kindly neighbour. As soon as she spoke your name, I knew it. She thinks she fucking owns you David. She tried to get me to leave. The worst of it is that she has used Amélie to get to you. You might be twenty years older but you're still a stupid idiot!"

I was so angry but, being a woman, this translated into tears and that in turn made me even more frustrated. David frowned at me darkly, got up and went over to close the door. Then he sat on the edge of the bed and clasped my hand between his. He intended for me to listen to this and to accept it.

"Audrey is irrelevant to this conversation. Besides, how can I "trade you in" when I have never owned you? Not that I have wanted to own you. If I have learned one thing from two marriages it is the futility of all that thinking. Now listen to me Waif, you are always going to be an important part of my life. I have loved you, always. Still do. You will always be a part of Amélie's life too. It was what Celeste wanted and I won't let her down. But you and me, we've missed every opportunity there was. Somehow, in spite of our love, we have just not been a fit and being older and wiser than you, and I AM older and wiser than you, I want to do what is right for the both of us. And the right thing to do is to accept that we can't be together, not like that."

He was making a brave, heartfelt speech, spoken with true feeling but I was stuck on Audrey.

"Have you had sex with that woman? I mean, I bet it was good, better than with me but I'm young, I can improve. She is just going to shrivel up soon and me I'm still improving, I haven't even reached my potential. Let me prove it to you now, come on."

I grabbed at him but he pushed me back.

"Stop it Claire. Just stop it. Have you listened to anything I have just told you? What? You think I need a lesson off a youngster about sex? I'm trying to talk to you about FEEL-INGS, like you're a mature adult. This jealous fixation is ridiculous. It makes you look childish."

I grabbed at him again, the tears running faster and faster and inside me a terrible rage.

"But I'm Waif. You love that I'm younger. It's the way we are. I need you."

He removed my hand carefully but firmly and squeezed it between his.

"No, no you don't. It's time to fully grow up, to realise your potential. That court case yesterday was just the beginning. From here, you get to soar. Trust me."

"If you say that one day I will meet someone, I'll kill you. There is no one else David. Only you."

This made him hesitate but he had already said too much. It was over. I felt it even if I could not accept it. He stood up, moved to the door but then turned back to deliver the final punch.

"I was a chapter, that's all. I'm tired. I'm going to bed. You should go home. Take some time to think about it all. Get used to it. I'm offering you friendship but no more. It's up to you now."

He clicked the door quietly shut. I cried into my pillow for a while but then did the inevitable. I left, on the motorbike Rob had given me.

DAVID

You felt rejected and inevitably there followed a period of anger which only gave way to loathing. Audrey was not the reason I put an end to "us". You imagined her powers far

231

greater than they were. To give you up was like making a decision to give up an addictive substance and I could not have contemplated such a change if it had not occurred to me that she was the healthier, synthetic version, designed to ween me off something which was harmful to both of us. She was from the outset a poor substitute, but enough to get me started on the road to Waif-free life. I used her unashamedly but she was absolutely a grown up and she took the deal for what it was; embedded in its small print enough to make her decide I was a worthwhile transaction. In any case, she stayed, as you know. More importantly, the one thing I desire for you to understand and accept is the fact that I did what I did precisely because I loved you, because twenty more years of life experience and two marriages had delivered important lessons on love. Watching you sleep, I saw exactly how young you still were and, taking our whole story into consideration, the right and honourable course of action was to admit to myself that I had been a formative experience for you but it was time for you to move on. You were beautiful, intelligent, formidable, not yet at your peak. I am not sure what Celeste had ever intended by making you Amélie's Godmother but when she died it had compelled me to find you and aside from your disastrous decision to marry Rob, it was a tie, a commitment difficult to erode without making me feel guilty. And now Amélie loved you so we would have to work it all out. It was the riskiest element of my decision but I trusted in your love for my daughter and believed we would find a way. You had loved Celeste and you adored Amélie and I did not believe that anything could break the bond. A man of reason, I pushed you off the ledge and waited in faith.

CLAIRE

Six months after my divorce was finalised, Rob contacted me by means of a very humble and polite letter and asked if we

232

could meet (if I wanted I could bring a friend for support), as he wanted to express a few things as part of the "healing process." I was not afraid of him. Actually, I felt mostly nothing about him. I had no need to consider David's feelings and yes, perhaps almost to spite David (for I had no doubt he would find out about the encounter), I agreed to the idea.

I thought it over dramatic to have a friend chaperone me and to be frank had not confided in many of my so called friends about my shady past and elected instead for him to come to my Chambers. He could come to my office, much like a client and the whole event could be kept professional.

He turned up in his biking leathers. He had lost weight almost to the point of seeming frail but the same fair looks, charming smile and an American tan. He had settled there and this was just a brief holiday to sort out various, small matters. I was an item on that list. So small?

I did not suffer any horrible flashbacks on seeing him but just the thought that I might made me nervous, and I was glad to have the expanse of a substantial oak desk between us. He nodded at me and promptly sat down, avoiding an awkward handshake.

"Thanks for doing this Claire. I realise it was a big ask."

"Well, let's get on with it. You want to know that I will not judge you for all eternity for what you did, so let me reassure you there are no grudges. I totally understand that you were not in your right mind and I am pleased that you have managed to get help. Honestly, I wish you well."

I had instinctively adopted the voice of authoritative reason used on clients. I noted the odd emotional detachment I felt toward the man I had been married to. It was so apparent to me that I had never really loved him. He must have been reading my mind.

"Actually Claire, I wanted to try to understand why you wanted to marry me when you were in love with David and I suppose I am also left struggling to grasp why you two are not together. I've met Audrey by the way."

I clasped my hands together and straightened my back. These were the gestures that went before a speech about how I felt confident we could win this case in spite of various shortcomings.

"You said in the letter you wanted my forgiveness. You have it. Are you now suggesting that I might need yours?"

In the past, his forehead would have tensed as a preamble to irritation and from there short, sharp stepped increases to rage but he remained serene, unmoved.

"Perhaps, yes. You pressed for marriage but you loved my brother. Did you just use me to make him jealous or just to hurt him or what?"

My shoulders dropped. My hands pulled apart. The voice that came out of me sounded distant. It was smaller.

"I developed real feelings for you. I found you attractive, charismatic, exciting to be with. We had fun, didn't we? When I first met David I was practically a child, so unworldly and he was married of course. Later, after poor Celeste died and he got back in touch, I had a crush on him. If it was more than that, I certainly depended on *him*, being older and more experienced, to show me that. He advised me not to become involved with you but he just never made it clear that he was offering me love. In the end, it became one huge emotional tangle. Had you and I had an honest conversation about serious things such as finance and children and the future, we might still have been happy and you know Rob, you are still ten years older than me, so you need to take some responsibility for all that. As to why David and I are not together now, I think he needs to explain that. As far as I am concerned, he just gave up on me and Audrey is clearly ticking all the right boxes so good luck to them."

Just in those last few words, some more of the hatred spilled and every time it was as unpleasant as vomiting and left me exhausted. Would it ever end? I started to crave a drink, a familiar antidote.

Rob looked plainly sorry for me.

"So you still love him. I'm sorry, Claire. I hate to say it but I think Audrey is good for him and she is brilliant with Amélie. Does David love her? My brother is a closed book to me on that but I believe he still cares very much for you, perhaps just not in the way you want him to. You shouldn't have married me. That said, in the interests of closure, I would just like to say that I intend never to forget the good times Claire. Let's shake hands and part amicably, yes?"

He stood up and it caught me off guard. I suddenly recalled how I had once felt about him and now we were going to separate perhaps for the final time. It was this and not two signatures on a piece of paper that ended our connection. I was not ready but he was and perhaps I did need his forgiveness after all. So, I stood up, shook his hand, smiled kindly and let him leave. I slumped back in my chair and poured the first drink. As it vanished down my throat, I understood that the hatred and loathing I had been feeling towards David was more properly directed at myself. As a barrister I was lauded for my intelligence, skills and impeccable judgment but as far as my personal life went it had been an unmitigated disaster. I thought of Celeste and alabaster hearts and the intricacies of the game of human love and had she been there she could have made me laugh at the absurdity of it all but I was alone. I carried on drinking.

DAVID

It seems cruel to talk about how content my life became because of Audrey Hopper so I will spare you the details but you know me well enough to understand that "content" was rarely enough. Audrey grasped this about me, saw and disliked the restlessness but was sufficiently mature and wise to give it a long leash. Her love was by no means unconditional and I was obliged to make concessions in many domains but she never asked me to put her before my work, only that I prioritise my daughter and she very importantly accepted that I still loved you and would never let you go entirely. When Caroline Summers gave me worrying reports, Audrey encouraged me to express my anguish. Sometimes, I said I would have to go and see you and she never told me not to which was enough to stop me from doing exactly that. I waited. I endeavoured to be patient.

After Rob's visit to you, he told me how angry and hurt you were but was quick to stress just how perfectly likeable Audrey was and surely, in time, you would find someone else and be happy. Yet, it was my daughter that proved the chief sticking point. For all that she adored Audrey, she never forgot you. "When will we see Claire again?" was a regular, stinging question.

Audrey patiently endured the torment of this and waited for me to choose a course of action but I was stuck. After a decent amount of waiting she reasonably concluded that enough was enough.

"You know David. I've made an important decision. I'm going to go and see Claire and arrange some visits for Amélie. It's what your late wife wanted and it's obvious Amélie loves her."

"I'm not sure how she'll react to that."

"Well neither am I but I guess we'll find out, right?"

She had pushed her spectacles up into her hair. She was wearing long earrings and they danced against her cheeks. She looked lovely and it was this more than her decisive attitude which persuaded me to yield to the idea.

"Ok. Fair enough. See how you get on. Could be interesting. You will be kind to her?"

She came over, took me by the chin and planted an inoffensive kiss on my mouth.

"Sure thing. This is entirely about Amélie, as far as I am concerned. Trust me."

She walked off, ever the slender panther. What she felt about you was a mystery but I did trust her love for Amélie and I did not trust myself to see you, not yet.

CLAIRE

It was a very wet day but not cold. I was in Chambers, surrounded by papers, adopting my usual chaotic way of ordering a case in my head. It was not one of my more interesting cases but not entirely straightforward either and the weather did not aid motivation, nor the remnants of a hangover from a particularly intense drinking session the evening prior. The temptation to have another drink, with the excuse it would even me out was a very present gnawing at the back of my mind. I was aware that my drinking had grown problematic, and trying to pull back from the precipice, but this was in and of itself a constant irritation. I kept checking my watch without ever registering the time.

The clerk then appeared at my door and introduced my unexpected visitor, Ms Audrey Hopper. She ignored the stunned look on my face and set about clearing files from the chair on the other side of my desk. She positioned herself in said chair with the poise of a duchess and smiled at me serenely and it struck me that I would find her very likeable if I did not resent her so strongly.

"This is not a very convenient time to drop in unannounced. Is it something very important?"

"Yes, I can see you are busy. Apologies but this doesn't have to take long. Amélie would like to see you and I want to arrange visits."

"Why you? David afraid to show his face or are you the one

that's afraid?" She took her time before responding, all the while holding my gaze.

"David does feel kind of awkward yes though not afraid and no, I do not regard you as some kind of threat Claire. Would you prefer me to or can we just agree to be nice to one another?"

It pained me to admit it to myself but I liked her direct method of communication and she was an overall attractive package. The pig of it was that I had few close female friends and here was someone I would like to know better. I wanted to know her story and I was sure that David had every good reason to enjoy her company. Yet, still I blamed her for leading David away, as if she had cast some wicked spell over him which was of course absurd. I retreated into a business-like manner.

"What do you propose? I cannot imagine Amélie needs to see that much of me. I've grown rather boring. Once a month, a Saturday?"

"Why have you grown boring? An ambitious, brilliant career woman like you must know how to let her hair down in this city. You have interests, aside from work?"

I suddenly became self-conscious, as if I had forgotten to brush my teeth and my breath maybe smelled.

"My private life is hardly your concern. I really do need to get on with this case. First Saturday of every month, collect her at 11? Does she still love the zoo?"

She stared at me, as if doing so might reveal every secret. Yet, her expression was not unkind. I supposed her to be a self-possessed patient type. Unlike me.

"Ok let's try that then Claire. I am sure Amélie will be happy to do anything. She's devoted to you. I know things are still painful for you to process right now but you'll find a way to make your peace with David, for Amélie's sake. Even better if we could be friends, though I understand you might find that challenging. Here is my mobile number. Any change to the plan, just let me know."

She put a pink slip of paper on the desk and glided away. I stared at that piece of paper and then lifted it to my nose. There was no particular aroma, not of her, not of David, just the number. That was it then. She was officially the gate-keeper. It had been handled very smoothly.

Amélie was a huge injection of fun into my life. A combination of her mother's vivacity and charisma and her, open, curious and hilarious take on life rendered whatever we did together highly entertaining. I held the privileged position of only see-ing her in her leisure time, much like a divorcee that didn't get custody. Moreover, there was scarcely ever a need for me to chastise her, nor did I concern myself with correcting or im-proving her behaviour and to all intents and purposes we were mates and she was by far the best friend I had had for years. London, though still not a city I loved, offered endless possi-bilities and soon our monthly meetings became fortnightly. Audrey always greeted me when I arrived to collect her and was there again when we returned. Occasionally it occurred to me that my time with Amélie afforded her and David qual-ity time together and that I was complicit in growing their relationship, a relationship that continued to hurt me. In one particular regard I maintained superb self-control, never ask-ing Amélie anything about her father.

Beyond the joy of these outings, I began to pursue physical fitness as a distraction from the drinking and became suffi-ciently in shape to accept invitations to play squash which proved useful for networking too. Caroline Summers would manage to "bump" into me fairly regularly and I knew full well that this was David checking up on me and was extremely cautious about any information shared with her. The months passed and I managed to create an existence that was above endurable, seasoned with the occasional flirtation or one night stand but apart from Amélie my life was dry and love-less. It was a life lived by many professionals in that city and as long as I did not see David it allowed me to function.

Then, one Saturday, after a fabulous picnic in Hyde Park with my god-daughter which had involved lots of bubbles and run-ning and chasing, I returned her to the house and was greeted at the door by the very man. It was a June day, warm, condu-cive to a shut-down in national productivity and he was in-congruous in a suit and tie but the labelled luggage we pushed past in the entrance hall explained that this was him just re-turned from a business trip. The initial eye contact had been fleeting and as I followed him into the house I had a chance to slow my racing heart, repeating a well-used mantra "he's a middle-aged bastard. Get over him."

The dilemma was that I was still in love with this "middle-aged bastard." He was no less attractive to me and every memory of our shared past, every sinew of our connection remained intact. Believe me, I wanted Audrey to be there. I needed her to curtail the rush of feeling, to dampen the chem-ical attack pulsating through my veins but neither she nor Mrs Jones were at hand and Amélie was of no use. She was ecstatic to have the three of us together and her excitement escalated so that she began to jump around David until he sternly in-sisted that she go upstairs, change out of her barely muddy clothes and wash her hands. She resisted at first but then the orders were repeated in French and evidently that meant that she really must do as she had been told. As soon as she left, I felt pressed in on every side by conflicting emotions, enough to make me feel nauseous and uninvited, so I took a seat at the kitchen bar, relieved to have something to lean against. David silently uncapped two bottles of chilled beer and pushed one toward me. It may seem ridiculous but this casual, unroman-tic gesture confirmed for me that I was in love with this man. Nothing had really changed. With the feelings of love were woven the inevitable hurt and anger.

"You look very well Claire. Amélie always loves her time with you. I'm so glad she has you in her life."

"I do it for Celeste. It's what she wanted."

"Yes, yes of course. I hope that you enjoy being with her too and that it is not just some sort of duty."

"Duty? No, of course not. I do it out of love for Celeste and for Amélie. She's a great kid."

There followed an awkward silence in which the absence of my having included my love for David hovered like a cloud of musky perfume.

Amélie rushed in and redeemed us. She was hungry again and demanded that her Daddy make pancakes. There ensued a battle of wills centred on mealtime routines and Daddy's fatigue and lack of enthusiasm for such a project. She negotiated for a toasted teacake instead and purely to annoy him I insisted that I should like that too. He frowned at me and I just grinned back, the beer emboldening me to flirt a little. If I had to suffer, then he could too.

"Where's Audrey today?"

He had his back to me now, preparing the teacakes.

"Out with Mrs Jones, doing something. You were not expected back just yet. Neither was I. "

Ah, so I was to understand that this entire meeting was without the knowledge or approval of Audrey and was entirely by chance. He did not feel pressed to have me leave either, signalling that this was his home and the gatekeeper would have to deal with the lapse in security.

Amélie was colouring a picture, the scene a picnic at Hyde Park, with lots of bubbles and artistic license included David in the scene.

He turned and presented us with slightly singed teacakes. He had not made one for himself but licked the butter from his fingertips. It was actually quite a funny picture, him still dressed for a business meeting but immediately plunged into domesticity.

"Would Madam like tea with her teacake?"

"No thank you. The beer is an interesting combination. Cheers." I took a hearty swig. I was in danger of starting to relax and enjoy myself.

"Good. Well, if you'll excuse me ladies I think I'll take a shower and change. Don't feel you have to rush off Claire. Actually, I think Audrey wanted to discuss the summer holidays with you and the possibility of Amélie having a week in Brittany with you."

I put down the beer bottle, suddenly tense.

"Or we could have that discussion now, the two of us and you can just fill Audrey in later. You are authorised to do that, I presume?"

"Audrey has specific dates in mind and I do defer to her when it comes to holiday plans. If you don't mind, I've just got in after a long trip and I'd like to get changed out of this suit."

He was on edge. I had put him there. As he walked off it felt like a hollow victory.

I remained at the counter, half listening to Amélie as she chatted away, not much fancying the teacake but then prompted by the child to eat. I could hear the water system turn over as David showered. I could picture him, soaping himself. I wanted to go to him but it was impossible. Amélie insisted that I draw a picture too and I was half way through my pathetic attempt when Audrey and Mrs Jones arrived, loaded with shopping. Mrs Jones gave me the usual unemotional greeting and took charge of putting things away. Audrey had seen the luggage, could hear the shower and saw the three of us in Amélie's vivid picture.

"Claire, this is an unexpected surprise. Where's David?"

Amélie wanted attention and was happily oblivious to adult matters.

"Daddy is having a shower and Claire is drawing pictures with me. Do you want to draw one too?"

Audrey leant over and studied Amélie's picture more carefully, perhaps trying to determine quite how we had engineered to spend time blowing bubbles together.

"No thanks honey. Not just now but I love the colours of the bubbles and you've made Claire's hair very pretty. Please go and ask your Daddy what time he wants to have dinner and let him know we are back."

Amélie did just as she was told. She had a clear respect for Audrey.

"We had a lovely picnic today. David must have got back just before we did. He made us teacakes."

My report and the way I felt obliged to give it made me sound pathetic and perhaps even guilty.

"Great. You know Claire, I've been meaning to suggest it for a while but we two girls should have lunch together some time. What do you say?"

It struck me that neither of us was a girl, least of all her and this seemed obviously a manoeuvre aimed at keeping me in check. She intended to sound me out further and clarify the limitations of my connection with David. Perversely, I found myself fascinated by her and keen to accept. Perhaps I simply understood the importance of knowing my enemy although I despised the notion that David Sutton had two women competing for him. It did not occur to me that she had any genuine desire to be my friend.

"Sure. Why not? I have your number. Let me check my diary and get back to you. Talking of diaries, I had better get going. I'm meeting someone at half six."

I was meeting a female colleague for squash and drinks but I was fine with letting the "someone" be a point of speculation. Amélie rushed back in all flushed with excitement. Daddy wanted Claire to stay for dinner. Without bothering to see how Audrey received that news, I calmly repeated that I had plans and knelt down to hug and console an extremely disappointed child. It was important to leave before David could persuade me to stay and Audrey was more than willing to usher me out. Just before the door clicked behind me I heard David ask where I was. It was hard to say he sounded concerned. Certainly, he did not come after me.

I met up with Audrey about ten days later. She had a passion for London and had explored it extensively so I deferred to her knowledge when it came to choosing a venue. This turned out to be a small, Iranian establishment where we were required to sit on colourful cushions, surrounded by vibrant murals, the menu predominantly vegetarian. Fortunately, I had opted for the loose trousers and not the figure hugging pencil skirt. I liked her bohemian choice and the enormous, jade and orange beaded earrings which swung from her lobes like chandeliers. I thought of Celeste and how she would probably enjoy painting Audrey. She had scooped up her long silver hair into a casual bun and loose tendrils caressed her strong, elegant neck. I thought of David stroking it and kissing it.

She led us through a polite exchange about our setting, the weather and made some casual recommendations about the menu. I decided to order a soft drink and keep my wits about me.

We chinked glasses, only slightly awkwardly.

"This is just great Claire. It's so good to spend some time together. I really want to get to know you."

"You're very diligent about Amélie and her welfare. It's admirable." I was determined not to become her pal.

She had ordered a gin and tonic but took only small, measured sips.

"Oh well today, us meeting like this, it has little to do with Amélie you know. It's because David loves you and you are still in love with him, right?"

I was about to take a gulp of my soft beverage but stopped just in time, preventing a choking incident.

"Oh, oh ok. That's a very direct approach. Straight down to business eh?"

I suddenly felt squashed and uncomfortable on my cushion. There was simply no support. My legs seemed too long and awkward and I probably looked like a new-born foal contemplating the need to get up but still too weak.

She, by contrast, appeared queen-like and I wondered if she had practiced on cushions at home.

"This is not business, there are no agendas and I want to make it clear that I am not here to engage in some sort of pathetic battle over a man. I'm with David yes, but he doesn't belong to me, nor I to him, so I am not here to ward you off my property. I just hope that we can be friends."

"That's an odd proposition. Look, David has chosen you over me. If he loves me it's a weird way to show it. As for my feelings, yes, I still love him and despise myself for it. It's hopeless. I know."

The waiter arrived and placed various dishes before us. We held a polite silence, only the rather spiritual background music offering any respite from the tension. The waiter was probably glad to move away.

"There's nothing conventional about any of this is there? You met him when he was already married, a man twenty years older than you. Subsequently, you chose to marry his younger brother. David is with me yes, but I don't feel chosen. The choice was not to be with you. He sees this as doing the right thing and I find that understandable. I myself have never married and never intend to. That I admit is also not too conventional but I value my independence. We are two, intelligent strong women and we can decide how this all works out. I don't expect you to stop loving him but I need to understand what you want going forward."

What did I want? Did I want Audrey to disappear and to get back on track with David? What I felt I really wanted was something far less attainable. I wanted to rewind to the house in Scotland and I wished to stay and not run away and to have never written a cowardly letter about needing space. The moment had gone and perhaps there was simply no way back from that wrong turn or all the others, not least the impetuous marriage to Rob. Under Audrey's intense gaze, I realised I had only myself to blame for being alone. I could not just cease to love David Sutton but I could accept it was a lost cause and attempt to find love elsewhere.

"What I want is to get over David but still be in Amélie's life which is not going to be easy. I suppose I need to meet someone else. I see people but nothing ever comes of it."

It was strange yet helpful to be honest with her. I felt some relief. She made me be open with her. It was not my usual way and I marvelled at her subtle powers.

"What about the rest of your life? Do you enjoy your career?"

There it was, the moment that revealed everything to me. What she was doing, the same way David always had, was mentor me. I was an orphan, estranged from my family, my roots, lost in London. I saw the gulf of years, wisdom and experience spread open between us and it made me giddy with vertigo.

"Look Audrey, you may be old enough to be my mother but I am not looking for one. I don't want David to be like a father to me either. I left my real parents a long time ago and to be honest I am pretty done with the whole parental thing. If you want us to be friends, well I am not sure we can be. Let's aim for amicable associates. Yes, let's try for that."

She saw it then, I am certain. She saw past my appearance and my age and what she understood of my vulnerability, the cherished "Waif" and her mind's eye falling upon that something else which Celeste had adored, ramparts of strength and resolve guarding it all. She saw my potential, felt its energy. She smiled. It was a smile that said "I yield", though I did not doubt that the woman opposite me possessed her own remarkable resources and this was only a temporary surrender.

"Ok Claire. I'll drink to that. Come on, let's eat. It all looks so delicious."

So we ate and it all tasted good and whatever questions I asked her about her business, family life and birth country she graciously answered and by the end of the meal, I understood perfectly why she had been allowed into David's life. What was not to like? Yet, to like is not to love and I held on tightly to that notion, though to do so was a kind of torture.

DAVID

I postponed returning to my home in Scotland for a while but a visit there was inevitable. It had become "your house", the place I returned to in my imagination whenever you crept into my thoughts. Though Celeste had died there, for me she was in her beloved France, her energy, passion and dark beauty at rest in a cemetery bordered by fields of lavender and sunflower. Whereas you were in the passenger seat of my car, heading up a Scottish driveway. Or giving a speech at the dining table whilst holding an orange, ridiculously poised and confident. You stared down from a wall, monochrome and stylised, breath-taking in your youth and beauty. You glanced about the loch from a rowing boat, slightly overwhelmed. You were hung-over and pale in my office but still defiant. You were naked and yearning but not quite mine beneath those floral sheets, rain dripping somewhere. These scattered thoughts and images always concluded with that cleverly composed letter of escape and then the drunken episode in London and my decision to release you or me or us. More rarely, I allowed myself to remember you on a beach, flying a kite with my daughter, a time when you offered yourself up to me, but that was the most precious and most painful moments combined, and it hurt to remember Brittany perhaps more than anything.

Celeste had once remarked on Mrs Stewart's talent for the perfect placement of objects, a vase of flowers positioned at just the right angle or intersection, a bronze bust in an aptly lit corner. Now, as though you were my possession, I wrestled over where to put you, not in the principal drawing room of my life but in a favourite occasional room, reserved for quiet introspective days. Crucially, I could not dispose of you. You were a valued treasure. Arrangements in London were awkward and temporary and Audrey was pushing me to make a better plan.

So it was that I needed to return to Scotland, with so much on my mind. Audrey wanted to see the house, of course. Our relationship was tenuous, intimate and connected yet so faintly defined and there was no strict convention which compelled me to invite her along, yet not to do so would create unhelpful suspicion and intrigue. Amélie was asked if she would to like to go but she declined. Audrey felt strongly that my daughter should go but I was not for leading Amélie to what seemed dark waters and making her drink. Her mother had died there. She would go when she was ready.

I eventually set off to Scotland with Audrey, my golf clubs and some sense that I would need to decide on the future of that great house.

Audrey is the sort of American who gives a grudging respect to the history and heritage of Britain and remained tight-lipped as we pulled up in front of the house, but this degree of control crumbled as we entered the hall, greeted warmly and yet all so correctly by Mrs Stewart. In that space, you can smell the history and it knocked her sideways. Her eyes expanded trying to comprehend it all. Then of course her eyes came to fall upon the portrait of you.

"My God, is that...?"

"Yep. Claire. Celeste painted it. What do you think?"

She moved closer and took a while to study it or you.

"Well, I am no art expert but I am guessing it is not considered your late wife's best work. There is no denying Claire's youthful beauty though."

"Yes, still at university then." I did not disguise the enchantment very well and awkwardly began to fuss with our hand luggage. Audrey's eyes were now upon me.

"Of course, she still IS very lovely. No wonder you fell for her."

I went over to her. She did look very old then and yet somehow this made me feel protective.

"Look, my feelings for Claire are what they are which is pretty complicated but it is you and me here now, so let's try to forget what is in the past, including Celeste as well. I want you to enjoy being here and love it the way I do."

What a ridiculous idea it sounded, to forget the past when the entire building was set into it. Audrey sliced me with her razor, blue eyes, not someone to be deflected or managed.

"Well, I can certainly do my best but I want to understand the past. Did Celeste love this house and what does it mean to Claire?"

"I don't think I should try to speak for Claire but as for Celeste, she was not so very fond of here. She laughed at me for wanting such a huge place. She said the light upstairs was good for painting. Of course, she ended her life here so that says a lot."

At this she stepped back from me, clearly shocked. Mrs Stewart appeared with a tea tray and scones and was perhaps sur-

249

prised to see that we had not progressed from the hall, or was it just the expression on Audrey's face and now an awkward silence? In her professional manner, she cheerily persuaded us to enter the sitting room, deposited the tray and made a suitably quick exit.

Audrey had sat down but was perched, ready to flee. The teapot was ignored.

"David, I thought, or at least I had assumed that Celeste died as the result of an accident."

"Yes and that was the coroner's verdict, that she went out in bad weather, got into difficulties and drowned. However, it is my belief that she went out to deliberately end her own life. She was emotionally imbalanced, especially after the birth of Amélie, though trust me, I very much want to believe the coroner."

"Well some women can be really affected by childbirth but you think that even prior to that she had problems? What do you mean?"

There are times in life when a teapot can prove a very helpful distraction and I started on serving tea as if this was the most natural of my offices and contemplated whether Audrey would get more truth than you. We had never fully discussed my late wife's obsession with you, or her peculiar ideas about our previous lives, nor much of the manner of her death.

"Well, she was an artist. She could be intense and she had a vivid imagination. After Amélie was born, I should have sought more expert advice but what did I really know? I always had Mrs Jones or Mrs Stewart keep an eye on her. I'm not really sure what happened that day. Maybe the coroner was right. She adored Amélie. Why would she abandon her? Do you mind if we don't dwell on it any further?"

I presented Audrey with a scone and a cup of tea. For a moment she regarded me as if I were losing my mind.

"Ok. I'm not hungry though David. Thank you. Perhaps you could tell me where to find a bathroom?"

So, Audrey took herself away from me to think it all over and I went to my study for a cigarette and a whiskey. What a horrible mistake to take Audrey to that house. For a while, even I hated its silence but then I summoned Mrs Stewart and had her update me on things and I rediscovered the love of it all and came to the simplistic conclusion that the house just needed a new dog to reanimate it, two even. One of the game-keepers had just acquired a litter of cocker spaniels, not my preferred breed but they would be patient with Amélie. I took Audrey with me and allowed her to choose and for a while we were happily distracted but I knew that Audrey would never love that place. It was full of ghosts.

I decided to take Audrey to Turnberry which she loved. She had played golf in the States and was naturally competitive. When we returned to the house, she tried to lose herself in the business of puppies or walked the grounds, content to chat to the gardener and expand her knowledge of British shrubbery. One day it rained very hard and she asked Mrs Stewart to talk her through the collection in the library. We spent that time together like an old married couple and there was a tangible lack of passion.

The house was costing me a fortune to run, the revenue from the estate hardly adequate. To keep it was folly but I was not ready or capable of letting go. Like you, it was in my blood now. One sombre evening, after a meal neither Audrey nor I had much enjoyed and when we were most of the way through a second bottle of wine, she finally found the courage to challenge me again.

"So tell me, what do you think you will do with this place? It deserves to be a happy home but do you think it ever can be?"

"One day yes, perhaps. I've had an offer to lease out the shooting rights. That would free up a lot of capital to carry out maintenance and I could reduce the staff. I've already spoken to Mrs Stewart about it. Either way, I can't easily justify keeping this place but I don't think I can stomach letting it go, not yet. I'm determined to bring Amélie here for Christmas. I'd like you too of course and well, you could invite your family naturally. I'm sure they'd love it."

"And Claire?"

"Claire? She has been invited before. She seems to prefer Christmas alone but I will invite her I suppose."

"What about her own family?"

"She walked out on them a long time ago. She has come from nothing, you know. She's a fighter."

I stopped myself from adding that this was what I loved about you, partly out of consideration to Audrey and partly because it was only one of several things.

Audrey lit a cigarette. She was not in the habit of ever smoking and it signalled that she was about to surprise me in other ways.

"You know, there was a book missing from a collection in the library and I happened to find it today, amongst some things of Celeste. She had made notes and well, to get to the point, seems like she thought you had lived here before, in another life, married to another version of her and the most far-fetched bit being that Claire had been your brother and the three of you were in some very dramatic love triangle. The photo of the brother carries some bizarre resemblance to Claire but of course the entire theory is ridiculous and well, slightly deranged. Did you know about it?"

I wanted a cigarette too but refrained. I made every effort to look Audrey in the eye.

"Yes, Yes I did. I'm not sure I am happy about you going through my wife's things but putting that aside, what of it? I told you my wife had a vivid imagination."

"Oh well, let me assure you I have been very proper. I did not "go through her things." I asked Mrs Stewart to accompany me to check if the book had been placed with them. David, the story aside, you must see that it is not a good thing for you to hang on to this place."

Now I began to feel a threat and anger rose in me.

"Thank you for your concern but I'm not ready to sell it and allow strangers to inhabit it."

Audrey seemed to regard my anger as though it were a curious fault in my genes and was calm and not to be deflected.

"Have you considered a third option? Why don't you give this magnificent house a fresh purpose? It can be a temporary thing, just maybe let some time pass. Celeste was an artist, so what about allowing the house to be used by artists, as a retreat? You could set up some sort of charitable trust and manage it that way. It could even be for artists from a struggling background, a therapeutic and nurturing setting."

"Wow, you *have* been busy. You are also sticking your neck out."

She inhaled and blew smoke unashamedly toward me.

"I don't think I have anything to lose. Frankly, you can and will do exactly what you choose and I shall do the same. It is how we two are, isn't it? We are both too old to mess about. I'm not sure what kind of future we have, if any, but I know it can't be tied up here. If it were me, I would listen to the wishes of Amélie's family in France and consider educating her there, not in London. You have a beautiful house there, Europe is expanding for business all the time. You can get an apartment in Paris as a base and fly down to be with Amélie whenever. If you don't want to sell this place, well you have my suggestion."

"I'm sorry, are you saying you want to move to France with me?"

"Oh no, well I haven't decided on *that* yet. I am certainly not in love with this place though and I already have plans for Thanksgiving and Christmas thank you. I'll be in the States. I'm not inviting you because I think it would be better for you to spend Christmas with your daughter and find out what she wants. Whilst you're at it, you may want to talk to Claire and decide once and for all where she fits into the equation, for her sake as much as yours."

I laughed. She was impressive and I had underestimated her. I was not laughing *at* her, it was a nervous reaction to her audacity, her plain talking. She understood this and for a while we both laughed. There was also a clear sense of relief.

"Ok ok. I hear you, loud and clear. Believe me, I am going to think about everything you have said. I respect you Audrey. You are an extraordinary woman and now with your permission, I would like us to go to bed."

Perhaps it should have been you going up to bed with me but your portrait was disregarded as we climbed the stairs and you did not appear again until the early hours. I thought of you as Audrey lay sleeping next to me. What was to become of us? In every equation I tested, you were an integral part. Nothing would balance without you.

CLAIRE

I didn't really have much appetite for the Law Society fundraiser that year and was inclined to just write out a cheque and rehearse some good excuses. However, a senior partner popped his head in to say that it had been unanimously agreed at a meeting I had missed that we should put in a strong appearance this year and tickets had been block booked in anticipation. His hard, fixed stare signalled that any resistance would be futile. He liked to regularly remind me that I was a sparkling jewel in their crown. He meant that I was an attractive woman and my percentage of wins was still above average. He chose to ignore any rumours about a bottle of scotch in my desk drawer, the days when I was grey with exhaustion. Being thirty years my senior I think he thought I was practically invincible and the stats sheets told him what he wanted to hear. He liked to dance with me and had bad breath. My job depended on being able to think quickly and adapt so I explained that yes, of course I would be going but I had already agreed to go with a public school chap from a rival firm, the sort of person he would want me to "mingle with." He would know his father naturally. If we could lure him over, he would be a prize. He was right to be shocked but I had convinced him. The younger man in question was pretty stunned himself when I later called him and asked him to be my partner at the event. He had flirted with me for months, with no success. Of course, he said yes.

I was going to wear black but something made me choose the green dress, one of those dresses a woman buys in a spontaneous head rush and which often stays on the hanger, label attached because the confidence to wear it never returns. It was the kind Celeste might have chosen for me, with a funny speech about the winning ways of a woman's back. I almost lost the courage but my date arrived early and eager. I felt his hand graze my back very lightly as I stepped towards his car.

Three quarters of that evening was dull, almost boring though I smiled on cue, laughed at all the jokes, navigated the treacherous waters that can be the company of men, the cool stares of some women mere raindrops against my glass exterior. There were a few friendly faces here and there but I must have checked the large, wall clock a ridiculous number of times. I was leaning against the bar, easing some of the strain from my poor cramped toes, trying to decide if another drink would make any material difference to the passage of time. Then, I yawned, a huge gaping one, no attempt to repress or disguise it. A hand took me by the elbow and I instantly blushed, embarrassed to be such a disobliging date. I turned to apologise, thinking that it wasn't my fault I was numb with boredom but perhaps he deserved better. It was David.

"Oh David. Bloody hell, it's you. I didn't know you were here. Where's Audrey?"

"In America, doing Thanksgiving. I came as a favour to Caroline. I am an expert at disguising the boredom, unlike you. Would you care for a dance?"

I was still so flustered that I just said yes. I took his arm and he led me away from the bar to the dance floor. We passed my date on the way. He was getting hammered with old school friends but looked a little perturbed as I glided past.

The band were banging out something lively and I was about to apologise for my poor dance skills but my partner launched me out, pulled me back in, twisted and twirled me and though it was apparent that he certainly could dance and I clearly was inept, I found myself laughing and unable to resist and thanks to him we put on a passable performance. That music ended and I rubbed my sides which were aching from the laughter. Some slower music began and he pulled me in closer, positioning my hands like any dance tutor would and it was entirely natural to rest my head against him. We didn't speak. We swayed in some kind of magical mist and as the music progressed I began to feel afresh the agony of losing him, of being cast off. What was this moment to him? I wanted to let tears fall, I wanted to play him, longed to manipulate him but when the music stopped and we looked at each other, my eyes were dry. Nothing.

"I think I had better go and find Caroline."

"Yes of course, you should. That was lovely and fun. Thank you."

He lifted my hand, kissed it and then squeezed it. It was the parting of an old friend.

"Take care Claire. Enjoy the rest of your evening."

He stared across the dance floor which made me turn and look.

My date was approaching. When I turned back, David had walked away. My date planted an unwanted kiss on my shoulder but I managed not to recoil.

"Someone said that was David Sutton. Filthy rich business guy. How do you know him?"

"Oh you haven't done your research. I was married to his brother and I was friends with his late wife. I'm god-mother to his daughter as it happens."

"Really? I didn't think a girl like you would have such connections. Makes you even sexier."

I gave him my most withering stare.

"Does it? Shame. Any man that underestimates me is a bit of a turn off. Sorry, but you will have to do better. I'm very bored so I am off. Good evening."

Though all I could think about was having danced with David, I managed to enjoy walking away from my crest-fallen partner. I caught a taxi home. Before I removed the green dress, I was pleased to observe that I had looked rather good. I hoped that David agreed.

DAVID

When Caroline asked if I might be her plus one at the Law Society Ball, I was inclined to say no but Audrey was there too and insisted that I acquiesce to doing the gallant thing. Caroline had requested if she could "borrow" me and there was something undignified about the arrangement but I realised it meant I would probably see you so I offered only minimal resistance. I am not sure if Audrey subsequently made the connection but she departed for her homeland in good spirits.

On the evening in question, Caroline decided to mention you, in the car en route to the venue.

"So, I suppose Claire is likely to put in an appearance this evening."

I stared away, out of the window to avoid her scrutiny of my face.

"Yes, probably. Let's play it cool. No need to go out of our way to say hello. I should like to observe her a little first."

"Really? What will you be looking for?"

"I don't know. I suppose I just want her to seem happier than the reports you have been feeding me."

"You don't owe her anything David. You have nothing to feel guilty about."

This made me turn to look at her. Caroline had always been a straight talker and her opinion would always matter to me.

"It is not a matter of conscience. I still love her."

Her brows bunched. She was perplexed.

"I really thought it was all about Audrey now. I thought you were moving on."

"Honestly Caroline, I am very fond of you and admire you for many reasons but when it comes to matters of the heart you do rather see things in black and white."

"Surely there is nothing else more black and white? Either you love her and want to be with her, in spite of everything, or you do not. It is reasonable to be concerned for her welfare but that is not the kind of love we are talking about is it?"

"No, when I say that I love her I mean absolutely that I love her. It's not a sort of kindness or goodwill thing. I love her enough to know that being together is no longer the best thing for her, or me. I had hoped that she would enjoy her career and meet someone else, someone younger of course. It's early days. "

"Look, I've told you, everything I have heard and seen with my own eyes. The job is going to burn her out. She drives herself too hard. I certainly don't think another man is what she needs, though there are plenty trying."

Our driver had pulled over and was opening the door and so we left the conversation there. Caroline didn't strictly require a plus one. As soon as we entered we found ourselves surrounded by her colleagues and friends. Our table was tucked away from the main section and you were easy to spot in that lovely, green dress. You looked thin but radiant. I enjoyed watching you though I could see past every smile, every forced bit of laughter. Perhaps you were not blatantly miserable but you were almost certainly bored. Maybe this was just a sign of your maturity? Was it inevitable that you should discover life's limitations and that the curiosity, exuberance and sparkle of youth should diminish? I might have convinced myself that I was in love with the idea of you and less so your actual, mature self, but then every time that chap stroked your back and you moved away, I felt a strange sort of relief. I held back, I bided my time but there was no question of me avoiding you altogether.

I chose my moment carefully, waited until you were alone at the bar. Just for a moment, I saw Waif in your eyes and our dancing together, well it was fun wasn't it? Then, when the music slowed and you leant against me, I felt the defeat; you were broken or we were broken, hollowed out by every bad decision, trampled by every part of circumstance which had conspired against us. Celeste, Rob, your pride and my pride and fear where there had needed to be trust. I loved Audrey but it was nothing like this. Whichever way I looked at things though, I could not escape my own wisdom, carved into me. If I loved you and loved myself even a little, then nothing had changed. The moment, the opportunity for "us" had passed.

I left you on the dancefloor but because I loved you so very much I was prepared to make one last effort to secure your happiness and Audrey had planted the seed. I had it in my power to move you away from London and to give you a fresh start but you would have to surrender to me, fully, properly. It seemed improbable but I decided I would try.

Audrey returned from the States, energised, renewed. She had no strong desire to return to live in her native country but she needed the occasional fix of its culture and she thrived on short, intense doses of her family. She would return again for Christmas. So far, I had not been introduced as her partner.

We were having a lazy Sunday morning, strong coffee and blankets of newspaper. Amélie was watching a cartoon, transfixed.

"I made a decision David."

"Oh?"

"If you go to France, I'll come with. You WILL try to talk to Amélie about it during the holiday?"

I removed the spectacles I had started to need.

"Yes and actually I have started to have people look at that idea for Scotland."

She was taken aback. It wasn't very often I could do that to her. I saw her mind conjecture and process rapidly.

"Wow! I really didn't think you would go there. What has made you decide to think about it?"

I did not need to be honest with her at that stage but I was not willing to play a game of cards over this.

"If the idea has any wings, I am going to ask Claire to head it up."

Now she was more than taken aback. She had never foreseen this move. She was better at composure than you, her feelings speedily handled. Only a momentary flash in her eyes gave anything away.

"Ok. That's a strange idea. I mean, what would persuade her to leave London and her successful career for a job that really has nothing to do with any of that?"

"Claire isn't happy. Caroline thinks she will burn out and I happen to agree. She loves the house in Scotland, she certainly loved Celeste and the notion of doing something to honour her might appeal. I agree, she may not leap at it to begin with but I want to at least give her the choice."

She folded the newspapers carefully and thoughtfully, without comment.

"If you don't support the idea Audrey, please, now is the time to say so."

"It is a very kind and loving gesture David and I would not dream of telling you not to do it. If you truly believe it would be good for Claire and I mean PRIMARILY good for Claire, then go ahead. I agree with you that she probably won't accept and I'd respect her for that."

I began to blush. Audrey could do that to me. She was fierce.

"You think she still loves me?"

"Yes, David, of course she does and you still love her. You want your damn cake and eat it and I hope she sees that."

I slammed down my coffee cup. The situation was running away from me.

"If that is really how you see this, then why do you stay?"

She stood up. Her hair was loose and she was like some powerful goddess about to pronounce judgment.

"You mean why don't I ask you, no DEMAND that you put her out of your life? Well, apart from the fact that your daughter loves her, I guess I just keep hoping that you will figure out the difference between loving someone and possessing someone."

"I have never tried to possess you."

"Well that has kinda been the deal from the start. You don't get to possess me."

"I would never cheat on you. What I feel for Claire is not like that anymore. I made a choice. She knows that."

Amélie had now stopped watching the cartoon and was staring at us, aware that something was happening.

"Make the proposal David. Do as you wish. Amélie, would you like to go for a walk? Shall we go check out the pond?"

Whilst they went off to do that, I should have been thinking about you and examining my motives for trying to lure you away to Scotland but in truth I had made that decision already and nothing would dissuade me. I actually felt strangely uplifted. Audrey may have tried to dress it up as woman to woman solidarity but it seemed to me that she was jealous, and that was a betrayal of her depth of feeling for me, and to be loved by Audrey Hopper was no mean feat. Did I want my cake and eat it? If she were a cake then I wanted more. I could not think of you as cake. Never did, never would.

CLAIRE

David wrote and invited me to spend Christmas with him and Amélie in Scotland. There was no mention of Audrey. It felt like a complicated, stressful situation and I had already decided to spend a quiet Christmas in Brittany. If he had come to see me and leant on my desk and I had looked into his eyes, I could have been seduced. I was still processing fleeting images of dancing with him and then leaning on his shoulder and memories of his smell were particularly unhelpful. Besides, we had a tradition of me not spending Christmas with him. I was so worn out by life and one needs energy to overturn traditions.

So, I spent Christmas walking on cold beaches and actually thinking a lot about Celeste. In particular, I thought again about the fact that she had painted me as a mermaid. A dangerous temptress? To David or to her? I decided the mermaid had to go, though Amélie would be cross and I worked hard to cover it with cream paint. I knocked in several picture hooks and covered the wall with framed photos of local scenes but in strong light I could still see a faint shadow of the painting. Celeste would always be in my life, like a shadow. For the most part however, I was alone, felt alone and it was a tonic to my weary soul. This was not the loneliness of London.

It was two days after Christmas and I was walking into a stiff, cold wind, all hunched up yet exhilarated and then I saw them, Amélie running and laughing and David chasing her and then the two of them waving at me.

Amélie arrived first and in her usual manner threw herself at me and spoke at me, fast, over excited and of course all I could do was appear overjoyed. She grabbed my hand and made me run towards her Daddy, though I did my best to not seem too keen.

"Hello Claire. Merry Christmas. Sorry about the intrusion but we are headed to the French family for New Year and we thought it might be rude not to pop and see you and well, we have your presents with us."

I laughed. It was hard not to.

"Well, I didn't think Brittany was on the way to the south of France!"

"Well, let's face it, Brittany isn't on the way to anywhere much and actually we are meeting the family in the Alps. Same country right? They want Amélie to ski with them."

More laughter. All of us. It felt so good.

"Ok well it's freezing. Let's get up to the house. I don't have much food in or anything."

David had brought food of course and insisted on cooking, whilst Amélie made me open my presents and though it was warm inside I was obliged to put on the penguin sweater and the even more ridiculous woolly hat. Thankfully, I thought that they would not be staying and she would not see the vanished mermaid.

After eating too much, we were content to sit around the woodstove and Amélie amused us with the curious anecdotes of her life. Then, David insisted she draw me a Christmas picture and she was installed at the kitchen table to produce the required masterpiece. I put on some Christmas music to help inspire her.

When I joined David again, he produced a large brown envelope.

"Happy Christmas Claire."

"What is it?"

"Open and see. It's just an idea at the moment but I hope you will like it."

Inside were some drawings of the house in Scotland and plans for interior alterations and then a rough draft of a business proposal. I was shaking, somehow suddenly anxious and it was hard to grasp any details but it seemed that David was planning to turn the house into some sort of Artists Retreat and all in memory of his late wife, Celeste Aubia Sutton.

"It, it looks incredible David. I mean, what a wonderful idea and a very generous one but I don't get it entirely. I mean, how is this a gift to me?"

"Well, I need someone bright, intelligent and driven to head it all up and I want to offer you the job. Of course, it will come with a very attractive package. Strong talent costs."

I must have stared down at those papers for only a few further seconds but it felt like minutes of impenetrable, stunned silence. I did not dare look up at him.

"But I have a career. I'm a barrister and bloody good at it actually and I have a house and a life in London."

"You hate London. I know you." Those particular words cut me.

"Ok, I won't pretend I love the city but I love my career and I like seeing Amélie at weekends…"

He hushed his voice now.

"Amélie is going to go to school in France."

Now I looked up, shocked.

"You're sending her away?"

"Well, she will have her French family close by and I will be moving to Paris so I can fly down any time. Naturally she can holiday here in Brittany with you."

It was taking a while for all this information to slot together but I was smart enough and a picture was emerging.

"And will Audrey be joining you in Paris?"

"She has decided she will, yes."

"Ah so all you need now is for the other woman to agree to go quietly to Scotland and your conscience is clear. I see."

If this annoyed him, he managed to remain calm, implacable.

"Yes, Audrey said you might see it that way. Look, you're going to burn out in London and this is an amazing opportunity I'm gifting you and only a fool would let pride be a stumbling block."

"Pride?" I found his stupidity breath-taking.

Amélie rushed in and leapt into my lap, crushing the papers which I made no effort to rescue. She waved a beautiful picture in front of me, the three of us next to a Christmas tree which was absurdly on the beach but in a child's world everything is possible and easy.

Despite my efforts, I had started to cry, silent, furious tears. I didn't care if the child saw them. She should know how cruel her father could be. One day, she would know what it felt to be controlled by him. She put up her hand and touched them, mortified.

"Don't you like my picture?"

"Oh I love it darling. These are tears of happiness but you know I am also very tired and I think maybe you and Daddy need to continue your journey."

David looked devastated. He had not been prepared for this depth of emotion.

"We had planned to stay the night and travel tomorrow but I can see how tired you are. We'll find somewhere near the airport." His tone was flat, lifeless.

I stood up and let the papers cascade to the floor. I picked up Amélie and hugged her and kissed her and told her I would see her soon and that I could not wait to hear all about the skiing, how exciting it all sounded. She was crying too now, just softly. She knew that there was suddenly unhappiness in the room and then she gave her Daddy an angry glare, her childlike instincts so powerful. Daddy had spoiled the game.

He made no effort to redeem the situation. He was not accustomed to failing at much but he knew when to accept that a battle had been badly lost and retreat was the only option.

Later, I burned the papers one by one. I needed to exorcise the very notion and yet the papers had been duly served and it was just possible that this summons could not be ignored, only postponed. Time would now test my resolve. Christmas would soon be over and the New Year loomed dark and grey. When I arrived back in London I found another envelope from a solicitor. My mother was dead. She had wanted me to know that I was unforgiven. I wanted not to give a damn but of course I did. For a while I wallowed in self-pity and considered myself cursed but the machinery of law must keep turning and my New Year's resolution was to work even harder. It was my only means to grace.

PART SEVEN

CLAIRE

After that, I carried on working in London for about another two years. That's how long it took for David to be proved correct and for me to burn out. It was a toxic blend of the demanding work, an ungratifying social life, too much booze (the restraint had not endured) seasoned with a kind of loneliness that ran through to my very marrow and yes, the tangy taste of bitterness. I continued to despise an image of David which stood centre stage in my imagination like a cold, marble mausoleum which I was compelled to visit over and over again. He was that hard, impenetrable structure and buried inside my unfulfilled love, unreachable. The real David Sutton was only an occasional visitor in my life. I saw him but once or twice a year depending on Amélie's visits to Brittany. He was kind, civil, concerned for me and bore scant resemblance to the man I felt inextricably linked to. He executed this detachment ruthlessly. Every time we were scheduled to meet, I prepared myself to launch an emotional ambush, to declare my deep and abiding love for him because of course it was this love which made me despise him. I wanted to shatter the status quo but something in his demeanour deterred me every time and so I felt a renewed loathing. It was an exhausting and appalling circle of damaged emotions. I actually resorted to seeing a counsellor but it became evident that I simply was not committed to "moving on".

All the while, David's offer of a job in Scotland lingered, never spoken out loud between us but it had survived its virtual form to be a phantom brown envelope marked "open in emergencies", grubby at the edges where my mind kept fingering it, trying so hard to resist.

It was on a suitably dark, damp, inhospitable February evening when I finally reached out to Caroline Summers, to begin the surrender proceedings. I confessed the sin of desperation to which she was sympathetic and above all she was a reliable and efficient envoy. I hated London, I was losing my way with the career and I was exhausted. Would she speak to David and ask if by any chance the opportunity in Scotland were still available? In fact, any opportunity would suffice, though I did go to the trouble of making a flimsy list of terms and conditions, as if this were some sort of regular business transaction. She did not ask me why I did not approach David personally because she understood perfectly and her discretion was a solid given so I had no need to refer to Audrey.

A few days later, she came to see me. She was only momentarily horrified by the scruffy pyjamas, my evident weight loss and ashen complexion and presented me with a hefty, detailed contract of employment which against her advice I signed unread, with it a letter, handwritten, from my new boss.

Dear Claire,

Of course the job was still yours. No question. There will clearly need to be a staged hand-over with the present incumbent, an old friend Mike Grainger who will be delighted and relieved to step away from what I have kept insisting was a temporary assignment. Please take your time to make the transition to what I hope will be a challenging yet fulfilling role for someone with your vast array of talents. Once you have sorted your affairs in London, I insist that you take at least 3 weeks holiday. Mrs Stewart has now retired but I enclose her address should you wish to visit her, something I know she would be pleased about.

Mike has put together a strong and highly skilled team but naturally you are free to consider changes. My next scheduled visit there is at the end of March for the end of financial year review and I shall look forward to perhaps seeing you at that meeting. Mike will stay until the end of April/beginning of May but only for as long as you find helpful.

Celeste would be delighted to have you on board. We have developed a fantastic place for aspiring artists in which to explore and develop their potential, many from under privileged backgrounds and with you in charge, I am confident the project will continue to blossom.

I know that this has been a very difficult decision for you and has taken enormous courage. I am, as ever, enormously proud of you.

With Love,

David

It was friendly, respectful, slightly paternal. The parts I found myself stuck on were "temporary assignment" and "Celeste would be delighted." David knew me and had waited, patiently. He had let me circle in the futile canopy of trees that was my London life, confident that it was only a matter of time and the little bird would weary and descend to perch in the pretty, gilt aviary he had carefully prepared. I was willing to concede that it was bigger than a cage. I had signed the contract and soon I would be held and secure. Would Celeste be delighted? My first reaction was to say "no". She would be disappointed at me, yielding to David's plan and it was all together too safe and predictable. Yet, I was troubled by another perspective. I was going to return to the house where first she had beguiled me and the three of us had rowed out in a boat. It seemed that my entire story was bound up in those powerful opening lines.

DAVID

I should say something about how I felt when you reached out to me and asked for the job in Scotland. Do you suppose that it felt like a moment of victory and that I toasted it smugly with a glass of my favourite malt? No, I felt initially relief. Watching you had felt like having to see fire destroy a priceless structure but finally a part of you had emerged and you were not beyond saving. My other feelings, they were deeper and more complicated and it was necessary not to explore them too much around Audrey. I kept them buried but secure like a pile of old love letters. Just a few weeks prior to you signing the contract, Rob had remarried in the States and Audrey had finally agreed for me to meet her children and there was a sense in which everybody was moving on apart from you. Even Amélie spoke of you less. In truth, I was not moving on quite so much either. If there was a clear emotion other than the relief then it was joy but it was managed, not allowed to shine forth. I wrote you a courteous, kind letter. The problem was this. I loved you more than Audrey but I loved Audrey very much. When I saw her with her children, on her own territory I appreciated just how magnificent she was but I realised this was her entirety whereas you were still elusive, had never truly been mine and you were an unfinished masterpiece. What did I want to do? What was the honourable thing to do? Was I honourable? With each passing week, I grew into a tangled torment. Audrey saw it expressed in a type of distraction and irritability and assumed this was a male, midlife crisis. To almost endorse her theory, I bought a Vespa and insisted we whizz around Paris on it which she found very entertaining. I concentrated on loving her and hoped that the resurgence of my feelings for you would pass.

CLAIRE

As David's employee, Mrs Stewart had always been a little stern, efficient and understandably guarded. She had stayed at David's request, in the early stages of the redevelopment of the house, tending to the domestic requirements of Mike Grainger but then happily retired into an ample cottage in the nearest village, a home in which she finally gave full expression to herself. Not for her lace trimmed chair coverings or crochet cushion covers. She was a woman of refined and progressive taste and proudly displayed over her mantelpiece one of Celeste's early abstract paintings. I am not sure if she appreciated that it was now worth thousands but it was daily enjoyed.

I arrived, not the wet and bedraggled orphan of what seemed a prior era, nor a bruised and battered wife but now just tired, defeated, clinging on to hope, the hope of something. She made tea and I apologised for my habit of being rather a pathetic case but she just laughed it away and it was wonderful to warm myself on her contentment and her steady, centred existence. She quickly made it clear that she no longer worked for David and there would be no proprieties between us. She intended to speak frankly.

"I think it is just grand that you are going to take charge because I know your connection with the late Mrs Sutton, poor thing, well I know it is genuine and well, to begin with I was horrified at the plans but I will admit it has given that old house a fresh purpose and put a few ghosts to bed. Mr Sutton is deeply fond of you and this is a wonderful opportunity he is giving you but if you want my advice and I will give it anyway, then you should look forward now and not back. Make this your thing and be strong and independent."

"You mean forget the fact that I still love him?"

The former Mrs Stewart would have held her counsel here and retreated behind the blank face of servitude but she was enjoying her freedom and expressed it to the full.

"Aye, I know. If you give yourself time and you settle on it, then you will find a way to see him differently and maybe even find love somewhere else."

"You don't think he and I belong together then?" It sounded absurd even as I said it.

"In my opinion, there is not one right way to go in life but some paths will be easier and from what I have seen of Mr Sutton, he is not an easy man to be with. Of course, he blamed his first wife for that marriage breakdown and true enough she was a greedy, untrustworthy sort but you know he was not there most of the time and with Celeste, he tried to manage her like one of his businesses. Now this American lady he's with, she's not my cup of tea but I will say this, she has the measure of him and that's maybe what he needs."

All the while, as she spoke, she studied the expression on my face which to some would have given little away but I could not deflect her perception. She sighed. She could see that for a while at least, it was a hopeless cause and only time could draw me away.

"And you don't think I have the measure of him?" I said it with a little laugh, to draw out this last important drop of honesty.

"I'm not sure but I am afraid he has the measure of you, very much. I mean, you wrong footed him that last time, going off back to London. He was pretty shaken but only briefly. I'd like to think that the better part of him will let you be now. You're a lot younger than him. He should focus on his life in France. You know, love can be a very selfish thing sometimes but there is certainly more than one way to love."

I noticed a wedding photo on a side table. There had been a Mr Stewart.

"Mmm. You know Celeste once told me to have an alabaster heart but I don't think I can with him. Maybe he does have the measure of me. We'll see."

We then agreed that there would be no further discussion of David Sutton and I began a three week holiday that was balm to my soul; good food, healthy walks (with the dogs David had picked out with Audrey and then handed over to the care of Mrs Stewart!) gentle, idle chatter, mindless television and just a soft, background hum of anticipation at what lay ahead of me.

Mike Grainger was one of the high calibre individuals David was skilled to place at his disposal. Older than David, he was hugely experienced, astute but not the brash, domineering sort and crucially he quickly demonstrated that he knew how to be a right hand man and how to work me in. Three weeks holiday had not cured me of stress but he read me beautifully and I never felt overloaded with information or overwhelmed by the adjustments I would need to make. He quickly homed in on my particular skills set and repeatedly emphasized every good quality, carefully and tenderly building my self-confidence. He managed our relationship such that it was entirely professional and so, unlike with Mrs Stewart, I never had the slightest clue as to what he made of me, or David's subjective decision to hire me. Perhaps, upon our first encounter, there was a brief glance that revealed that he saw me as a woman, a look away because he wished to quickly process the fact that I was young and attractive and then dismiss such thoughts. There, it was gone, dealt with. Of course, he had already seen the portrait of me and had time to speculate about the object of David's peculiar devotion. This ability of his, to be entirely professional, lifted an enormous weight from me. My being a woman would not be regarded as a disadvantage, or an asset, or anything worse. He made it irrelevant. He made my connection to David irrelevant. He did everything he could to ensure that my new role would be a success. Of course, this would be aided by the team of experts he had assembled. Guided by his lead, they too were helpful, open minded and above all professional.

By the time David's scheduled visit was to take place, I knew I could certainly do the job but I was still lonely. Busy, challenged, but lonely. Mike found me staring out of a window and read my mind.

"You know as director, this can feel a bit of an ivory tower up here. Now that you know what the job entails, why don't you cut yourself loose a bit? I know you've been introduced to all the current artists in residence and you probably felt a bit like the Queen at some grand opening, shaking their hands, asking polite questions but you don't have to run things that way. Take some time to meet them individually, open yourself up to them a bit more. Get to know your team as individuals too. There is nothing in your contract which says you can't have friends here. It is up to you."

I do not know what prompted me to respond so frankly but I did.

"You know, I am not entirely sure I know *how* to make friends, not any more. I think I am a bit locked into my ivory tower."

"Well, to make friends you just have to be yourself."

"And what if I don't really know myself? I ran away from home when I went to university and after that I am not sure who I became."

"Then decide who you are from today. Take a lead from those artists down there and start creating. You can do this job standing on your head but if you don't forge deeper relationships you won't have a proper life here. This place is not for everyone and I have got to be honest with you, I can't wait to get back to city life. I've only survived by spending weekends away but I think you might actually find you fit here. David thinks you will."

I think it was the first time we had mentioned his name.

"He certainly wants me to. He wants me here, contained."

At this, Mike recoiled slightly. I had undermined his profound sense of loyalty to David Sutton perhaps.

"What you make of this has nothing to do with him. I am not going to begin to question his motives in inviting you here but it seems to me you accepted the invitation and now how it works out is entirely up to you."

He made me feel bad, guilty.

"I'm sorry. I sound bitter. Thank you for everything Mike and I will try to take your advice."

He nodded at me and was going to leave but then wavered and turned back.

"When David arrives, I'd like to sign off on my involvement here and take the lead at the meeting etc so can I politely suggest that you take a bit of a back seat?"

"Yes, of course. That sounds fine. I will. Thank you again."

He left me pondering the possibilities of friendship but also with a powerful sense that at the last moment, he had felt a need to protect me, not from the demands of the job or myself but from the man himself, David Sutton.

DAVID

I flew to Scotland for the board meeting, my car delivered to the airport so that I could drive myself. I rarely liked to use drivers and it was a drive I particularly loved. On the way there, however, you were the subject of all my thoughts and perhaps the scenery was a little wasted on me. In my imagination, you would be there to welcome me, smiling but actually it was Mike who emerged, suited and business-like. He offered me a firm handshake but I felt grateful for his loyalty throughout and so pulled him in for a hug. Perhaps there was a sense that he held back slightly but I assumed he was just being British.

"So, where's my new director?" I looked up at the house

eagerly, perhaps hoping to see you pressed up against a window, waving.

"Claire is waiting with the others. We agreed this is my show until the official handover. Where's Audrey?"

I detected something then, a slight edge in his voice. Mike had never been an open book to me but I knew this was somehow a loaded question.

"Audrey is in London dealing with some of her own business matters. So, as per all our previous chats, you ARE happy with Claire's appointment?"

"Absolutely. David, you have a fantastic record at picking great people and she is no exception. She is bright, a fast learner. Of course, she clearly went through something in London and it may yet take a while for her to run at 100% but even at 70% I think she can do this. What I think is important is that you just let her fly."

There it was again, not *what* he said but something in the way he delivered it, a slight tone. It irritated me but the important thing was that you were there and Mike had done a good job.

"Ok. Well, come on Mike. Let's get on with business."

We went into the great hall where your painting was still hanging and from there into one of the sitting rooms which had been sympathetically remodelled into a conference room. There was the usual aroma of coffee. People were standing around talking, not eager to sit down until the meeting was actually underway. I glanced around and was greeted with suitable nods and smiles but with the first sweep of the room I could not see you. Then, the slender woman, leaning against the end of the long table, in a sharp trouser suit rotated to see what her colleague was staring at, stood up properly and turned and it was you, a serene, composed smile on the lips. You had cut your hair short and I will not lie, it was like a slice to my gut and yet, how powerfully beautiful it made you. Is there anything more incredible than a confident woman in her 30's? If Mike was right and this was you at 70% then 100% might be more than I could handle and yet, I knew you, every soft part behind those pristine edges and the fragility woven into your strength. I gave you a nod of approval and taking my seat at the head of the table signalled that the meeting should commence.

I could have done that meeting on automatic pilot and charged through the agenda but this was a special and unique occasion. We were in a work setting together and here was an opportunity for me to show you a little how I operated and no one achieves my level of success without being a consummate leader. My hands-off dealings are never fully hands off and I will shine the light of scrutiny into every corner and so everyone around that table, including Mike, was made to shift a little in their seat, was obliged to answer a question they never saw coming. The bar was being held high but no harm in pushing it a little higher. Mike had apparently briefed you to let him take the lead and you were largely silent but attentive. Finally, we came to the last but most important matter on that agenda, the formal handing over of the reins to the new director, Claire Sutcliffe, at which point, unprompted, you stood up and delivered a slick, eloquent speech. This was quite some improvement on the girl who once held an orange and bluffed her way through, charming and utterly captivating though that had been but, whilst I savoured every word from the former Barrister, what I was most acutely aware of was Mike's eyes, burning into me from my right side and it dawned on me the reason for his slightly off attitude. He had decided we were lovers, that you were my mistress. He disliked the hidden, unprofessional agenda or perhaps just not being party to it. The reality was far more complex and nuanced but I knew I would not be leaving Scotland without having to explain myself. I had been open with him about the fact that you had been unhappily married to my brother and he had known that this job was a favour to you, however solid your credentials. Somehow, he had come to understand that there was a connection between US, something of greater significance, something I had not confided in him and I could scarcely blame him for objecting but what now intrigued me was what he felt he knew and how he knew it. What had you said to him?

The meeting concluded in a buoyant atmosphere. An exhibition of the current resident artists' work awaited our viewing. There was no question of Mike and I having that critical conversation yet and meanwhile, the three of us were destined to be joined at the hip as we admired art work, meeted and greeted, sipped at refreshments, nibbled at canapés and after the thinly disguised strain and awkwardness of that, you and I were required to deliver further speeches. It was late afternoon, running into early evening before people began to disperse. I can only apologise for seeming to coldly dismiss you but Mike was an old friend and I had no choice but to face his questions. I invited him to join me for a drink in that part of the house I had retained as a private apartment. I poured us a large whiskey each and made myself comfortable in front of the blazing fire.

"So Mike. Let's have it. What's on your mind?"

"What do you mean? I thought it all went very well. I'm patting myself on the shoulder and I expect that big bonus from you."

"So you are totally happy with Claire's appointment and you have no reservations whatsoever?"

He drained his glass and placed it on the table carefully, thoughtfully.

"Look, at the end of the day, it is none of my business but I admit I am disappointed that you only told me part of the story as far as Claire is concerned."

"Ok. So what is the story as you understand it? I'm curious to know."

"Oh I'd say she has been more than your sister-in-law and I don't think she took this job easily. I wouldn't mind betting Audrey doesn't even know she's here, that you have put her in charge."

I poured him another and considered my response.

"This whole project was Audrey's idea and I always intended for Claire to head it up. She was very fond of Celeste and is Amélie's God-mother. It made sense to give Claire the opportunity. I knew she wasn't happy in London."

He took another swig and stared at me. He had known me too many years.

"I saw the way you looked at her David. Other people may not know how to read your poker face but I know you are more than fond of her. You put on the full performance in that boardroom and I would bet it was for her benefit."

There was still every chance I could bluff my way out but it had been tiring and difficult to avoid telling Audrey that Claire was now in Scotland and the whiskey inclined me to let down my defences if only a little, that and the huge trust I placed in Mike.

"It's complicated."

"Sounds like it, yep."

"If she hadn't married Rob..."

"But she did."

"Look, after she left Rob, I was willing to explore things but Claire wasn't clear what she wanted and then I met Audrey."

"And you *love* Audrey, right?"

"Yes, yes I do. The problem is that I also love Claire. I admit it."

"Do you? Do you *really*?" This threw me, set me off balance.

"Well, you claim to have observed that for yourself, haven't you?"

"Listen David, I will tell you straight. Claire is very lovely. I get the attraction totally and I bet she has always looked up to you, right?"

"Yes, I suppose so. And?"

"Compared to Audrey, she's a child. She has stuff about life to figure out, things that you and I worked out a long time ago. I think you have done a kind and generous thing by giving her this opportunity and I think she won't let you down but beyond that, I advise you to let her go. If you care for her, let her go. In time, she will fall in love with someone else and I think that is the best thing for her and I think you should focus on wanting what is best for her."

"You make her sound like my daughter."

"Well, you are old enough to be her father! Audrey is incredible and you would be a fool to lose her."

"Audrey doesn't love me the way Claire does."

"You mean she doesn't worship you? That's what makes Audrey right for you!"

Was that it then? Had my ego failed to grasp the key fact that what held my attachment to you was your worshipping me? I had pretended for a long while that I would love you unselfishly but perhaps I really had brought you here because there was something overwhelmingly compelling about the age gap, about the power I could assert. Was it all about possession? Did you worship me? Really?

I drank the whiskey. It burned but it helped me to regain my composure.

"Look Mike, I really value the honesty and I trust you. However, affairs of the heart are not business matters but something far messier! I am not sure what I want from Claire but I intend to make my own decision about it and I suppose Claire will also decide for herself. She may be younger but she is hardly a child. Audrey has promised me nothing and I have promised nothing in return. I can only thank you for running things here and for helping Claire make the transition. I think you can go back to London with a clear conscience. I will hold myself responsible for whatever happens."

He stood up and offered me his hand. He was resigned to my position, knew I would not be influenced further.

"Very well David. As ever, you make your own decisions. I'll say good evening then."

He left me to my brooding. I had planned to speak to you alone but decided it was not wise. Not yet. Mike had not only said that you looked up to me. He had described it as love. I hoped that you still loved me. I had to plan the next move carefully.

CLAIRE

David walked into the meeting, my new boss and but for that first look across at me, he duly behaved very much like a boss. He was confident, assured, impressive. He had been unprepared for my short hair but not disappointed overall and the attraction between us ran the length of the table, a tight, buzzing wire, only Mike obviously aware of it. I wasn't sure if David was aware of the little side glances from his old friend. Mike disapproved but would he say anything?

The meeting was concluded successfully and we moved on to the art exhibition. Drinks, canapés, polite introductions, questions and comments, these type of events are never relaxing and I think we were all relieved when things began to wind down, though it occurred to me that there might now be a rather frank exchange. Yet, David practically ignored me. It was Mike he wanted to be with, to talk to and I was dismissed from his presence.

How on earth was I supposed to go to bed and sleep? I went for a walk in the grounds, took a hot bath, drank half a bottle of wine (I had been staying off the drink for a while, so this was a relapse) and tried very hard indeed not to speculate about their conversation but it proved impossible. My imagination churned up a multitude of scenarios, none particularly positive. I drifted asleep eventually from the sheer exhaustion of so much angst.

I descended into a dream world; a mad disjointed realm with unsustainable plotlines and muddled endings and at some point washed up onto a beach and stopped fighting the bed covers. Three firm knocks on my bedroom door made me sit upright abruptly and set my heart pounding with the shock. The sleeves on my bathrobe were turned the wrong way, so I just wrapped it around me and cautiously opened the door, just enough to peek out. It was David, washed and dressed. I could smell the soap and he was clean shaven.

"David? What time is it?"

I probably looked dreadful but it was too bad.

"Just turned five thirty. I have to make an earlier flight to get back to a situation in Paris. Get dressed and come with me to the airport. You can drive my car back. I'd like us to talk."

I felt horrible and the idea of this scheme did not appeal.

"I'm tired. Let's talk another time. I'll send someone to get your car."

"Just shove some clothes on and do as you're told. I'm your boss now, remember?" He said it with a cheeky smile but I did not find this amusing. However, I agreed to go with him. I wanted to hear what he what he had to say.

The house was beautifully still as we made our departure. Plenty of drink had been consumed. The car was freezing but soon warmed up. I liked watching him drive and for a while we said nothing at all. We shared an enchantment with the awakening day in such panoramic surroundings. Eventually, the sun was risen and I decided silence was no longer golden.

"So, how's Audrey?" He turned and frowned at me.

"Really? You want to talk about Audrey?"

"Well, it's the polite thing to do, to ask after someone's other half."

He laughed but it was a hollow, bitter laugh.

"Well that is very bloody polite of you Claire. Yes, she is fine though I don't regard her as my "other half". We are together but in no way joined."

A silence, long and tense, followed.

"So, you said you wanted to talk. What about?" I tried my best not to sound very interested.

Another frown from him and then a shorter silence.

"So, you *are* glad you took this job and you're starting to find your feet?"

"Yes, I am thankful for you yet again coming to my rescue David. First, the impoverished student, then the beaten up wife and now the nervous wreck. I hope you never feel obliged to rescue me again."

I sounded so bitter, so angry and these emotions crowded into the car like strangers. David looked across, perhaps not confused but frustrated at me.

"You know it has never been an obligation. I love you." He said this with absolute sincerity but this only stirred up my rage.

"Ah yes, but it's not a normal kind of love is it? I mean you chose to be with Audrey and don't expect me to be glad that you don't even love her properly. I think, for the sake of my own sanity, we should agree that we are first and foremost work associates now, good friends perhaps. I don't want you to love me. I want it to stop."

He let out a long sigh. We were on the main road now and he speeded up.

"Well, if you are no longer in love with me Claire, then it does stop."

"If I were in love with you it would be pointless and stupid."

Another, long pensive, unbearable silence before he was willing to respond.

"You want me to leave Audrey and choose you. Right?"

That he asked me that, that he expected me to confess my love for him and worse, my NEED OF HIM it sent wave after wave of rage crashing over me. Yes, he had rescued me countless times but he had also rejected me several times. It had always seemed about him being the one in control and now, once again, he required me to ask him to choose me. Taking the job in Scotland had not destroyed all of my dignity but asking him to leave Audrey and choose me might. I suddenly thought of Celeste and felt her telling me to resist.

"Whatever you want me to say David, I am not prepared to say it."

He laughed perhaps partly out of admiration, partly exasperated.

"I see. I hear you. Not much else to say then. Not for now."

When we arrived at the airport, my rage and every other confused emotion had subsided into a sullen sulk. He pulled over and I went to get out of the car but he grabbed me by one arm and stretched over and directed my head round to face him. He regarded me with what I can only describe as tenderness and kissed me, deeply, passionately, not a kiss of friendship or the kiss of a fatherly mentor. It was a kiss which drowned me in further confusion and I think he may have liked that because he gave a satisfied smile.

"Right, well I'll be off then. See you again."

He got out, took his bags from the car and walked off, no backward glance or wave. I didn't know whether to love or hate him. I climbed into the driver's seat, still warm from where he had sat and something made me rest my head against the steering wheel and scream. It helped. My senses gathered themselves. It was time to go. I was in a drop off zone and my passenger had gone, leaving me with the somewhat onerous responsibility of driving his car back to the house. It was probably worth about a quarter of a million and so far hadn't picked up a single scratch.

DAVID

As far as I was concerned, the trip to Scotland had been pretty successful. I had got you there and you had settled in and looked amazing. No one could accuse me of letting you down, or abandoning you in your time of need. Mike had confronted me about keeping two women in play but about this my conscience was clear. Audrey and I shared an understanding. Though she did not want me to love Claire, neither did she offer herself up as a worthy replacement. Perhaps Audrey loved me but it was a half-hearted, reserved kind of love. Most importantly, it appeared it was all she had to offer. I cared deeply for Audrey, held her in high esteem but it was nothing like the torrent of feeling I had for you. You still loved me. I could smell it, taste it, feel it in every word spoken between us. It was a messy love and had taken a lot of knocks. I may have gone to Scotland unclear about what I really wanted from you but on the flight back to Paris, in clear skies above the clouds, I understood that our love hinged upon one simple thing. You had once asked me for space. Well, you had had plenty of time and space in which to make up your mind and if you wanted even more then you could have it. It was easy enough. I would choose you but importantly you would have to ask me, beg me, one final time. I wanted total surrender, nothing less, not a drunken proclamation nor a half committed fumble under the sheets. Your power and strength were lovely yes but I desired your vulnerability and I wanted you to latch on to MY strength. These were the two halves that needed to come together. No compromise, no watered down deal. In my life, how many times had I fought for a deal, done everything I could and then waited? This was not so very different. I had made my final pitch. The rest was up to you.

CLAIRE

David was embracing new technology and had gone to extraordinary lengths to make sure the house in Scotland was connected to the internet and email communication which began as a slightly absurd novelty in the working world was becoming the norm. I looked for his messages amongst the others. Many were brief and business like but now and again he liked to tease me with something flirtatious, just enough to remind me that he was more than my boss. He was waiting for me to make the next move. All I had to do was tell him that I loved him, wanted him, needed him. I held off, afraid. I told myself that if it were ever to happen then it would be face to face, when he next visited. There were no scheduled visits in the diary, so if I wanted to have it out with him soon, I would have to concoct a reason. I had a tentative conversation with the Art Director and proposed a summer exhibition, asking David Sutton to attend with possible corporate clients who might be interested in purchasing work. She was not as enthusiastic as I might have hoped. So far, the focus had been on exhibiting the artists in Glasgow or Edinburgh and whilst naturally she wanted her protégés to sell their work she talked of the importance of timing and delicate stages in their development. Far easier for me to jump on a plane and go to see him but this sort of desperation was my least preferred solution. I procrastinated and David waited. He was used to waiting. Of course, I could just ask him to come to Scotland, no pretence that it was about work. He would love that. I resisted.

Then, one day I discovered an email from someone else, Celeste's friend Gary. I opened it, saw how long it was and decided it would have to wait. He contacted me again, two weeks later, asking me if I had read his email and what did I think? It was a wet and blustery evening in May when I finally decided to open the original communication. Every line carried his voice to me and with it echoes of a distant past. He was still quite a character, full of dry wit. I remembered him and Celeste huddled together, laughing. After quite a long introduction during which he talked of his current life and London, expressed his incredulity upon learning that I had moved to "bloody Scotland" and hoped that I was in a strictly professional relationship with David Sutton, he began to talk about an artist he had met, an artist he believed would benefit from a placement with our charity. He believed Celeste would have loved said artist. He was eager to send a portfolio of work for us to see. I was quite engaged until he went on to describe that he had met the artist behind his wheelie bin! The man was a homeless drunk. Gary explained how he had initially limited his involvement to making the chap an occasional sandwich or a hot drink. Then, one day the man had been unresponsive and Gary had called an ambulance. When the hospital was happy to discharge the man, Gary had decided to take him in.

At this point, I decided it all sounded rather pathetic and impatiently forwarded the email to the Art Director with a short explanation; probably a waste of her time but I would leave it with her to consider. I messaged Gary to explain that such decisions were made by the Art Director and lied, saying I had naturally put in a good word.

It was the beginning of June when the Art Director came to see me and announced that she was captivated by the portfolio of Gary's new stray. Gary had offered her assurances that the thirty year old former tramp was dry and now she wished to propose offering the man a placement at our next meeting, subject to her meeting him first in London. I agreed to her going to meet him but stressed that I did not consider a recently reformed, homeless alcoholic a suitable candidate. At a subsequent meeting, I argued that he had only been off the booze a short time, was older than most of the other artists, that we could not offer him the on-going support he would probably need. I was out-voted. The others liked his work, saw the potential and it was decided that suitable accommodation could be provided at the cottage in the grounds and our in-house counsellor was willing to take him on.

The evening before his arrival, I decided to look through the portfolio myself. He drew and painted people. They were the faces of his street existence and the images were powerful but I questioned how coming to a remote corner of Scotland was going to help him develop. The Art Director said it was about creating a stable, secure backdrop and encouraging him to grow and explore other media. She spoke with compassion but I remained highly sceptical.

I made up my mind I would be the one to collect him from the station. I intended to vet the man, though at this stage it was a little late. So it was that I set off in the rather dirty four by four pool car, to meet and greet Aidan Dolan. I had a picture of him in my mind. If Gary had taken in him, he would be slim, pale and pretty. At a wild guess, he had been thrown out of an Irish Catholic home because of his conflicted sexuality. Yes, I went armed with every prejudice and preconception. It was the third week in June. We were having a dreadful summer and when I pulled up at the station, it started to rain.

I walked up and down the platform but no sign of a pale, pretty man. Slowly, the small gathering of passengers dispersed. I waited. Checked my watch several times. I let out an impatient sigh. Of course he was a no show. He had probably started drinking the moment the train had left London, perhaps fallen asleep on the train. I was heading back towards the exit when a tall, bearded man, smartly dressed in jeans, cotton shirt and a linen jacket emerged from the coffee shop. I did not expect him to speak to me.

"Sorry but would you be Claire by any chance, Gary's friend? "

The accent was Irish, so it had to be him, but he was nothing remotely like the person I had expected to find and it threw me off balance.

I looked him up and down. He was holding a takeaway coffee and some smart luggage.

"Er yes, I'm Claire but are you Aidan Dolan? " The disbelief rang out.

He laughed at me.

"Not what you were expecting maybe? Gary insisted on buying me clothes and stuff. I refused to shave off the beard though. Sorry, I just had to buy a coffee. Would you like one?"

There was something immediately appealing, charming even about that accent but every fibre of my being was charged with resistance. So, Gary had cleaned him up a bit but this man was a nobody and an alcoholic to boot. I decided to be honest with him.

"No thank you. Let's just get going. Did you need a coffee to sober up?" I gave him a formidable, disapproving stare but he didn't flinch.

"No, I did not. Haven't touched a drop. You don't have much faith in me then, Claire?"

His steady brown eyes fixed on me. If I wanted to try and look into his soul, he wouldn't try to stop me. I looked away, announced "Let's go." and started a quick march back to the car. He did not attempt to keep pace but followed slowly, making me check over my shoulder several times. I got in and left him to deposit his luggage in the boot and to see himself into the passenger seat. I considered telling him to sit in the back but was too late. I waited for him to put on his seat belt.

"As I'm overall Director, you should refer to me as Ms Sutcliffe please and no, I am not one of the people rooting for you. I fully expect you to fail. One slip and you're out, is that clear?"

The steady brown eyes wavered now. He was taken aback by

my ferocity, as was I in fact.

"Yes, Ms Sutcliffe. Hear you loud and clear."

We drove some of the way in a frosty silence. He had fidgety hands which further irritated me. He eventually found some courage to speak again.

"Gary didn't warn me about you. I was expecting a friendly face."

"If it were up to me you wouldn't be here. Take it as a challenge."

"Ok, fair enough. Am I what you expected?"

I glanced across at him scornfully.

"Cleaner I suppose and less delicate shall we say."

He laughed again. He had a nice, cascading musical laugh.

"Ah so you were expecting a gay man perhaps? Because of Gary…"

I refused to join in with the humour.

"It would be wrong to stereotype of course but yes, I expected someone more Gary's type."

He laughed again. One of us was trying to enjoy the conversation, in spite of my hostility.

"Oh I think I could have been Gary's type if I'd wanted to be. I think he's quite flexible you know? We agreed to be friends. I'm sorry if I presumed we would be friends too. If you want respect, then you've got it. Nothing but respect from now on."

In spite of his words, he was being sarcastic and probably thinking I was a stuck-up bitch. The scenery around us was changing and he started to comment on this and explained how glad he was to have left London. It struck me that we had something in common, seeking escape in the Scottish hills but I said little. I didn't want his friendship, nor need it.

When we pulled up in front of the house, the sun had come out and the Art Director and some others were eagerly waiting. They greeted him warmly and ushered him inside and perhaps they expected me to follow them in but I got back in the car and drove his luggage down to the cottage. I carried it up into the bedroom and placed it on the bed where David and I had once been lovers. Unashamedly, I unzipped the bag and searched carefully for any bottles. Nothing. I saw that he wore boxer shorts.

I returned to the house and passed the key to a staff member with instructions to show Mr Dolan where he would be staying. From there, I climbed the stairs to my offices, past the portrait which by now he would have seen. I had piles of paperwork to see to but when I finally slumped at my desk I was overcome with fatigue, put my head down and fell asleep. I dreamed of wine, red wine.

DAVID

Audrey and I had grown into a strange partnership. She loved living in Paris and for an American was learning to speak a passable level of French. Our individual schedules had expanded around new and enthralling opportunities. When it came to Amélie, she remained scrupulously committed, ensuring that I continued to deliver as a father whenever an opportunity arose, willing to take a back seat to this relationship and not just my marriage to work. It all fitted together but after my visit to Scotland I was reminded that my love for Audrey was somehow shallow and second rate. It was a compromise between two people set against union, individuals who valued their emotional sovereignty. This status quo depended on her believing I had mostly given up on you, that my scheme to put you in Scotland, at my disposal, had failed. She counted on your relative youth, and the separation, to place you in the arms of another. I believe she even hoped you would secure happiness. Whilst I had been disciplined and maintained the stand-off myself, convinced that it was the honourable thing to do, the delicate alliance with Audrey had endured but after the visit to Scotland it was hard to look at her and not focus on the fine lines and the wispy ends of her hair. It was difficult to patiently tolerate her erratic, hormonal moods. She had a libido that had to be nursed like a baby. Sometimes, when I watched her sleeping I felt a deep, protective compassion which I wanted to place over her like a blanket and when she made me laugh, or wrong-footed me intellectually I felt a great shield of loyalty rise up to protect her, but the fact remained that you only needed to bow now in surrender and the alliance with Audrey would shatter. I loved you more than Audrey, the sweet deal that kept evading me. I waited.

CLAIRE

The next morning, I had a terrible headache. I drank two glasses of water and decided to go for a run. I avoided the route that would take me near the cottage. I had had time to consider what set me against the Irishman. His story was about working class roots, broken family ties, needing a helping hand to avoid the streets, drinking to numb the pain, the loneliness. My story had thus far been more successful but I couldn't be entirely sure that it was *all* down to hard work. I had definitely put everything into my studies and my career but look at how much my life was entwined with David Sutton and generally I could be fairly accused of trading on my looks. It was irrational but I began to imagine that Gary had sent his artist here to taunt me, to remind me that but for the patronage of Celeste I would have been a sorry failure and David Sutton still controlled me, still had hold of the strings. Then there was the drinking. I was confident I had it under control. I could manage without it, was better without it but it had been a friend who always stayed in touch, no matter how long I maintained a silence. Aidan Dolan had got into bed with it, caught a disease. The others, including the Art Director, they were all kindly middle-class, well intentioned individuals who wanted to "make a difference." I was put in charge of a charity to help others when I was the one who probably needed help and someone like Aidan Dolan would see through me. Or, the idea that he might disturbed me. I pictured him stood on the edge of the driveway, watching David Sutton get out of his car, observing the way David took hold of my arm and knowing that this was the only difference between us; she sleeps with the boss, I see.

These were crazy, paranoid thoughts and I ran faster and faster, trying to erase them. It wasn't fair to taint Mr Dolan's chances, to expect him to fail and it was madness to imagine that he had any thoughts about me other than the obvious one, that I was a snooty, sceptical, dogmatic boss lady that he would be wise to avoid and should be determined to prove wrong.

When I had returned and showered, I decided to email David. After several drafts, I settled on the following.

"Hi David. All good here. I have some ideas to discuss. Are you planning another visit?"

Minutes felt like hours, waiting for him to reply. Was he online? Would he see it?

"Hi Claire. The prospect of discussing "ideas" is not all that enticing but in any case my schedule is very full for the next month or so, including a three week trip to California. If you have anything compelling to say, you could call and I might just come running. Otherwise, let's aim, in principle, for a visit early August."

I stared at the phone. All I had to do was make one call. I went to the window and looked out. I could see the loch. The early clouds had cleared and it would be a beautiful summer's day. Aidan Dolan was crossing towards the house. He had been instructed that he should take all his meals here and prescribed a rigid timetable. I wondered if he had what it would take to succeed. I also decided I would not be making a phone call. Not today.

As the weather improved, most of the resident artists chose to carry out some work outside and I started to enjoy meeting them and having a window into their creative minds. Naturally, there was also more leisure time lived outside and I was reminded of summer on a university campus. For the most part, I was careful to confine myself to socialising with my staff and always found excuses to opt out from the artists' barbeques, picnics etc. Mike had advised me not to isolate myself and to forge friendships and this seemed to be the best compromise. There were rare occasions when I found myself remembering the past, when the house had been a home but I quickly shut down such nostalgia. Yet, what I could not avoid were the split second flashes which would jump me, Celeste's ringed fingers running up the bannister, the back of David's neck as he gazed out of a window, water parted by an oar, the splatter of rain against the cottage window pane. They were a terror and a pleasure and of course, David wanted me to remember.

It was the middle of July and it had been a particularly warm, humid day. I had trudged through a thorny thicket of numbers with the Finance Manager so that we could present David with an up-to-date picture of how we envisaged the charitable trust's sustainability. David was the principal and most generous benefactor but he and Mike had been adept at finding other sponsors and there were various grants that could be chased. Energy bills were still too high and we wanted to put the case for expenditure on improvements to energy capture and efficiency, all of which would be initially costly and implementation would be problematic in a listed property. However, it was a good day's work and when the Finance Manager proposed sitting out on the lawn with a glass of white wine I was severely tempted but the artists had already gathered there. They had downed tools in the middle of the afternoon and there had been shrieks of laughter on and off ever since. Now, they were quieter, more reflective and one of the women started to play an acoustic guitar. It was an inviting scene but I could not imagine myself in its midst. Mr Dolan was absent, probably to avoid being around crates of beer and a box of wine. I told the Finance Manager I had a slight headache and he may even have looked a little relieved as he left. I was not known for being fun.

Actually, I was hungry, so soon I departed for the staff kitchen conjuring a green salad in my head, with avocado and olives and some buttered baguette. I took the quickest route, down one of the side staircases and on the second floor found the Art Director stood to the side of a door, slyly peeking in at a studio space. She heard me, turned, put her fingers to her lips indicating that I should be silent and then ushered me over in a manner that recalled childhood conspiracies. She then spoke in a whisper.

"It's nice to watch him working. He is totally in flow. We mustn't disturb him but take a look."

She moved me into her position and I felt slightly silly playing the game of spy but I complied.

This was Aidan Dolan's studio space. He was not alone. Out of my line of sight was the object of his. He was sketching quickly with a compelling intensity, in big, free movements, almost with a sort of desperation, as if his life depended on the outcome. When he had filled the paper, he tore it off and began again. It was as if he were searching for something. He was sketching what appeared to be the shoulders of a woman from behind and her hand reaching over one of those shoulders.

"Who is she?"

The Art Director frowned at what she considered to be an irrelevant question or perhaps my unemotional reaction.

"Oh, probably one of the cleaning ladies. He likes his subjects to be ordinary, regular people. Anyway, we must come away."

She pulled at me and we crossed to the stairs together. She was buoyant, uplifted by what she had seen. I was still processing the image. I kept remembering Celeste and the way she had studied me, her subject. The Art Director wanted to make a point.

"You see Claire, we were right to give him a chance. There are so many ways in which he can improve and in which he needs to grow. This is an exciting journey for him and you know he has the best work ethic. He also has that depth of lived experience to draw upon."

"We'll see. He has the sense to mostly stay away from the others and their afternoon drinking. I still think he needed rehab and that coming here is a huge risk."

"Claire! Why are you so fixated on his drink problem? Do you have to define him by it?"

We were near the kitchen and I felt empty.

"Look, it is my job to provide oversight. You only see the artists and creative potential. I know how much it costs to run this place daily and so each place granted to an artist is very precious and we have to assess the likelihood of a desired outcome. I really hope he *does* succeed and that we are not wasting our resources but he is a huge risk and I do not ignore the challenges. What does the counsellor say?"

She had been so bright and hopeful but I had drained it out of her. She shrugged her shoulders.

"Not much. It is all confidential, as you know. She has promised to alert us if there are any risks to his wellbeing or to the wellbeing of others. She has to follow protocol."

I glanced into the kitchen, towards the fridge.

"Fine. Well, I need to follow my stomach. I am ravenous. Care to join me?"

She pulled back.

"Er, no thank you. You enjoy."

Was I a bit disappointed, as she walked away? Not really. I only had one ripe avocado and I wanted it all to myself. As I prepared the salad, there was another flash, David's hands slicing onions. He was a good cook, better than me.

It was later that same day, the light beginning to fade, when I decided to run past the cottage and check up on Mr Dolan. I moved stealthily through the trees nearby and stared across towards the lit windows. I don't know quite what I expected to see. The silhouette of him drinking from an upturned whiskey bottle? What I certainly did not expect was for him to walk up behind me.

"Good evening Ms Sutcliffe. Anything I can help you with?"

To be discovered like that was embarrassing. To jump half out of my skin and scream like that was humiliating. He put up a hand apologetically and stepped away. I was the one who needed to apologise but it would require further shame so I opted to front it out.

"I was simply running this way, saw the lights on and thought I would check you were ok. Only, I didn't wish to intrude."

"Ok. Well, as you can see I am just fine. Just been for a run myself. Would you like to come in for a cup of tea?"

"Er no, no thank you. I'll leave you to it."

"Are you sure? I can go to the bathroom and take a shower and you'd have plenty of time to search the place for bottles."

My front crumbled away and I felt a huge blush creep up into my face.

"That won't be necessary thank you. I suppose I should apologise for my unprofessional behaviour."

"Well yes, go on then."

I saw the defiance in his eyes and I wanted to hit him and my irrational feelings just made me blush deeper.

"I'm sorry. There, well, I'll say goodnight."

"Goodnight Claire."

I turned and set off at a jog and focussed on getting out of his line of sight. It was only once I was calmer that it registered that he had called me Claire and not Ms Sutcliffe. The man did not respect me and after that shambolic episode it was scarcely surprising. Did his respect matter to me so very much and if so why? These were questions that could wait until the morning and the clear light of day.

Yet I didn't return to such matters. I ploughed a deeper furrow into my work and what little time I allowed for my mind to wonder I devoted to thinking about David. I tried to imagine what it might be like to be Mrs Claire Sutton and, truly, the only way I could picture this was to suppose that he would surrender his career and retire here, to the house in Scotland. The alternative was that I would be required to give up this new role and replace Audrey, except that unlike her I would not have my separate business interests to help consume the hours that David would be working. I had already walked away from my career as a barrister and felt there was no conceivable way I could give up on this work too. Besides, David had predicted accurately that I would enjoy the role and thrive in the position. A third option was that we would continue as we were, our lives largely separate yet intertwined, but if he wasn't going to be much physically involved with me why on earth would he give up Audrey? What actually were we? I did not much care for these complex, hard to solve questions so I indulged in hopeless, romantic ideas of us rowing out on the lake, driving over to Turnberry, kissing amongst the heather and the fact that part of me delighted in this empty-headed activity tormented another part of me to the point of rendering nights half sleepless. I had developed a habit of going to the kitchen for warm milk and found myself pathetic.

Another week passed in this way. The weather had cooled, there had been some light rain but then another mini heatwave descended like a stuffy, damp blanket. The atmosphere was tangibly subdued and the artists seemed to spend a great deal of time wandering the grounds, distracted. The Art Director proposed taking some away to Edinburgh on a field trip and I agreed. This had the effect of creating an even greater sense of hush and suspense, waiting for a weather front to come and break the spell.

I took a walk down by the lake one morning. Out of sight from the house, there was a small stony beach area and I made my way round to it. Aiden Dolan had been in for a swim because his hair was still wet and there was a damp towel thrown over one of the small rocks. He was skimming stones now and it was not my desire to intrude upon his happy privacy but he sensed me and turned.

"If you want to bathe, it is safer to do so from in front of the house, so that you can be seen."

I sounded like an old school ma'am though my advice was well intended.

"Oh don't you worry. I'm a Connemara man. I float like a duck."

He turned and nonchalantly skimmed another stone, managing four bounces. He turned and grinned, pleased with his effort.

"Want a go? I can show you how."

I stooped, selected a flat stone, walked over and launched it, producing a very impressive five bounces. He was suitably taken aback.

"Practiced a lot as a kid. It was a cheap way to pass the time."

"Wow. I'm impressed. The hard work paid off."

He was staring not just at me but into me and for a couple of seconds I let him take a good look but then I lost my nerve. I straightened up.

"So you see Mr Dolan, hard work produces results. I hope you will continue to demonstrate a strong work ethic. The Art Director has been feeding me very good reports." I was the stern headmistress again.

He frowned, put off by the shift in tone. He gathered up another stone, turned and propelled it, with greater force than before. It flew and skipped six times, an admirable distance from the shoreline. He picked up another and off it went and it was only when he had bent down for a third that I realised he was in a rather passive aggressive way dismissing me. The conversation was over.

My instinct was to walk away and let him sulk but I didn't.

"Sorry, have I offended you in some way?" As soon as the question was asked I regretted it.

He carried on with skimming stones and I wanted to throw one at his head.

"Tell me Claire, do you actually have *any* friends?" It was mostly rhetorical. If I said yes, he would take some convincing.

Fortunately he did not look at me as he asked this impertinent question because I was starting to blush again.

"A few, yes. I admit I left several behind in London when I took this job. If you are implying that I am a bit formal with you then you must get that we cannot be friends as such. I am Director here and you are a client."

He faced me and his expression was not unkind. However, his words were cutting.

"Gary told me you were a bit of a tight arse but I like to form my own opinion. I think you like to act tough but you're actually very defensive. You see, I think there's a wee bit of a connection between us two. Wouldn't you like to explore that maybe? I mean, fair enough if you prefer to keep it all business like but I think it's a shame, I do."

"If you mean something romantic... I mean, do you actually mean something romantic? Because, I'm in love with someone, as it happens."

He didn't seem surprised, wrong footed, or taken aback, as if my being in love were common knowledge. He stared beyond me over my shoulder. Someone else was there. I turned. It was one of the secretaries, out of breath.

"Sorry to interrupt but Audrey Hopper has just turned up at the house. No one knew she was coming. I thought you would want to know."

"Oh, ok. Yes, I'll come right away."

There was scarcely any time to process it all. His reaction to my announcement. What had the secretary overheard? Why on earth was Audrey suddenly here?

"Sorry. I have to go."

"No worries. Good luck." He said it in such a knowing tone and I made my way back to the house trying to second guess just how much Gary thought he knew about my life and how much he had shared with the Irishman.

Beads of sweat formed like buds on my forehead and my throat felt dry and cracked. The house came into view and as I crossed the lawn I was certain that this was not about to be a random, social call. Audrey Hopper had come on business, serious business.

She was in the hall, leaning against the bottom of the banister on the stairs, gazing up at my portrait. Someone had left the front entrance propped open to allow a breeze to circulate and so she did not immediately realise I had arrived. I took a few seconds to admire her. She was elegantly dressed, as ever, her slim, tall athletic frame purpose-made for hanging clothes with style. Her long, silvery hair had been gathered up in the usual casual but effective manner and this was a woman with a strong and striking side profile. From here, I could not see fully into the pale, piercing blue eyes which had the power to arrest anyone. Yet, even without the impact of those sapphires, she was a lovely woman and David had chosen her over me. She was an accomplished mother, had successful businesses, she exuded strength and independence. She was examining the portrait of me, the working class upstart who had traded on her looks for many a favour from the mighty entrepreneur David Sutton, my job here the latest gift. Her problem was that I was young, not the girl in that painting true but always younger than her and David refused to give up on me. He loved me and "all" I had to do was tell him I loved him and wanted him and it was over for them.

She sensed me then, turned and perhaps a little surprisingly gave me a warm, welcoming smile. She strode over and embraced me, a confused, slightly stiff recipient. She stood back, still smiling and as if I were her daughter stroked the back of my neck affectionately.

"You cut your hair! It looks so pretty. How are you?"

Perhaps she thought she could hide her true feelings strategically until she had conducted her own appraisal of matters but I saw the eyes were cold pools in spite of the smile and kind words. I touched the back of my neck instinctively, as if it were burned.

"You have come a long way to enquire Audrey. You could have just phoned or sent an email but I suspect this is not about my wellbeing at all, is it? Let me guess, David didn't tell you I had taken the job."

All the warmth drained away from her other features and she suddenly looked every bit older than me, but this was not hostility I met but sadness or disappointment. She sighed.

"Well I guess we were never gonna be best buddies you and me, though I hope you recall that I did try. Yes, it was a surprise when I called in at your chambers to see how you were, only to discover that you had left , maybe less of a shock to find out that you had come here. I hope you understand that I am mainly disappointed for you. David got what he wanted. Did you know the whole idea for this place was originally mine?"

She looked about at her surroundings as if she owned them.

One of the artists entered behind me and so I suggested that we go up to my office. It was a long, awkward journey. She tried her best to comment on the changes to the building but I obliged her with only perfunctory responses. I felt anger rising, perhaps a normal defence mechanism but it shamed me. It was a lack of self-control and I despised feeling that way. Audrey had said it, David had got what he wanted from me. The words ran on and on, over and over and the anger could not be diffused. As soon as I had closed my office door I needed to release it.

"What did you mean when you said that David got what he wanted?"

She clearly felt my fury and paused but remained calm, untouched by it.

"I mean that he wanted you here, at his disposal. He didn't tell me because he probably wanted to explore his options before neatly removing me from his life. He is a typical successful man. In other words, an arrogant, controlling bastard. Still, if you love him and he loves you, I suppose that's that."

"If David loves *you*, then the same applies."

Now she grew a little irritated, frustrated at me.

"Don't be deliberately stupid Claire. David loves me like he loves his morning coffee, or closing a business deal. Our relationship makes sense. It works. You, you're the risk, the adrenaline ride, only he doesn't want to be controlled by you. He wants to possess you, the ultimate acquisition, a drug he can shoot up his arm whenever he wants it but with no nasty fallout or side effects. It has probably always been you, even when he brought you here to Celeste. When you married Rob, you think you just hurt his pride, his feelings? No, you showed the folly of youth, weakness, vulnerability, things he never gets with me and finds so irresistible. I myself thought you were stronger but it doesn't matter. You're the entire package for his male ego. I came here to tell you that I won't get in the way unless YOU want me to."

This was an astonishing offer and left me speechless, so she went on.

"I mean that in the unlikely event that you come to your senses and realise that being married to David would not be happily ever after for you, well then I get that you probably enjoy this job and your life here and are loathe to sacrifice it, and as you can't just put aside your feelings for him, how to manage the predicament, right? Well, if you decide to reject him, I will push to marry him myself. You see, I love him just about as much as I could love anyone which might be enough for him if you are not an option. As his wife, I can ensure he never comes here again. He will be out of your life. I can take his position here. There's Amélie of course but the two of us can figure that out."

It was audacious but delivered so calmly, as if this were the most rational, logical course of action but none of this leant itself to pragmatic compromise. David had left me with a kiss and time to think and to decide but she was shouldering me into a corner, applying pressure. However, she had added confirmation. David was waiting for *me* to choose.

I found myself standing taller, shoulders back.

"I'm sorry Audrey but I haven't decided what I want and it takes as long as it takes. What I will not deny is that I do love David and you *are* right, being married to him would not be easy but unlike you I have at least dared to marry before, so I know that sacrifices are required. If I just give up on him, I may never love another in the same way. That also requires sacrifice and courage. If you are unhappy with the current situation and uncertainty, you might be courageous yourself of course and walk away. Now, I think we have said enough and I would like you to leave."

For the first time, she looked at me with loathing albeit fleetingly.

"The words of a very clever lawyer. I'll take my chances and leave it in your hands. I'm counting on you seeing sense. David underestimates you but that's his problem. I'll see myself out. Goodbye Claire."

She put out her hand, we shook hands and she left. I took hold of my desk. I was shaking. I waited for this to settle a little and then made my way to the bathroom where I was promptly sick. For some reason I kept remembering the face of Aiden Dolan and his words "Good luck." I considered calling Mrs Stewart and seeking her counsel but could not act on the thought. The truth was, I needed a friend and in spite of what I had said to Aiden, there were none. Not really.

DAVID

We were thousands of miles apart, existing in different time zones but you were daily in my thoughts. I only required you to express the tiniest degree of need and I was willing to fly to Scotland. I waited for you to give in, to admit that you not only loved me but that it was a love rooted in need. Several times, I either picked up the phone or composed an email, just a few, clever words to entice you over the line, to clinch matters, but then I recalled every prior false turn and resisted. You were not so much a thorn in my side as a cold blade pressed up against my rib cage, threatening to end me. It was reasonable for me to desire surrender and I would have it. In return, I would offer you love, devotion, protection. In the intense, Californian sun, I continued to wait.

CLAIRE

Not surprisingly, I did not easily fall asleep that night and even then it was a restless, unhelpful kind of sleeping. I am not sure what woke me at two but I immediately needed the toilet. Returning to my bed, I observed that the room was bathed in a blue haze of moonlight. I pulled back the light, golden curtains and saw that the culprit was indeed very full and breathtaking, floating above the trees. We had an excellent display of stars, unpolluted by urban lights but a cloudless sky was rare. Tonight there were no clouds to diminish this stunning lunar display and it would have been wonderful if my mind had not quickly returned to Audrey's visit. I turned from the window and observed that the moon was practically casting a spotlight on my bed and the probability of going back to sleep was slim. I dragged on my dressing gown and scuffed downstairs in my slippers, headed for the kitchen and some tea and toast.

I glanced over at the door to Aiden's studio space and saw that someone had left a light on in there. I approached, already rehearsing the reprimand he would receive but at the door I discovered that it was not a casual over sight. He was there, working. He had a talent for putting me on the attack.

I hissed at him, not wishing to wake anyone else.

"Er what the hell are you doing?"

He did not jump, nor did he bother turning to look at me but the hand that had been working furiously did pause and hover over the paper. He sounded equally annoyed at me. I was interrupting a process.

"I'm working. Foxes woke me up. I thought hard work was what you encouraged."

I had destroyed a moment and now he turned and tossed down the piece of charcoal. He was wearing a t-shirt, boxers and flip-flops. It was a warm night and I suddenly felt overdressed in my robe but tightened it nevertheless.

"Who gave you a key to the building and the code for the alarm?"

He raised an eyebrow at me, signalling that I was being dim and folded his arms, leaning against the corner of the desk.

"Well now you're the big boss so what is Diane then? Would you say my line manager?"

"Right well, the Art Director shouldn't have done that. It compromises security. If we were burgled…"

He scowled at me but overcame this to try to change tac.

"Look, as you're here and clearly unable to sleep, why don't you take a look at my hard work and tell me what you think? I imagine you're a tough but honest critic."

Sensible me was headed for the kitchen but something more adventurous in me drew me over to accept the invitation. This was not the first time I had looked at his work but with him leaning in beside me the drawings gained a different energy. I flicked through, determined to feign detachment but in truth his drawings provoked many feelings. He tended not to draw beauty and yet there was something compelling and magnificent about his subjects. He did not attempt to explain anything but waited for me and I felt under pressure to say something insightful and intelligent but my words ended up just coming from another part of me, less thinking more feeling.

"You make a cleaning lady seem powerful. You seem to see the animal in people but there is also a sense of loneliness."

"Yes, well the Bible says we're like sheep but I see us more like lone wolves, trying to manage in packs but essentially loners, wanderers in a wilderness, not eating grass. Course, some are more obvious, never really belonging, circling the pack."

There was a long silence. I continued to turn pages. Now there were more joyful sketches, people laughing. Most of these figures were people he had met on the streets.

He sensed and predicted my questions.

"So laughter goes a long way to help us survive. It's not a weakness, it's actually one of our greatest strengths. It has real power over darkness."

Now I looked at him.

"Do you a laugh a lot then?" It was the first time I had dared any proper intimacy with the man and my heart was pounding. He made it skip faster by putting out a hand and just lightly touching the outward corner of one of my eyes. It made me step back but he remained bold.

"More than you Claire. You have scarcely any laughter lines. I've noticed that about you."

He had a way of looking into me and I realised that my attempts to treat him professionally, like a client, had been a waste of time. He didn't do protocol, proper conduct, guidelines. He had lived on the streets, dropped below. He could not be managed, kept in line. I held his gaze and felt my body relax and yield under it. If he wanted to kiss me now, then I would let him. Damn the rules.

He moved closer but then swerved away, scooped up the charcoal and moved back to the easel. In the process, I caught a faint smell of him which I liked. He smelled of the woods.

"Sorry but I really do need to work now, so perhaps we'll leave it there. Diane wants a painting soon and I need to go with this. Goodnight Claire. Hope you manage to sleep ok."

Great. Now I had his rejection to process too. By the time I made it to the kitchen, there were tears building in the eyes with no laughter lines, not from sadness but from total confusion and perhaps just exhaustion. As I sipped my tea I tried so hard to focus on David and decide what I was going to do but my thinking was contaminated. On the one side, Audrey, appealing to my common sense and rationality. On the other, Aiden, stirring up emotions, yearnings, drawing out the animal in me. Just then, he had made a clever move. By being the one to step back, by showing restraint, he had just augmented my curiosity, my desire to know him. He was no academic, not my intellectual match but he had innate powers, not rehearsed and learned. Like David, he saw me but whereas David perhaps wanted to tame the beast with the normal conventions of a committed relationship, perhaps Aiden just wanted to explore, to know. It was very tempting. He had been a temptation from the very first moment. That was why I had been so set against him. The temptation was not a good or sensible thing in my pragmatic, rational universe. I may have abandoned the Law but I lived my life like a true lawyer, always thinking of the small print.

I moved past the door to the studio and back up to my room and went to sleep pondering my love for David. Was there any real depth to it, after all? Aiden had presented me with the true test, not Audrey.

David was back in Europe. He had gone to the south of France because Amélie was on holiday but he sent an email to confirm that he would visit Scotland soon. It was brief, business like. He would not make it easy for me, or perhaps he was just constrained by Audrey? Would she confront him about me?

Then, that night, I had a dream about Aiden Dolan. I was making my way down to the cottage, feeling confrontational, determined. If it was my intention to put our relationship back on a wholly professional footing then this was contradicted by the flowing dress and new underwear. I did not need to look in a mirror. I felt beautiful, radiant, desirable.

The door to the cottage was open and I glided upstairs but the dishevelled bed was empty and in a peculiar sort of panic I suddenly regretted being there, sensed danger and went to leave. As happens in dreams, Aiden magically appeared, naked to the waist. We were nowhere in particular, the background of the cottage faded and now irrelevant. Aiden seemed to find it entirely natural that I was there and started to kiss me. His beard was rough against my face but his tongue was brutal, pushing about in my mouth and a little appalled I tried to push him away but then his hand was running up my leg and deftly squeezed its way into my knickers and I felt a surge of ecstasy and my whole body relaxed and opened to him. Now I loved the feel of his tongue which moved in synchrony with his curved hand which worked rhythmically to open me, to ready me. Even in a dream, a part of my mind still insisted on logic. I wanted him so much, but why wasn't I undoing his trousers? How would we get from A to B? Dreams work strange solutions and do not obey logic. Now he was naked and entering me, apparently not needing to be shown the way. Naturally dream Aiden felt huge but nothing I could not handle or did not enjoy. However, the terrible groaning I was making bothered me and I suddenly felt an unhelpful shame and tried to pull away. To this point there had been no talking but now I heard him speak into my ear, saying "It's ok. It's ok." Though I did feel ashamed, I also felt irritated by this expression, its reassurance, and I was about to shout something at him when he started to push harder and faster and breathlessly repeated "Its ok" and I thought "It's not ok. I feel like I am going to fall somehow or is it explode? Something is coming towards me, a great curtain of water and I won't be able to withstand the force. Why doesn't he realise that it isn't ok?" Then another Claire, a calm reasoning version spoke to me from somewhere. "It's ok. It's just an orgasm. It's good. Let him carry on. David won't mind." So, I listened to her. In fact I was grabbing onto him and I practically begged him to keep going. It was going to be immense, washing me away like a tsunami...the clock radio alarm woke me up and just for a few seconds I tried not to be awake and to fall back into the dream but the light of that world diminished and the reality of my bed, the furniture in the room and me in old pyjamas came into full focus and between my legs only the faint sense of pleasure lingered. I thought about taking a shower and trying to rekindle the feelings but who would I be conjuring to do the honours? Which man? Sex with David had not been like in the dream but might be. Dream Aiden was not a real man but the creation of my imagination. My body grew fed up waiting and my stomach put in a plea for breakfast and so one hunger replaced another and I got up. I got up to a day that I will never forget.

DAVID

I went to California partly to revisit a new tech company that I had tried to buy out on a previous occasion. Since rejecting my offer, the owners had managed to grow the business but very slowly and the market was fast and competitive. They had approached me about making an investment for a thirty per cent stake. I knew the business had huge potential but something made me resist. An American colleague accused me of being unforgiving, holding a grudge against the owners' initial refusal. Actually, I had begun talking to a potential rival enterprise in Europe and had negotiated a better deal. In the plane, high over cloud, I considered whether I was a forgiving person. I thought immediately of your marriage to my brother and was inclined to conclude that I was open to second chances but something kept taking my mind back to Brittany; a wonderful image of you on the beach, with Amélie, trying to fly a kite. It was a poignant and happy memory and seemed a long time ago. That was when you drank a little too much and I decided to back off. Why the hell did I do that? Sometimes, I miss out on deals because I want it to feel a certain way, because something in my gut tells me "no" or "not yet". It had been a costly, ill-judged decision by me. Maybe I could have won you back in Leeds but I let my pride and feelings about my rival being Robbie get in the way. Damn it. I had been over and over this so many times and always inclined to make you so responsible and maybe it was a lack of forgiveness that made me require you to ask me into your life now, to spell out that you wanted Audrey to go and for us to be together. Soon, I would see you and there would have to be a definitive conversation. I was twenty years older. Shouldn't I just decide on our future?

On the connecting flight to the south of France, I considered Audrey once more. I held her in high esteem. I respected her and yes, I was fond of her. I just didn't love her the way I loved you. Yet, if I did respect her then why put her fate in your hands? On the way home from the airport, I resolved to end my relationship with her. She did not deserve to be a boobie prize or a life boat or any kind of secondary option. Frankly, if you did not want me after all of this, maybe I was done with women and love. It may just have been the jet lag but I felt exhausted. Yet, the words Mrs Claire Sutton kept repeating in my mind and I knew the notion of any rest was futile until I had been to Scotland.

CLAIRE

I was standing at my office window, nursing a mug of tea, procrastinating. Every now and again, my wandering mind meandered back to an image of Aiden but I pushed it away and tried to think of David. I kept glancing at the wall clock, as if doing so could fast forward the time to his arrival here. Aiden was just symptomatic of sexual frustration whereas I loved David. People could be fickle and treacherous. I lived my life according to that assessment but it had never struck me until then that I was "people". How easily I had been lured into an attraction for the Irishman and how quickly I had ceased to yearn for David. Another part of me, a raspy nagging voice, complained that my thoughts were centred on two men and the rest of me had no better explanation than biology and the age old predicament of loneliness. I saw that the shrubs alongside the lawn had still not been trimmed back and were encroaching further on the path and started to compose in my head a suitable reprimand of the gardener and oh yes, I needed to complain to Diane about giving a key and the alarm code to Aiden. I remember I was thinking about overgrown bushes when the telephone rang.

I grabbed it, suddenly charged with excitement. I thought it had to be David.

"Hello. I thought you might call." I regretted saying that straight away, of course. There was a measured pause by the caller.

"Hello Claire. Caroline Summers. Ok to talk?" She was stern but no more than usual.

"Oh hello. Sorry, yes, go ahead."

"Audrey Hopper has asked me to call you." I froze. What the hell was she up to now? Caroline was completely loyal to David. Why would she get involved?

"Oh? What about?" I did not disguise my disdain.

"She called me a short while ago to inform me that David suffered a heart attack yesterday evening."

I fell into my chair and my heart started to pound madly but not as fast as my racing mind.

"Oh my God. I'll go straight away. Which hospital?" Sounds pathetic but I think I briefly thought about what to wear.

"Listen Claire. No hospital. I'm afraid he didn't make it. "

There was a brief pause but not a long enough one.

"Audrey said they had an argument and he stormed up the garden and she left him to think stuff over but when the house-maid went up to find him they found him on the ground. They called an ambulance of course but I'm afraid there was nothing they could do. He'd gone."

She had not actually spoken the word "dead", so it wasn't real. It was some sort of mistake or sick joke. David was too strong, too alive, too real to me.

"This is ridiculous. David can't be dead. No one just dies like that, not someone like him anyway."

"I am so sorry Claire. So very sorry. I know this is very hard to process but I am afraid it is true."

Her voice broke slightly and lifted the curtain onto a new reality. She was upset. She was close to David. She was telling me the truth.

"I need a moment Caroline because my brain is just not working. You are telling me that David died last night, just like that and because of some stupid argument with Audrey and she, she just left him, what, up a bloody garden? I mean this is fucking madness..."

When she spoke, you could feel the strain of her trying to stay composed.

"An official announcement will shortly be emailed to everyone who needs to know but out of respect you have been informed in person. Diane and the others will help you. You're not alone. I will email Audrey's suggestions about what should happen next and you have time to think it through and decide what you want to do. Amélie is with her French family, being comforted. Audrey wanted me to tell you that."

"Amélie. Oh my God, poor Amélie." I started to cry a little then but it was all about dear Amélie and still had nothing to do with me and David and this reality of loss. I pictured Celeste briefly but turned my back on her.

"Yes, indeed. Look, I'm going to ring off now. There is a lot to do. Take a few moments and then just wait for Diane and the others to catch up and they'll support you. Ok?"

She sounded stressed now and I imagined the machinery of David's empire snarled up and alarm bells ringing. Without much thought, I just put down the receiver and as though holding the phone had kept me in some kind of delicate balance, I found myself dizzy and the room swaying. I gripped hold of the desk, fumbled open the top drawer, uncapped the bottle of whiskey and started to drink. The burning to my throat and first kick of alcohol in the blood rallied me but only briefly. If I wanted to stay in control I needed to keep drinking. It was like leaning up against a door and David's dead body weighing down from the other side, trying to get in. I had to keep him back. It wasn't over. Not until I said so.

Diane duly came, and others, but I had locked the door and I screamed at them to just fuck off, hurling a few objects at the door for good measure. They just didn't get it. Once I let them in and the conversation began, about David and arrangements then I had to enter a whole new reality, a life post David. Here, in my office, it was just me and him suspended and all I had to do was think of him on a garden path, not breathing and that was impossible which meant that it just wasn't true and all I had to do was wait for a plausible explanation. I carried on drinking as though the answer were inscribed at the bottom of the bottle. It helped to numb a distant pain that was my heart breaking. Now and again, I had to let a little of the misery escape so I thought of dear Amélie, an orphan now. I allowed myself to feel sorrow for her but my own sorrow was pushed back, denied an exit. Better in than out.

I am not sure how much time passed. I avoided the clock. It measured reality. I was slumped over the desk, trying very hard not to think about anything, to somehow float away, when Aiden arrived.

He sounded very calm, older maybe.

"Claire. It's Aiden. Open the door please. We just need to know you are ok."

I took another long swig from the bottle. The kick from it made me momentarily alert. I remembered I was Claire Sutcliff, Director of the Art Institute and decided I could be her for the next few seconds at least. I unlocked the door and staggered back behind my desk, a large oak desk which gave me authority, my throne.

He walked in. I had never seen him look so serious.

"What do you want Aiden? Why are you here?"

He turned and clicked the door quietly shut. Something made me take another swig from the bottle rather defiantly.

"Oh I heard that the love of your life had just died and thought you could do with a friend."

There were so many things wrong with that statement. The barrister in me circled them with red pen. Let's start with the word "friend."

"Piss off. You're not my friend. Here's my friend right here."

I held up the bottle and shook it at him, suddenly powerful with anger. He moved to grab it away from me but I had incredible superpower reflexes and thwarted his attempt.

Why did he look at me then as if I were a child?

"That's not a friend Claire believe me. Now give me the bottle."

He put out his hand and waited.

"No, I want it and in the circumstances I think I am entitled. Don't worry. I'm not like you, not some loser alcoholic." The last two words were spoken with true venom.

It was a vicious thing to throw at him but he just sighed, pulled up a chair and folded his arms in a casual sort of way. He had time, time to talk sense to me.

"You're right about that Claire but drinking still isn't the solution... Oh it will buy you a few hours, might even let you fall into oblivion for a while but sooner or later you are going to have to face this. Now, I know we haven't known each other long but I care about you and if you'll let me I'll help you do this."

"Do what?" I took another swig but he saw his chance and pulled the bottle away from me.

"I'll help you face the loss Claire because you know it's coming. It's like a huge wall of water and the longer you put off facing into it the bigger and stronger it grows."

He got up and walked out of the room with the bottle. In so doing, he crossed some sort of red line, broke a serious rule which enraged me. I ran from behind the desk and met him coming back in, slamming into him. He took hold of me but I pulled back and struck him and he just seemed to absorb it, so I started to pound at his chest and he stood there like a punch bag and allowed me to do so a few times before one blow made him tilt back and then he grabbed me by my wrists. With no outlet for my anger, I started to scream.

"Give me back my drink! Give me back my drink!" Those were the words coming out of my mouth but in my head they were "He's not dead. Bring him back to me." At some point the words in my head came out of my mouth and as Aiden had promised a wall of water came up behind me and washed me into his arms. I do not know how I even remained on my feet then because I felt so overcome and the whole of me started to shake. There were no tears, just some sort of primordial crying from deep within, the response of a lonely human who has suffered a very deep loss, a terrible wailing muffled only partly by Aiden's sweatshirt. I thought the shaking would never stop but as it began to ease, so I began to weep, as if the water had entered me and now escaped by the only logical route. David was dead. It was real. It felt like the end of everything.

After that I entered the fog of grief, a valley with the shadow of David's death hanging over it. Aiden managed to get me to lie on my bed and stayed with me until Mrs Stewart arrived. Though she had clearly been crying herself, she was her efficient, capable self and he was promptly dismissed. Days passed before I saw him again.

If anyone wanted proof of the formidable strength of Audrey

Hopper, well she revealed it in the days that followed. She rebuffed the demands of the French family to have David buried with Celeste. Instead, she organised a small ceremony to cremate his body (which I declined to attend) and announced that his ashes would be taken to Scotland, to the place he most loved (to the woman he most loved). They would be scattered on the loch, as part of a ceremony of thanksgiving. A great many people could be expected to attend. The Art Director saw to it that even those artists who had not made holiday plans did so promptly. Their rooms could be cleared to create accommodation and Turnberry agreed that they would accommodate as many as possible; what a superb marketing opportunity for them! Mike Grainger arrived within a couple of days and began to coordinate efforts. I could not quite grasp that David himself would not be appearing on a podium to deliver a speech or that the guest of honour would be arriving in an urn. Audrey had set in motion an event that would suitably honour a very successful and powerful man, an occasion that would create a crowd in which two women could be lost; we might even avoid having to speak to one another. Just in case, she insisted that it was in Amélie's best interests to attend, knowing that the child would be an additional buffer. Above all, she did not want me to ask about that argument with David I suppose. If I were curious, it was dampened by grief and cold logic; whatever had been said, David had a heart attack because he smoked, drank, and worked too hard.

The day before the sombre event, the weather changed and beautiful skies yielded to clumps of cloud and heavy showers and just the slight occasional chill of an autumn that hovered eagerly. A summer in Scotland can leave on a whim. Aiden came to see me and found me seated by the lake. I had put on a raincoat but it had no hood and my hair was wet. Not that I cared much. We looked at each other. I found myself dumbstruck.

"So everyone is leaving but they say they don't need the cottage so I could stay if you really wanted me to."

"But?"

"Well, Gary has leant me some money and I want to go over to Ireland. It's time I sorted out a few things of my own."

"What things? Your family?"

He looked tired. He stared out at the expanse of grey water which was rather uninspiring.

"It would take a lifetime to mend some of those bridges. I was left a small house by an Aunt who adored me and a bit of land. Connemara land, near the sea, so it's not fit for much more than ponies. The house must be in a right state by now. Anyway, I need to finally do something about it, that's all. Still, it can wait if you need me."

It was a question too immense for me to begin to answer. How could I suddenly be at ease with needing this man when I had fought so hard against fully needing and depending on David? Aiden peered over at me, and saw fear in my eyes.

"Look, you don't need me. You're strong and Mrs Stewart and dozens of others will help you through it all. It wouldn't have been polite not to offer. I've been avoiding Ireland for years and the fact is I have to go while I have the courage."

"Yes, you should do it, of course."

He stayed for a while longer. We said nothing. Just stared out at the water. Then he got up.

"Right then. I'll be going then."

I just nodded and he began to walk away. I turned back to the water and didn't watch him leave but when I walked back to the house later I suddenly felt a sense of panic and wondered if I would ever see him again. I rushed quickly down to the cottage. It was empty.

Audrey looked more attractive than me in black and conducted herself impeccably. To the extent that we communicated, it was a polite, professional tone, set by her. We might have been embassy colleagues. Amélie looked so much older than I expected and I hoped that this was not the abrupt end of her childhood. Strangely, she also resembled Celeste more than David now. It was hard to talk to her because the French relatives kept a close guard but her English was actually very improved. I promised her we would have a holiday in Brittany soon and this conjured a faint smile.

The great David Sutton had been reduced to ash and placed in a pot and this struck me as so absurd that I quickly decided that it simply wasn't him. Though not religious, I kept my bedroom window open later that night and wondered if I would be visited by his spirit but it was just the crisp air that made the hairs on my skin rise up. He had definitely gone, in entirety. A local minister spoke briefly during the ceremony and talked of David's legacy and how he would live on in hearts and memories but my heart had broken apart and he had left it and for now, I did not welcome the memories.

It was only when the few of us chosen to go out on the boat to scatter the ashes had lined up on the small wooden jetty that I noticed Robbie was even there. A pretty young woman had a firm grip on his arm but had to let go to allow him to board the boat. She would remain on shore. She stayed on the jetty and watched us until we slipped out of view. We were going to the far side. Someone had produced a boat with a small motor and this was nothing like a rowing boat. We moved quickly and the breeze was fresh and damp in our faces.

Once in position, Audrey passed the urn to Robbie. He paused and looked over to me but in answer to his unspoken offer I shook my head and started to cry. Amélie moved over awkwardly, lifted my arm and wrapped it around her and so we cried together and neither of us really watched as David was committed to the loch, the loch which had taken the life of Amélie's Mother. A stretch of water which had once filled me with wonder was for now a cold, graveyard. If there were spirits then David had joined Celeste now.

In every possible sense, it was over. Caroline Summers spoke to me briefly later on and explained that David had been very clever and had secured most of his estate for Amélie, neatly avoiding much of the possible death duties, and the future of the Art Institute was reasonably secure for the foreseeable future. David, at least, had understood his mortality. He had already signed over the house in London to Audrey before they had moved to Paris. He could afford extravagant gifts. He had apparently bought Robbie a house in the States. For me there was nothing because who was I really?

Except later, about a month after the funeral, Caroline came to the house in Scotland again. I assumed she had come to brief me about the Institute and who would replace the governance of David Sutton which she did do but then she produced some other documents and placed them very carefully on the table in front of me.

"What's this then?"

She was solemn and looked uncertain.

"I thought you should know that David had taken steps to prepare a new will which was contingent upon you becoming his wife. Most of everything would still have gone to Amélie because that was the best way to protect assets and she is his daughter of course."

I stared at the papers but David was not there. He had gone. I did not need to read them.

"He told me he was waiting for you to propose! However, you know David, not a patient man. I think he was also preparing to be the proposer because he arranged to have this made for you and asked me to collect it."

She produced a ring box, opened it and placed it on top of the papers. Right on cue, the morning light struck the diamond and sparkled at us, making us both gasp. What could you do but marvel at its beauty? She laughed.

"He intended to make it very difficult for you to refuse!"

I hesitated, unsure whether to try and pick it up. She pushed the box towards me.

"I think it rightly belongs to you. It is what he wanted. I think I knew him sufficiently well to say that he loved you very much indeed Claire."

I closed the lid on the box. I could not bear to look any longer.

"I didn't know what to do with such love. I squandered it. It's too late now. Sell the ring and donate the money to the Art Institute."

"That would be a very sizeable donation..."

"Enough to purchase my forgiveness and see off all the ghosts that haunt me? "I sounded desperate, a little mad.

She frowned at me. I am not sure she had ever really liked me.

"There are no such things as ghosts and David would not approve of such thinking. However, I suppose a donation to the Institute is fitting nonetheless. I will see to it. When will you next see Amélie? David would expect you to keep in touch with her. Audrey has returned to America so she only has her French family now."

"Yes, yes. It is all in hand. We are spending a week in Brittany."

And with that we resumed our discussions about the Institute. The ring was removed and I never saw it again. We had a vacancy at the Institute and candidates to consider. Aiden Dolan had never returned.

I met David when I was a girl and had grown into a woman. In all that time, in spite of his marriage to Celeste, my sorry marriage to Robbie and then David's choice to be with Audrey, David had fundamentally been the focus of my life. Now he had been cut out like an abnormal mass and only trace cells remained, and the prognosis was that I had a lifetime still stretching out in front of me and I should not be defined by what had happened. His greatest gift had not been an intricate, diamond ring, nor the love it symbolised but as it happened the job in Scotland, perhaps intended to contain me, so that I could be his wife on his terms but beyond that a fundamentally good call by a wise, experienced man. The job and the place were a good fit for me but it was only in the months after David's death that I fully began to see that. There was nothing for me apart from the job and the place and the people and I allowed myself to be moulded to them, liberated from all other hope, any other possibilities. I discovered a fresh purpose, grew into the vision of the place and the people around me drew me in, blanketed me with friendship and for the first time in what had been my entire life I encountered a feeling of belonging and security. David was gone but I had been saved.

In a similar way Amélie was absorbed into her French family and it was tacitly understood that if I wanted to maintain contact with her then it would be on French soil and so Celeste's decision to provide me with a house in Brittany proved visionary. Our first holiday there was a painful, sad affair, traces of David hanging in the spaces between us, in spite of the rough blustery weather but there was a bond between us, deep and mysterious perhaps but real, and we agreed that we would have another holiday there the following summer.

When she returned, she had altered. More and more like her mother and less of a child. The weather was gracious and allowed us to have an aimless schedule, dividing our time between the house and the beach, until the floor of the hall and sitting room seemed to be covered by the beach and smelled of the sea. Amélie was an only child but she had lots of cousins to grow her social skills and the natural confidence of both parents and by the middle of the week she had begun to befriend other beach regulars and I was happy to retreat into a holiday book when they departed on their little adventures.

I was relaxed and sun kissed and had started to gather up our possessions to head back to the house for lunch and Amélie was down by the water saying her temporary goodbyes and scheming for the late afternoon, when I spotted a tall figure ambling in our direction. I recognised the beard. The eyes were obscured by shades. That was a relief.

"There you are. Thought I'd never find you. How are you doing?" His Irish accent was rather wonderful. It had not occurred to me before.

"Aiden! Good grief. What on earth are you doing here?"

"Well now, that's a long story which you would probably prefer to hear with a glass of something cold in your hand but…"

Amélie had spotted him and had run up the beach. She jumped in front of me.

"Hello, I'm Amélie. We're going to have mussels for lunch. Who are you? "

She had the vivacious energy and charm of her mother which sort of sparkled out of her and the childlike directness was of course rather disarming. She spoke it first in French and when he stared blankly blurted it out in English and stuck out a hand because someone had told her that English people like to shake hands and she assumed he was English. He hesitated but gathered his senses and shook the small hand politely.

"Well, I love mussels and my name is Aiden."

She looked him up and down and I am sure the accent had not gone unnoticed.

"Yes but WHO are you monsieur?" She tried very hard to pronounce the "H" and this made the nature of her question even more imposing. He glanced at me for advice but I just shrugged my shoulders.

"Well, I'm Claire's friend, and it's nice to meet you Amélie."

She really did not care for the accent and frowned at him.

"Yes I am and you can share mussels with Claire. You are only HER friend. Allons y."

She walked off leaving us to catch up. Which was really a bit rude but also quite funny.

Aiden took some of the bags and we set off to the house.

ACKNOWLEDGEMENT

My heartfelt thanks to the many people who have helped, cajoled, encouraged and inspired me, in life, and in the writing of this book.

To all the women who have touched - and are yet to touch - my life. For shaping my views, and inspiring me with your insights, your optimism, your zeal, your fortitude. For persisting through thick and thin.

ABOUT THE AUTHOR

S. Ridgway

As a young child I was a daydreamer. As a teenager, I began to read my Mum's romantic fiction until I was encouraged by my teachers to read "great literature".

After studying for a degree in Modern Languages, where I met my husband, I worked as a university lecturer but found this unrewarding. I decided to have four children, and to focus on being a mother.

I lived a lot of my adult life with great intensity until, in 2008, I started to feel unwell. In 2012, I was diagnosed with M.E.

A combination of reduced energy levels and living in the North Pennines created a desire to journey inward, and I began to explore creative writing.

When I write, I feel free, I feel limitless.

Printed in Great Britain
by Amazon